MERCY'S REIGN

By: Jess L. M. Anderson

Acknowledgements from the author:

To those who have been working just as hard as me on this series, you are my heroes! I want to give a shout out to the talented voice actor Patrick, who brings the audiobooks to life in new and amazing ways every time. Also, Viyanca, who has worked very hard bringing Cal's sketches and the cover art to life, taking every bit of feedback with a smile. A shout out to April who has created all the beautiful character portraits for the website and Cartographybird Maps who brought the Ozran map to life in a way never before seen! Lastly, Mike, my awesome stepdad who helped me with editing (especially the fight scenes) to create a story that flowed smoothly!

I want to show some love to my beta readers Brittney, Allison, Julia, and Jessica "Scout." Without them I wouldn't have been able to create a deeper and more meaningful story. Their feedback and ideas are beautifully reflected in the pages.

I also want to acknowledge the fans and readers of the first book in the series. You all are driving me forward and keeping this series going. Without you, there wouldn't be a second book, let alone a whole series in the works. A special thank you to Nic, Paige, Sara, Curtis, Miranda, and Chandra for being huge parts of the fundraising for this novel!

Lastly, a huge warm thank you to my friends and family who have supported my journey and a HUGE thank you to my parents for letting me take this time to follow my dreams while getting back on my feet.

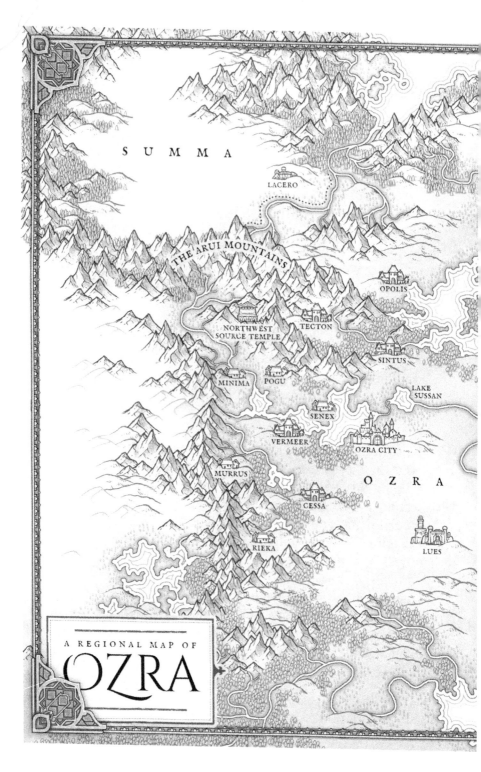

SUMMA

LACERO

THE ARUI MOUNTAINS

OPOLIS

NORTHWEST
SOURCE TEMPLE

TECTON

SINTUS

LAKE
SUSSAN

MINIMA

POGU

SENEX

VERMEER

OZRA CITY

MURRUS

O Z R A

CESSA

LUES

RIEKA

A REGIONAL MAP OF

OZRA

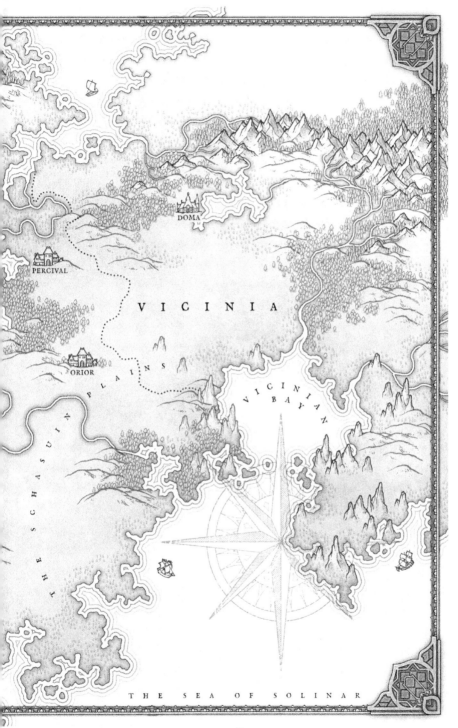

DOMA

PERCIVAL

ORIOR

V I C I N I A

VICINIAN BAY

THE SCHASUIN PLAINS

THE SEA OF SOLINAR

e

Chapter One

Jolting up in bed, Mercy tries to stifle his screaming by cupping his hand over his mouth. He hadn't even realized he'd been doing it until he startled himself awake. With his eyes darting around the room and his breathing heavy, he lets out a sigh of relief. He was alone in his bedroom with the wooden floors and pale walls still intact. The sheets and hand-made blanket from Pippa were still there too. No one was in here to attack him. He was safe.

Nearly every night Mercy had been plagued with nightmares. He wouldn't even go as far as to call them nightmares actually. It was more of terrible replays of all the horrors he had lived through before and during Spheara. They varied from night to night, but the pain of reliving the agonizing memories never ceased. Even his waking hours felt just as unbearable.

Tonight, he had been haunted by the gruesome memory of fighting Caligo in the courtyard of the royal estate. The memory of Cal's corrupt mind was an eerie one to relive. Not only was he at war with a friend that day, but he had felt helpless against him. That day he was fighting for his life and became part of the machine that murdered

1

his brother and nearly took his best friend's life as well. It was a day he hated.

He squeezes his eyes shut trying to shake the images. He could still feel the blades as they pierced Trust and Sylas even more than a year later. The violence and terror were enough to make his stomach hurt.

Taking a shuddering breath, he turns on the light beside his bed. His eyes scan the catwalk he had crafted for his cat, Soot, that trailed up the wall and along the ceiling, but the feline was nowhere in sight. With the room illuminated, he closes his eyes, taking a steadying breath, inhaling on an eight count, and exhaling on a seven. This was the same breathing routine he did every time he thought of Spheara or the traumatic events leading up to it. He had hoped he'd at least stop screaming in his sleep at this point, but that was a lost cause. His cries would wake the girls more often than not and he hated worrying them.

He gives a soft smile as Soot finally appears and jumps up onto his bed. She begins to nudge her head into his palm, demanding his attention. He gives her a scratch between the ears and relaxes. He always found comfort in his small friend and appreciated her ability to recognize when he needed a little cheering up. He continues to stroke her soft fur as she curls up in his lap, happy to be receiving his attention.

Hearing a small cough, he glances up to see Ruby standing in his doorway with worry on her face. Mercy takes a deep breath and forces a smile at the eight-year-old. She was dressed in her nightgown with her dark hair a mess from tossing and turning all night. She was small for her age and had dark skin like her father. Her slightly pointed ears mirrored Mercy's, showing she was a human/Aitian mutt as well.

After the death of her parents, the little girl had gotten attached to Mercy. He was familiar and had become her guardian. After school she would often go to the

2

blacksmith shop he owned to watch him work. Once home, Ruby followed him around the house relentlessly. She would even ask him to read to her before bed when he was able to. Every waking moment Mercy was around, she wanted to be with him. She tended to be quiet and reserved like him, while her sister Saphie was loud and domineering. It was a contrast that reminded Mercy much of his friendship with Sylas.

"Did I wake you?" he asks, keeping his voice low.

Ruby shakes her head as she enters the room. In her hands she held a small stuffed rabbit that her mother had made her. It was one of the few things they were able to salvage from the burned remains of her childhood home. Mercy had tried his best to patch up the charred legs of the plush animal, but it still seemed to bear the scars of the day Rieka fell. All of them did. This was a home full of broken people.

"Did you have a nightmare?" Mercy questions as she climbs onto his bed.

The young girl nods her head, getting under his blanket. This had become a routine as well. Ruby seemed to remember the Fall of Rieka much better than her older sister, which caught Mercy by surprise. She was even able to recollect how her parents were killed, unlike Saphie who had blocked out the gruesome day all together. When Ruby had nightmares about it, she always refused to sleep in her own bed. She wanted the security that Mercy or their housekeeper, Charlyn, offered and would walk around the house until one of them stirred.

Curling up beside Mercy, Ruby nestles into the crook of his arm and stares at the door numbly. He puts his arm around her and rubs her shoulder trying to offer some support but knew it was just going to be the same cycle tomorrow. Ruby got just about as much sleep as he did during the night.

Taking care of Brokkr's girls had been his blessing in disguise. If he had to come home to an empty house at the end of the day, he may have fallen deeper into the ever-present misery than he already was. He needed them just as much as they needed him.

"What was yours about?" Ruby mutters.

"Uncle Cal," Mercy confesses as Soot hops off the bed.

"He's scary," she admits.

"Just sometimes," he says with a small smile, his tone flat.

He was happy the girls didn't understand the events of Spheara. While they were teaching it in school, they weren't giving the grisly details. Telling Ruby about fighting Cal would surely paint a terrifying image of the man that came around often and was meant to keep her safe. They knew he was strong and fierce though. They had seen him spar with Mercy more than once, proving he would be an intimidating opponent in a fight. That was enough to get across how nerve wracking a battle against the King of Novus Aitus could be.

Continuing to sit with Ruby, Mercy closes his eyes. He was tired. He was beyond tired. The last few days had been busy at the shop, and he hadn't been sleeping well. The nightmares combined with his Source buzzing more than usual created a very unfit week of sleep. Having not been called to help Cal or Sylas on any assignments lately had made the use of his Light Source infrequent, and that made his connection antsy. He would most likely need to head to the arena in the morning to get in some training, or he risked an outburst of his Source happening.

Though he was encouraged to use his connection for day-to-day tasks, it felt wrong. His Source was meant to protect, not heat steel or light up the room on a dark night. He also didn't want to rely on the ease his abilities gave him with mundane tasks. After Spheara he had come to

4

realize how easy it could be to lose his connection if things went bad. He had gone through two grueling weeks when his Source had been taken then returned to him before those events. Adding on the six months he had willingly let it stay with Cal, his body still seemed to feel the strain when he called for it, the sensation feeling somewhat harder than before.

The sound of a loud crash downstairs startles the pair. Knots automatically begin to fill Mercy's stomach as his mind goes to the worst-case scenario faster than he cared to admit. It always did.

"What was that?" Ruby whispers, distress in her small voice.

"It's just Soot," Mercy assures as another clatter resonates through the house and several thuds follow.

Scanning the room, he spots the white cat sitting up and alert by the door. The loud noises had startled her as well and she was ready to take on any intruder. He furrows his brow at another disturbance downstairs that prompts Soot to bolt from the room to investigate herself. Mercy pulls away from Ruby, getting to his feet. Could someone be in the house? Had the Sentry Guard stationed outside perhaps come in?

He goes to the door and sees Charlyn peeking out of her room. Both adults wince at the sound of glass shattering on the first floor. Powering up his Source, Mercy's eyes begin to glow. He puts a finger to his lips toward Charlyn as he beckons her over. The woman quickly enters his room and goes to Ruby. With a flick of his wrist, Mercy puts a shield up around the little girl and the woman and exits his room to approach the staircase.

Moving soundlessly, he pushes the door open to the girls' room beside the railing and spots Saphie asleep in her bed. Paranoid, he puts a shield up over her as well. No one was going to harm his family if he was there. He was going to protect them with everything he had.

5

His shields were one of the first skills he had worked to perfect over the last eight months. Being able to keep his friends and family protected was a priority. The precision he had been able to reach with them was impressive. He could even conjure one for himself that hovered just above his skin. It was like an armor made from the Light Source and it was impenetrable by everything he had come into contact with thus far.

Descending the staircase slowly, he takes in the main room. From the bottom of the steps, he could see the front door was wide open, the lock broken. The books on the shelf in the living room were strewn across the floor, along with the small knickknacks that lived on the shelves. His heart sinks wondering where the Sentry Guard that had been stationed at his home had gone. Sander had been keeping watch every night for over year. Why hadn't he stopped the intruder or given a warning of anyone entering the house?

His eyes buzz with his Source as he hears a crash and shuffling coming from his office. Moving slowly down the hall, his hair begins to stand on end as the sensation of an unfamiliar Shadow Keeper hits him. Who could be in here? With a deep breath, he pulls a solis orb to his hand as he rounds the corner to the room. He locks eyes with a hooded figure, the genti tome held tightly in their gloved grasp with a bag draped over their hip. The figure says nothing as it begins to march toward him, the dark black combat suit becoming clear in the glow of his Light Source.

Fear in his eyes, Mercy launches the orb at the individual causing them to drop the book at his feet as they put their hands up. Taking the moment to grab the tome, he gasps as the person shoots a wave of spiritum fog at him. It was then he realized the only reason they dropped the tome was to free their hands for an attack. Using their smokey tendrils, they grab his leg, pulling him to the ground with a thud. His hands burning from the genti, he releases the

6

book, letting it hit the floor with him. The intruder snatches the genti clad tome away once again.

As the intruder stands in front of him, Mercy gawks, unsure what to do. He should have been prepared for a break in. While he thought he was over this whole freezing thing, it was suddenly entirely different in his own home.

The figure pulls what appears to be a blade from their belt and uses Mercy's moment of confusion to jab the sharp metal into his arm. He lets out a hiss of pain as he feels blood soak into his night shirt but relaxes as his Source heals him. He could feel a continual stinging as the cut healed over into a jagged glowing scar. He puts his hand to the raised bump that now rested on his upper left arm as the person darts past him into the hallway.

Fighting a Shadow Keeper was probably Mercy's biggest weakness when he started his Keeper training. He had spent the last few months working with Cal to figure out how he could defend himself against a Shadow and vice versa. With the emergence of Keepers of Light came a new fighting style Cal had to learn too. It had taken some time, but Mercy was able to discover his advantages to battling his opposite Source.

While he wanted to stay on the floor, he knew he needed to go after this person. They were in his home with his family upstairs and the tome he was trusted to protect in their possession.

"Get up, Validus," he mumbles to himself.

Getting to his feet, he takes a deep breath and rushes down the hall, shooting another solis orb at the figure. The burn of the orb does nothing as they take the hit to the back of their shoulder and continue forward. Seeing his Source do little against the jumpsuit, Mercy runs back into his office and yanks his father's sword from the wall before turning back into the hall. He needed to act and not think before this person walked out of his house with the genti tome. If he lost that tome, there was no knowing what the consequences could be.

With an angry scream, he rushes the person. This gets the figure to stop and turn toward him. They quickly flick their wrist, tearing the blade from his hand with their fog. With their face completely covered in a dark mask, Mercy was unable to make out who was in his home. He hears a small, annoyed growl from the figure as they shove him away, the touch feeling like a battering ram as he flies back down the hall, slamming into the wall at the end with a crash. His body flying back breaks the small wooden table and vase that decorated the end of the hall. The painting hung behind him also falls from its nail and hits him on the head making him let out an audible groan of pain.

The suited Shadow Keeper spews another wave of fog at Mercy, pinning him. As the fog begins to eat away at his skin, Mercy switches his tactic. Aiming his palms at the floor he calls his Source again. He hated using it, but this was his best defense against a Shadow Keeper.

His irises going completely white, he begins to turn the dark fog into a white cloud. It was a move he had discovered at Spheara and was something only he seemed to be able to do. No other Keeper of Light he had spoken with could quite grasp how he could manage such a feat. Not only could he turn a Shadow's fog into a Light Source weapon, but he could control it. Being able to manipulate a physical fog was only known for a Shadow Keeper, the fact Mercy could turn the fog into his own was unheard of and a scary thing for anyone to witness. It had even shaken up Cal the first time he attempted to replicate the move.

The solis fog shoots toward the Shadow and pushes them into the living room, knocking them into a bookcase, the books clattering to the ground around them. Mercy takes a stance and enters his living room, his Source lighting up his veins and eyes. Keeping the solis fog tightly to the Shadow, he stops and looks at the genti tome still held firmly in the Shadow Keeper's hands.

"What do you want?" he questions, keeping his focus on the thief. With no answer he pushes his fog harder. "Why are you here?"

"You'll learn soon enough," a woman's voice taunts him.

Before his eyes a cloud of spiritum fog comes up behind the figure. In a panic, he uses his solis fog to grip the genti tome and yank it away, his Source rejecting the cold metal, dropping it to the floor. Suddenly the figure was seemingly pulled into the wall, the Shadow Keeper leaving no trace behind. The solis fog Mercy had created hits into the case, knocking the remaining books to the floor as the thief completely vanishes. He pulls the white smoke back to his hand and into his palm, the act seeming to recharge him in an instant. Looking around completely dumbfounded his breath shudders. Where had she gone? How did she simply vanish?

After taking a moment to catch his breath, he throws a small blanket over the genti tome and picks it up before walking back to his office. Moving his eyes to the mahogany book stand, his stomach drops. Why would they even want the genti tome? Hardly anyone could read that book and make sense of it. Even Sylas struggled some days, and he was fluent in Ancient Aitian at this point. Moving to his desk he sees a drawer open. Digging through it, he registers that the four notebooks full of translations from the book by Sylas and Pippa were missing.

"Shit," he breathes, moving to the bookcase.

Scanning the books still on the shelves and the ones on the floor he notices the Riekan Tomes were also among the missing items. He takes a step back in panic. Why would someone take his tomes? Those were Elder Rom's tomes. Sylas had spent the last year adding more information to those pages. 100 years of Riekan Source

9

history was collected within those books and now they were gone.

He drops the genti tome to the floor. Moving to a cabinet in the corner he hastily opens it. Inside were a few cases, none seeming to be disturbed. Moving a few to the side he opens an intricately carved pine box. The Pura Blade was untouched and still nestled on the velvet cushion Cal had given him. Pulling it from the case, he puts the sheathed crystal dagger into his pant pocket, not wanting to let the item stray too far from him. Moving to the next box, a carefully carved chest, he opens it to reveal the dagger Master Novi had gifted his brother the day of the battle in the courtyard. He lets out a shuddering breath, and closes it slowly, happy to see the last item his brother held was safe and in his possession.

Leaving the study, he moves to the front door to assess anymore damage. The lock was completely broken meaning brute force was used to enter the home. That must have been the first crash he had heard. Looking out on the porch he confirms Sander, his Sentry Guard, was gone. His stomach drops again at the thought of Sander being hurt or worse. That man had become more than just a bodyguard, but a friend since Spheara. He was the first Keeper to stand down in the battle and had fought alongside Trust until the end. His eyes look over the porch, at least there was no visible blood.

Closing the door, he looks around the living room, trying to calm himself. He could feel the fear beginning to set in. Why would someone break into his home? What did they want with the genti tome? What if they had hurt the girls or Charlyn? He could feel the adrenaline beginning to subside as fear took over.

"Char!" he shouts, forcing himself to power down and drop the shields.

He watches as the housekeeper and the girls appear at the top of the steps. The woman registers the fear in his eyes and quickly rushes down the stairs with Saphie at her heels. Mercy begins gasping for air, his chest locking up as the debilitating anxiety began to sink in. With the adrenaline leaving his system, all he could feel was a sensation of intense, immobilizing terror. It felt like his heart was going to pound out of his chest.

"Mercy, it's okay," Charlyn states, rushing toward him as he falls to his knees. "Saphie, get the lights," she instructs.

The eleven-year-old nods her head and begins to turn on all the lights in the room. They had witnessed Mercy go through this multiple times, and all were aware of what needed to be done to bring him out of it. While he had been able to control his fears and anxieties in a fight, once it ended, it seemed the world would come crashing down, and there was no stopping it once it started.

"Try to breathe, Mercy," Charlyn encourages, sitting beside him on the floor.

He nods his head, but the air didn't want to come into his lungs. The more he tried to inhale, the harder it became. Even with the lights on, the state of his living room was only accelerating his dread. As his eyes dart around the room all he could see was the destruction and how unsafe his home had suddenly become. He grabs Charlyn's arm and points toward the kitchen.

"Saphie, get the door," Charlyn requests, getting Mercy to his feet and leading him into the other room.

The young girl turns on the lights to illuminate the kitchen as they enter. The sight of the clean and safe space begins to ease him as the air finally gets into his chest. He begins to count again, inhaling on the eight count and exhaling on the seven. He needed to get this under control.

"Sander is gone," Mercy gets out between gasps. "Sander's gone."

Chapter Two

The city of Orior laid on the edge of the Eastern Quarter of Ozra, just across the border from Vicinia. The town wasn't small by any means, but it lacked the splendor of the larger cities. The Eastern Quarter was known to be a wealthy, purist sector, but Orior was one of the few that didn't fit the mold. The city was mainly mutt populated, many of the citizens crossing the border from Vicinia into Ozra to escape from the harsher areas of the neighboring country. Vicinia had proven time and time again to not accept mutts or humans and that was an issue Cal's governing was working to repair. This made Orior a safe haven location for many of the citizens seeking refuge.

In Orior a number of residents had been complaining of a large animal scaring livestock and residents, just along the border. While the claims had gotten put to the side, the capital assuming it was a bear or some other large animal, it became clear a few days ago that this was anything but.

A young girl who had been out feeding the chickens early in the morning finally caught a glimpse of the beast, the creature moving to attack her. A large, dark, shrouded creature that she could only describe to her father as a "spiritum fog monster." This was enough to spook the Ozran Council into sending Sentry Guards to search the area for any sign of the creature.

Leading the assignment was Sylas Bellator. After parting ways with Cal and a few months of soul searching, the young man had found himself back in Ozra signing up for the military. No matter how he played it in his head, serving Ozra and protecting his people was where his calling seemed to be. Being in the new steel and purple uniform felt like the right choice given his circumstances. His shaggy curls were partially pulled back to keep them out of his face, the longer length showing he gave little care for a haircut. The image of a military man never did feel right to him, even if the fighting did.

Cal was wary about sending Sylas on a mission without Mercy, but since the break in at Mercy's house two weeks prior, the Keeper had become timid about leaving the village. He even sent Abtal to the Ozran Council meeting that week, the Council Member noting an increase in paranoia with Mercy. This caused concern from both Sylas and Cal, but they understood his apprehension. Mercy had created a family and a life in Rieka, and he was fearful of losing it.

Scanning the tree line of the farm, Sylas lets out a sigh, pausing to try and make sense of the situation. Over the last couple of weeks, the reports were getting stranger and stranger. Mercy reported some type of portal in Rieka, something that had never been heard of before. Not to mention the neighboring country of Vicinia was reporting rogue Shadow Keepers in more frequency than ever. Now Orior was reporting a beast supposedly made of spiritum fog. The more he tried to make sense of the strange reports, the more he wondered if they were even real.

"Bellator!" He hears a voice from behind him.

Turning he locks eyes with Zero Skerrick, his second in command on this assignment, and a Light

Keeper. The Keepers of Light who fought in Spheara were the first Keepers offered military positions in the new and improved Sentry Guard by King Caligo, wanting to balance the ranks. Zero wasn't Sylas's favorite Keeper that Cal recruited at first, but he took his job seriously and was starting to grow on him.

While Zero wasn't particularly strong, his demeanor set others on edge. Having only been around a mutt Light Keeper, seeing an Aitian Keeper of Light like Zero was peculiar. While his complexion was still ghostly, he retained a purple hue in his skin. The only item Zero wore that showed his pride in being a Keeper was the Light and Shadow Source runes he had carved into the leather hilts of two blades he wore at his belt. He had a scar that ran across his face from his hairline to his upper lip from an old injury, and despite being a Keeper of Light and a Sentry Guard, he wore nothing but black. Even with threats of being written up for being out of uniform, he never cared, and Sylas paid no mind to the clear rebellion against authority. In fact, he admired it.

In a way, Zero reminded Sylas of Caligo. He always seemed to be brooding over something that he never could quite grasp, but his blunt, sarcastic remarks were refreshing compared to the Sentry Guards he usually had to work with. Overall, he enjoyed being put on assignments with the wise cracking Keeper.

"We've been here for nearly four hours and have turned up nothing," Zero states in annoyance. "I think we should leave. Mainly because *I* don't want to be here."

"I was hoping to find something related to the incident in Rieka," Sylas admits.

"The sooner you and your Light Master realize Sander isn't coming back, the better," Zero sighs.

Sander's name brings a pained expression to Sylas's face. Sander had been the first member of Mala's Shadows to yield to their cause during Spheara, and he knew how

14

much his best friend had grown fond of the man. Sander going missing after the break in was a much harder hit than losing the Riekan tomes by a landslide. What made his vanishing even worse was that the tracking device Cal had issued in the Sentry Guard attire had been cut from his tactical suit in Rieka. The device was found about 100 yards from the house. This meant whoever had orchestrated the attack knew where the issued tracker was located.

"Where's your sense of adventure, Zero?" Sylas chuckles, trying to keep the mood light.

"My sense of adventure died the last time I was put on an assignment with you," Zero bluntly retorts, folding his arms.

"Liar. You always have fun with me," Sylas teases, with a smirk.

Zero glares at him and dryly laughs. "The times I almost die are the most fun."

Giving a small eye roll, Sylas shakes his head. "Just keep looking," he orders. "We don't leave here until we have some idea of what the girl saw."

"Come on, Cap," Zero groans. "How do we know she didn't just make it up? It could have been a black bear. They're common in the Eastern Quarter," he suggests, not wanting to waste any more time. "We should be spending our time more wisely. I really don't want to be here longer than I have to."

"You never want to be anywhere," Sylas scolds, shaking his head again. "Just keep looking."

"Fine," he growls, "but I want you to know I'm not having any fun."

"According to you, that just means you aren't dying yet," Sylas playfully retorts.

He watches as the Light Keeper flashes him the middle finger and walks toward a group of Sentry Guards to direct them. Turning his attention back to the trees, Sylas moves forward. They needed to find something. There had to be proof of what the girl saw. While he wanted to agree with Zero that it was only an animal, this was different. This felt like something dark. There was something brewing in these woods, and he was going to figure out what it was.

Breaking into the tree line he keeps himself alert. The forest behind the farm felt strange and ominous. Scanning each tree trunk and patch of dirt he could, he looks for a sign of the beast. The thing seemed to have vanished into thin air. Considering how large it was, he couldn't grasp how it just disappeared.

He begins to think about the wall of fog that had helped the thief escape Mercy's home. Mercy insisted he had the thief pinned to a bookcase and suddenly they were gone. How had that happened? A peritia was a psychological or spiritual manifestation, not physical. A Keeper of Shadows being able to create a gate to another place made no sense to him or anyone else.

He pauses at the sound of a creaking. The sound reminded him of an aged tree about to fall. Pulling his bow from his back, he readies an arrow. If Cal were here, he'd probably say he was being paranoid. He was starting to feel like he was always paranoid though. After Spheara he didn't have much choice. He wasn't going to put himself in another situation where his life was on the line. His near-death experience in that courtyard was the last one he was planning on having for a while.

The creak sounds again, and he turns his head swiftly as a tree begins to topple toward him. He jolts to the side and dives into the brush as the large tree comes crashing down beside him. Getting to his feet in a hurry, he scrambles to adjust his bow and aim it toward the tree's base. While it could have been a natural occurrence, it seemed too coincidental to write off. He narrows his eyes at the slight glint of a cloaked Shadow. He knew that sparkle better than anything else.

Letting loose an arrow he hears a woman scream as the cloak drops. A Shadow Keeper glares at him as they pull the arrow from their arm. He smiles at his ability to hit the invisible target. It was a woman by the sound of her voice, but she wore a black combat suit with a hood and mask. Clearly, she was trying to hide her identity.

Pulling another arrow, Sylas readies for a counterattack but the Shadow vanishes again. He looks around trying to detect the small disturbance of a cloaked Shadow Keeper in the forest around him. Suddenly he hisses in pain as a sharp sensation hits his left arm. The sting felt like someone had quickly carved a blade into his skin. Pulling his arm away from the unknown feeling he sees a bleeding wound. He couldn't quite make out what made the mark on his arm, or even what it was of, but it was there and putting a red streak down his forearm. A sudden wave of dizziness hits him as he stumbles, but he shakes it off keeping his bow taut.

The figure quickly pops up to his left. He lets loose another arrow, but she uses her fog to block it. She seemed unconcerned with him as she pointed her finger in his direction. He stumbles again as the ground below him begins to quake and a deafening screech rings out behind him. Turning frantically, he sees the creature the girl had reported. Standing at least nine feet tall, swirling in dark fog, with eyes as red as rubies, the creature stared at Sylas as it moved forward. What the hell was this thing?

Feeling a chill on his ankles, Sylas looks down to see spiritum fog creeping around his feet from the woman behind him. Panic ensues as he realizes his shield wasn't reacting to her fog. How? Why? He turns to try and get a shot at her as his feet are swept from under him and the beast barrels in his direction. His bow clatters to the ground as fear takes over. He was not ready for this type of ambush. A Shadow he could handle, but whatever this was, wasn't of this world.

He lets out a scream as the beast pins him down and pauses just inches from his face. Why wasn't Mercy's Source protecting him? Even though his Keeper wasn't there, it should have still been active and protecting him from the Shadow Source. He lets out a shuddering breath as the air from the beast blows in his face, paralyzing him with fear.

The woman appears beside him again, her hand outstretched toward the beast seeming to control it. As she crouches down to look at him, she pulls the black mask from her face to reveal her dark Aitian features and black hair. Her eyes and sclera were completely dark as she stayed powered up beside him.

"Sylas Bellator," she nods with a smile. "We were hoping to get the Supra Keeper himself, but I guess you can relay a message for us, can't you?"

He was terrified. His life was flashing before his eyes all over again. He couldn't move and there were no other Sentry Guards near him. This was it.

"Tell Mercy, Iana thanks him for the Source Tomes, will you?" she grins, pulling a sword from her waist, "and let him know Bryer would like to speak with him." She watches him a moment, waiting for a remark and frowns. "I heard you were the witty one. I was hoping to at least have some banter with you. Is my friend here a little too much for your simple Riekan mind?"

Taking a deep breath, he scowls at the woman. Not only was she attacking him but now she was insulting his intelligence? He could take a physical blow, but not a stab at his intellect. He feels another gust of air from the beast breathing above him and grimaces.

She looks him over again. "I'm actually disappointed with how easy you were to take down," she sulks. "That Shadow Keeper in Rieka put up much more of a fight than you did. He was cute too…"

18

"Sander…" he mutters under his breath. "Get rid of your pet here and we can try again," he snaps, trying to calm himself.

He needed to focus. If he didn't focus this was going to end badly for him. How had no one heard the tree fall or the roar from this thing? Did no one else feel the ground shaking when she manifested it? He just needed to stall until someone got there. Zero couldn't have gone too far with the other Guards.

"I'm afraid you won't take me seriously without it," she sighs, looking at the dark figure. "You can thank your notes on the Aitian Source Tome for this beautiful creation. I wanted the genti tome itself, but those translations had just what I needed," she explains running her blade down his forearm. "What would send the best message to your Keeper?"

"Depends what message you want to send," he laughs tensely. "Is it a love letter or a threat?"

"Maybe both," she smirks, pulling the blade away from his skin. "Do you think he'd like me?"

"I don't think you're his type," Sylas retorts, trying to squirm free. "He doesn't tend to go for the spiteful, angry kind. That's more my department."

She looks at his arm and places the tip of her blade on his forearm. "A shame really," she frowns, looking him in the eye. "The best shot Ozra has to offer. What would happen if we took that title away?"

"I'd like to see you try," he snaps back.

She runs the tip of her blade over his arm again. He tenses as he realizes what she was implying. She laughs at the sudden flex in his arm as the fear sinks in. What was wrong with this lady? Was she nuts?

"You realize how vulnerable you are don't you?" she states, dancing her sword over his skin. "I could just take the hand. Or maybe the whole arm?" she suggests. "What's your preference, Nota?"

19

He sets his jaw as his mind begins to race. He watches in horror as she raises her sword and with force, crashes it down toward his arm. Adrenaline hits him as the creature eases up at the sight of the blade. With all his strength, Sylas yanks his pinned arm out. Unfortunately, it becomes clear within a second it wasn't quick enough. He lets out a gasp as the blade goes through his hand and into the dirt below. His eyes go wide as the shock takes over. While he couldn't feel the pain yet, he could still feel the blood rushing from his chest to his hand.

"Good enough," the woman glowers.

She gets to her feet and signals her beast to release him. As soon as the creature backs off, he pulls his bleeding hand to his chest, gasping at the shock of the injury. He looks at his hand and could see that his fingers on his left hand were gone as he lets out a scream. What had this woman just done?

"Let Mercy Validus know Bryer Nitesems, and Malice are looking for him, will you? If not, he has so many other loved ones I would love to meet," she smiles as her cloak goes up and she vanishes into the trees.

Sylas could feel his body begin to shake as his vision went hazy. The shock was setting in, and he couldn't control it. The pain was suddenly there, and it was excruciating. As his vision begins to go black, he sees two sets of boots rushing toward him, one being the familiar black boots of Zero, followed by a wave of calmness in his mind.

Chapter Three

Hurrying through the halls, Mercy holds Ruby on his hip with Charlyn and Saphie trailing behind. As soon as he felt Sylas's pain, he lifted his travel restrictions and rushed to Ozra. He didn't even need to be told what happened, he already knew and once he arrived, they only confirmed his fears.

Darting between the people in the halls he finally makes his way to the infirmary of the estate. Cal had added this wing after the events of Spheara to prevent any more lives being lost on the estate grounds. It was dedicated to those who had fought beside them and built to keep their families safe in these vulnerable times. Now it housed Sylas, Mercy's best friend and his Nota.

Breaking through the doors to the lobby, he ignores the front desk and rushes toward the area he knew Sylas was. He could sense both Cal and Sylas in that direction, so he simply needed to follow his feet. All the details had already been given to him, so he wasn't wasting time with a check in. Charlyn pauses at the desk with Saphie to speak with the woman as Ruby and Mercy continue forward.

Locking his eyes on Cal in the hallway, he slows his pace. He could see his Alia was speaking with a woman very diligently, taking her words to heart. This was Doctor Willa. She was one of the most praised and recognizable doctors in Ozra and now headed the estate infirmary. While she traveled when needed, the estate was her main place of practice. She also had an office outside of the grounds in the capital to aid those not associated with the Royals or Spheara.

Mercy didn't even care to let them finish their conversation before speaking. "What the hell happened?" he interrupts with fierce eyes on Cal, Ruby still clinging to his hip.

"Thank you," Cal nods as Doctor Willa walks away. With his friend rushing toward Sylas's door, Cal puts a hand on Mercy's chest to stop him. "You need to take a breath before I let you in there."

"Why was he alone?" Mercy snaps. "You promised me he wouldn't get hurt on that assignment! You said I could trust Zero! Why didn't the shield protect him!?"

"Calm down!" Cal scolds in a low voice. "Sophos, you sound like a mother."

The relationship Mercy had with his best friend made this whole ordeal more terrifying. After what happened in the courtyard, the thought of losing Sylas was all the more real. His best friend was his last connection to his childhood and the moment he felt his pain from this incident, he feared the worst. His hand still felt the dull ache, even after Sylas had been patched up.

"I thought he was dead," Mercy scolds. "Do you have any idea-"

"I know," Cal eases, giving Mercy an understanding look. "I already talked to Zero about what happened in detail. Remember, you're the one who wanted Sy to have his independence. You knew this could happen."

"Zero said a Shadow attacked," Mercy follows up. "My shield-"

"Did not work," Cal finishes harshly, his tone matching Mercy's.

Taking a trembling breath, Mercy nods his head. He could tell that Cal was just as shaken up by this as he was. His Alia still had feelings for Sylas, he had made that very clear. It was one of the few things Cal confided in him over the last several months. Every time Mercy went on a mission with Sylas, Cal made him promise he'd get him back safely and he always did. Neither one of them wanted to risk losing him again.

Mercy begins to chew on his bottom lip, trying to calm himself for his own sake and Cal's. The fact his shield failed was the least of their worries. He looks down trying to make sense of the situation.

"Can you heal him?" Cal asks, sincerity in his voice.

"No one healed him yet?" Mercy retorts, his eyes darting back up to Cal. He feels Ruby grip him tightly as the conversation grows more tense.

"You think they didn't try? He will not let a Light Keeper near him," Cal states with an annoyed tone.

"Why's he refusing?" Mercy bickers, confused.

Taking a deep breath, Cal closes his eyes trying to find the words. This was delicate and complicated, but he needed to try and rationalize it. Opening them again he looks at Mercy and speaks with a calm voice. "Whoever this woman is severed his fingers on his left hand. Half his hand is gone, Mercy."

"So, what's that mean?" Mercy interrogates.

He could see the exhaustion on Cal's face. He had been buzzing with worry long before Mercy arrived. The King's unease mirrored the Light Keeper's, but at the same time was much deeper. While Mercy feared losing a friend, Cal feared losing the man he loved.

Caligo takes another deep breath. "The fingers are gone, Mercy. He would not let Zero try to heal him in Orior so there was not any chance to..." he trails off, frustrated at the words he was saying. "With natural healing it is going to take quite a bit of time before he could potentially get back into a fight. Doctor Willa suggested we have a Light Keeper heal him, but he has to agree to it. Once he is healed, she will be able to assess the damage better, and look into alternatives for him."

"By the Elders..." Shaking his head, Mercy places Ruby on the ground as he begins to understand.

Archery and fighting were things Sylas took seriously and without his fingers on his dominant hand, he couldn't draw the string of his bow back. His bow and arrow was something he was good at and losing his talent and passion was a scary thought. Not to mention losing his left fingers meant he couldn't write, his main form of expression. Sylas most likely felt like he lost everything. He probably felt just as empty as Mercy did when he gave up his Source, but even then, Mercy had the option to take back his power whenever he felt like it. Sylas was sitting on the threat of never being able to do the things he loved again.

"They were looking for you," Cal continues to explain as Charlyn approaches. "This was supposed to be some sort of warning for you."

"What?" Mercy questions, shaking his head in puzzlement.

"I checked you in, Mercy," Charlyn announces. "I can take the girls upstairs to your suite." She looks to Cal. "Is it the usual, Your Grace?"

Cal nods his head, keeping his eyes on Mercy. Charlyn nudges Ruby away from Mercy, but she clings to him even tighter. The little girl was wary to let him go. With a steady exhale, Mercy crouches down and takes her hands in his. He looks her in the eye, his gaze serious. While he wanted to be there for her, he needed to be there for Sylas right now.

"I have to make sure Sylas is okay, Rubes," he explains to her. "Can you be brave on your own for a little bit? Be brave for Uncle Sylas?"

"I'll stay," she insists.

"No," he adds, shaking his head, letting out a sharp breath. He glances to Saphie who had a frown on her face as well. "This is grown up stuff. Go with Char and I'll come upstairs as soon as I can."

"Promise?" Saphie asks.

He nods as Charlyn takes Ruby's hand. She leads the two girls toward the exit of the infirmary as Mercy watches. He felt bad sending them away. Ever since the break in, both girls had been using him as a security blanket. Every chance they got they were by his side.

"Fatherhood suits you," Cal remarks.

"It terrifies me," Mercy retorts with a small smile.

"Those girls adore you though," Cal notes, watching them go through the door.

"I'm starting to wonder why anyone would willingly have kids. Ruby is *always* sticky. I don't even know what it is half the time," Mercy shares in annoyance.

"Do you want to know?" Cal pokes, using the break in their bickering to lighten the mood.

"No," Mercy laughs.

The two pause another moment before Cal nods toward the door and opens it. Mercy enters first and scans the room. It felt too small for the big personality that Sylas had. After he got back from his trip his personality seemed to have only gotten louder. His eyes fall on Sylas who was sitting cross legged on the bed reading a book as usual. Though today, instead of reading a history book or a Source Tome, he was enthralled in a fiction novel.

"How're you feeling?" Mercy asks, his tone soft.

"Hey," Sylas greets, closing his book. "High five?" he asks, raising his left hand to show off the bandages and splint he wore.

25

Noting Mercy's wary eyes, Sylas rests it back down with a wince. Seeing the injury brought a look of sadness to Mercy's face. His right hand goes to his left, the echo of the injury still fresh in his mind. The fear and pain still felt raw. Though there was distance between them when it happened, it didn't seem to make the feeling of pain any less intense. Even with the bandages he could see Sylas was missing a majority of his left hand.

"You realize I'm never taking leave on assignments again?" Mercy shares, going in for a hug.

He holds his friend tightly for a moment before letting him go. It was relieving to see Sylas alive and well. Mercy had been at the shop working on paperwork in his office when it hit. His apprentice, Yule, heard the screams and rushed to aid him. Not being able to run to Sylas's side right away was agonizing. It was one of the reasons they had always gone on assignments together.

"I asked if we could just regrow it," Sylas smirks as Mercy pulls away, "but I noted the lack of *palm* trees."

"Still bad, but I'll give you that one," Mercy chuckles with a small huff.

"Thank you!" Sylas praises. "No one here has laughed. They don't appreciate my humor here."

"It is an acquired taste," Cal shrugs, closing the door as Mercy stifles another chuckle.

"So are you, King Charming," Sylas adds, pointing at him with his uninjured hand, giving him a wink. "The taste of royalty isn't a bad one."

"Stop it," Cal scolds. "Whatever they gave you is making you unbearable."

"You," Sylas puts his attention back to Mercy. "The evil woman said this," he points to the bandage, "is a message for you from some asshole named Bryer. Interpret it however you please but next time, I'd prefer not to be the messenger boy."

"Bryer?" Mercy asks, staring at his friend's hand.

"Yes," Cal confirms. "Does the name mean anything to you?"

"No," Mercy replies.

The Light Keeper shakes his head lightly taking in the name. Whoever Bryer was, he wasn't a good person. This was a message of hatred. This was trying to get a rise out of the pacifist Light Keeper.

"The lady who did this also took the Riekan Tomes and the genti notes," Sylas informs, "and Sander."

"She has Sander?" Mercy questions, alarm in his voice.

"We are not sure yet," Cal deflects, glaring at Sylas for sharing the information.

"Did you page Pippa yet?" Sylas asks, turning to look at Cal, who was hovering by the door.

"I did," he nods.

"Why do we need Pippa?" Mercy questions, his voice seeming to go up an octave.

He wasn't about to let Pippa become a part of this Bryer person's agenda. If he was willing to do this to Sylas, who knew what he was willing to do to anyone else. While Pippa could hold her own in a fight, Mercy would rather her not be involved.

"The woman, Iana, was throwing around the term of Supra Keeper," Cal informs. "Sylas and the Ozran Elders have never heard of it, so we are hoping Pippa can make sense of the statement, or at least start looking into it."

"I'd prefer her stay out of this," Mercy notes.

"Why is that?" Cal inquires with a raised brow. "She knows our history and the Source readings better than anyone in Ozra. She has spent the most time with the genti tome, other than Sy. If anyone can make sense of what this woman meant, she can."

"We both know why he doesn't want her here," Sylas laughs in a sing song voice, batting at Mercy with a grin.

27

The chewing on his lip begins again. Mercy and Pippa had become close over the last year, beyond close, but a relationship wasn't in the cards. Not only was the idea terrifying to him, but he had no interest in the physical aspect of what a serious relationship involved, nor was he ready for that kind of commitment. Regardless, putting her in danger didn't sit well with him.

"He's in love with your little nonbiological sister, Cal," Sylas teases, unable to control himself.

Mercy darts his eyes to his best friend. The two of them had spoken about Pippa a few times, but he had purposely kept the subject away from Cal. He didn't want to make his Alia uncomfortable or have him make any remarks on the relationship.

"Like I said, you are unbearable," Cal rebukes toward Sylas. "I am going to tell them to cut you off."

"No!" Sylas frowns with a pouty lip.

"Mercy, can you just heal him please," Cal prompts, putting a hand to his forehead in annoyance. "I cannot take any more of this childish behavior."

"Not sure he's any less childish without the drugs," Mercy remarks. He looks at Sylas with stern eyes. "Give me your hand."

"No!" Sylas barks, pulling it to his chest. "I already told Zero 'no.'"

"Sy, please," Cal begs. "We need you."

The Nota's eyes dart between Mercy's hand and his face. Keeping a firm yet understanding look, Mercy nods his head. They needed Sylas out of this room and back on his feet, even if that meant he was coming without part of his hand. Seeing the apprehension, Mercy looks to Cal for help.

The devastation he had experienced when he lost his legs begins to play in Cal's mind. The helplessness he felt and the fear for his future were all he could think about while he healed. Even his first set of prosthetics gave him

28

little hope toward his future, but he learned to use them. He learned to fight with them. It was one of the hardest obstacles he had to overcome in his life, but he did it. With the help of Doctor Willa and Master Novi, he had been able to learn to see the injury as a way to progress forward and make himself even more deadly in a fight.

After meeting Mercy, the clever blacksmith had improved his fighting even more. The pair had gone through many models of prosthetics over the last year until they found the perfect match for his rapid fighting style and needs. With how often he needed to go from a casual pace to a fight, it made it difficult, but Mercy was up for the challenge. Mercy even altered his weapons to work better with his spiritum fog recalling or to be used as a crutch in emergencies. Honestly, the Light Keeper's mind was fascinating when he was allowed free rein of inventing and improving items. It took Cal time to see it, but he truly was a genius.

"You will get your perfect shot back," Cal states, staring at the pair.

Both Mercy and Sylas look to him with perplexity, Mercy souring his face quickly. How were they going to do that? He didn't want Cal giving his best friend false hope.

"I have been trying to tell you how childish and stubborn you are acting when in reality I should have just..." Cal trails off rolling up his pant leg. "You think I wasn't afraid that was the end of the line, Sy? I thought my fighting days were over."

The fun demeanor Sylas had been putting on quickly falls as he studies Cal's prosthetic. The strong metal frame had been made sleeker and the shocks and springs made each step smoother and quicker than before. Mercy had even painted them black and purple since they were Cal's favorite colors.

"We *will* get your perfect shot back," Cal repeats. "You are not the first person on Novus Aitus to lose a few fingers, and certainly will not be the last. It may be challenging, and you will need patience, but you can and will get it back."

"You can't guarantee that," Sylas responds in a quiet voice, looking at the bandage and splint.

"But we can try," Mercy nods in agreement.

"The worst mistake you can make right now is looking at this as something that will hold you back," Cal continues. "You do that, and you are going to lose yourself, Sy. We just got you back," he points to his own head, "do not get lost in there again."

"You know I hate admitting when Cal is right, but he is," Mercy sighs, looking at Sylas.

The last year had been taxing for all three of them, but for Sylas it was different. While Mercy and Cal were trying to establish their lives with their new responsibilities, Sylas was trying to figure out where he belonged entirely after Spheara.

Staring at the bandage on his hand, Sylas lets out a steady breath. He hadn't even thought about how Cal had to move past losing his legs. That thought hadn't even crossed his mind. Seeing Cal fight was astonishing, and he did it with grace. Not for a single moment did Cal look at the loss of his limbs as a weakness. Sure, he had his days where he would get frustrated, or maybe a few moments where he stumbled or had to take something slow, but it didn't hold him back. He used what happened to move himself forward. If Cal could find a way to work past that, then he could surely find a way to move past losing a few fingers.

"Minor inconvenience," Sylas nods, putting his hand up and waving it.

With another deep breath, Sylas leans forward and moves his left hand to Mercy. With some hesitation, Mercy unwraps the bandages, wincing at the sight. The top part of his Nota's palm was held shut with a mass of stitches. He

30

could tell the blade had cut at an angle, showing a slight slope of damage across his hand. The woman had cut slightly past the base of the fingers and through the top part of his palm. The fingers were completely gone.

Glancing up his arm, Mercy could see a symbol cut into the skin just below the crook in Sylas's elbow, one that he had never seen before. He furrows his brow at the strange lines, wondering why no one had mentioned them yet. The circle with a line and swirl through it was odd and not anything he had seen before in his studies.

He looks up to Sylas who seemed unconcerned by the marking and takes his eyes back to the stitches on his friend's hand.

"They need to take out the stitches," Mercy pauses, giving Sylas worried eyes.

With an annoyed huff, Cal moves forward, pulling an item from his pocket. He shifts out a small scissor on a utility blade and hands it to Mercy. Looking at the tool, Mercy begins to chew on his lip again. Why couldn't Cal just go get a nurse or something?

"Just do it," Cal demands with frustration in his voice. "Get it over with."

Taking the blade and steadying his breathing, Mercy cuts each of the stitches and lets them drop to the floor. He could feel his own hand begin to ache with each passing moment. Once the last one was out, he places his palm to the wound, holding the hand as steady as possible, and begins to heal it. While usually healing Sylas would send a wave of relief through him, that wasn't the case this time. As he attempted to heal the injury, nothing was

31

happening. The more he tried, the more obvious his failure was becoming. After another moment, he drops his hand and looks at his Nota in confusion.

"Why didn't it work?" Cal asks, alarm in his voice.

"I don't know," Mercy admits, looking at his own hands in puzzlement.

Pulling his hand away, Sylas's eyes bolt between his hand and Mercy's face. Mercy quickly registers the look of fear in his best friend's expression. The more Sylas stared at the injury; the more fear crept into his eyes.

"Go get Doctor Willa," Mercy orders Cal. "She needs to restitch him."

Without a second thought, Cal leaves the room to find the doctor. The same fear in Mercy and Sylas was echoing in Cal. The trio were completely baffled by what they had just witnessed.

"What the hell..." Sylas mumbles to himself.

"Don't panic yet, Sylas," Mercy heeds, trying to keep his own voice steady.

Mercy could see the anxiety bubbling up in Sylas with each passing second. The more Sylas stared at his injured hand, the more restless he became. The severity of the injury was creeping in slowly, and then all at once.

"The Light Source doesn't work on me anymore?" he asks, looking to Mercy. "What's happening?"

"Sylas, you're gonna be fine," Mercy states, trying to make sense of this himself. "Cal is going to get Doctor Willa and we're going to figure this out."

"My fingers are gone, Merc!" Sylas shouts, looking between his hand and Mercy again.

"It'll be okay, Sy," Mercy assures him.

"I don't have Source powers like you do!" he shouts. "I'm useless!"

"You're not useless, Sylas," Mercy retorts, unsure what to do in that moment. "You'll never be useless."

They both look up as Cal comes back into the room with Doctor Willa. The woman moves to the Nota without saying a word and begins working on his hand. She appeared annoyed but kept her professionalism.

"You can't heal me, I lost my shield, my archery days are over. What's the point in me even being in the Sentry anymore?" Sylas continues, locking eyes on Cal.

"Sy…" Cal closes his eyes trying to hold back his own emotions. Seeing Sylas like this made his heart ache.

"Please leave," Doctor Willa states to the pair. "You are only making him more upset."

Mercy looks to the floor, unsure what to say. Why wasn't his Source working on Sylas suddenly? This made no sense. Staying silent felt like the better option right now. He winces as Sylas continues to shout.

"What am I supposed to do!?" Sylas screams at his Keeper.

"Go!" Willa barks at the pair.

Getting up, Mercy moves to the door and grabs Cal's arm, yanking him along. They both step outside the door and stand in silence for a moment. Their minds were reeling. What on Novus Aitus would take Sylas's shield and render Mercy's Source useless on him? Mercy glances to Cal who mirrored his confusion and worry. None of this made any sense. What the hell happened in Orior?

"Did you say Zero tried healing him, or Sylas refused?" Mercy questions, looking up to Cal.

"Refused," Cal clarifies.

"What the hell?" Mercy mumbles, looking to Sylas's door.

He takes his attention to the blade in his hand and grabs Cal's arm. He shifts the utility blade into a knife and without prompt, he makes a small cut on Cal's forearm, his Alia hissing in pain in response.

"Sophos, Mercy!" Cal protests.

Putting the blade away, Mercy puts his hand to Cal's arm and attempts to heal him. He keeps his thoughts steady, making sure to focus on positive energy. After a moment he pulls his hand away to see the cut was healed, the scar nearly invisible on Cal's dark skin. Realizing what Mercy was doing, Cal takes a deep breath, but keeps an annoyed expression on his face.

"I don't get it…" Mercy whispers to himself, pulling out the knife again.

"I swear if you cut me again, I will kill you myself," Cal snarls, snatching his utility blade away from Mercy. "If you want to use me as a test subject, ask next time."

They hear a crash in the room, followed by the door opening and Sylas storming out. His hand was partially bandaged as he shoves Mercy out of the way. He glares at the two of them shaking his head. Seeing that Sylas was losing it brings a pained expression to both Keepers' faces.

"Sy, try to calm down," Cal pleads. "We can figure this out."

"You want me to calm down? Why don't you calm down!?" Sylas snarls, pausing to look at Cal.

"Please," Cal begs.

"Back off or I'll touch you," Sylas threatens, putting his good hand up.

Caligo quickly backs away in fear of the shield that would blast him. He wasn't sure if the shield would still affect him or not, and neither was Sylas. Just because it didn't work in Orior, didn't mean it wouldn't work now. It causes Cal to lose his footing and stumble into a cart as Sylas moves past them in a rage.

"Sylas!" Mercy shouts after him.

Moving to his Alia, Mercy steadies Cal's feet. The two pause a moment taking in what just happened. While both of their initial reactions were to chase after him, they knew it was better to let him simmer down. Sylas needed time to collect himself before he would even think to listen to their words.

"That did not go well," Cal mumbles, pushing Mercy away from him.

"You thought it would?" Mercy retorts with agitation. "Never tell him to calm down. It just makes him more upset."

"Noted," Cal sighs in annoyance.

"He isn't discharged yet," Willa states to the pair, appearing in the door.

"We will get him back as soon as we can," Cal assures. "He just needs a moment."

The woman nods her head as Sylas shoves through the infirmary doors, leaving his friends behind.

Chapter Four

The technology of the capital never ceased to amaze Mercy, and the conference room was no exception. While usually he would be captivated by the touch screen in the table and Cal's ease of using it, today his mind was elsewhere. He couldn't even concentrate on his friend's words. His mind had been foggy the last couple of weeks and had only been getting worse. On top of the brain fog, all he could seem to really think about was Sylas and the sudden inability to use the Light Source on him.

In the conference room sat Mercy, Cal, Master Novi, Pippa, Tristia, and Zero. The group had come together to try and make sense of what happened in Orior and to piece together what Bryer and the woman who attacked Sylas were trying to accomplish. There was clearly a plan being enacted by this woman and they were desperate to get ahead of it.

"Captain Bellator gave a fairly good description of the beast in Orior," Cal shares with the group, pulling up an image that had been rendered of the creature and projecting it into the air at the center of the table. "While it's something we've never encountered before, he is confident it was manifested by the Shadow Source, which means we have a rogue Keeper of Shadows."

"I told you we needed to do licensing or at least regulations on Keepers," Princess Tristia adds, the anger clear in her voice. "This would fall under improper use of a Source connection in the proposal I brought to the National Council months ago."

"I'm starting to agree with the prissy Princess more and more," Zero admits.

"I agree as well," Pippa adds, looking from Novi to Cal. "You know I respect the Sources and our Keepers, but we need to protect ourselves against those who use it maliciously. This creature is not a proper use of a Source connection and a crime against the balance."

"Crime or not, we need to figure out their motives," Cal notes, looking at the beast with solemn eyes.

This thing had aided in hurting Sylas, and he wanted it tracked down and destroyed. Whoever was controlling this was their enemy and needed to be dealt with accordingly. The threat it posed to his people was not something he was going to take lightly, especially with the clear threat made by the woman controlling it.

Scrolling through the file Cal brings up a new image. The eerie face of a man they were assuming to be Bryer illuminated the tabletop, his image projected into the space above it. The King looks at the image with a serious gaze. There didn't seem to be much information on Bryer other than a birth date and his last known location. The only image they had of the man on record, he had a hood over his head that was shadowing his face, making his features hard to decipher.

"Bryer Nitesems," Cal nods to the image.

"He looks friendly," Zero scoffs, leaning back in his chair.

Tristia gestures toward the image, "What do we know about him?"

"Not much," Cal discloses, swiping the image off the screen and bringing up more information on the man. "He appears to be a dishonorable discharge from the Unity Council, from a small village in Vicinia called Doma. He has kept a fairly low profile after his discharge until recently. It appears he is one of the minds behind the rebel group in Vicinia that call themselves Malice."

"A rebel group?" Tris questions, raising a brow.

"Yes," Cal confirms. "We don't have much on them either unfortunately. They have a few branches popping up in Ozra these days, but they seem harmless."

"Harmless my ass," Zero snaps. "You need to get better at gauging your threats, Caligo."

"Why was he discharged?" Tristia continues, leaning forward to look at the information closer.

Giving Zero a quick glare, Cal goes on. "Unfortunately, our mother was not the best at keeping records," he states, taking his gaze to his sister as she scrolls through the file. "I have someone from the Sentry Guard Recruitment Center working on locating a physical file on Nitesems from the UC archives in hopes it may clear things up."

"What would they want with Validus though?" Zero asks, gesturing to the Light Keeper as Mercy stares at the table numbly, clearly not even paying attention. "He's hardly been involved in anything since Spheara. He's actually pretty incompetent."

"He is not incompetent," Cal snaps in a low voice, his irritation with Zero showing through. "I have Pippa looking into that."

"I have a few ideas, but I would prefer to speak with Sylas in private before bringing them to you or the National Council," Pippa shares, giving Cal a smile and small bow of the head.

"I would like to get a handle on this in general before involving the National Council," Cal confesses.

"You're forgetting to mention one crucial detail, Your Highness," Zero eyes Cal.

"And what is that?" Tristia asks.

"Bryer's daughter," Zero shares, swiping his hand over the table to bring up her file.

"She is dead," Cal differs.

"Seemed pretty alive to me in Orior," Zero retorts.

"What is he talking about?" Master Novi questions.

"Bryer has a daughter. Iana," Zero explains, pulling up an image of her. "Archives claim she died four years ago in one of Mala's suicide missions, but somehow Bellator gave her name and identified her as his attacker."

"We are not going to start chasing ghosts, Zero," Cal stresses. "She is dead."

"Is she?" Zero tests with a frown. "I was dead for eight years according to your records, but last I checked I was still breathing this shitty air."

As the group continues to bicker, Mercy focuses on an ant walking across the table. The small insect had avoided the detection of the others in the room, but not Mercy. He had his eyes on it ever since it crawled onto the surface. Usually, he would listen to the meeting but today he couldn't even act interested in the topic no matter how hard he tried. His mind was jumbled, and his feelings felt more and more disordered the longer he sat there.

As the little bug makes its way toward the center of the table his ears begin to ring as his heart begins to beat in his skull. Closing his eyes, he welcomes the sensation knowing what it was leading up to. This was going to be a vision from the Elders, and it was perfect timing. At least he'd have an excuse for not listening to Cal.

He had only had a handful of visions over the last year. He had been able to predict an injury Cal risked on an assignment as well as a large fire in Cessa. There never seemed to be a pattern to what he saw, but each one was triggered by being in a location or being around someone involved in the outcome. Spirits on the other hand were another story. Since the return of his Source, he hadn't seen a single spirit, which seemed to concern Pippa and Sylas, but he paid it no mind.

He lets out a gasp of pain as his skull begins to ache. What was this? When he had visions before they never hurt. Why was this hurting him?

"Mercy, are you okay?" he hears Cal's voice ask as the ringing drones louder.

Attempting to shift his gaze, Mercy's vision goes blurry as he's thrust into a new setting. Scanning the forest, he was now in, he attempts to figure out what he was meant to see. The forest around him was empty and after the first few trees in his line of sight, everything appeared pitch black. This was strange. Usually, his visions were clear and vast, not limited by a blackness.

Taking a few steps forward, he spots someone laying in the grass. With a deep breath he approaches the motionless figure. It was a man with brown hair wearing an all too familiar dark purple vest. Getting closer he could make out the face.

Filled with panic he stares back at his own corpse. He lets out a sharp breath and takes a step backward. Blood soaked the purple vest from a wound on his side and his entire body was drenched in water. There was another point of blood seeping from his head. Had he bled out, drowned, or had head trauma? He couldn't even tell from the state of his body. All he could tell was he was unresponsive, and his chest was no longer rising.

As he continues to take in the scene, trying to connect the dots, he feels the familiar grasp of the Elders pulling him back to reality. Frantically he looks around for a clue to where his body was, but there was nothing. All he could see were trees and a river nearby, the black haze keeping him from seeing more than 20 feet in any direction. His future self was alone and dead in the forest with no explanation of how or when he got there.

With a gasp he comes back to himself in the conference room. The plunge back into his body causes him to push back from the table and his chair to jolt into the wall. He looks around frantically grabbing his chest to make sure he was still alive as his breathing goes into heavy gasps. A searing pain hits his head as he squeezes his eyes shut. Just as quickly as the pain came on it eases, but the panic was still there. His eyes were ablaze as he looked around the room trying to calm himself.

"Sophos! What was that?" Tristia shouts.

"He had a vision," Cal snaps at her, keeping his eyes glued to his Alia.

"Mercy?" Pippa moves toward him, but he puts a glowing hand out to gesture her to stay back.

His eyes dart to Cal who gives him a concerned look. Had Cal been able to see his vision through their Voca? The sight of his own body was horrific. Why would the Elders show him his own corpse? Cal takes a step toward him, but Mercy gives the same response with a slow head shake. He needed a moment to process this. He needed a moment to breathe.

Suddenly he feels Cal in his head trying to encourage him to relax. He squeezes his eyes shut attempting to get his Alia out of his mind. The uneasy sensation Mercy could feel from the comforting gesture indicated Cal knew what he had seen. The images were probably painted in Cal's mind unwillingly. It was something he hadn't been able to control when he was around Caligo. It seemed the more the pair used their Voca, the more difficult it became to turn it off when strong emotions were involved.

The familiar terror begins to creep in as Mercy gets to his feet, his eyes scanning the table for the small ant he had been following before the interruption. Looking around, the room suddenly felt too small. He couldn't breathe in here. He was suffocating in this room.

"I need to go," Mercy mumbles to himself. "I-I have to- I need to go. I'm sorry."

He rushes toward the door as his breathing goes ragged. What was he supposed to do with this vision? It was too vague and unclear to be helpful. There were forests and rivers all over Novus Aitus. There wasn't a single sign in the vision to indicate where his body even was to try and avoid it. All he could muster was that he was going to die alone on the forest floor.

Slamming the door behind him, he moves to the wall on the opposite side of the hall and leans his head against it. The cold stone felt good against his burning skin. He needed to calm down. Freaking out over this wasn't going to prevent it from happening. Going into a panic would just make things worse. He begins calming himself down again with his breathing exercises.

What would Saphie and Ruby do if he were killed? They relied on him for care, comfort, and safety. Not to mention what would happen to Brokkr's Forge and the two apprentices he was teaching his craft to? He needed to keep the techniques going to keep his mentor's memory alive. His students still needed his guidance and knowledge. He couldn't leave Sylas, Caligo, or Pippa behind either. They needed him. He couldn't die. Not yet. Not anytime soon.

As the door behind him opens, he winces at the realization someone followed him. He just needed a moment to get over the initial shock and sort out the meaning of the vision. If they would just give him a moment he'd come back to the room and the meeting could continue.

"Mercy, whatever you saw…" he hears Pippa's small voice chime behind him. "You know it is not set in stone. A Keeper's visions change all the time."

He turns to her quickly, trying to force a smile. He couldn't let her know what he had seen. Not yet anyway. With everyone shaken up over the incident with Sylas and the fear of Bryer and the beasts, he couldn't add more fuel to the fire.

"It's fine," he assures. "Everything's fine."

She studies his face and could see the fear in his eyes. Whatever he had seen had shaken him up quite a bit. "What did you see?" she asks, putting a hand toward his cheek, only to have Mercy pull away.

He watches her closely, trying to take in the familiarity of his close friend. Her features seemed more defined now. He hadn't seen her in a couple of months, but it was plenty of time for her face to age just enough to be noticeable. She had darkened the purple streaks in her hair and had taken the time that morning to put it into an elegant braid that draped over her shoulder. Her shoulder had an intricate white tattoo on it now, symbolic of her continued studies of the Sources and spiritual ranking. She had gold painted around her right eye to try and distract from the foggy pupil in her left, something she often did since they had met, the injury still something she was self-conscious about at times.

"Nothing," he snaps, trying to stay calm while his eyes were big.

"This does not look like nothing," she replies, attempting to approach him again.

"I need space, Pip," he mumbles, trying to back away again, but the wall holding him in place. "Please. I'm sorry."

She watches him a moment and nods her head as Cal comes into the hall. The look on Mercy's face was all he needed to confirm what he had seen in flashes. Mercy saw his own death and he was terrified.

43

"Pippa, why don't you go find Sy," Cal suggests, keeping his eyes on Mercy. "You two can discuss what you need, and I will get Mercy back to his suite."

The woman looks between the two of them. She could tell Cal was aware of what Mercy had seen and she disliked getting shut out of their conversation because of it. Their Alia connection and Voca made it impossible for them to hide things from each other. The psychological bond the pair had made her angry at times, but she respected it.

"Fine," she sighs, backing away. "I will be sure to come by and check on you later, Mercy."

He nods his head, still trying to regulate his breathing as she turns away and heads down the hall. As soon as she turns the corner, Mercy begins to slide down the wall having lost his ability to hold it together any longer. Suddenly standing felt impossible.

Grabbing him before he hits the floor, Cal pulls him up. "Stay on your feet, Mercy. Let's take a walk," he directs with an understanding tone.

This had been happening often with Mercy lately. Cal had begun to refer to it as "going boneless." When something shook up Mercy, he seemed to lose all ability to hold himself together and would just become a pile on the floor. It was usually coupled with a feeling of terror or an episode of crying. While it was annoying at first, he had begun to understand the worry and fear that was afflicting his friend. It was something he was becoming familiar with himself. He honestly envied Mercy's ability to be so open with his emotions, even if it wasn't necessarily being done on purpose.

Letting Cal keep him steady; Mercy nods his head and lets him lead the way. He hears the door to the conference room open as they begin to wander down the hall. His vision had completely ended the meeting. How were they going to accomplish anything if his unstable mind was enough to sidetrack a meeting like this? They needed to get a handle on this Bryer situation, not worry about him.

Leading him to a door at the end of the hallway, Cal takes Mercy out onto a balcony that overlooked the city. Mercy pulls away from his friend and leans on the railing trying to take in the fresh air as Cal closes the door and watches him. They both stay quiet and somber for a moment, Cal aware that Mercy just needed time to collect himself. After what Mercy had put in his mind, he needed a moment himself. The idea of losing his Alia was daunting. The friendship they had forged since they met was important to him and he didn't want to lose it.

"I would ask if you are okay, but I think I already know the answer," Cal finally speaks. "I will *not* allow that vision to come true."

Mercy nods his head in understanding. He knew Cal would do everything in his power to prevent something from happening to him, or anyone else he cared for. When you had Cal's adoration, he'd fight to the death for you. His loyalty was something Mercy admired. He knew when Cal was around, he had someone there to watch his back and seeing someone care for Sylas the way Caligo did kept him at ease. With the King of Novus Aitus's heart set on his best friend, he knew he would always be surrounded by the most trustworthy and strongest people.

"I'm not ready to die," Mercy mumbles, rubbing his hand down his face and taking a deep breath. "I can't die. Too many people depend on me."

"You will not," he assures. "You know as well as I do those visions can be changed."

"I know," Mercy agrees, bowing his head with a shuddering exhale. "This was different though... This didn't feel like a warning, Cal. This felt like...a promise."

Coming up beside him, Cal places a reassuring hand on his friend's shoulder. Based on what he could see in the vision, he wasn't exactly sure how they were going to prevent it. There wasn't any way to know exactly when or where it was going to happen, and they both knew something as simple as him not wearing that purple vest couldn't resolve the nightmare they saw.

"I'm tired, Cal," he adds, closing his eyes. "I'm tired of fighting. My entire life has been one fight after the other. I just want to take a moment to-"

"Breathe?" Cal finishes.

"Yeah," Mercy nods, leaning his head on the cool metal railing.

"I wish you could," Cal agrees.

"Sometimes I get so tired of everything that I start to feel like I'm drowning," Mercy adds, forcing a laugh. "I feel like a child trying to live up to an unrealistic expectation. Everyone wants something from me, and I don't know if I can give it."

"We are simply a couple of kids who had to grow up too fast," Cal states, looking out at Ozra. "Forced to take on these leadership roles we should not have had to."

Mercy shakes his head, standing up straight. "I thought I could do this, Cal. I really did. I thought I could handle the responsibility of being a Keeper of Light, but now... I have a family I need to worry about and a village that depends on me... I can't... and Sylas- I can't..."

The King watches Mercy for a moment. His Alia looked tired, but not just physically. He was emotionally and mentally drained as well. The last year he had been trying to put his life back together and heal himself. While they had both lost so much to Mala, what Mercy lost was different. Mercy had to live every day wondering if he'd make it to the next morning and now that he had freedom, he didn't know how to use it.

"I thought after Spheara I was done hiding," Mercy confesses.

46

Cal nods, looking down. "I am afraid you cannot hide from this one, my friend. Bryer is going to find you, and when he does-"

"I know," Mercy replies with a heavy exhale. "He's dangerous. I don't even think I can take the girls home."

"You and the girls are welcome to stay here," Cal adds. "You are always welcome here."

At least having the girls in Ozra meant they would be guarded and difficult to get to. The woman Bryer had working for him could easily take the girls in his sleep. Being here they were under constant surveillance and safe from any enemies he may have lingering out there.

"Thank you," Mercy breathes, giving a small smile.

"Try not to dwell on this vision too much," Cal emphasizes. "The future is forever changing, and nothing is guaranteed."

"That's the scariest part," Mercy admits. "I was given these visions to try and help people but half the time I'm worried sharing them won't even matter. One change in a decision, one factor shifting, and the entire outcome is different."

"I don't find that scary," Cal shrugs. "I find the uncertainty of the future endearing. It means nothing will last forever and anything can happen."

"Like maybe winning Sylas back?" Mercy asks with a raised brow and a playful smile.

Cal laughs at the statement and nods his head. "That is one thing."

"Something his report said is bothering me," Mercy adds, looking down. "That woman told Sylas I had more loved ones she'd like to meet…"

"I saw that," Cal replies.

Mercy thinks another moment and turns to Cal with big eyes. "Meera…"

"What about her?" he questions, as the terror in Mercy begins to echo through him. "Oh no…"

47

Chapter Five

Walking out onto the back lawn of the estate, Pippa spots Sylas. He was attempting to shoot his bow, but his look of frustration proved he was struggling. He was attempting to draw the string back with his thumb and what was left of his hand. The blood seeping through the bandages was indicating he shouldn't be pushing himself so soon. It had only been a few days since the injury, and he was not giving himself time to heal.

Releasing a shaky arrow, Sylas lets out an annoyed scream as it misses the target. In frustration he slams his bow into the grass and begins to fiddle with the bandages that were covering his hand. At this point he had removed the bulk of the dressings and splint and was doing more harm than good to the injury. He huffs at the sight of blood seeping through but showed no sign of letting up on his efforts.

"Perhaps you should allow yourself time to heal before getting back into your craft?" Pippa suggests, approaching him.

"I'm not patient enough for that," he retorts, retrieving his bow from the grass.

"Odd," she notes. "Your patience has always been something I admired about you. Strange it would vanish in such a short amount of time."

She hears him let off an annoyed huff. Learning to shoot without his fingers was going to require practice and time. At least he was trying, even though he should have been resting. Seeing his efforts this early in his recovery showed he wasn't ready to give up.

"Do you have a moment to speak?" Pippa asks, stopping beside him.

She notes the messy curls that were nearly to his shoulders now. He usually took time in the morning to tame them or pull them back, but he had clearly come straight here after being discharged from the infirmary. He wore a dark brown sleeveless shirt and black pants with a brown leather bracer on his left arm. He even had on his chest guard to protect his shirt from the string's draw back.

"I'm a little busy," he mumbles, pulling another arrow from the quiver, and fumbling with it.

"I see that," she notes, assisting him.

He gives her an annoyed side glance but accepts the help before drawing back his arrow. There were about fifteen arrows strewn across the lawn, none of which were stuck in the target he aimed for. Cal was right, he seemed to have lost his perfect shot, or at least Sylas thought he had. There was no doubt in Pippa's mind he would find it again, he just needed time to let his injury heal.

"We can talk while you practice," she states, understanding he needed to do this.

He takes aim at the target again and watches his hand and bow shake from the pain and strain as he tries to steady it. The longer he tried this, the more his hand ached and the worse the shaking became. He closes his eyes for a moment trying to calm himself, hoping this was all in his mind. He opens them again and shoots the arrow. He watches as it skims the target and imbeds in the grass with the others. He lets out a hiss, feeling the pain from his hand resonate through his arm.

"Damn it!" he groans, releasing his bow and letting it hit the ground with a thud.

"It will not come back over night," Pippa comforts, picking up the weapon for him. "You just need time."

"I should have never gone on that assignment," he sulks taking the bow from her and walking toward the estate with rage in every step. "I was stupid to think I could handle myself. I never should have gone into the woods alone."

"You are perfectly capable of handling yourself," Pippa adds, following him.

"Yeah, that explains why I get my ass kicked every other week," he snaps back.

"Defending your people," she stresses as he picks up speed. "You seem to have forgotten how big of a component you are in every battle you have seen. Your scars are proof of your bravery, Sylas. Your intentions are always good, even when you fall short."

"Having good intentions isn't enough to save anyone," he shoots back.

She could hear the frustration in his voice. It had been difficult enough for him to find his place after Spheara, and now the Elders were just putting more roadblocks in his way. It seemed the more he tried to separate himself from Mercy, the more he was pushed toward him. While he loved his best friend, he didn't love being his Nota.

"The Elders are only trying to help you," she stresses, trying to hurry her pace to keep up with him. "Things like this happen to support you in your journey."

"The Elders are punishing me," he growls.

"I disagree," she retorts. "The Elders would not punish someone with a heart as good as yours."

He rolls his eyes at her words and speeds up his walk more. He wasn't in the mood for her acolyte wisdom. While he believed in the Elder Spirits, in that moment he wanted nothing more than to curse their existence.

"Sylas, can you stop for just a moment," Pippa pleads, unable to keep in stride with him.

He pauses and turns to her with steely eyes. "What do you want, Pip?"

"I was hoping we could speak about what you saw in Orior," she explains. "From what you described in your debriefing; I fear those beasts that are being reported are called obscurums."

He nods his head and looks down to refocus on the topic. As much as he wanted to pout about his hand, he needed to help his friends. He lets out a steady exhale and nods his head again before looking at her.

"An obscurum?" he asks.

"Yes," she confirms as Sylas begins walking again, this time keeping in pace with her. "I remember studying them in the genti tome. There were partial instructions on how to make them, of which I translated. If she took the notes as Mercy says, then she has access to that information. They are created by the Shadow Source, and they are powerful. If this Iana woman has our notes, Sylas, she can easily overpower anyone we send after her, including Mercy and Caligo."

He shakes his head in disagreement. "Cal can take care of himself, Pip, and Mercy is smart. He knows how to use his Source better than ever. I'm sure they can take care of this. Especially-"

"Mercy is still a novice," Pippa warns, her tone showing her worry. "Yes, he has improved, but he has a long way to go. He is far from being a Master Keeper."

"You saw what he did at Spheara. You've watched him train with Zero, Cal, and your mother a dozen times. He's powerful, Pip. He just needs confidence," Sylas reminds her as they walk through a door into a small weapons room in the back of the estate. "If Bryer or anyone else is after him, it's probably because they think he's a threat."

The power Mercy had was beyond any Keeper of Light they had encountered thus far. The things he could do were unheard of. No Light Keeper could absorb another's power like he had done, especially one from an opposite Source. His ability to control and manipulate a Shadow's spiritum fog and convert it into his own weapon was something they didn't even understand, Mercy unable to explain it himself. Any Keeper who encountered him mentioned the sheer ferocity of the Source power he exuded being overwhelming. The only ones who didn't seem to get anxious around him after long periods were Cal and Zero. Though Zero had voiced he had a challenging time being around Mercy on multiple occasions.

"I fear what he did at Spheara," Pippa explains as they come to a stop at a locker.

Noting the concern in her voice, Sylas furrows his brow. She wasn't just worried for her friend; she was fearful of him. He had to agree that Mercy had the aptitude to do dangerous things, but was it something to fear? Was his best friend's Source connection really that big of a deal?

"Why?" Sylas asks, narrowing his eyes, removing his chest guard.

She looks away from him for a moment to collect her thoughts. After seeing what Mercy had done in the courtyard, her fears had grown with each passing battle. Mercy's full potential mirrored Caligo and they already knew Cal was capable of tremendous things. Being able to take the lives of over 100 UC Guards in Rieka was an unimaginable feat. Mercy being of equal power on the opposite end of the Sources meant he could do things they couldn't even grasp yet. Having access to the Aitian Source Tome and the other materials at the Northwest Source

Temple had painted a truly horrific picture of the pair of Alias that she had kept to herself. If either Cal or Mercy unlocked their full potential, it could end poorly for everyone involved.

"Pippa, what do you know?" Sylas pressures, seeing the worry on her face. "What aren't you telling them?"

Her eyes dart to him. "I fear it may be easier to show you," she states.

"Show me?" he questions.

"I cannot explain it," she admits. "Follow me."

"Where are we going?" Sylas asks, confusion evident on his face as he shoves his gear in the locker but keeps his bow at his side.

She smiles. "We have some reading to do."

As they enter the library of the estate, it felt fuller than usual with many of the books placed on the shelves coming from the Northwest Source Temple. Fiddling with his bow, Sylas watches Pippa move along the wall searching for something. He glances over to a locked case on the other side of the library where the genti plated tome was held securely, taken from Mercy's protection. He could see a camera aimed at the book that was displayed below thick glass to protect it. He wondered if he'd ever be able to hold the book in his hands again.

"Caligo has been letting myself and other Ozran acolytes study the Aitian books here until the Northwest Source Temple is restored," Pippa explains, walking along the wall. "There was one book in particular that I have been keeping to myself, fearful of Cal or Mercy discovering it. Though if this Iana woman also knows about what I have determined, it may be time to share the information with them."

"Why hide it?" Sylas asks with a raised brow, as Pippa pulls a few books from the shelf to reveal another she had hidden behind the stack.

53

"Because of what it depicts," she enlightens him, moving to a table.

She sits down, opens the book, and begins to shuffle through it. She gestures for Sylas to join her. He does as requested and sits in a chair to her right, leaning his bow against his leg. He watches her scan the pages with concern in his expression.

"Most of the books in the Great Library of the Source Temple are from the old world of Aitus," she begins. "We still cannot quite figure out who brought these to Earth 400 years ago. Well… you know the story."

Sylas nods, finishing the history lesson with an exasperated tone. "Answering the human's beacon wasn't supposed to involve Keepers. They sent the distress call, we answered, we found the planet in complete chaos. I know the history, Pip. What's that have to do with Merc and Cal?"

"I believe someone had very different plans for our planet," Pippa enlightens. "Perhaps a Keeper like Orlo Validus, who could see visions of the future. Perhaps one who saw Mercy's potential on Novus Aitus. Their decision to bring these books and Mercy and Cal discovering them has given us information we never had access to before. Information that Mala would have relished in if she had taken the time to actually look through that temple."

"Maybe she would have treated Cal a little better," Sylas laughs tensely.

"I very much doubt that," Pippa retorts with a frown.

She continues to flip through the book as Sylas watches her. She pauses on a page with a depiction of a Keeper of Light and slides the old leather hardback toward him.

"We always knew Mercy and Cal were powerful," she states. "My mother and Orlo made this very clear when enacting the Spheara vision, but I think Mercy may be more powerful than we thought."

Sylas begins to read the page as his eyes get wide. "This is impossible."

"Is it?" Pippa asks, turning to the next page. "Read here," she requests, pointing to a paragraph. "Mercy can take the Shadow Source and convert it to the Light. He can use it as his own or recharge himself with it, Sylas. That should not be possible, but we have both witnessed it. You said Cal was exhausted after he ended the Fall of Rieka, but you also noted he was able to use his Source the next day. After unleashing the Shadow Source on such a mass level, not once but twice, it should have taken him days, if not weeks, to recuperate. What they are doing is not normal. Not just to our knowledge, but to the knowledge of our ancestors."

Continuing to take in the information, Sylas nods his head. The claims depicted on the page were unimaginable. It spoke of a combined level of Source magic that could create an unstoppable Keeper, one that could seemingly bend reality to their will. A Keeper that was above all others and exhibited abilities gifted from both Sources. A being who could supposedly create life itself. One phrase caught his attention, the word "Supra Keeper" was cited multiple times. This was the same word Iana had used in the forest in Orior. If Mercy truly was a Supra Keeper, then it made sense why Bryer was after him.

While Mercy was good at what he did and was constantly showing skills beyond what other Keepers of Light could manifest, controlling the Shadow Source was something Sylas was skeptical of. Converting spiritum fog to solis fog was one thing but controlling the Shadow Source all together seemed outlandish. Then again, the book formulated it oddly. It wasn't so much that a Supra could control both Sources but instead could seemingly mimic the abilities with the aid of a small spark. Sylas turns the pages, he craved further explanation, but the text was limited.

"This could mean they are more than just a Shadow or Light Keeper," Sylas laughs with nerves. "This could mean they're practically gods."

She nods her head, taking the book back from him. "A Supra Keeper of the Sources," she states. "I have never witnessed Cal trying to manifest a Light Source weapon without being a Penumbra, but we both know he is beyond what a Keeper of Shadows should be. He is stronger and can push himself further than others. My mother has even admitted she has knowingly limited him out of fear." She pauses a moment before continuing. "It is doubtful they are both Supras. It would be more likely that Cal's Source is simply attempting to mirror Mercy as best it can. If Mercy is a Supra, this means he can create Keepers, manifest peritias," Pippa informs him, "he could restore drained powers, take them away, practically do whatever he pleases. There would be no limitations, Sylas. His only confines are what he can think of and what his body can physically handle. A Supra is untouchable, and dangerous if they cannot figure out how to control their abilities. This would explain why no action by the Spirits was taken when Mercy killed Charity or Trust."

"That was a Keeper's Judgement," Sylas reminds her. "Those lives weren't taken on purpose."

"I do not believe that," she differs, shaking her head. "A Light Keeper in Resili took the life of a barn cat when it scared her last winter, and she lost her connection. The act was unintentional, it was just a cat, yet the punishment was still given."

"You're basing this off of limited encounters, Pip," Sylas speculates, calling out her conjecture. "There isn't enough information to call either of them a Supra."

"A Penumbra is a bridge between the Light and Shadow Sources, but a Supra is above them. It would explain why Mercy has two peritias and why the Elders are so in tune with him," she adds. "You have seen Mercy when they speak with him. He zones out entirely, like he is on a different plain of existence. He can hear their voices like he hears ours. I have spoken with at least a dozen Light Keepers, including Zero, and not one was able to say they have heard the Elder Spirits speak to them. Not even yourself, and they have helped you in the past. Why else would he be gifted a person as a Nota when nearly all other Keepers born during these times are given an animal. It would also explain why Orlo chose him to live over his other two children. Even you have to admit it seems heartless for Orlo Validus to let such a gruesome fate play out for his other children. This would explain his choices, Sylas."

He shakes his head and looks down, taking a deep breath. He knew Orlo, he grew up with him, he didn't want to believe that Orlo purposely let Charity's fate play out the way it did. He didn't want to accept that Orlo trained Trust to be used as a pawn and Mercy to be some cosmic hero. None of this held up with the picture he had of Orlo Validus in his mind, and it never would.

"This is insane," Sylas mutters. "How long have you been speculating this?"

"Since I found the book," she informs him, closing it. "I was afraid if I spoke with Mercy about it, he would become fearful of his Source again."

"Good call," Sylas nods, sitting back trying to take in the material.

"I fear Bryer knows about this based on what you told Caligo and Zero," she stresses. "If he has access to the obscurum beasts, then who knows what else he has figured out. The events of Spheara were publicized, and what Mercy did has been speculated about ever since. If someone with knowledge of a Supra is in Bryer's court, then that may be why he is trying to reach him."

They both pause as Mercy comes to a stop at the door and enters the library. He looked out of breath and worried, like he had been rushing around.

"Sophos! We've been looking all over the estate for you two," he scolds.

Seeing and feeling the fear coming from Mercy, Sylas perks up. "What's going on?" he asks as Pippa slides the book off the table.

"We need to go," Mercy pants. "Now. Preferably 30 minutes ago."

"Why?" Sylas asks.

"You said that lady was looking for more people to help send me a message, right?" Mercy asks, his eyes ringed with white light.

"Sophos," Sylas gasps, understanding his friend's concern.

Chapter Six

Moving to a secluded area of Ozra felt like the right way to cope after losing Trust. Being alone was something Meera valued, but until Spheara she had never felt truly lonely. Part of her regretted having Trust sever her connection before he passed instead of just gifting her his. When she had made that agreement with him, they had planned on Trust still being there to keep her out of harm's way, but things quickly changed that day.

He had pulled her aside on the way to the arena to tell her what he planned to do. While Orlo's vision had predicted the death of Mercy's friend Sylas, Orlo hadn't shared with Trust that the young man was Mercy's Nota. Having gone through losing his own to Mala, Trust couldn't let that happen to his brother. Especially knowing Mercy's Nota was an actual person, and someone they had grown up with. Letting Sylas die without trying to change the course of the vision felt unjust and a betrayal of the kindness Ezra and Wynna Bellator had shown the Validus family. It was just another selfless act the man she had fallen in love with had done for others. Trust had always put others above himself, knowing he was just a small stroke of the brush in the overall painting.

After that day, Meera had returned to Bernya, but her family had voiced their disapproval of her involvement in Spheara. Her parents supported Mala's tactics and all that she had done to the Keepers, including the fallen tyrant's treatment of Meera and Trust. This made the few months she spent in Bernya with her family exhausting, and she wasn't about to bring her child into a family who despised everything she and Trust were.

When she brought up the concerns to Sylas in a letter, he reached out to Mercy who offered to make her a home wherever she saw fit, and this was where she chose to do so. At least she had somewhat of a family in Ozra. While at first Mercy seemed hesitant to be around her, he eventually warmed up. After she had Velia, he became even more supportive and made sure to check on her frequently. The young man was quiet, but he made sure she, and Velia had all that they needed. Even though he didn't visit often, she knew Mercy cared for them.

Sitting on her front deck she takes in the late autumn night while sipping a cup of hot tea. The air was cool and the night quiet as the baby slept inside. This was her first taste of silence in months, and she wanted to enjoy it. Getting Velia to sleep was never an easy feat and raising her alone was even more strenuous. Moments like these were few and far between.

Closing her eyes, she takes a deep breath and places her mug on the table beside her. She takes a moment to pull her hair up into a messy bun before opening her eyes again. Looking out at the trees, she furrows her brow. For just a moment she caught a glimpse of something or someone in the tree line watching her. Getting to her feet she moves to the edge of the wooden deck and focuses her gaze on the forest that surrounded her small cabin.

She shivers in place, the wool shirt and pants she wore not quite cutting out the crisp autumn air as a gust of wind swept through. She was being paranoid. Spending so much time alone combined with her lack of sleep were bound to make her start seeing things.

Turning around, she picks up her mug as a sharp pain hits her in the back. She lets out a gasp and drops the mug, soaking her feet in the hot tea as it shatters. Putting a hand to her chest she feels the sharp point of a blade sticking just below her collar bone. Tears quickly come to her eyes. If she was under attack no one would be there to protect Velia.

Through the pain, she rushes inside and slams the door behind her, locking it. She looks around the room and spots Velia still asleep in her crib by the fire, the infant not even aware of her mother's injury. Moving swiftly, she grabs the baby and rushes to her room. While her chest was burning, the adrenaline running through her was keeping her feet going. Placing Velia into her buggy by the bed, she goes to the closet and pulls a crossbow from a case. Grabbing a small silver device inside the case, she hits a button to send a message to the capital that she was in danger. She wasn't going down without a fight.

Dropping down beside the buggy, she begins to shake at the sound of a pounding on her front door. This was exactly why Mercy had requested her stay in Rieka. In Rieka he could protect her and Velia, but here she was miles away. Here she was the perfect target. Alone and isolated.

"Meera!" she hears a familiar voice scream.

Grabbing Velia carefully, to avoid the blade in her chest, she gets to her feet. Cradling the infant she moves slowly back into the main room, keeping her cross bow aimed at the door. The voice sounded like Mercy, but how could it be? There was no way he could have gotten here that quickly.

"Meera, open the door!" his voice screams again.

She hears the sound of a deafening screech from outside as the pounding stops. She drops to the ground and pulls herself and Velia behind a table, keeping the crossbow ready to fire.

Outside, the booming noises from the creature had caught the attention of the group as Mercy scrambles trying to find an open window to the cabin. The broken mug and the drops of blood on the porch showed a terrifying depiction of what could have happened just before they arrived. The idea of Meera being injured or worse was sending surges of panic through the Light Keeper.

Sylas, Pippa, and Cal sat in a large metal vehicle, one of the many they had kept in the capital and main Sentry Guard locations. Cal and Sylas sat in the front with the door to the back open where Pippa was sitting. It was large, bulky, and painted a steely gray. The windows and vehicle were made up of sharp angles with large tires to maneuver off the smooth paths. Seeing one of the solar powered transports was rare, but they were needed when time was of the essence, like now. In fact, most missions that involved the King of Ozra called for the vehicle to keep him protected and moving quickly.

"That's the damn thing!" Sylas shouts at Cal from the passenger seat, covering his ears as another shrill cry shakes the group.

Hearing his words, Cal opens the driver's side door. With determination on his face, he exits the transport and begins powering up as soon as his feet hit the ground. They were taking care of this problem now.

"What're you doing?" Sylas shouts, following him out of the vehicle and around to the back. "Caligo, don't be an idiot!"

As another tremendous roar wracks the forest, Cal scans the area. He comes to a halt beside Sylas at the back of the transport, ignoring his friend's worry. If the beast was already here, that meant Iana or Bryer weren't far behind. They had been trying to draw Mercy out and had finally succeeded.

Frantically looking around the trees, Sylas opens the back doors of the transport. He glances at Pippa who was sitting quietly with a look of worry in her eyes as he begins shuffling around items. Moving the bags wasn't going fast with his injured hand held close to his chest. Pippa quickly goes to help him knowing full well when Mercy brought Meera and the baby out, they needed to leave fast.

"We can't let them get to Mercy!" Sylas shouts at Cal. "Do you hear me, Caligo?"

"I thought that was self-explanatory, Sy," he snaps back, moving away from the transport and into the front yard. "Note to self... Do not let the Light Keeper die or the Nota will kill you," he mumbles to himself with a small laugh. It seemed like that had become his job since he met his Alia.

Cal watches the trees in the direction the beast's call came from as spiritum fog begins to seep from his fingertips. He was ready to take on whatever this was. It had been a while since he was in a good fight, and he was ready to break back into the action. He just needed to buy Mercy some time to get Meera and the baby into the vehicle. The odds of this thing being able to outrun the transport or best his driving skills were slim.

At the back of the cabin, Mercy was now growing more impatient. Realizing the back door was locked, he draws his Source to his hands and places his heated palms to the hinges. He lets out a hiss of pain as his shoulder begins to ache. Why was his shoulder hurting?

The hinges now hot orange, he backs up and uses his shoulder to ram the door, breaking it away from its frame. The pain in his shoulder rings through his body as he stumbles into the dark room hearing his niece begin to cry at the loud crash.

"Meera," he speaks into the darkness, jumping as an arrow comes barreling toward him. "Meera, it's me!" he shouts, putting a shield up to block the blow. "It's Mercy!"

She pops up from behind a table, aiming a crossbow at him, a serious look on her face and a crying infant cradled to her chest. His eyes get wide at the sight of the blood soaking her wool sweater. Seeing how on edge she was, he yanks off his gloves and puts his hands up and quickly draws his Source to prove it was him. The intricate glowing veins in his hands and forearms light up his white tactical suit, the standard uniform for a Light Sentry Guard, showing he was safe and who he claimed he was.

"It's alright," he reassures her. "Me and Cal are both here, okay?"

She nods her head as she drops the cross bow to her side. Mercy being here meant someone would be able to protect Velia from whatever just attacked her. She lets herself fall to her knees as another loud roar echoes through the house.

"Wha' es that?" she pleads in her Bernyan accent as he comes up beside her, looking toward the front door.

"I don't know, but maybe we should go before we have to find out," he remarks, getting her to a standing position.

She yelps at the pain in her chest and her legs start to give out, but quickly gathers herself. Mercy grabs the baby, cradling her with one arm while supporting Meera with the other. They needed to leave. He'd have to heal her once he got her to the transport.

"I got you," he reassures.

As they approach the front door, Meera unlocks it. Mercy pulls her through the doorway, grabbing the attention of Cal who was on the front lawn at full power. He looks to them, taking in the blade protruding from Meera's chest and sees the blood that was now starting to soak Mercy's white uniform. Rushing over, Cal takes Meera from his Alia and helps her toward the vehicle.

"Iana is trying to send another message I see," Cal grunts, guiding the woman toward the back of the transport, her blood soaking his dark uniform as well.

"Her messages just keep getting friendlier and friendlier, don't they?" Mercy snaps with sarcasm.

Sylas runs over and meets the group as the beast breaks through the trees. All of them pause and look up at the horrifying creature that Sylas had described. It seemed bigger than what he portrayed and much more menacing. The dark smoke that surrounded it obscured the night sky, making the entire canvas of stars go hazy. Peeking out of the back of the wagon, Pippa's eyes go wide. The sight confirmed that this creature was truly an obscurum, and a powerful one at that.

"Sy, get her and Pippa out of here," Cal orders, handing Meera off to him.

Keeping his Source at the ready, Caligo trails Mercy and Sylas as they rush toward the transport, Cal keeping his eyes on the obscurum. Mercy hands the baby to Pippa, who clutches the small bundle to her chest, worry plastered on her face. Her eyes go to the beast as Mercy moves to help Sylas hoist Meera in. As Meera sits across from Pippa, Mercy climbs in and swiftly yanks the blade from her back. She screams in pain as the beast lets out another screech. Eyes wide with panic, Sylas gets into the back of the wagon, leaving Cal to protect the vehicle on his own.

Working on healing Meera, Mercy gives his Nota orders. "Sylas, whatever happens, you keep Meera and Velia safe. You do not come back here under any circumstances. You take them straight to Sintus. Got it?"

"We can't leave you here," Sylas argues, moving to the door that separated the wagon from the driving cabin.

"That is an order from an Ozran Council member and the Keeper you serve, not from your friend," Mercy adds, finishing his healing. "Do you understand me?"

"Merc, I-" Sylas begins.

"I said, do you understand?" Mercy snaps with a glare.

Seeing the severity in Mercy's eyes, Sylas nods. "Yes, sir."

With an irritated glance at his Alia for his choice of words, Cal bolts away from the transport. Mercy on the other hand, hesitates. He hated pulling the Nota card on Sylas, but situations like this called for it. It made him feel even more guilty for their situation. Deep down he knew that if he gave Sylas an order as his Keeper, his best friend wouldn't be able to deny his request.

"Sorry," he mutters to Sylas before leaving the back of the transport.

As Sylas watches the pair get ready for a fight, he swallows his anger. After closing the back door, he looks at Pippa. "You can drive this thing, right?" he asks, his voice rushed and breathless.

She nods her head with big eyes as Sylas moves through the steel door to the driving cabin. He waits a moment, but Pippa doesn't follow. Popping his head back through the door he stares at her.

"Let's go!" he snaps.

"What about-"

"They can handle this!" Sylas barks. "Let's go!"

With that, Pippa hands Velia to Meera and heads to the driver's seat. While she wasn't as skilled at driving one of these as Cal was, she could handle getting them to Sintus. Buckling in, she pushes the accelerator with one hand and steers with the other. Speeding away from the action, the transport moves toward the main road, leaving Cal and Mercy behind.

As Mercy comes up beside Cal, they both look up at the beast. It had come to a stop just outside the trees watching them closely. It appeared to be frozen, but the sight of the creature was menacing enough.

"Is this thing made of spiritum fog?" Mercy asks, the fear clear in his tone.

"You should really start paying attention in meetings," Cal snaps, his eyes dark. He looks Mercy up and down and could see his suit lacked the metal plating his own had. "Didn't I tell you, you needed to wear armor?"

"I am," Mercy breathes, tapping his chest to show the light shield hovering just above his skin.

"Not exactly what I had in mind, but that works," Cal admits in annoyance.

If the monster was here, where was Iana? How close did she need to be to control this thing? Mercy's Source begins to illuminate the area as Cal's fog coats the ground. It created an eerie image with the obscurum's own fog filling the air around them. They stare at the beast as it pants from the edge of the trees.

"Mercy Validus!" they hear a woman's cheerful voice say from the forest. "It's about time you came out to play."

Glancing to Cal, Mercy waits for instruction. While he was improving his combat skills, he still relied on Cal or Sylas to tell him what he needed to do in a real fight. He wasn't bold enough to let it go the other way around. Other than Spheara, Cal always took the lead, but it seemed for once he wasn't sure what to do. He could feel the hesitation in his Alia's mind as he tried to analyze the situation. This was a new threat, and Cal wasn't sure what to do to win this fight.

"Show yourself!" Cal shouts.

About 20 feet in front of them a woman uncloaks. She wore the same combat suit and mask Mercy had seen at his house indicating she was the one who broke into his home. Pulling the mask off, she smiles at the pair, her slim face focused on Mercy. He probably looked more scared than brave in that moment with Meera's blood running down the side of his suit.

"I'm so excited to see the Supra Keeper himself," the woman fawns, taking a step toward Mercy.

Cal pulls his blades from his back and quickly puts up a wall of spiritum fog, sending a message for her to keep her distance. Mercy looks to him and could hear the clear instructions for him to stand back. If these people were after him, Mercy needed to mind himself. He nods his head to signal he understood Cal's request as his Alia quickly drops the wall.

"Going after an infant seems a little low," Cal snarls, moving in front of his counterpart, snapping his blades into their signature polearm.

"I wasn't going to hurt the baby," she frowns. "The woman on the other hand? I could see her being much more fun than that Nota. She has much more at stake."

The comment puts Cal on edge. This was the woman who had attack Sylas which meant she needed to be taught a lesson. No one went after Sylas without facing a brutal consequence and Iana was no exception to that rule.

"Why are you targeting Mercy's family?" Cal interrogates.

"I don't like when people demand things from me. Especially you," the woman scowls, her voice sounding sweet. "Your Majesty must understand that not everyone agrees with his politics, myself being one. You trying to order me around is only going to anger me."

"I do not really care if you agree with my politics," he snaps, gripping his weapon.

"I'm not sure why you brought him with you, Mercy," she sighs, taking her attention back to the Light Keeper. "Someone of your power should be able to take on an obscurum with little effort."

Mercy looks to the large creature standing behind her. It was simply staring at the pair as Cal spoke with the woman. What was she even talking about? How was he supposed to fight that thing?

"If it's made of spiritum fog, how did it touch Sylas?" Mercy mumbles to himself.

Cal shoots his eyes to his Alia, annoyed that he spoke. He wanted him to stay quiet. Anything he said to this woman could be ammunition for her to attack. Being quiet shouldn't have been a problem for him. His natural state was silent.

"Inquisitive minds deserve answers," Iana yields, gesturing toward her creation. They both take a defensive stance as the beast begins to move toward them. "You see, even a Nota's shield can have flaws," she smirks. "Those notes you so kindly handed over to me have a very special rune in it, one that I'm sure your acolyte friend would love to see in person. Have you looked at your Nota's arm lately?"

She moves her eyes to Caligo, a smile drawn on her face as she pulls a dagger from her belt. This prompts Cal to pull his polearm into two blades again. The polearm he had now was altered quite a bit. He and Mercy had worked on it for months trying to come up with a design that matched his fighting style and needs. He had even fashioned the blades hilts with a few straps to make them easier to recall with Cal's fog when he was disarmed. They could also be fashioned into a crutch in case he was to lose or break a prosthetic in a fight.

"I just want to see your arm for a second, Your Highness," she mocks.

Both Keepers dive out of the way as the beast lunges toward Cal. Mercy quickly creates a solis orb and launches it toward the woman, sending her several steps back. She shrieks in irritation as the beast continues to go after Caligo, seeming to absorb any attack he gave it.

This thing mimicked the fighting style of a Shadow Keeper. It could use the fog that built it as a weapon and with each attack Cal threw at the obscurum, it simply mirrored his efforts. Each tendril of spiritum fog was met with one of equal or greater power. Trying to take any blows with the curved blades Cal held was pointless, the weapons seeming to slice through thin air. Each attempt Cal made at trying to ward off this thing was useless, meaning it was just a waiting game before Cal wore himself out.

Watching his friend try to fight off the creature it becomes clear Cal was making no advances. It seemed her creature was adding his spiritum fog to its form, which meant the more Cal tried to defend himself, the more fuel he was giving it.

"Stop!" Mercy orders through their Voca, putting a shield up around his Alia as the beast goes to strike him. The attack bounces off the shield as Cal pulls his fog back toward him.

Whatever message Bryer was trying to send, it was clear it involved taking out those Mercy cared for. While he only knew Cal for a little over a year, they were bonded. Not just as Alia Keepers but as friends. Cal was like a brother to him. He was family and he was done letting people take away his family.

Registering that Mercy was protecting Cal, the woman turns the beast's attention toward the Light Keeper. His eyes get wide as the monster begins to take steps toward him, causing the ground to rumble at his feet. He needed to come up with a plan, and he needed to do it quickly. If Cal's Source was useless against this thing, that meant the outcome of this fight relied on Mercy.

Glancing to Cal, he gets the message he needed. "Solis fog." If this beast was made of spiritum fog, perhaps he could use his Source to sway it over to his side.

With a look of determination, he rushes toward the creature, pulling as much of his Source to his right hand as possible. He needed to make this count. As he comes up to the beast, he drops to skid across the grass under it and forces the energy from his hand into the spiritum beast's legs as he slides below it. The dark purple mist quickly turns into a white cloud at his Source's touch. His stomach drops as he comes to a stop in front of Cal. The energy coming from the beast was one he knew. It belonged to Sander. He gets to his feet beside Cal and drops the shield.

"Never put me in your stupid solis jail again," Cal scolds, powering down. "I was about to stop."

Mercy couldn't help but let out a small laugh. It wasn't the first time he put Cal in a shield, and it wouldn't be the last. As the beast turns back to him, only one leg turning into the ghostly white, Mercy pulls his Source to his hands again. He winces at the burning in his arm, grabbing Cal's attention.

"Are you hurt?" he questions.

"No," Mercy growls through gritted teeth.

Just as Mercy begins to move forward the beast suddenly backs down, moving quickly into the tree line. Turning wildly, he searches for the creature and the woman, both seeming to be gone.

"Did you see where she went?" Mercy asks Cal, keeping his Source at the ready.

"Maybe if you had not turned your back to the enemy, you would have seen yourself," Cal lectures him. "How many times do I have to tell you to-"

Cal turns quickly feeling his hair stand on end as Iana appears behind him. He quickly puts an arm up to block her hit with his forearm. Grabbing her wrist in response, he twists it and shoves her to the ground. She lets off an annoyed groan as she gets to her feet and starts a series of rapid kicks and punches at Cal, the King easily fending off each blow. Watching in shock, Mercy takes a few steps back to let Cal move freely without the worry of hitting him. Each hit Cal delivered to Iana seemed more and more powerful, his rage and Source fueling his body.

Narrowing her eyes, the woman finally gets a good hit in, punching him in the face, causing Cal to stumble back. Taking the moment, Iana cloaks herself. Cal looks around trying to focus in on her Source energy but struggled with the pain from the hit. This girl hit like a battering ram. It was in that moment he started to realize just how out of practice he was from a real fight.

She appears behind him, kicking him in the back of the knees and using her fog to rip his weapons from his hands. This causes his legs to buckle out from under him and he swiftly collapses. In the same rapid motion, she pushes Mercy back further with a tendril of fog to put space between him and Cal. Reaching for his blades, the woman uses her fog to pin Cal, pulling his arm out straight as she begins to carve into his skin. He screams as the blade cuts him, sending a searing pain through his forearm.

Swooping down from the trees, Nex goes in to protect her Keeper. The sudden ambush from the crow causes the woman to slice through whatever she was doing on Cal's arm and release him. Cal scrambles to his feet and rushes toward Mercy who puts a shield up over him again, this time Cal thankful for the protection. He needed a moment to collect himself.

Turning, Cal watches Nex as her talons continued to rip at the woman's face. After a moment he whistles for his Nota to pull back as Iana flails her arms around trying to get a hit at the crow. Nex had gotten a good scratch at her eye, blood trickling down her face as she held it tightly shut. This was the first time Mercy had seen Nex attack someone trying to harm her Keeper. Whatever this woman was doing, Nex was scared of.

Anger on his face, Mercy keeps the shield on Cal and sends a wave of Light Source energy toward their enemy, knocking her back. With an angry scowl she discharges her spiritum fog in response toward Mercy, Cal quickly powering up to wall his Alia off from the attack. Now completely furious, Mercy pulls his Source to his hand, shining his lit palm toward the woman. With his

72

Light Source bright, it made it more difficult for her to call her Shadow Source and every attempt he simply converted it into his own weapon. He watches as Cal's dissipates as well, his Alia pulling back knowing Mercy had the upper hand here.

"I can kill her," Cal suggests through their Voca.

Mercy shakes his head. The two had sworn Cal's killing days were over, which meant he wasn't allowed to use his Shadow Source to take any more lives. Mercy would prevent that at all costs.

The Light Keeper lowers his arms, keeping his Source in his veins, the vessels in his hands dancing with the soft white glow. "I'm here to receive your message," Mercy snaps, projecting his voice. "Give it to me before this goes in a direction you won't walk away from."

He places one of his hands to the blade at his waist. Hidden within a leather sheath was the Pura Blade. Since the break in, he had kept the ipdum close, feeling he needed to protect the last item his brother gave him. While he had never been willing to use it before, now he may have. This woman coming after Meera and his niece was too much. Velia was the last blood family he had left in this world, and he wasn't about to let this woman or anyone else take that away from him.

"An actual threat," she chimes, putting her own dagger into its sheath. "He might get what he wants from you after all, Supra Keeper of Light."

"Which is what?" Mercy asks.

She laughs. "He just wants the world to see you both for who you truly are. You are a threat to the balance."

"We restored the balance!" Cal barks.

"Oh, shut up, pest! You'll be gone soon enough!" she snaps, wavering in her peppy tone for the first time. Putting it back on she speaks to Mercy. "You see, Malice knows what a Supra Keeper is capable of. You are only beginning to understand your full potential. You have more power in your little peacekeeping finger than most will ever have in their entire body."

"What are you talking about?" Mercy inquires, looking at his glowing hand.

"You'll understand soon," she smirks. "He'll draw it out of you. I'm glad we had this chance to meet, Mercy. If only you didn't take my new toy from me," she frowns, looking at Cal. "I'll get him later. I know when I'm in over my head. The King and your Shadow Guard will be so happy to be reunited."

"What'd you do with Sander?" Mercy snarls, launching an orb at her.

With that, she cloaks herself, the orb hitting a tree behind her. The two Keepers stand on edge for a moment, but Cal soon relaxes as her energy leaves the area.

"She's gone," he announces. Looking to his Alia, Cal's face quickly goes to irritation. "If you are not going to listen to me, why do you even bring me along on these little outings? I told you to keep your mouth shut."

"Sorry," Mercy mumbles.

"How is it you manage to screw up the simplest of orders, Mercy?" Cal retorts, walking toward the cabin. "I swear, you are going to get us all killed one day."

Chapter Seven

The group had stopped in Sintus for the night, staying at Master Novi's house. While Sylas was out picking up some food and a few supplies, the young women were upstairs trying to wind down. It didn't take Mercy and Cal much time to catch up with the group after their departure, Meera's horse still being at the cabin. After the obscurum and its puppeteer ran off the two had grabbed a few necessities for Meera and Velia before heading to Sintus to meet the rest. It had gotten late, but at least they were somewhere they felt comfortable.

Beside Mercy and Cal was the infant, wrapped in blankets, lying in a small bassinet Novi had from when Pippa was a baby. The two had left in such a hurry that Cal didn't even bother to have Mercy heal his cuts until they arrived at the house. They were reluctant to waste any time before getting somewhere safe. Now being in a secure and familiar location, Mercy was able to take the time to get a good look at what the woman had cut into his Alia's arm.

"The symbol on your arm looks similar to the one on Sylas's," Mercy notes, finishing his healing session. "Unfinished, but she tried."

"Sylas has a symbol on his arm?" Cal questions, watching the glowing scar dissipate.

"I noticed it in the infirmary," Mercy nods pulling his hand away. "It was by his elbow."

"I wonder what it is," Cal voices in concern.

"Whatever it is, can't be good," Mercy sighs.

The baby begins to fuss as Mercy looks at the fire. The King watches his friend get to his feet and scoop up the little bundle. He begins to shush her with light rocking, not wanting her cries to disturb Meera upstairs. She quickly begins to settle in his arms.

"They are trying to get to you. First the break in, then Sylas, now this," Cal adds.

"Clearly they have plans for you too," Mercy adds, nodding at his friend. "She threatened you at the cabin tonight."

"Threats are useless on me," Cal smirks, leaning back on the couch with a stretch. "I am far too stubborn to die."

The pair exchange a small smile as they fall silent. Mercy continues to rock Velia in his arms, keeping his attention on the baby. Finally looking at the infant, Cal furrows his brow. He had yet to see Meera and Trust's daughter, and Mercy hadn't spoken much about her. His Alia had been insistent on hiding the newborn but had neglected to tell him why. He had even requested the birth records be kept out of the public archives, which Cal gladly agreed to. While he assumed it was just Mercy being paranoid, now he wasn't so sure.

"Am I seeing what I think I am?" Cal asks, getting to his feet.

"I told you I was hiding her for a good reason," Mercy shrugs, pulling her away from his chest.

Moving closer, Cal's eyes get wide. He had assumed Velia was marked based on who her parents were, but this was not what he was expecting. Her hair was a peppered mix of white and black, her skin patched with both pewter and porcelain, and each eye was marked for one of the Sources. Her left was a light silver and the other obsidian. It reminded Cal much of himself when Mercy had left his Light Source with him. While his skin had kept its pewter tone, his hair and eyes mirrored what he was seeing in Velia. Had Trust and Meera's daughter been born a Penumbra? Was that even possible?

"Meera was scared," Mercy explains with uneasy eyes, "and so was I. So… I got her the cabin hoping to the Elders no one would see Velia until we were sure. I wanted to tell you… I just… I wasn't sure how you'd react."

"Does Master Novi know about this?" Cal questions, keeping his eyes on the baby.

Mercy nods his head, pulling Velia close to him again. Meera had told Novi in hopes she would be able to help them. They decided the secret be kept between the three of them to keep Velia safe. The less people who knew about her, the better. Even Sylas was left in the dark. When Mercy would bring Sander or the girls by the cabin, the baby was kept out of sight. Any whispers of her getting out could cause a stir that he wanted to avoid. If something happened to her, he would never forgive himself.

"Novi's heard of her future, Cal," Mercy shares. "We're scared of it."

"What did she hear?" he asks as Mercy goes to sit on the couch.

The Light Keeper shakes his head. What Novi described put Velia in a similar light as Mala. She was an angry woman on a power trip with hatred in her heart. He needed to change her future, but how could he do that if the vision he had in the conference room came true? How was he going to save his niece if he lost his life?

"What is it?" Cal asks, noticing the waiver in his expression.

With a steady exhale, Mercy shakes his head again. "I'm going to change it. I promised Meera I would."

"Change what?" Cal asks, staying on his feet and keeping his eyes on Mercy.

"That's all you need to know," Mercy warns, getting defensive. "I need you to trust me on this, Cal."

"If she is going to be a threat to-"

"She isn't a threat," Mercy snaps, "she's a baby. Can you please just let me handle this."

"I trust you," Cal yields, "but you cannot hide things like this."

"Wouldn't you?" Mercy inquires with pleading eyes. "If you had a daughter like this, wouldn't you want to hide her? Didn't your mother hide you out of fear of what her people would say?"

Cal's concern quickly shifts to understanding, the softness reflecting in his eyes. Mercy was only trying to protect his niece. Penumbras were a new term for most of their people, including themselves. A Keeper who could access both the Light and the Shadow Source was completely unheard of until Master Novi and Cal came to light. Even Novi had kept her connection to the Light Source to herself until the day she came to Mercy in Vermeer. One born like this, not created, was an entirely new threat. How would her powers even react?

"I think having Meera and Velia stay at the estate might be the best move right now," Mercy shares as the baby begins to fall asleep. "Can you do that for me?"

"You want everyone under one roof?" Cal questions, skeptical of the idea.

The girls were already there with Charlyn, and now he wanted his niece and Meera there as well? It seemed a little too easy of a target. Not to mention it was seeming like Mercy and Sylas would be extending their stay in the capital upon their return. Sylas was wary to head back to

Vermeer alone, and Mercy would likely go insane in Rieka without his girls.

"It's the most protected place in Ozra," Mercy states. "I need them protected. Especially if I'm going after Bryer."

"*We* are going after Bryer," Cal corrects as the door to the house opens.

Sylas enters with three large bags, the smell of a hot meal filling the air. They both turn to look at their friend as he begins to struggle with one of the bags. Guardia comes out of the kitchen with a grumpy face, rushing to aid him before he drops it.

"Why not ask me to cook?" she reprimands, steading the bag in his arms.

"Pippa strictly requested pie from Letti's Kitchen, and I wasn't going to argue with her," Sylas laughs.

Guardia takes one of the bags into the kitchen to prepare the plates. Sylas smirks at the woman as she moves away, and he places the other bags on the floor by the door. Removing his boots and coat he lets out a quick shiver.

"Sy, come here," Cal requests.

"Hey! You guys made it out alive!" Sylas beams at them. "You already have two feet in the grave, Cal. The odds are starting to look grim for you."

"And you are still annoying," Cal retorts with an eye roll. "Come here."

Mercy gets to his feet again and places the sleeping infant back in the bassinet. Without hesitation, Sylas walks over to the pair. There was a clear tension between Sylas and Cal as he got closer, but Mercy disregards the reactions.

"Let Mercy see your arm," Cal requests. "The injured one."

With a cocked brow, Sylas puts his left arm out. Mercy's eyes fall on the bandaged splint wrapped around his Nota's hand, but he moves past it quickly to locate the lines of the symbol. Once he finds it, he signals for Cal to move closer. They both stare at the arm as Mercy points to the cuts on the back of Sylas's forearm, just below his elbow.

"There," Mercy states to Cal. "Something like this is what she was trying to put on you."

Sylas moves his arm away to look at the scabbed over wound himself. He hadn't even noticed the marks. He had been so focused on his hand he hadn't detected the lines sliced into his skin. His eyes get wide at what he was seeing. He recognized this symbol. The sudden alarm on his face piques both Mercy and Cal's interest.

"Pippa!" Sylas screams. "Pippa, get down here! Now!" He shouts in panic.

"Sy, what is it?" Cal asks, the nervousness clear in his voice.

"Pippa!" Sylas yells again.

After a moment the young woman appears at the top of the steps in a nightgown. "Yes?"

"Come here!" Sylas shouts, fear in his voice.

"What is going on?" Cal asks, his eyes bolting from Sylas to Pippa in anticipation.

They watch as the woman descends the steps quickly and walks over to Sylas. He sticks his arm out and points to the symbol on his arm. While he was fairly sure what he was looking at, he needed her to confirm.

"An exua rune?" she questions, looking up to Sylas with a shocked expression.

"What is that?" Mercy asks as the baby begins to fuss again, Sylas's shouting startling her.

The Keeper sighs and takes his attention back to his niece, scooping her up into his arms again. He rocks her slowly, moving back to the group. While he wasn't upset to have the extra time with Velia, he was hoping Meera would come down to get her soon. He could feel his mind start to fog over as his heart began to race from the worry around him. The unsettlement in Cal was echoing through their Voca, something that frequently happened when Sylas was involved.

"The exua rune. It's uh… It's a fail safe," Sylas explains quickly, gawking at the marks, gesturing with his other hand. "They used it to strip Keepers of their Source on Aitus when they committed crimes against the balance. Like a Keeper tempting someone to kill in their stead or maybe using their peritia in a dark way that it wasn't meant to be used. The only place I've ever seen it was in that genti tome from the Source Temple. Not a single book has had that rune in it. At least not that we've looked at."

"Your notes," Cal breathes in understanding.

"With no Keepers meant to be on Novus Aitus the use of the rune was not needed," Pippa adds, shaking her head. "The Elders lost knowledge of the symbol hundreds of years ago. The fact it is currently on Sylas's arm is completely bizarre."

"This is why my shield wasn't working, Merc. It's why you can't heal me," Sylas explains, showing him the rune again. "Your Source can't protect me anymore. This explains ev-"

He stops speaking as Cal quickly darts his hand out placing it on Sylas's cheek. He gawks at his friend's black tipped fingers before moving his gaze to Cal's face. The Shadow Keeper could actually touch him. He stares at Cal with wide eyes as the Shadow keeps his eyes on his hand making contact with Sylas.

"By the Elders…" Cal mumbles.

The two hadn't touched since that night on the balcony. Their interlocked fingers that snowy night was the last bit of contact they had in over eight months. That night Mercy took his Source back and the pair had to cease all physical contact again. It was something that killed Cal. That entire night was seared into his mind. It was the night he had to walk away from the only person he ever truly loved.

"So… I can touch you?" Sylas questions, a playful smirk coming to his face.

With a small nod from Cal, Sylas puts his hand out to touch his face in return. This prompts Cal to pull his hand away. Though there was no shield between them, the touch still felt charged. As much as Cal hated to admit it, he wasn't over Sylas. Though they had become friends again after their somewhat messy break up, there was still the pull of a lover there.

Mercy clears his throat and looks away, not sure where this was going to go. He knew the two still had feelings for each other, but he also knew there was some unspoken resentment from both parties. He exchanges a look with Pippa realizing she was also wary of this newfound discovery.

The smile on Sylas's face quickly falls to a scowl. Without hesitation he pulls his right fist back and punches Cal right in the jaw. The blow causes Caligo to take several steps back and to fumble into a chair. This results in both Cal and the chair clumsily falling to the ground.

"What the hell, Sylas!?" Mercy shouts as the baby begins to scream again.

"I probably deserved that," Cal admits, getting to his feet, his hand going to his now bleeding lip.

Sylas shakes his fist out as he walks over to Cal and pulls it back again. Now that he could touch Cal, he was going to get out some pent-up aggression. This time when he goes to swing, Cal dodges the fist and throws his own, hitting Sylas in the face.

"Sorry, Mercy," Cal notes, as Mercy reacts to the hit himself.

All this does is add fuel to Sylas's anger and he goes in for another punch. In frustration, Cal grabs his arm, twists it, and locks it behind his back. He wasn't going to hit Sylas again. He knew Mercy was going to feel every punch, and this was between him and Sylas.

Cal had a good feeling about where this was coming from. The two had argued about it multiple times when Sylas had come back from his trip. It didn't matter how many times Cal insisted it meant nothing to him, Sylas still couldn't let it go. It honestly made this even more infuriating. He had even broken off the relationship before seeing where it could go to appease Sylas, not wanting to cause anymore unneeded tension between himself, Sylas, and Mercy. The three of them knew they were connected, and Cal needed to do his part to keep the peace in any way he could.

"Need I remind you that you broke up with me?" Cal snaps, tightening his grip on Sylas's arm.

"Doesn't make me any less pissed," Sylas snarls, trying to use his leg to swipe Cal's out from under him, but failing.

"How am I the bad guy for trying to move on?" Cal asks as Sylas jabs his elbow into the Shadow's stomach.

"It wasn't moving on! It was a rebound!" Sylas rebukes, Cal releasing him in annoyance.

Sylas stumbles forward but quickly regains his footing. He was ready to keep going. Knowing he could get physical hits in on Cal just fueled his bitterness. For Mercy's sake, Cal was going to hold back, which meant Sylas didn't need to.

"I am not going to argue about this again, Sy," Cal growls, ready to block the next punch.

The screaming from Velia gets louder as Sylas clenches his fist and goes for another hit. The longer this went on, the angrier it was making Mercy. He actually couldn't even tell if he was angry or just frustrated with the pair. Nevertheless, he intervenes and uses his Source to shoot a wave of energy at the pair. The blast a bit heavier than intended, shooting a visible wave of light through the room. The move offsets his best friend's footing, making him stumble again. The entire room shakes, causing objects to rattle and a painting to fall from the wall. The use of his Source connection causes a pain to radiate through his arm, forcing him to quickly power down.

"Stop it!" Mercy warns, keeping his hand aimed at the pair as Velia screams in his arms. "I'm not above using my Source on you two idiots again!"

"What are you going to do? Blind us?" Sylas laughs, glaring at Cal.

"Doesn't sound like a bad idea!" Mercy retorts, light flickering in his eyes.

"He's the one who slept with someone a week after we split up!" Sylas growls.

"That was eight months ago," Mercy scolds.

"Well, I couldn't punch him eight months ago," his best friend scowls, rotating his shoulder.

"Sophos," Pippa finally interjects. "If you two want to spar it out later, then so be it, but not in my parent's house and certainly not at Mercy's expense."

The disturbance brings both Meera and Pippa's father, Emidio, out. Emidio had been in the study and looked more agitated than Meera by the noise. He was a tall, daunting man. Working with the Ozran International Trade meant he wasn't home often, and when he was, he liked his quiet. Just like Novi, he demanded the same respect as his wife, the two complimenting each other well.

"What on Novus Aitus is going on out here?" Emidio barks, moving toward the group as Meera descends the stairs. "It is far too late for this kind of noise."

Meera goes to Mercy and pulls Velia away from him, rocking the infant as she heads back toward the stairs, not saying a word. The baby was still crying from the outburst but eased in her mother's arms quickly. Meera had no interest in what was going on, her only focus being her daughter. He wondered why she even left the baby with him this long.

"Sorry, Master Emidio," Cal states, giving a small bow, his thumb to his palm.

"Caligo, you are a King," the man disciplines. "You do not bow to anyone, especially me. That goes for all of you. You are heroes; therefore, you bow to no one."

"I apologize," Cal states, straightening his posture.

"Sorry, Master Emidio," Sylas adds, shaking out his hand again. The punch to Cal's face really did hurt, his knuckles showing a hint of irritation on his purple skin. "We got a little riled up."

"Understatement of the damn year," Cal mumbles under his breath.

Emidio looks between Sylas and Cal and stifles a laugh. The man knew the history between the two and seeing Cal's bleeding lip, one of his canines having sliced it, confirmed the pent-up hostility. Emidio's laughing brings Cal's attention to the stinging, and he puts his hand to his lip again as the taste of blood fills his mouth. He sours his face at the realization.

"Pip," Emidio sighs, "I expect you to get your guests in line."

"I apologize, father," she adds with a small bow herself. "We are all excitable after what happened earlier this evening."

Mercy looks up the steps as Meera disappears into Pippa's room and frowns. While he had welcomed her distance after Trust's death, he suddenly didn't want it anymore. After this last week he didn't want any distance from any of his friends or family. In fact, he was aching to get back to Ozra to see the girls again. For some reason being around them felt like it was the only thing grounding him.

85

Chapter Eight

Sitting on the couch in the Dror home, Mercy leans forward watching the fire. Everyone had turned in for the night except him. His mind was racing. He needed to put these pieces together so he could calm his nerves. Why was Bryer trying to get to him? Why did Iana try to strip Cal's Source? Why did she remove Sylas's protection? What was a Supra Keeper anyway?

He jumps as someone comes up beside him and sits on the couch. He glances over to see Pippa, giving her a small nod of the head. She had worry on her face as she scoots closer to him, leaning her head on his shoulder. He takes a deep breath and puts an arm around her, leaning back on the sofa. Having Pippa there made him feel a little more at ease.

"You asked me to come down once Meera was asleep," she reminds him.

"Right," he nods with a heavy sigh.

They stay quiet, listening to the fire pop for a few minutes. Sitting in silence with Pippa gave him time to take a few breaths and collect himself. He felt like he had no control over his emotions recently. Even his outburst on

Cal and Sylas with his Source felt over the top. Sure, he was frustrated, but unleashing his Source like that in the middle of the house with so many people inside, was irresponsible and he wasn't even sure why he had done it.

"War is waging in your head, Mercy," Pippa notes in a quiet voice, glancing up to his expression. "I can tell by the look on your face."

"It's a full-on blood bath up there," he retorts with a soft voice.

"How can I help to calm it?" she questions, wrapping an arm around his chest and getting comfortable in the crook of his arm.

"Someone's targeting me, Pip," he sighs. "I don't think you can calm that."

"Unfortunately, recognition is often followed by intimidation," Pippa notes.

"Very helpful," he huffs.

He shakes his head with a small laugh. That was one of the worst parts about post-Spheara. While he spent the first 23 years of his life trying to stay under the radar, he was now thrust into a spotlight. No matter where he was, people knew who he was. They called him things like "savior" and "liberator," both titles he didn't feel worthy of. While what he had done in that courtyard was heroic, there was more to that day than others realized. Without the support of his friends and others he would have been powerless that day, and no one seemed to understand that.

"You are far more resilient than you believe yourself to be, darling," she explains, looking at him.

Keeping his eyes on the fire, he lets out a heavy sigh. While he would normally take her words to heart, something in him was continuing to nag that he needed to push further. He needed to try harder to keep his family and friends safe. Simply accepting these recent events and letting Cal take care of it wasn't enough this time.

"What's a Supra Keeper?" he finally asks her, knowing she would have the answer.

"I will only tell you if you promise not to grow fearful of yourself," she states.

"I don't know if I can promise that," he laughs nervously, shaking his head. "I think I deserve to know what someone thinks I am though."

"You do," she agrees.

He gives her a moment to respond, but she sits in silence. With a heavy sigh, he nudges her. "Come on, Pip."

"Okay," she concedes, taking a deep breath. "A Supra Keeper is one who can control both the Light and Shadow Source abilities."

"A Penumbra?" he asks, his body growing tense at her words.

"No," she adds, shaking her head. "It is different." She pauses a moment to think through her words. "A Supra is above all Keepers, including a Penumbra. While they can manipulate both Sources, they do not exhibit them the same as a Penumbra would. A Penumbra is still bound to the rules of the Elders Spirits and has their limits. A Supra though? They are the beings of legends, but maybe that is not so true anymore. You have shown many abilities that have proven to be something more than a Keeper of Light."

"Should I be worried?" he asks, not sure he wanted to know any more about the subject.

"You are cautious with your Source, which will aid you in learning more of your craft," she shrugs, trying not to show her skepticism. "At this time, I see no reason to be wary of your abilities." He lets out a steady exhale and nods his head as they both fall silent for a moment. "I will let you read my books when we return to Ozra so you can process it in your own way."

"Right," he breathes with a small laugh.

Somehow her words didn't ease his mind. If anything, this just made him more frightful. He barely knew how to use his Light Source… How was he meant to master the Shadow Source as well? What did Bryer even want with his abilities to begin with?

His mind wanders to what his brother had said about his power being more than anything he had ever felt before. Others had commented on it as well. It was one of the reasons other Keepers tended to avoid him. The energy he emitted was sometimes more than another Keeper could handle. While it concerned him in the past, he never thought much of it. He had Novi and Zero to help him master his Light Keeping, but now he wondered if even that was too much for the two. He glances to Pippa wondering what else she may have been keeping from him.

Over the last year he had grown fond of Pippa. She was smart, kind, and understood his way of thinking. On top of that, she forced him out of his comfort zone. One of the main reasons he had grown confident in his voice was due to her persistence in making him speak. She had helped him to understand his words had value and people respected what he had to say. With that in mind, he feared her involvement in this situation may just cause more emotional confusion in the long run. His feelings already felt scattered and misplaced the way it was. Adding Pippa or anyone else to the mix could very well make things worse.

"I think you should stay out of this one, Pip," he breathes. "You and everyone else. This is my fight."

"You cannot be serious," she replies, pulling away from him in shock. "Last I checked you, Cal, and Sylas were a team," Pippa reminds him with a raised brow.

"It'll be safer for all of you to stay in Ozra," Mercy stresses. "Especially with Sylas's hand and Cal's Source useless against those monsters. I need you to keep them in Ozra while I figure out what Bryer wants."

"You are not exactly the most coherent in a fight, my dear," she adds. "You need what Sylas and Cal bring to your battles, even if you fear they will be incapable."

"Please keep them out of this one, Pip. I'm begging," Mercy pleads, closing his eyes trying to remain calm.

"What if I refuse?" she tests, folding her arms.

"Please don't," he sighs, leaning forward again. "Mercy-"

"Can you just listen to me for once in your damn life?" he snaps, unable to control his frustrated tone. "We don't know what we're up against and after what that woman did to Sylas I can't just-"

"You are not going to negotiate with Bryer, are you?" she asks, furrowing her brow. "Do not change your tactics based on one altercation."

"People who threaten my family can't be reasoned with," Mercy retorts, trying to keep his tone as calm as possible as he gets to his feet. "Sylas and Cal are my brothers. They need each other and I need them. I need you. I can't just sit here and watch her- The girls- Meera- I-I-I can't, Pippa. I can't."

"You are scared," she accuses.

He lets out a flustered groan as pain shoots through his arm and his Source comes to his eyes. He puts his hand to his arm and rubs it, trying to focus on his next words. They come out harsher than intended.

"Yes, Pippa. I'm scared," he snaps in a low voice. "I'm actually terrified. When I felt Sylas's hand... I saw him dying all over again and Meera- When I saw the blood and then I saw her, it was Trust and I'm not- I refuse to go through that again. I can't handle the guilt or the pain. Velia is already growing up without her father because of me, she can't lose her mother too."

"What happened to Trust was not your fault," Pippa explains as she gets to her feet. "I thought you had moved past this. That was Shay's doing."

"But it was my hands!" Mercy shouts, looking at his palms, wincing at his volume. He calms his tone and takes a steady breath. "My hands, Pippa. His blood is on my hands."

Her face softens at his words. With compassion in her eyes, she moves toward him, pushing his hands down. She gently wraps her arms around him to offer some security. He accepts the embrace and buries his face in the crook of her neck. No matter how much he tried to accept that Trust's death wasn't his fault, it still felt like it was. Trust's entire life was his fault. He spent ten years in a prison being used as a pawn because of him. How was he supposed to accept that his death wasn't his doing as well?

"You spend so much time trying to save everyone else, when has anyone ever stopped to save you?" Pippa questions. She could feel him tighten his arms around her at the words. "Please do not leave us behind on this, Mercy. You need us. You need Caligo and Sylas."

He pulls away, keeping his eyes to the floor. Why couldn't she just listen to him? She was just as stubborn as Cal was. He felt he could handle this on his own and it was better if he did. Even if she thought he was being irrational, he didn't see it that way.

"Speak your mind," Pippa begs, keeping her eyes on his face.

He continues to think over the encounter with the beast in Opolis. One on one he could take that woman and maybe the obscurum. Though Cal could easily end her with a flick of his wrist, that wasn't how Mercy wanted things to play out. Cal's days of killing were over, and he was determined to keep it that way unless absolutely needed. If Cal went with him, he would surely kill that woman and possibly Bryer.

91

"Mercy," Pippa pleads.

He looks at her and nods his head. "We need to find a way to outsmart these people before they try anything else," he voices. "We need something that isn't going to be expected and will give us an upper hand the next time Iana or anyone else shows up."

Looking to the floor again, Mercy continues to collect his thoughts. What could they do that Bryer and the obscurum woman wouldn't expect? Who or what could give them an upper hand going into this fight? His eyes shoot to Pippa.

"I have an idea, but Cal isn't gonna like it," he admits, biting his lip.

"And what is that?" she asks, skepticism in her voice.

Chapter Nine

Walking through the corridors of the Ozran Prison put Mercy on edge. The last time he had walked these halls was as a criminal running from the Unity Council Guards with Trust. The memories of his time in this place were what built him into the Keeper he was though. Without the isolation that Mala had put him through, he may have never worked up the confidence to do what he had to in the courtyard that day.

"This has to be the dumbest idea you've ever had, Validus," Zero states bluntly.

"Yeah, I'm starting to agree with our resident pessimist here," Sylas admits from behind him.

Giving a roll of the eyes, Mercy huffs in annoyance. "Thanks, mom." This prompts a small smack on the shoulder from Sylas in retaliation at the comment.

"Pessimist?" Zero questions. "That stings, Bellator."

"You're just gonna need to have faith in me on this one," Mercy retorts. "Sylas, stay outside."

"Are you kidding?" his Nota protests. "I'm not leaving you alone with-"

"Your shield is gone, and I can't protect you," Mercy pauses, turning to remind his friend. "That means your mind is wide open."

With a frown, Sylas stops in the hall and watches Zero and Mercy approach the cell door. After seeing what Shay could do to Cal, Sylas had no interest in being part of her mind games. The emptiness and hatred she had instilled in Caligo still shook him over a year later. Seeing how cold and lifeless Cal had been was something he would never get out of his head.

"Keep your distance," Zero instructs Mercy, giving a nod to the two Light Keepers guarding the cell.

Unlocking the deadbolt, Zero gestures for Mercy to enter. Taking a deep breath, Mercy grasps the handle and pushes open the steel door. It felt heavy and cold in his hands. Keeping his eyes down he closes it behind him and hears it latch. This was their way of keeping Shay in her cell, even with a visitor.

"Mercy Valldus?" Shay's voice chimes from the cot on the opposite side of the stone cell. "You have got to be kidding me."

Her voice causes him to shudder. While he hadn't gotten much time alone with the girl, he knew what she could do. He knew what she had made Cal do. There were days he still asked Mercy and Sylas for clarification on the events that led up to Spheara. Shay's peritia had such a long-lasting effect, that even healing Cal's mind couldn't repair that. Caligo was permanently damaged by her abilities, questioning himself now more than ever.

"I'm giving you a chance to get out of this cell," Mercy shares, folding his arms.

"I find that hard to believe," Shay sighs.

She looked thinner than when he last saw her, but at least she seemed rational. Her hair was pulled up into multiple braids to keep it from tangling. Somehow her face looked harsher, but maybe it was just the fact she aged another year. She was now 18, a fact that made Mercy feel guilty for locking her away. She was no older than Cal's sister, and Princess Tristia had proven to be an ally since Cal took over.

While some went stir crazy on level three from isolation, Shay seemed unbothered. The time in prison didn't wear too heavily in her expression which was odd to him. It seemed everyone he had encountered who had spent time in level three had aged physically and mentally during their stay. Even Zero seemed much older than he was, the man holding himself much more mature than 27. Then again, Cal's treatment of prisoners was much more kind than his mother's.

"Remind me how your peritia works," Mercy questions, averting his eyes to the floor.

"It's simple," she explains with a smirk. "Those who are untouched by the Light Source I can bend and mold to my will. I can see their thoughts, alter their memories, shape them into whatever I want. Your King was wise to place Light Keepers at my door."

He nods his head. This was exactly what he needed. If he could get Shay close enough to Iana, he could get her to hand over the Riekan Tomes as well as Pippa and Sylas's records and maybe even control her beasts. He would also be able to get the woman to lead him to Bryer and shut down his rebel group. Shay was young, but based on her history, was looking for recognition in her skills. If Mercy offered her the opportunity to gain the favor of the Royals again then perhaps this could work.

"I need your gift for an assignment," Mercy informs her, trying to sound confident. He looks up at her and they lock eyes.

"What makes you think I'd help you?" she laughs. "You're the son of a bitch who put me in here."

"Helping me could get you the freedom and recognition you want," he bargains. "The King trusts me more than any other person on the Ozran Council, the planet even. If I say you deserve your freedom, then you get it. It's that easy."

"Under what conditions?" she asks, her interest piqued.

"You do what I ask and don't cause any problems," he offers, keeping close to the door. "The only minds you touch are the ones I say you can."

She lets out a laugh. "Let me get this straight. I use my gift to get you the information you want, and you will set me free?"

He nods his head in assurance. He wasn't sure what freedom he could get her, but he would figure something out. There was no way they could let someone so close to Mala run rampant in Ozra with a peritia as powerful as hers, but they could come to an agreement, he was sure. All he had to do was convince Cal letting her aid him on a mission was needed.

"In a matter of speaking," Mercy edits.

"More conditions," she scoffs.

How was this girl so smug? If Mercy was in her shoes, he'd be leaping at the chance to walk outside of these stone walls.

"I'm giving you a chance to redeem yourself, Shay," he states. "How you earn that is up to you. I'll come back tomorrow with an offer."

Backing toward the door, he keeps his eyes on her. He knocks to signal he was ready to leave. Behind her steely gaze he could see the pain. She knew she was wasting her true potential behind these walls. He couldn't help but see a little bit of himself in her eyes.

As he exits, Sylas grabs him and yanks him down the hall. Zero watches them as he nods to the Light Keepers watching the cell and follows the pair.

Harshly, his Nota lectures him. "You said you were talking to her, not breaking her out."

"I need her," Mercy stresses.

"No. What you need is a mental wellness check," Sylas snaps back, bopping his friend on the side of the head.

"I already talked this through with Pippa and she agreed," he shrugs, pushing his friend off and starting to walk. "Shay is our best option right now."

Sylas looks to Zero. "He's lost his damn mind, right? You're seeing this?"

"I'm staying out of your lovers quarrel," Zero yields, keeping his distance.

"You realize Pippa doesn't have one of your magic shields, right?" Sylas questions in an angry tone, taking his attention back to his Keeper. "Shay can get to her when you saunter that *witch* out of prison. She can get to Cal and now she can get to me."

"I won't let her touch any of you," he informs his best friend, feeling his own irritation come through.

"You're willing to risk Pippa?" Sylas asks, grabbing Mercy's arm, trying to stop him.

"She can handle herself," Mercy shrugs, pushing Sylas's hand away again and keeping his pace.

"Don't bullshit me," Sylas laughs.

"I'm not bullshitting," Mercy retorts. "She's stronger than you think she is."

"No one is strong against Shay," Sylas warns. "You didn't witness firsthand what she can do. You didn't have to watch Cal go through that and-"

"I'll keep her under control," Mercy snarls, coming to a stop and glaring at Sylas with a flicker of light in his irises.

"You don't get it do you?" Sylas continues.

"I understand completely," Mercy nods with a sigh, blinking his Source away and moving forward again. "Did you ever think that your feelings for Cal are clouding your judgement?"

"Clouding my judgement? I'm not the one trying to release a damn war criminal!" Sylas rebukes. He continues to push his point by stressing Mercy's relationship with Pippa. "She could hurt Pippa, Merc. She could-"

"I'll find a way to protect her if that's what you're so worried about," Mercy groans.

"Me? You should be worried," Sylas clarifies. "It was one thing watching Shay control Mala's army, it's another thing watching her control the person you love."

Mercy stops and takes a deep breath. Sometimes he forgot just how strong the emotions between Sylas and Cal were. They were more than friends and he needed to remember that. Seeing Cal go through what he did was much worse for Sylas than what he witnessed.

"I'm sorry," Mercy states with a heavy exhale. "I didn't... I'm sorry."

"You can't do that to Cal. You can't let anything happen to Pip either," Sylas warns, a tinge of pain in his voice.

"I won't," Mercy affirms. "I won't let her near you or Cal or Pippa..."

His Nota nods his head as the two begin to walk again. Glancing back, they could see Zero had left them at some point during their walk out of the prison. They didn't blame the Light Keeper; anyone was a third wheel to Mercy and Sylas.

"You ever think that maybe... Just maybe, you like Pippa?" Sylas suggest, trying to change the subject.

"Of course I like her," Mercy states in confusion. "She's one of my best friends."

He watches Sylas roll his eyes. The Nota collects himself and lets out a small laugh. He couldn't help but laugh. Was Mercy really that dense?

"Sophos, you're an idiot," Sylas sighs.

"What?"

98

"I mean in a girlfriend sort of way?" he clarifies, talking with his hands again. "You two are both socially awkward. She had a normal childhood, yours was traumatic, yet somehow… You complement each other in a very strange way."

"No," Mercy bluntly retorts.

"I'm just saying," Sylas shrugs. "Have you two even talked about it?"

"Have you and Cal talked?" Mercy shoots back with a sly grin.

"Don't try to turn this on me, Validus," Sylas replies, shaking his head with a chuckle.

"There was more behind that punch than just pent-up aggression," Mercy adds with a shrug. "Who did he sleep with that got you so riled up?"

"That's none of your business," Sylas retorts. "I saw how Pippa fell asleep curled up with you on the couch the other night," his best friend adds.

"Shut up," Mercy scolds with a smirk.

A smile comes to Sylas's face. "I know you love her." Mercy snaps his eyes to Sylas in shock. "I'm not an idiot," Sylas laughs. "I know what it's like to be in love. I know the risks you'd be willing to take with their life on the line… You've seen how I react when Cal's in danger."

"Can we not do this?" Mercy sighs, closing his eyes.

"Would it kill you to just admit how you feel for once? Saying it out loud that you love that girl isn't the end of the world," Sylas presses.

Admitting his feelings for Pippa felt like it though. If he spoke those words, it meant it was real. Giving into how he felt would just end in pain, like it always did. He couldn't bare losing another person he loved. It was enough worrying about Sylas, Cal, and the girls, adding Pippa to the mix felt like a recipe for disaster.

"I know you've been through a lot, Merc," Sylas comforts, nudging his arm. "I know it probably feels like you're opening yourself up for a world of pain, but loving someone is special, and she deserves to know her feelings are shared."

"Shared?" Mercy asks.

"You're really that oblivious?" Sylas laughs.

"No," Mercy retorts.

Pippa was special to him, and she always had been. From the day he met her she had been someone he cared for. At first, she was a little odd, but once he got to know her, he realized just how alike they were. She understood his pain, without having ever lived through it. She reflected him in a way he couldn't quite explain. While before his person to go to when he was upset was Sylas, it was now Pippa. Every time he was scared, confused, or angry he went to her, and it had been that way for the better part of the last year.

"Say it," Sylas encourages, pulling him to a stop again.

"Say what?" Mercy asks, trying to pull his arm away, but Sylas was holding his ground.

"Say, 'I'm Mercy Validus and I'm in love with Pippa Dror,'" he nods with confidence. "We aren't going anywhere until you admit it."

He relaxes his shoulders with a small smile. "I can't just… say that," Mercy replies, forcing a laugh.

"I'm Sylas Bellator and I'm still nauseatingly in love with Caligo Tenebris," his friend adds, folding his arms and raising an eyebrow. "I also hate him, but that's beside the point. Not that hard."

"I can't," Mercy mumbles, starting to walk again.

"Yes, you can," Sylas persists, pursuing.

Mercy lets out a groan. Sylas didn't understand. Though they had both seen their fair share of trauma in the past, Sylas never seemed to falter in his ability to share his affection for anyone. Expressing his admiration for those he cared for was part of who Sylas was. It was never who Mercy was though. He was quiet, kept to himself, and just hoped the people he cared for knew he was sticking around because of that.

"Come on, say it," Sylas continues to pressure him. "It's just words."

The pestering was starting to weigh on Mercy. He picks up the pace to try and flee from the encounter all together. He missed the days when Sylas respected his silence. Ever since he began speaking more, his best friend had been digging for more and more words, but he didn't have them for this, and he didn't want them. For the first time in a while, he just wanted to stay quiet.

"Mercy, seriously," Sylas laughs, grabbing his arm.

Flinging him away, Mercy glares. "It's not just words to me, Sylas," he snaps, his eyes lighting up in response to his annoyance. "You don't seem to get that. You've known me since you were born, but there's still shit you don't understand about who I am," he explains, his voice getting frantic. "I can't say it because I'm terrified of it. Caring about anyone else is just…I don't even understand why I'm like this," he shrugs feeling his emotions take over.

"Okay," Sylas nods, realizing he had pushed too far. "Talk me through this… What's happening?"

"I don't think you understand how stressful it is to try to explain what's going on inside my head half the time. I don't even understand it myself," Mercy laughs, reining in his emotions. "I can't just… I can't, Sylas. I can't do that."

"Mercy…" Sylas breathes, his eyes going soft.

"I wish I could be like you," the Keeper admits, trying to calm himself. "I wish I could just tell her everything, tell you everything, but I can't. That's not me. It never was and never will be. I can't take any more pain in this lifetime, or even the next. Loving someone? That's pain. It already is."

"Loving someone isn't always going to end in pain, Merc," Sylas tries to comfort.

"Really?" Mercy laughs condescendingly. "Tell that to our parents or maybe Trust and Meera. Hell. Tell that to yourself. Love *is* nothing but agony, Sylas."

Looking at his best friend with wide eyes, Sylas was at a loss for words. How was he going to argue with that? In a way, Mercy was right, and he couldn't debate that fact. What examples did he have to prove him wrong?

"Nothing else to say?" Mercy scoffs with a disappointed laugh.

Exhaling heavily, the Light Keeper turns to continue the walk toward the estate. He wanted Sylas to retort with something to change his mind, but Sylas couldn't. Pippa had done a lot for him over the last year, from helping him learn his Source to decorating his house, to taking the girls shopping for him. Both Saphie and Ruby loved her, and the admiration was returned by the young woman. She was thoughtful, considerate, and was willing to guide the conversations when he didn't feel like speaking.

"Bringing Shay into this is a bad idea," Sylas stresses, changing the topic. "She's dangerous."

Mercy lets out a deep breath feeling the frustration return. If this plan didn't work, he wasn't sure what their next move was going to be. Pulling Shay into this was a risky move though. If using Shay failed, he was going to be at square one again.

They walk in silence the rest of the way back to the estate, Mercy trying to think through his plan meticulously. He had to have this plan well thought out before bringing it to Cal for approval. If it wasn't detailed and straight forward, he would no doubt decline his request.

102

As the two enter the estate they are greeted by a rage filled Caligo sitting on the entryway steps. He looked like he had been stewing in his annoyance for some time before they showed up. Someone must have told him they were going to see Shay, and it was no doubt Zero. Perhaps that was why he had vanished when they left the prison. "Are you two daft?" Cal snarls. "Shay Tract? Really? That girl is a menace."

"He's the crazy one this time, King Charming, not me," Sylas informs, offering Cal his hand to pull him to his feet.

"She can help," Mercy retorts, walking past the pair as Cal takes the gesture. "Her peritia is useful."

"Need I remind you she's the one who murdered your brother, and nearly your best friend?" Cal questions, yanking Sylas along by the hand as he keeps on Mercy's heels. "She turned me against you like it was nothing at all. Who is to say she won't do it again?"

Mercy closes his eyes at his Alia's words. He knew what Shay had done. He relived it in his head at least once a day. The image of his brother falling back after taking the blade was something he would never forget.

"I try not to dwell on the past," Mercy states, looking to his feet.

"All you ever do is dwell on the past!" Sylas adds with a shocked laugh.

"Forgetting the past will only put you in line to repeat it," Cal snaps, quickening his pace to block his path, Sylas's hand still in his. "History is there to learn from, Mercy. Shay cannot be trusted."

Narrowing his eyes, Mercy takes in the words. As the annoyance intensifies, he feels himself begin to speak without thinking. "You've made mistakes too, Cal. You've killed thousands of innocent people, but I don't hold that against you."

Sylas's jaw drops at the statement. "Merc!"

"I was manipulated," Cal defends.

"And how do we know she wasn't?" Mercy snaps back, his tone steady.

The comment sends a wave of sympathy through the King. He hadn't thought about why Shay had done what she did. His mother had influenced many to do her bidding. Who was to say Shay wasn't one of them? Deep down he felt for the girl he once trained with. He had spent a year training with her, teaching her how to use her Source connection. At one point they were even friends. It was one of the reasons he had spared her life.

"Anything else?" Mercy asks, eyeing his Alia.

As his friend shakes his head, the Light Keeper shoves passed him and continues down the hall. He leaves Cal and Sylas behind as the pair watch him disappear around a corner. Sylas lets out a heavy sigh. Whatever Mercy had going through his head was causing him to make some bold moves.

"I'm sorry he said that," Sylas apologizes, glancing to Cal, seeing the pain on his face.

"You do not apologize for him," Cal snaps, letting go of Sylas's hand. "He is foolish if he thinks I am going to approve her release," he states, folding his arms.

Sylas shakes his head. Seeing Mercy like this made him nervous. While Mercy said he talked through the idea with Pippa, the young woman had little experience with situations like this. Like Mercy, she was trained for peace, not war.

"Shay should not be toyed with," Cal stresses, looking at Sylas.

He had to agree with Cal on that, but he couldn't help but defend his Keeper. His duty was to protect and guide Mercy, and while usually he could feel the Elder Spirits urging him forward, there was nothing now. There was no indication on needing to change Mercy's mind so perhaps this was the path he was meant to be on.

"Merc has a good head on his shoulders," Sylas assures him. "He acts with his heart and with the guidance of the Elder Spirits."

Looking to the floor, Cal nods his head. If there was something off with Mercy, Sylas would know. He shouldn't have been doubting his friend. His Alia would always be on his side, even in hard times like this.

As Mercy makes his way down the hall toward his suite his mind races. This entire situation could end with his death if he wasn't careful. He pauses his steps at the idea of that. The sacrifices he had already made, he was still working through. Charity's death, the Fall of Rieka, fighting Caligo, losing Trust for the second time, Sylas nearly dying, Spheara… It was all still raw. Now on top of that his own life was on the line.

Mercy tries to calm his rapid breathing, feeling his chest begin to get tight. His arm begins to ache as his eyes begin to glow. He puts his hand to his shoulder, feeling the scar that had been left on his arm from his office. This wasn't the time to have a panic attack.

The image of his corpse begins to play in his head. His own body lying on the forest floor was chilling enough to make him rethink this. He couldn't risk putting anyone in danger again, especially if this risked losing his own life.

While Sylas and Pippa were skilled fighters, they were just mortal. With the use of the obscurum beasts, he wasn't even sure if Cal could help in a fight. Plus, the risk of Bryer and his minions stripping Cal's Source was still a threat. They had already tried it once. Whether or not he was dying, he was the only one who could face Bryer head on and possibly win.

Chapter Ten

Mercy looks down to the official request form in his hand and lets out a heavy sigh. He had thought through this assignment carefully and detailed his plans thoroughly. He couldn't give Cal a reason to deny his request. Though knowing Caligo, he was going to deny it no matter how much he tried.

Approaching the open door to Cal's office he nods to Zero who was the Sentry on duty to watch over Cal while he worked. Part of him was getting tired of seeing the Light Keeper. He always seemed not to be far behind when it came to Cal. Why did Cal even keep him around? He wasn't approachable and tended to just glare at anyone who walked by. He did very little for the poised and put together image Cal had worked so hard to construct.

"This'll be good," Zero mumbles to Mercy as he frowns in response. "Go on. I'll be listening."

Eyeing Zero, he knocks lightly on the door frame. Cal looks up from his desk and waves him in. Mercy gives one last scowl to Zero before entering the office and closing the door behind him.

"Sorry it's late," Mercy apologizes, looking to the window to see Nex perched on the sill.

"It's alright," Cal assures, keeping his eyes on a document in front of him. "Is everything okay?"

"Fine," Mercy shoots back, quicker than intended.

The sun had set several hours ago, and it was well past Cal's working hours. It seemed Caligo was always working. From sunup to after sundown he was at his desk or in a meeting. Mercy couldn't remember the last time his Alia didn't look exhausted. He may have never seen a well-rested Cal in his life now that he thought about it. There was always something weighing on the King that made him seem tired regardless of getting a good night's rest.

Taking a seat, Mercy fidgets in place. He looks over to the window again and watches Nex swoop to the back of Cal's chair. The crow eyes Mercy closely, cocking her head at his presence. Looking to Caligo, he notes the gold hoops that now slinked down his right ear. With less fighting and more desk work, Cal started sporting the jewelry that came with wealth. The most notable was the three gold hoops that cuffed his right ear, the last one connected to a shimmering chain that ran to a gold stud in his lobe. Only one hoop was mirrored on the other side. Cal's hands were also embellished with a few rings, several having been made by Mercy himself and he wore a pendant with the Shadow Source rune carved into the complexly wrapped stone. Seeing Cal embrace his life of status with an added flare instead of constantly keeping himself fighting ready was still strange to see. It did mean Cal was getting a moment to relax and heal from his days as a warrior though.

"What are you working on?" Mercy asks, trying to make small talk.

"The National Council is calling for an official solution for the Reintegration Stopgap," Cal states, keeping his eyes on the pages.

Mercy nods his head. The Reintegration Stopgap was put in place shortly after Spheara to help Keepers and humans merge back into society. Since many had been in prison, hiding, or forced to work for Mala, they needed time to get their footing in the real world. The National Council had opted for a temporary solution at the time of their formation to funnel military funds toward these individuals to give them a basis of survival. Now with the frequent displays of unrest and anger toward the throne, they were wanting the funds to come from elsewhere. Perhaps this was another reason Cal had kept Malice from the National Council this long.

Rieka had become a principal recipient once they became a human settlement about six months ago. Rieka had grown to nearly 800 citizens, 60% being human, 36% being mutts, and 4% being Aitians. Mercy himself had been a beneficiary of the funds until he filed to have them halted. Being so close to Cal, his friend paid for a majority of his needs until he got the shop up and running. Once Brokkr's Forge was reinstated to its former glory, he no longer needed the financial aid.

"What are they looking to do?" Mercy asks, unable to hide his interest in the topic.

"Unfortunately, discussing it with a Riekan Elder would be a conflict of interest," Cal states bluntly, looking up from the paperwork. "Regardless, it is taking far too long to come to an agreement on the national standpoint, so I may have to call in a royal decree, which is going to anger quite a few people," he explains.

"Wouldn't be the first time," Mercy shrugs.

"Certainly will not be the last," Cal agrees with a shake of the head.

The two go silent as Cal continues to read over the papers. Glancing up to Mercy he sees the document in his hand and shakes his head lightly. He knew what he was in here to ask, it was just a matter of time. Every part of him had been begging with the Elders for his Alia to change his mind on this idea.

Keeping his eyes on the stopgap paperwork he speaks. "If you are here to ask me to allow the release of Shay Tract, my answer is no."

"You don't even want to hear my proposal?" Mercy asks, his voice already frantic.

"I have no interest in your proposal," Cal replies with a disgusted scoff.

"Shay can use her peritia to end this," Mercy retorts, his voice rising slightly.

"As could I, but you will not allow that," Cal counters, marking something on the document.

"Your days as a killer are over," Mercy adds.

With some frustration, Cal puts his pen down and lets out a steady exhale. What Shay had done to him and so many others was sickening. She had forced his hand to kill Trust and nearly Sylas, not to mention the days he spent completely lost in the mental breakdowns she caused. She had changed so many of his key memories he wasn't sure how he was even able to function during those days. Even though Mercy had healed his mind, he still felt hesitant about things and had to constantly ask others to confirm he was remembering properly.

"You are putting your faith in the wrong Keeper, Mercy," Cal heeds. "If she chooses, she can make this whole situation much worse than you care to imagine."

"I'll make sure she won't," Mercy rebukes.

"You cannot guarantee that," Cal argues. "You know the damage she can cause if she chooses."

Looking down at the paper, Mercy nods in understanding. While he wanted to agree with Cal, he couldn't. They had a solution to getting rid of Bryer and that woman's obscurums staring them in the face. There was no harm in trying.

"I've thought this through," Mercy speaks, avoiding his friend's eyes. "She can stop Bryer and-"

"I do not think you have," the King differs. "This is about more than Bryer, this is an entire rebel group consisting of thousands or more. I think you are too focused on the chance of having an easy solution that you are forgetting the real threat here. We can protect your family from those spiritum beasts and Bryer. We have proven that. What we *cannot* protect them from is Shay or the backlash potentially received for releasing her. It would be irresponsible of me to allow."

"Sometimes being irresponsible is the solution," Mercy states, gesturing to Cal, feeling his annoyance overtake him again. "You're sitting here today because you chose to give up your responsibilities as the Prince. You chose to stop following orders and-"

"This is different, Mercy," Cal snaps, rubbing his temples. "I was choosing to help bring down a tyrant, while you on the other hand are asking me to release a criminal. A criminal who is responsible for countless citizens and military members needing counseling for the horrors she put in their heads. She made our people do horrible things. She made me do horrible things. Things that I still cannot get out of my mind."

Taking a shuddering breath, Mercy pulls back. He needed to see this from Cal's point of view. What Shay had done to him caused him an inner pain that Mercy couldn't even dream to understand. Cal nearly lost the love of his life because of the influence of Shay. As much as Mercy, Cal still blamed himself for the death of Trust. Even the execution order for Mercy had come from Cal's lips because of Shay. The King wasn't just afraid for his people; he was afraid for himself.

"I can't sleep some nights because of what she did to me," Cal admits, looking at him with fatigued eyes. "I cannot tell you the last time I got a good night of sleep. It may not have been since Sy moved out. I honestly do not know. Her being out of that prison is only going to make things worse for me. I am already overwhelmed and-"

"I know. I'm sorry for asking you to do this, Cal," Mercy interrupts, "but we can't just-"

"I just replay that day over and over again in my mind," Cal shudders, ignoring his friend's words as he stares at the desk. "I am fine when I am asleep. *If* I can sleep anyway. When I am asleep, I can't think about it but as soon as I wake up…"

Realizing Cal was starting to go off on a personal tangent, Mercy collects himself. For once Cal needed him to just listen. "It's like reliving that nightmare all over again," Mercy states, looking down at the floor.

Nodding his head, Cal lets out a heavy sigh. "My life has never been easy, Mercy," Cal adds, taking a steady breath, "but I would do anything to go back to a time where things were simpler. Before that day in the courtyard."

Looking back to Cal, Mercy shakes his head. "We all need to stop trying to be the people we were before Spheara. Those people are gone," he addresses as Cal looks to him. "Healing doesn't mean going back to what you had before the injury. There will always be a scar there. You have to find who you are with that scar… where your normal once was."

"Finding a new normal," Cal nods with a small smile. "You have done a fantastic job at that, haven't you?"

Mercy nods his head, averting his eyes again. Building his small family and reopening the shop kept his day to day feeling somewhat ordinary. While his life wasn't how it had been before Spheara, he had found a way to care for a family and continue his mentor's legacy. He had simply taken aspects of his old life and reinvented them into something new.

"I envy you," Cal voices.

111

"Envy me?" Mercy questions, locking eyes with his Alia. "I envy you. You're the strong and confident one and I-"

"The confidence is all an act," Cal confesses. "No one doubts my actions more than I do. I simply portray myself as resilient and self-assured when in reality I am weak and fearful of the future. Some days I wish I could just quit being King and abandon the capital. Everyone said I was destined to be this great leader, but time and time again I am made out to be a failure."

"You're great at what you do," Mercy corrects.

"No," Cal disagrees, shaking his head. "I am constantly angering the masses, I have rebel groups wanting me off the throne, I am repeatedly battling the National Council on every move I make. It's like they want me to fail. Some days I wonder if we made the right choice putting me on the throne. Some days I wonder if it should have been you instead."

"Me?" Mercy asks, wrinkling his brow at the statement.

"The people love you, Mercy," Cal clarifies, folding his arms. "They see you as a hero. You defeated the villain in their story, while I... I aided in her horrible acts for much of my existence. No matter what I do, there will always be those who see me as the Prince of Death. I fear the day I die will be a day many celebrate."

"That's not true." Mercy could see the misery in his friend's eyes.

Taking his gaze from Mercy, Cal tries to calm himself. It didn't seem to matter how much good he did, his past was always there to be thrown in his face. He had limited his appearances in fear of being rejected. Even the members of the National Council would, out of spite, make his life hell at meetings. The Reintegration Stopgap was a perfect example of the mistrust his people had in him. While he had offered to take a pay cut for the estate and the

Royal family, it still didn't seem to appease them. Every solution he offered was denied time and time again to the point he wasn't sure how he was even going to fix the tattered remains Mala had left behind.

"That's not who you are anymore," Mercy adds, leaning forward in his chair. "You are a good person and a remarkable leader."

"But that is *not* enough," Cal frowns, staring at the pen on the desk. "I think we would have been better off if you had just killed me in the courtyard."

"No, we wouldn't," Mercy scolds with worried eyes.

"I have done nothing but cause pain in my life," Cal admits, looking at Mercy with tears dancing on the edges of his eyes. "What I have done to our people is unforgivable and they are making that very clear. I wear my failures on my skin." He pulls up his sleeve to reveal the dark veins that marked him as a killer. "I am a murderer, Mercy. That is all they will ever see me as. Even when I look at you, I see the pain I have caused."

"Cal, please stop," Mercy mutters, shaking his head.

Why hadn't Cal told him about this sooner? If the National Council had been treating him like this, why wasn't it voiced? Perhaps Mercy could have stepped in and offered support for the things he was trying to do. The fact others could see anything but the strong and compassionate person he knew Cal to be was painful to think about.

"You're my friend, Cal. You're my brother," Mercy reminds him. "I'm alive because of you."

"But Trust is dead because of me," Cal states, pulling back his tears. "Sylas's father and brother are dead because of my actions. Just as you said earlier, I have slaughtered thousands, yet somehow, I sit here acting like I have the best intentions for you and our people. I am a fraud, Mercy."

"That wasn't you," Mercy argues.

113

"But it was!" Cal snaps. He takes a deep breath, quieting himself. "Doing this job... Being a leader... a King... It constantly makes me relive the things I have done, and I do not want to do this anymore."

The tears in Cal's eyes begin to reflect in Mercy's. He wasn't sure if it was due to genuine compassion or if Cal's emotions were sweeping over to him through their Voca. Either way, he understood why Cal was feeling the way he did. His Alia's past was painful and full of bloodshed. Ever since he had met Cal, the Shadow had been trying to put space between himself and the horrid acts he had committed under his mother's influence. All Cal wanted to be was a good person.

"Then stop," Mercy suggests. "Why put yourself through this?"

Cal laughs at the idea. "I do not get a choice."

"Your wellbeing is more important than Novus Aitus having a King," Mercy corrects.

"But it is not," Cal chuckles at the suggestion. "I cannot put the wellbeing of millions below myself," he explains. "The unrest that would follow me stepping down would no doubt cause a power struggle. There would be even more riots in the streets. Novus Aitus would break apart and we would end up right back where we were last year, if not worse. I cannot do that."

"You deserve to be happy though," Mercy whispers, feeling his words deflected.

"Success does not equate happiness," Cal discloses, finally reining in his emotions.

Mercy frowns. How had he not noticed Cal falling apart? How had Sylas not noticed? Or had Sylas caught on and simply not said anything?

"I guess it does not matter though. My actions and my happiness are insignificant in the grand scheme of things," Cal divulges with a shrug.

"What do you mean?" Mercy asks, giving his friend room to vent.

Cal stares at the pen again, zoning out on his own words. "Did you know the universe is around 13.8 billion years old?"

"No," Mercy replies.

"Novus Aitus? It's less than five billion years old. The human race? Just over 215,000 years. The Aitians have existed on this planet for even less, just 406 years. The Aitian on our home world though, they have been around for over 350,000 years," Cal lectures. "One of the few planetary life forms to actually come together to prevent their own extinction. We used that knowledge and experience to help others, traveling from planet to planet, answering call after call, and for what?"

"I don't know," Mercy mutters, looking down.

"I do not quite know the answer either," Cal admits. "Maybe my grandmother did? Perhaps yours too. Some days I wish Prima had not cut off our contact with Aitus." He pauses before speaking again. "I bet in another billion years this planet will not even exist. So here I sit, wondering what the point was in our ancestors saving this planet? In letting this broken system continue to exist? Actively destroying an infrastructure and rebuilding it sounds horrific when you think about it. The cities and towns we decimated to thrust our own beliefs and politics on are countless. Humans wanted a savior, and while we gave them one… What was the cost?"

"Their lives I guess," Mercy acknowledges, sadness in his own voice.

"I am not surprised it led to genocide in the least," Cal goes on. "Once you paint the image of an enemy in the mind of one, it will spread. 400 years ago, our ancestors came here and saw what the humans had done to their planet. While the masses were not to blame, the image of a greedy, selfish creature was already created."

115

"I see your point," Mercy confesses shamefully.

With the idea of humans being vile and greedy set into the minds of their people, it made it difficult to see they had the capacity to be more. Even Sylas had proven this. While Mercy's mother had done nothing but show kindness and love toward the Bellators, the propaganda the capital had put out skewed her image and forced his best friend's family to see Aalin as an enemy to their existence. Cal was just like the humans in a way.

"We are all going to die eventually." Cal looks at Mercy. "Think of all the planets that the Aitians did not save. Think about if we had not come to Earth. No one would even know this planet died…"

As Cal trails off, Mercy nods, unsure what to say in response. "I guess you're right."

Coming back to reality, Cal apologizes. "I'm sorry," he laughs, trying to get back on task. "I should not… You came here for a formal meeting, and I completely lost it. I am very sorry."

"Shut up," Mercy scolds. "I'm your friend before your colleague."

Cal gives him a small smile and nods his head. That was one thing he appreciated about Mercy. Even though his Alia wasn't one to show his compassion on a normal day, he knew when it was needed. Over the last year he had watched him improve on being a guiding voice instead of just staring blankly at his friends while they confided in him. It was growth Cal appreciated and deeply needed from someone he was close to.

"Thank you," Cal whispers, taking a shaky breath.

"The people who know you, see the good heart you have," Mercy stresses. "Screw anyone who can't separate you from Mala."

Glancing at the paper Mercy still had clutched in his hand, Cal reaches for it. Seeing the interest in the document signals Mercy to change his demeanor and hand over the paper. The vulnerable King was now putting his professional face back on.

Looking over the paper, Cal frowns. The request indicated that Mercy wanted Shay for a private assignment, one that would involve only himself. It didn't specify where they would be heading, but it detailed the plan to use Shay's peritia to infiltrate Malice camps and locate Bryer Nitesems. He shoots his eyes to Mercy who was averting his own to the floor. This request denoted that Mercy was planning to go after Bryer without Sylas or anyone else. Was he insane? He was still learning his Source. He couldn't do something this risky, especially with the idea of him being a Supra being thrown around.

Pippa had spoken with Cal when they got to the estate about the threat Mercy possessed. If his Alia couldn't get a handle on his abilities or was pushed too far, it could be deadly for anyone around him. He wasn't shocked at the idea of Mercy being as powerful as she was speculating, having been around him and seeing what he could do. Mercy was powerful, and he could feel that every moment he stood beside him. Allowing him to go on an assignment without himself or Sylas was completely out of the question.

"I cannot approve this," Cal declares.

"I can keep Shay in line," Mercy stresses.

Cal shakes his head. "I cannot approve the assignment, Mercy. I'm sorry," he repeats, handing the document back. "I cannot allow a novice Light Keeper to go after a threat like Malice *or* handle a criminal like Shay Tract. Not even you. That would be negligent of me."

"Cal-"

"You have my answer," Cal sternly retorts, picking up his pen and going back to his document. "You are excused."

117

"I can handle this, Caligo!" Mercy snaps, getting to his feet and feeling his Source come into his eyes in response.

Looking at Mercy, Cal furrows his brow at the white glow in his Alia's eyes. Why the hell was he powering up? Surely, he was upset by him denying the request, but this was a bit much.

"I can have you escorted out if you would prefer," Cal warns, trying not to react to the threat.

"No," Mercy retorts, taking a deep breath, blinking away his Source. "I can see myself out."

Trying to hold his composure, Mercy nods his head and turns away. While Caligo was hiding behind regulations, Mercy knew the real reason he was denying his request. He didn't trust him to handle this on his own. As far as Cal was concerned, every assignment Mercy had gone on was as backup. Even with a high standing in the Ozran Council, the truth of the matter was Mercy was ill prepared.

Chapter Eleven

Glancing up to Nex, who was perched on the foot of the bed, Cal puts the finishing touches on his sketch of the black crow. His entire sketchbook seemed to be filled with her lately. Usually, he had more than enough he wanted to sketch, but recently he was just exhausted. Though he lacked inspiration and drive, he didn't want to give up the hobby he loved dearly. Drawing had always been an escape for him.

He lets out a steady exhale as Nex perks up. A light tapping on the framed arch door to his bedroom grabs his attention, causing him to power up in anticipation. He had been jumpy all evening it seemed, the recent events keeping him on edge. Looking up quickly, his eyes going dark, he sees Sylas. For just a moment Cal feels himself activate his peritia without intention, causing Sylas to freeze in fear.

The images Cal put into Sylas's mind force him to gasp as his eyes glaze over for just a moment. What he was seeing made his blood run cold. He was standing in an open field, his bow in hand, surrounded by hundreds of dead bodies, each of them with an arrow between their eyes. The only faces near him he could make out were Cal's,

Mercy's, and his brother. Within seconds the image is yanked from his mind as his vision comes back and he is able to register the room. His eyes shoot around for a moment before they land on Cal in fear of what he just saw.

"Sophos," Cal pulls back, powering down. "I am sorry, Sy. I didn't know it was you. It's not real. What you saw isn't real."

He watches as Sylas takes a few quick breaths while nodding his head and looking to the floor, trying to refocus on the moment. He had never been on the receiving end of one of Cal's nightmares and he was happy he hadn't. Not only were the images frightening, but the panic that he just felt through him was hard to shake. His body wasn't even reacting to the nightmare, it was like Cal's peritia drove his emotions to the highest level of terror.

"Sy?" Cal questions, moving to grab his prosthetics so he could go to him.

"I'm fine," Sylas gets out, breathless. "It's okay. It wasn't real. You're right."

Calming himself and watching Sylas for another moment, Cal could see he was collecting himself quickly. They lock eyes again, Cal wanting to confirm that Sylas was okay. Sylas's shield truly was gone.

"What did you see?" Cal questions, the briefness of the encounter not letting him look into the manipulation he just used.

Shaking his head, Sylas takes a deep breath and puts on a playful smirk, looking Cal up and down. "The question is more what haven't I seen?" He laughs as Cal narrows his eyes. "After sleeping with you for six months, there isn't much left to the imagination."

With irritation, Cal looks back to his sketchbook. There went the jokes. It didn't matter that he knew Sylas had just witnessed something horrifying, he was still going to put on the happy go lucky front and act like he saw nothing.

"Who let you in here anyway?" Cal asks, keeping his focus on the page he was working on.

"I bribed Zero," he winks, entering the room.

With a laugh, Cal shakes his head. "I doubt that. He finds you just as annoying as I do."

"Ouch," Sylas chuckles.

Moving into the room, Sylas looks at Cal and notes he is ready to turn in for the night. He lets out a sharp exhale and sits down on the bed causing Nex to let out a disgruntled squawk and flap her wings. The bird takes off, moving to her tree in the corner in annoyance. Sylas scoots forward, until his knee touches Cal's, causing the Shadow to glance at the interaction. Cal was wearing loose shorts and hadn't gotten under a blanket yet, meaning his amputated legs were on full display to the room.

"You got your nubbins out," Sylas teases, poking at his leg.

Cal smirks at the remark but keeps his eyes on the sketchbook. He was working on smoothing the lines with his finger, covering his already black tipped fingers in smudges from the pencil and charcoal. While usually he enjoyed Sylas poking fun at him, he wasn't in the mood tonight. He was still irked from his meeting with Mercy and just wanted the day to be over with.

"Are you just in here to pester me?" Cal asks, his tone flat.

"I wanted to apologize for punching you the other night… repeatedly…" Sylas admits, watching Cal work. "It was uncalled for and definitely inappropriate."

"You have a keen grasp of the readily apparent," Cal mocks, cleaning up the edge of Nex's wing in his image. "Is that it?"

He waits for a response but hears nothing. Cal lets out a sigh and looks up at Sylas who was staring at him intently. While part of him was happy to be able to interact with Sylas again, another part was wary. Sylas had hurt him. He had made the decision to not even try when Mercy took his connection back. He had good reason, but that didn't make the sting any more bearable. Even though Sylas had said he wasn't going to abandon him, it felt like he had.

"What?" Cal asks, Sylas's orange eyes locked on him.

"Just looking at you," he shrugs.

Closing his sketchbook, Cal takes another deep breath. What was Sylas doing in here? What was his strategy? Was this about more than an apology? His eyes get wide as Sylas leans in and kisses him. Cal lets it happen, closing his eyes. Sylas slowly pulls the sketchbook away from Cal and pushes him back. This moment was something neither of them thought they would ever get the chance to experience again, and Sylas didn't want to waste it.

In Cal's mind though, the only reason Sylas was doing this was due to the shock of the situation. With the injury to his hand and the loss of protection from Mercy, Sylas was probably close to another mental breakdown. He had come back to Ozra with a purpose, and now that purpose was gone. If he knew anything about Sylas, it was that he craved having meaning in his life and right now, it seemed like it was fading away.

"This is a bad idea," Cal warns through the kiss, pushing Sylas away lightly.

"What is?" Sylas asks, hovering over him.

"This," Cal gestures between them, "is a bad idea. We should not be doing this."

"I'm sorry... I didn't... Why?" he asks, confusion on his face. "The only reason we broke up was the shield and-"

"No. We broke up because *you* said you needed time to work on yourself," Cal reminds him, agitation in his tone. Was Sylas that clueless?

"And I had time," Sylas retorts.

"Did you work on yourself though?" Cal questions with a raised brow, still leaning back. "From what I can see, when you came back from that trip you simply fell into the same routine, serving Ozra and protecting Mercy."

"Maybe I realized my place in life," Sylas shrugs, sitting back.

"You really want to spend the rest of your life as a soldier at Mercy's side?" Cal questions with a cocked brow as he readjusts into a sitting position himself.

"No, I don't-"

"Then what are you doing?" Cal asks, shaking his head and eyeing Sylas's bandaged hand. "You are seeing this injury as an excuse to fall into old habits, and I refuse to play into that."

"That's not what I'm doing at all," Sylas defends, hiding his hand behind his back.

"Yes, it is," Cal insists. "I am not about to be your crutch, Sy."

Pursing his lips in annoyance, Sylas folds his arms. "You're being ridiculous."

"*I* am being ridiculous?" Cal chuckles but quickly gains his composure. "I am not interested in another fling with you."

"A fling?" Sylas questions, his voice tinged with hurt.

"I didn't mean it like that," Cal backpedals.

"Then what did you mean?" Sylas questions.

It wasn't a fling, that was a poor choice of words on Cal's part. The relationship the two of them started over a year ago was serious. No one had ever cared for Cal the way Sylas did, which made the outcome of their relationship all the more painful.

"I saw a future with you, Sy," Cal enlightens. "I was ready to commit to a relationship with you, but you were not ready-"

"I wanted to commit," Sylas defends, interrupting him in frustration. "I loved you. I still do. I never stopped but the shield-"

"You broke up with me, Sylas!" Cal shouts, his irritability from the day pressing on him. He takes a deep breath and repeats himself calmly. "*You* broke up with me. Remember that."

Looking down, Sylas stifles a sniffle. He wasn't about to let himself cry in front of Cal. He couldn't do that. Crying would only make this worse and he didn't want to look weak or force an apology out of Cal. That wasn't what he came in here wanting to do.

Cal shakes his head and continues. "I was willing to try. That is what hurt me the most. I was willing to try and you just… gave up."

"I didn't give up," Sylas corrects.

"Yes, you did," Cal accuses with a shocked scoff. "Sophos. I don't want to do this right now…" he mumbles, grabbing his sketchbook. "I am exhausted, and I just want to finish this drawing so I can go to sleep."

"Talk to me," Sylas begs, keeping his eyes on the Shadow Keeper. "Please, talk to me."

"There is nothing to talk about, Sylas," Cal replies, opening the book to the page he had been working on.

Sylas closes the sketchbook quickly, his eyes firm. "You're not running away into sketchbook land right now. Please talk to me."

"It is *not* running away, it is my way of observing things," Cal defends, feeling his emotions shoot through him from the frustration. Sylas always had a way of pushing his buttons, even when he wasn't trying.

"You didn't like that I never wanted to talk about stuff, well now I do," Sylas informs, setting the book to the side. "I want to talk right now."

Grabbing the sketchbook, and placing it in his lap, Cal glares at him. They had more important things to worry about right now than their relationship. There were people after Mercy and Sylas wanted to suddenly talk about their feelings? For the last eight months Cal had been trying to move past this and now Sylas wanted to try and ignite the old flame they had. It was horrible timing as usual.

"Talk to me," Sylas begs, his voice sincere. "Please, Cal."

"You wanted to fix me!" Cal accuses, wincing at his volume. He pauses for a moment to calm his tone again. With his luck the frustration he was having was causing his thoughts to leak over to Mercy across the estate. Why couldn't he get a handle on their Voca when emotions were high? "You saw a fragmented, traumatized, wounded person and you wanted to fix him, and I let you. I let you make me feel safe and whole for the first time in my entire life, and then you just left. *You* walked away from *me*. You helped heal me and then left the biggest hole in my chest and I am afraid of you now. You make me scared. Do you understand that?" he questions, Sylas's eyes big. "On top of that, I was forced to idly stand by and watch you slowly fall apart and that was agonizing for me." Cal shakes his head and looks at the sketchbook in his lap. "I cannot do that again, Sylas. That is a form of torture I never want to relive."

While Cal would always be there to support Sylas, he needed to remember to protect himself. The breakup made the last eight months more difficult than he wanted to admit. He was serious about where things were going with Sylas, and Sylas just left him. While he wanted to be understanding of why, he couldn't lie about how it made him feel.

"I'm sorry... I didn't realize," Sylas mumbles, unsure how to respond.

"You were my future," Cal adds, the confidence coming back into his voice as he locks eyes with him.

"Were?" Sylas asks, his eyes laced with worry.

He didn't like the use of past tense here. Sylas still saw his future with Cal. He wanted that. Especially with the change of circumstances they were in with the exua rune. Now he could have his future with him, but Cal was using past tense?

Taking a deep breath, Cal puts a hand on Sylas's knee and keeps an intense gaze on him. "You were right in front of me, Sy, but you were not there. I really do want this to work, but I need your mind here for that."

Sylas looks down at his hand and sulks for a moment. The fact he kept his pain to himself had always bothered Cal. It was one of the biggest and most glaring issues in their relationship, but they still cared for each other. Sylas cared for him more than anyone else, that included Mercy. While he would be devastated if he lost his best friend, he wasn't sure how he'd continue forward if he lost Cal. This man was important to him, and no matter how hard he willed himself to move on, he couldn't.

"I still care for you, my love," Cal comforts, seeing the pain on Sylas's face. "I would do anything for you, but this... I can't do this. Not right now. I need to protect myself. You need to understand that."

"I do," Sylas nods, his face numb.

Scooting forward a bit, Cal puts a hand to Sylas's chin, forcing him to meet his gaze. They lock eyes for a few moments before Cal moves even closer, leaning his forehead on Sylas's. Cal takes a deep breath and closes his eyes, Sylas following suit. Sylas missed this. He missed Cal's touch and gentle moments. He knew Caligo wasn't refusing him out of spite or anger, he was trying to protect himself. He needed to make sure Sylas was ready for a serious relationship because Cal was in this for the long haul.

They sit in silence for a few moments. They hadn't been able to interact in eight months and the familiar touch was something they both wanted to take in. For all Cal knew the exua rune had an expiration date. The threat of Mercy's shield returning was still there until they could figure out the long-term effects of the symbol.

Taking a deep breath, Cal finally speaks. "You *are* my future. Do you hear me, Sy?" he asks.

"Yeah," he nods, leaning into the touch for a few more moments.

"Falling in love with you was the most inconvenient thing I ever did," Cal admits, with a small smile.

"I know," Sylas snickers at the remark. "Thanks for keeping in *touch* though."

"Do not ruin this," Cal states with annoyance but laughs. "You really are the most maddening man I have ever met, and I hate you for that."

"Sorry," Sylas snickers. Getting serious, Sylas keeps his voice quiet. "I love you."

"I love you as well," Cal replies.

For eight months Sylas had wanted nothing more than to be close to Cal again. He'd have to find his patience, but he was willing to wait. He was willing to work on himself and show Cal he was ready for the commitment.

Pulling away with a deep inhale, Cal changes the subject. "I will on the other hand let you sleep in here, because I know for a fact you came in here because you were anxious and over thinking, and you will not get a wink of sleep otherwise."

"Just admit *you're* anxious and over thinking and in desperate need of a cuddle buddy," Sylas playfully retorts, moving to sit next to him.

"Oh, shut it," Cal chuckles with an eye roll, opening the sketchbook again.

Getting comfortable beside Cal, Sylas puts his head on his shoulder and watches him finish his drawing. A small smile comes to Cal's face as he continues smoothing the shading out. Even if he was wary to get back together with Sylas, he did miss this.

Chapter Twelve

Stirred awake by a sinking feeling, Sylas sits up and looks around the room. Beside him, Cal was fast asleep, not bothered by Sylas's sudden movement. Taking a deep breath, he closes his eyes feeling his hand throbbing. Maybe that was what had woken him up. He slips out from under the blankets to get out of bed, trying not to wake Cal.

His stomach in knots, Sylas makes his way out of the suite. He closes the door quietly and waves to the guard standing outside the door. Without a word, he moves down the hallway to his own room to locate his pain medication. Furrowing his brow, he goes into his suite and lets out a heavy exhale. While he wanted to blame this on the pain in his hand, something felt off.

Finding the small bottle, he pops a pill and turns back toward his door to go back to Cal's room. As he reaches the doorknob the sinking feeling quickly turns into an intense anxiety. Why was he anxious? Letting go of the doorknob he closes his eyes and tries to calm himself. There was no reason for him to feel this way. Why was he feeling so upset and discontent suddenly?

To no surprise, his mind begins to wander to Mercy. With an eye roll he lets out a groan. Of course, the Elder

Spirits were trying to warn him that something was off with his Keeper. Why did Mercy have to start something now? He was finally going to get a good night of sleep for the first time in months, and Mercy had to blow it. With a heavy exhale, he exits his room, and makes his way to the stairs to find Mercy's suite below.

As he moves through the estate onto the second floor, he notes the silence that was wrapping around the manor. He hadn't bothered to look at a clock when he woke up, but it must have been later than he thought. Usually, the halls were bustling well into the evening hours with staff and guards prepping for the next morning's events or making sure no one was where they weren't meant to be. Coming up to Mercy's room he looks at the door in puzzlement as the knob begins to turn. Was he about to catch Mercy in the act of whatever the hell he was up to?

Exiting the room with her eyes down, Pippa runs directly into Sylas with a jolt. He steadies her as she lets out a small yelp in surprise. This just added to his confusion. Why was Pippa here?

"Pip?" he states in bewilderment.

"Oh, I am sorry," Pippa replies. "I did not realize-"

"Is Merc with you?" he asks, his eyes wide. "I woke up and-"

She shakes her head. "I was sleeping in his room, but when I woke up, he was gone. His Sentry suit and sword are gone as well. I thought maybe he was with you?"

"Sophos..." Sylas mumbles. "He's *gone* gone then."

"What do you mean?" she asks as he turns around.

"Come on," Sylas states in frustration.

The young woman follows him, wrapped in one of Mercy's robes. He couldn't help but find it humorous that she was sleeping in his room. Maybe Mercy was less of a prude than he thought he was. Shaking the thought, he drops the smirk and focuses.

Why were the Elders so concerned about whatever Mercy was up to? As he attempts to tune into their message the anxiety begins to signal an all too familiar warning. Whatever his Keeper was doing was going to put him in danger if he wasn't already. This prompts him to pick up the pace, Pippa trying to match his speed.

"How do you know he's gone?" she asks, jogging a bit to catch up with him.

"I'm his Nota, remember?" he reminds her with an annoyed laugh. "I swear, being his Nota has a very similar feeling to yelling at a bird to get out of the way when a wagon is barreling toward it."

She follows him as he walks down the hall and up a flight of stairs to the third floor. Sylas was on edge, and it was clear why. Over the last several months his connection with Mercy as his Nota had gotten stronger. The more Mercy unlocked his Light Source abilities, the keener Sylas became to his Keepers actions. He could sense dishonesty from Mercy, impending danger, and even an oncoming vision. It was remarkable to witness how in sync the two could be when they allowed it. It also meant Sylas was willing to risk his own safety for Mercy, often not even realizing he was running into the danger himself.

Being a Nota was an instinct and one that was difficult to fight. Sylas's purpose was to keep Mercy alive and help him to understand his gifts. This meant in his subconscious, Mercy's life held more value than his own. It was something Sylas often fought and made him feel closed in. Not having a choice in serving his Keeper had made him rebellious and irritable at times.

"Where are we going?" Pippa asks, following him.

"To wake up Cal," Sylas informs. "He can get a better read on where he is than I can."

"How do you know?" she questions.

"What else do you think Cal and I talked about the last eight months? Personal things? People don't do that after they breakup, Pip," he laughs out loud.

As they approach the door, Sylas's demeanor gets more and more agitated. Ignoring the guard outside of the King's suite, Sylas goes to open the door. A night guard had been put in place after an attempted break in at the estate by a few rebels a few months prior. The goal was to make sure that if anyone was able to get into the grounds, they wouldn't be able to get to Cal.

The Sentry Guard attempts to block him, but Sylas shoves him out of the way. "No one-"

"Oh, shut up. I was just in there and you know it, Quincy," Sylas snaps, pushing the door open and storming into the royal suite. "Caligo!" he shouts. "Rise and shine, King Charming!"

Pippa pauses to nod an apology to the guard as Sylas continues forward. What did he mean he was just in there? Was he sleeping in Cal's room? Realizing Sylas wasn't going to wait for her, she bolts into the suite after him. She attempts to shush him, but he had his volume and angst up to a level ten at this point.

He storms into the bedroom and turns on the light, slamming his right hand on the wall for added noise. "King Charming! Wake up! The light of your life is missing!"

The shouting causes Cal to sit up abruptly and Nex to begin to squawk from her perch. "Sophos! What the hell, Sy!?" Cal groans, putting his hand up to block the light.

"Our Light Keeper is gone!" Sylas barks, folding his arms as Pippa comes up beside him. "Get up! Get your legs! Let's go!"

"What?" Cal asks, unable to make sense of the statement.

"Mercy. Is. Gone," Sylas stresses, speaking slowly and clearly.

"What do you mean he's gone?" Cal asks, looking groggily between the two.

"Am I speaking English or Aitian?" Sylas asks Pippa who shrugs in response. "Never mind, he'd understand me either way. Your Alia is gone, Cal!"

They all turn as someone knocks on the arch framed entrance. Sylas raises a brow at the sight of Zero, who also seemed out of sorts. The man was shirtless and wearing loose cotton pants, showing he had come here right after being woken up himself. The idea of Zero having a room in the estate was odd, but he wouldn't be the first high ranking Sentry Guard to call the manor his home.

"Mind if I join the party," he mutters, rubbing his face.

"Zero?" Cal asks, still trying to make sense of the situation. "What the hell is going on?"

"By the Elders," Zero mumbles to himself before speaking up. "I got a call from the prison about ten minutes ago. They said that you approved the release of Shay Tract. Figured it was something I should look into. You're lucky I value my job slightly more than my sleep."

"What?" Cal gawks, finally comprehending what was going on. "I did no-"

"You did," Zero corrects. "They said Validus had the right paperwork. It sounded off so they paged me to see if I knew anything about it. Clearly you don't either, so can I leave now?"

"That little traitor…" Cal moves to the side of the bed and begins to put on his prosthetics.

Seeing Cal begin preparing to take action, Zero turns away to leave. He wasn't about to get dragged into another one of Mercy's escapades. Sylas watches him turn away and his eyes get wide for a moment. A large scar in the center of Zero's back showed the horrors he had once seen. While Sylas didn't know much about Zero's time in prison, he could tell it had been harsh on him.

134

"Zero, you are on this assignment too," Cal orders. "We might need a Light Keeper."

With an annoyed groan, Zero turns back around. Sylas keeps his attention on the Light Keeper to give Cal a moment. He must have had a look of unease on his face by the annoyed stare he gets back.

"Where the hell is he even going?" Sylas asks, trying to put this together.

"I don't know, and I don't care," Zero replies in exasperation.

"Orior," Pippa shares.

"The last attack was outside of Opolis," Sylas states, furrowing his brow at Pippa.

"Yes, but he's going to Orior," Pippa repeats, worry in her tone.

"Does Validus have any other friends or family that Bryer could be targeting?" Zero questions, accepting he wasn't going back to his room anytime soon.

"No, they're all here in the capital," Sylas assures. "I doubt they'd make any moves against Rieka itself."

"What about you?" Zero asks. "Hurting you would hurt him too."

"My mom maybe, but I don't know where she is," Sylas admits, shaking his head. "I haven't talked to my extended family in years. They probably all think I'm dead if they don't pay attention to the news."

"He is going to Orior!" Pippa reiterates louder.

"How do you know?" Zero questions the girl.

"Because he told me," she snips back. "When he talked me through why he needed Shay, it involved going back to Orior. He is assuming Bryer, maybe even Malice, have a base there."

Anger begins fuming in Sylas. He was furious at Mercy for taking the lead on this alone. Leaving Sylas and Cal behind was not what he should have been doing. The two of them existed to be his back up and he just

135

disregarded that. If something happened to him or if Shay turned anyone against him, he was alone and that made him vulnerable. How could he be so damn stupid?

"Why did no one question him?" Sylas snaps at Zero, his tone littered with frustration.

"Do you think my Light Sentries are idiots? Of course they did, but he had the proper documentation," Zero stresses. "An official seal and a signature were all he needed to get her out."

"He must have snuck into my office," Cal interjects, finally on his feet. He puts a hand on Sylas's shoulder to try and calm him. "Sy, we can track him. If he is in his Sentry Guard uniform, then it will be easy. That man cannot make a move without one of us knowing."

Letting out a sharp exhale, Sylas nods his head. Every Sentry Guard suit had a tracking device in it to make it easier to go on recovery missions. That plus Cal's Voca and Sylas's keen Nota senses meant Mercy couldn't get far without them knowing.

"That doesn't mean he won't try," Sylas grumbles.

"If what Pippa says is true, we will head to Orior," Cal informs them. "We will pack up and head there right away. He could not have gotten far."

"He doesn't want to be followed," Pippa adds to the conversation.

"No shit," Zero scoffs.

"He is not getting a choice," Cal states, moving out of his room, the group following him. "He is our comrade and now he is a criminal."

"Criminal?" Pippa gawks. "You have to be kidding, Caligo."

"He forged a document, Pippa," Cal clarifies, grabbing his circlet crown and placing it on his head. "I do not care if he is my Alia, your boyfriend, Sy's Keeper, or what the hell he to anyone else in this room. He committed a crime, and it will be dealt with as such."

136

"He is not my boyfriend," Pippa protests.

"I do not care," Cal snaps, opening a wardrobe to reveal his own black and silver Sentry suit. "He is a criminal right now and will be dealt with accordingly."

"Are you seriously going to arrest him?" Sylas asks, his eyes wide at the idea.

"Please arrest him," Zero begs.

"To scare him, I will," Cal laughs, turning to the group. "He is just being Mercy. He probably thinks this is the right choice to keep us out of trouble. What he has failed to take into consideration is that we are just as stubborn as him."

"This doesn't seem like him," Pippa speaks. "He's seemed off since that vision in the conference room."

The comment brings a falter to Cal's face. He was the only one in the room that knew what that vision was, at least that he was aware of. He glances to Sylas for a reaction but sees nothing confirming his fears. Mercy had kept the vision away from them and probably would have kept it from Cal if he had a choice.

"You're not going to actually put him in prison, are you?" Pippa asks.

Putting on a smug face, Cal shrugs. "Depends on how furious I am when we find him."

Chapter Thirteen

The rain was falling heavily as Mercy and Shay walked down the road. The two had on street clothes, trying to blend in with the other travelers between cities. The soft yellow hood of the jacket Mercy wore covered his hair and kept it dry, while Shay wore a knee length, green dress with the Shadow Source rune on her back. In the distance they could hear thunder cracking as a storm began rolling in. It cast a dreary journey for the duo thus far. The rain combined with the cold air set a chill in their bones and Orior was still a good two day walk.

The two trudged in silence as Sylas's horse Maple walked leisurely behind them, Mercy grasping her reins in his hand. He took Sylas's horse knowing she would be much faster and still trust him. Sylas had jokingly named her Maple Stirrup when Cal had gifted him the mare nearly a year ago. He would be livid once he realized Mercy had taken her without his permission.

Leaving his comrades behind made Mercy feel guilty. Forging the document made him feel even worse. Surely Cal would see him as a traitor when he got back. He wondered if anyone had followed him or if they stayed behind as he wished. Knowing Cal's short temper, they probably took pursuit not long after they realized he left, interrogating Pippa for any information on where he went. Not that she would keep it a secret anyway.

Though he had felt Cal try to reach him through their Voca, Mercy had shut him out. Cutting Cal off wasn't an easy thing to do, but he was getting better at kicking his Alia out of his mind with every passing attempt. The more Cal tried to pry into his mind, the harder Mercy pushed back.

"May I ask why you're going off on your own?" Shay finally speaks.

Her words catch him off guard. They had been silent for nearly eight hours, the only conversation the two had since her release was her shocked response to him removing the shackles and letting her walk freely. The cold, lack of sleep, and guilt were putting him on edge, so he had little interest in speaking with her further. She was simply there to be used to get the information he wanted.

He lets out a heavy sigh. "It's better this way," he states, a small shiver running through him.

"If I've learned anything, going into a battle with allies is better than going alone," she informs him. "I'm not sure what you have planned, Validus, but clearly you are expecting the worst."

"What do you know about allies?" he questions, his tone sharp.

"I know that Queen Mala fell due to the lack of support she carried as a ruler," Shay adds. "What has King Caligo done to lose your support?"

This was simply Mercy trying to keep Cal out of a fight. Facing Bryer or Iana again would surely cause Cal to use his Source for punishment or his peritia to get an upper hand, neither of which Cal wanted to do. Like most Shadow Keepers, Cal's gift was able to manipulate those mentally. All he needed to do was lock eyes with another and activate it. It was a peritia they hadn't been able to find in another Keeper yet, and Cal didn't have full control of it. He had accidently activated it on a few people, including Tristia, when they would catch him by surprise. Tris said what Cal put in her mind was chilling, something out of her worst nightmare.

"You seem conflicted," Shay adds. "Perhaps it would be best to talk about it?"

"With you?" Mercy questions, turning his head to look at her.

She gives a small nod and reassuring smile. He laughs but quickly pulls back and shakes his head in response. He knew talking to Shay could risk playing into her games, but why was he annoyed by her presence? Why was he angry in general?

"If I remember correctly, you wanted me dead," he accuses. "In fact, you tried to walk me right to my execution."

"You survived," she shrugs.

"No thanks to you," he retorts smugly.

Shay watches him as he goes quiet. Being along for this journey made her feel like a pawn once again. While it was nice to be out of the prison, this didn't feel very freeing. Mercy was cold and stoic with her. Perhaps that was his demeanor all along, she wasn't sure. From what she had seen in Cal's mind though, he was a caring and kind man who had admiration for the new monarch.

"I wasn't always Mala's tool," she states bluntly.

He raises a brow and looks at her. Now that he thought about it, he didn't know much about Shay. All he was aware of was what she did leading up to Spheara. Cal never spoke about her other than her part in the events. After the toll this girl took on his mind, Caligo avoided talking about her as much as he could.

"Caligo and I were actually somewhat friends," she continues. "We trained together for nearly a year. I looked up to him. I wanted to be just like the Prince of Novus

Aitus. He was strong, brave, handsome, and seemingly loved by the people. Once I learned he was a Keeper of Shadows, he was everything I strived to be. The opportunity to train with him was the chance of a lifetime."

"You trained with him?" Mercy asks, prodding to get more of her story.

She nods. "We both studied under Master Novi. Every young Shadow Keeper going into the UC Guard wanted to study under her, but few were selected. You had to show promise and come from Noble birth to even be considered. It was quite an honor. I would do anything to return to her training. Master Novi is a gifted Keeper of Shadows and knows how to use her Source in ways a novice couldn't even dream."

"She does," he agrees.

Over the last year Mercy had gotten to work with her many times himself. While most were fearful to train him, Novi had offered guidance and aid in mastering his skills. At least once a month he would meet with her in Sintus to go over what he had learned and how he could improve his abilities. She also continued to train Caligo in his Source during that time, both still having much to learn. Watching her train Cal was a completely surreal experience. He could only imagine what another Keeper of Shadows could learn under such a knowledgeable woman.

"When my peritia manifested, I suddenly had the regard of Mala," she sighs, looking down. "The recognition I had been longing for was there. I felt like I was a step closer to being like Prince Caligo, but I was very wrong. Mala shrouded her malicious intent with words of admiration and praise, and I was blinded by it. I so craved the attention I was given from her, that I didn't even realize what was going on. Manipulating you and Caligo became part of my childish ambition."

Mercy watches her closely as she looks up to the sky. Through all of this, most people had forgotten how

141

young she was. Shay was only seventeen when she aided Mala. She was no more than a child. She still was. Her and Charity would have been the same age. How could they have expected her to be aware of what she was doing? He was correct in his assumption that she was manipulated into doing Mala's dirty work. Regardless, he couldn't forget what this girl was capable of.

"What you did to Cal... He still hasn't recovered from that," he informs her.

"As I'd expect," she notes. "I also have yet to recover from what he did to me."

He furrows his brow again. What Cal had done to her? What was she talking about?

"His peritia," she enlightens. "Being on the receiving end of such a gift is something I wouldn't wish on my worst enemy. While my peritia can mess with your mind, his can destroy it," she continues shaking her head. "Some gifts... I wonder why they were given."

"Sylas calls his peritia 'the nightmare,'" Mercy shares.

"As his Alia, you must have an interesting gift yourself," she mentions.

He shrugs, never really seeing what he could do as something extraordinary. "I have visions of the future and the ability to talk to spirits. Sylas likes to call me a 'seer.'"

"You have two?" she questions, thrown off by the statement.

He nods his head. He wasn't sure why the Elder Spirits had given him more than one gift. As far as he knew, he was the only Keeper given multiple. Though now with the term Supra Keeper being thrown around, maybe that was the reasoning. Mercy also couldn't control when or how he saw spirits or the future.

"You are powerful, yet you don't flaunt it like Caligo does," Shay observes.

142

He shakes his head with a smile. Cal was dramatic in every sense of the word. He spoke with enthusiasm and conviction in his voice. In battle he made a spectacle of what he could do. Even Sylas jokingly called him dramatic on more than one occasion. Was he flaunting it though? Or was that just how he was wired?

"You never answered my question," Shay reminds him. "What has Caligo done to lose your support?"

"Nothing," he confesses. "These people we're after are trying to draw out my power by hurting the people I care about, and I don't want to give them any more chances to do that."

"What do you mean?" she inquires.

"I'm not sure I understand myself," Mercy admits. "That's why I need you. I need to understand what they want and figure out how they're doing the things they are."

"And you feel your comrades are best left in the dark on this?" she pries for elaboration.

He nods his head, keeping his eyes on the muddy path. This was the right choice. It felt like the right choice anyway.

"I need to end this," he adds, looking to his hand with a heavy sigh.

"I know what it's like to have a future resting on your abilities," she adds. "You may not realize this but Spheara... Mala put that on me. She put her future as Queen and the continuation of the Tenebris throne on the shoulders of a child. I know what it is like to have that much weight on yourself. You can't breathe."

Not being able to breathe was an understatement. It seemed that over the last year he couldn't catch his breath. Every inhale felt painful, and every step forward felt like a sprint toward the end. Part of him welcomed the death that he had prophesized. At least then he wouldn't be in an unending battle with living every day.

A crash of thunder echoes through the forest causing them both to jump. The rain begins to pour, causing them both to let out exasperated sighs. With a shiver, Mercy looks down at the muddy path. They should have made camp ages ago.

Chapter Fourteen

About five miles behind Mercy and Shay were Cal, Sylas, Zero, and Pippa. The four of them had left as soon as they could, which unknown to them, was about an hour after Mercy had fled the capital. They all looked exhausted already. The group opted for a horse drawn wagon knowing Mercy had taken a horse himself, that way Sylas or Zero could guide the cart when the others needed rest. They were sleeping in shifts in the back of the wagon, worried that stopping for anything would cause them to fall further behind their friend.

Cal and Sylas sat in the driver's box of the wagon as Pippa and Zero slept in the back, the Nota keeping his eyes on a tablet mounted in front of him that was being used to track Mercy. Cal felt on edge as they rode forward scribbling in his sketchbook. Looking up from his book to the dark clouds ahead of them, Cal's face softened. He found comfort in the dark storm stirring up ahead. It wasn't far off from how his mind felt the last few months. He had been trying to work through things on his own, but it was proving to be a challenge.

Everything felt like it was just piling up on top of him with every passing day. Trying to repair the damage his mother had done to Novus Aitus was a job he wasn't even sure he was ready for. At first it came naturally but now that it was in full swing it was anything but. Even sleep didn't seem to help him recover from the stress or strain. No matter how hard he tried, the National Council wasn't allowing him to do the things he aspired. It made the recovery efforts difficult and long.

His mother and grandmother had done a lot to keep their people in the dark and reliant on the throne. Purposely keeping technology and amenities from the smaller, poorer areas of the planet had been all part of her plan to keep them under their control. It was something he had been working very hard to change. Even getting Sylas and Zero, who had some knowledge of Aitian technology, trained on the many devices and mechanics had proven to be difficult. Teaching Mercy was basically pointless.

Though the National Council appreciated Cal freely providing electricity and running water to their lesser privileged areas, they were all still very much against the reintroduction of the technology of their home world. Cal suspected that the NC fought him on this and several other suggestions in an attempt to retain power over him.

While a majority of the people were relieved to see Mala taken down, there were still many who agreed with her treatment of the Keepers and humans. They embraced her brutal tactics against the minority and wanted them to stay. Some had even tried to orchestrate a jail break for the fallen monarch, but Cal put a stop to that quickly. It also seemed those who were glad the tyrant was removed from leadership were upset another Tenebris had taken the throne.

With the pressure of everything lately, Cal actually welcomed Mercy going off on his rogue mission. It gave him an excuse to let Tristia act in his stead for a short time as regent. At the same time though, he felt betrayed. Mercy had become his closest and most trusted friend since they had met, yet he purposely disobeyed his orders. What the Light Keeper did was disrespectful and broke the confidence Cal had with him. How was he going to trust him after this?

Exhaling heavily, he glances to Sylas who had his eyes on the path ahead. The two of them hadn't spoken much since they left. Last night was the most they had talked in the last eight months now that he thought about it. Three of those months he didn't even know where Sylas had gone and when he returned their only interactions revolved around politics, damage control, or Mercy.

Turning his attention back down to his sketch, Cal suddenly hated what he saw. He had been working on an image of Nex flying above the trail as they rode through the trees, but now it seemed all wrong. The perspective felt off and the lines didn't seem right. He goes to grab the eraser from his pocket, but it was gone. He sighs and looks back at the page.

With a frustrated huff he scribbles his pencil over the image. Once he started, he couldn't stop himself. He wanted to let all of his aggression out on the drawing suddenly. The sudden shift in demeanor grabs Sylas's attention.

"Whoa! Whoa! Whoa! Why'd you go and ruin it?" Sylas scolds, watching Cal's pencil begin to rip through the page.

"It is my sketch, I can ruin it if I please," Cal retorts, frustration in his tone.

He quickly rips the page out and tosses it into the back of the wagon. He takes a deep breath, trying to calm himself, unsure where the sudden burst of irritation had even come from. With a steady hand, he begins the piece again.

Sylas watches him as he continues to trace a single line over and over. Cal was rattled, and Sylas understood that. Mercy pulling something like this made him angry too. Neither of them had ever had to deal with Mercy going against them like this.

After a few moments Cal repeats the disgruntled scribbling, letting out an angry growl. Nothing had been going the way he planned. He knew taking over the throne wasn't going to be easy, but he hadn't anticipated just how poorly it was going. He just wanted something to come simple for once. Sitting in dozens of meetings every week and hardly having a moment to himself wasn't what he wanted his life to be. It was probably why his relationship with Sylas had failed so miserably. How was he ever going to have a relationship with anyone if he hated his life this much?

"I think you should put the sketchbook away before it starts raining," Sylas suggests as a crash of thunder echoes around them.

Looking up again, Cal could see the storm clouds were growing closer with each passing moment. They seemed to be lining up with his own impending mental breakdown. He takes a steady breath and nods. He needed to calm down.

"Sure," he mutters, closing the book.

He leans into the back of the wagon and tucks the book away into a bag. It wouldn't have been the first sketchbook he ruined, but he had started this one last week which made him a little more wary about letting the fresh parchment get warped from rain. Coming to a rest beside Sylas again, he folds his arms and leans back.

"You seem a little… gloomy," Sylas notes, pointing to the dark clouds.

"Sorry," Cal mumbles.

Sylas frowns. Usually, his jokes got some kind of reaction, whether it be a laugh or an annoyed whine. "Are you feeling a little under the *weather*?" he pokes, nudging Cal with his elbow. "Did someone *rain* on your parade?"

Cal finally looks at him with a small smile and an eye roll. Sylas couldn't tell if the Shadow was annoyed or amused, but at least he got a reaction out of him. Caligo was always one to simmer in his brooding when things weren't going his way.

"You are insufferable," Cal sighs, sitting up straight.

"I take my weather puns very *cirrus*," Sylas laughs with a wink.

"I wish you took everything a little more '*cirrus*,'" Cal retorts, looking down at Sylas's boots. He furrows his brow at the laces being tucked instead of tied as his smile shifts to a serious look. His eyes go to Sylas's bandaged hand. "How is your hand doing?"

Sylas looks down at the bandages and splint. When they returned from Sintus he finally went and spoke with Doctor Willa about the injury. She was kind and listened to his concerns, she was also optimistic that they could find a solution once he healed. The fact he couldn't he healed by Mercy was still haunting him. He missed the simple solution to his injuries his Keeper's Source provided. Not having it made the risk of injury all the more fearful.

"It's good," he nods.

"You just need to find a comfortable way to draw your string back," Cal states, giving him a weak smile. "Mercy suggested a modified trigger release. I am sure once you two find a release aid that works for you, you will be fine with some time and practice."

"Are you trying to give *me* archery tips?" Sylas asks with a small smile.

"Just trying to remind you that you are lucky to be alive, my love," Cal retorts, his smirk falling at his own slip up. The use of the name causes Sylas to frown as well. Realizing what he did, Cal clears his throat and sits up straighter. "You know what you need?" he asks, taking the reins from Sylas.

"What?" Sylas questions, confused by the action.

The King reaches into his pocket with his free hand and pulls out a small purple gem. "Here."

"A rock?" Sylas asks, taking the small token from him. "Why do I wanna eat it?" His mind automatically comparing the gem to a piece of candy.

"It's not edible," Caligo scolds, but laughing at the remark. "Not everything is food."

"Is that a challenge?" Sylas asks, putting the gem up to his mouth with a smile.

"Be serious for just a moment, please," Cal begs, pulling Sylas's hand away from his face trying to stop his own laughing.

"Is this your way of saying I *rock* your world?" Sylas continues.

"No," Cal chuckles looking at the stone. "It is the only thing I have held onto from my days as the Prince of Death. It was the gemstone in the circlet crown I wore when we met outside Vermeer."

"You kept it?" Sylas asks with a raised brow.

"Yes. The circlet was a gift from Tristia just after my 20th birthday," Cal explains. "I was thrown off by the gift, but I treasured that circlet because of that stone. That stone was from my father's crown. The one he wore the day he was killed. It's one of the last things that belonged to King Emrys that I still have."

While Sylas still held Emrys's sword close to his side on assignments, it seemed odd for Cal to give him another token from the departed King. He knew that Cal letting him keep the sword had been a big deal when their relationship began. When he offered to return it, Cal insisted on the blade staying with Sylas. He even wore the sword on his hip in that moment. Knowing that Cal trusted him with it meant there was still hope in the two reconciling.

150

"Why are you giving it to me?" Sylas asks, looking at the gem in his hand.

"To remind you that even when times are difficult, the things that built you, created who you are, molded you, will still be with you," Cal explains, looking at the path ahead. "My father knew what I was capable of. He was the first person in my life who knew I was worth something. I have held onto that to remind myself that even when I feel the world is crashing down around me, my father would be proud of the man I have become."

Sylas studies the small oval gem for a few moments, taking in what Cal had just said. While he may not have been able to fulfill his duties as a Sentry Guard and was knocked back several degrees with archery, what those skills gave him would never be lost. There was no denying his time as a Junior Guard, Sentry Captain, and countless years of archery had helped shape him. Archery was something he had taken the time to master, not only because he had a natural talent for it, but because he enjoyed it. His years of practice had helped ground him, it taught him patience, it built his self-esteem, and overall gave him something to focus on when he felt his world was falling apart. Without it, he felt lost and even more alone than before.

"Your passions and aptitudes are still there, Sy," Cal continues. "Just like my father's love and compassion is still with me. The things and people who built you are never truly gone."

The two look at each other for a moment. They keep their gazes locked, Sylas wanting to move in on Cal, but not allowing himself. Cal had made his boundaries very clear last night, and he was going to respect them. A small sway forward from Cal indicated he was close to the same thing.

Clearing his throat, Sylas reins in their focus. "Thank you," he nods, giving Cal a small smile. "I'll keep this safe."

They go quiet as it begins to drizzle. Sylas tucks the gem away in his shirt pocket and turns to pull a small awning down over the front of the wagon to keep them dry. Cal gives an eye roll and stands up. He hands the reins back to Sylas and looks down at the path. He removes two dark leather bracers from his arms and begins to climb down as the horses continue forward.

"What are you doing?" Sylas asks as the King lands on the path clumsily.

"I am welcoming the rain," he replies as Sylas slows the pace of the horses.

Watching Cal, the rain begins to pour. The steady pace of the drops made a calming tapping noise on the tarp that protected the wagon and their belongings. Cal kept in stride with the horses, letting the water soak him. The dark cotton shirt he wore was quickly showing just how fast the rain was coming down.

"You'll catch your death!" Sylas reprimands jokingly with a laugh.

Being a Royal meant Caligo had to play a part. Even free of his title of the Prince of Death he was still expected to behave a certain way. Being well kept and put together was how he had to be every minute of every single day since the moment he was born. He missed getting grimy and roughed up on trips like this. While before he could hide behind his Shadow Guard armor when traveling, he couldn't anymore. In fact, leaving the estate for anything other than political travel was rare in the last year.

He looks to the sky as a crash of thunder echoes through the forest. He just wanted the rain to wash over him, inviting the chill it put in his bones.

Glancing to Cal, Sylas couldn't help but let a small smile slip onto his face. It was moments like this that Sylas had fallen in love with. While Cal was usually reserved and held himself gracefully, he was also impulsive and had a candid side. That was the side of Cal very few got to see, and it was the side he had grown to love the most. While he had fallen for the short tempered and bold Shadow Keeper, it was the compassionate, spontaneous side of Caligo that he had grown to adore.

After a few more minutes, Cal finally pulls himself back into the wagon. It was a little less graceful than he'd have liked, but he does, his clothes drenched. He lets out a small laugh, wiping the rainwater from his face as Sylas pulls a rag from the satchel by his feet.

"Feel better?" he asks, handing him the cloth with an amused smile.

The King nods his head, drying his face and arms. He felt calmer. He just needed a moment to himself. He begins to put back on his leather bracers, adjusting the straps carefully. The pair was a gift from Mercy for their birthday earlier in the year, a birthday that Mercy legally changed to reflect his true mirroring with Caligo. While Mercy continued to celebrate on the day his parents and Elder Rom had written on his false documents, he still wanted that symbolic birth date to reflect his connection to his Alia on record.

Sylas's smile quickly falls as he looks forward. He felt foolish looking at Cal the way he was. He made it clear he wasn't interested in restarting their relationship right now. Seeing the smile fall, Cal also frowns. The awkward tension that had been set in since their talk last night was back and he hated it.

"Why do you want to get back together?" Cal asks, watching Sylas's face. "I want to understand."

"I thought you didn't want to talk about that," Sylas shoots back, his tone even.

Cal lets out a heavy sigh. "Is it only because the shield is gone?"

"No," Sylas admits.

The truth was, getting back together with Cal felt right. Sylas had months to sort through what was going on in his head, and after the talk in Cal's bedroom he was starting to realize at this point he wanted to grow beside Caligo. Working on himself felt more doable with Cal helping him, just as he had helped Cal. He'd learn to accept the need to share his thoughts and feelings with Cal if it meant not having to sort through them alone. He would force himself out of his comfort zone for that.

Shaking his hair out, the rainwater from Cal's curls splashes on Sylas who lets out a laugh. Locking eyes, the Nota takes a deep breath. Maybe bringing this up now wasn't the best choice, but when was Sylas going to have another moment alone with Cal? As soon as they returned to Ozra Sylas would probably leave the capital. He certainly wasn't going to continue his Sentry duties until his hand was usable again. This meant he would either go back to Rieka with Mercy or to his father's cabin in Vermeer.

"I'm the one who chose to step away from the relationship. I came back from that trip ready to move on, but…" Sylas looks to the rune on his arm.

"Do you still want to move on?" Cal asks raising his brows at the statement.

"I don't think I ever wanted to," Sylas discloses with a small smile, thinking carefully. "Just because I said I wanted you to let go, didn't mean I was ready to," he explains. "I spent the last eight months trying to accept that what we had was over, Cal. That maybe we were just meant to help each other for a brief time. To ya know… help each other accept what we had been through. For eight months I've tried to convince myself of that, and now…"

"And now what?" Cal prods.

Looking at Cal, Sylas shakes his head. Right now didn't feel like the right time to start dissecting their relationship. In fact, it was the worst time. Pippa and Zero were just a couple of feet away and they were trying to find Mercy. While he wanted to have this conversation, it made more sense to wait until after this whole ordeal.

"We shouldn't be talking about this," Sylas laughs, changing the subject. "This is a wildly inappropriate time to be talking about this. We're supposed to be looking for Merc." He glances over to Cal and smirks. "You look like a soggy cat by the way."

Brushing his hair back with his hand, Cal lets out a tense laugh. What was he expecting? As usual, Sylas shut down his emotions. He shakes his head in annoyance, looking down at the horse's hooves as they meet a wooden bridge. Each hit of the hoof created a clopping noise on the drenched bridge. Maybe he needed to get over his own worries and offer a resolution.

"I think we should-" Cal stops himself.

Suddenly the Shadow could feel a surge of energy go through him as his hair began to stand on end. His eyes shoot up to the path ahead of them looking for the cause.

"Should what?" Sylas asks, anticipating the rest of the sentence.

He watches Cal shush him as he signals to slow the wagon. The pair look out into the rain. This energy echoed what Cal felt at Meera's cabin. This was the same energy. That meant an obscurum was nearby, which no doubt meant Mercy was too.

"Stop the wagon," Cal orders as he stands up.

Heeding his words, Sylas shushes the horses to a stop just as they exit the bridge. The rain begins to pour harder as Zero stirs awake from the same feeling. Sylas watches as Cal takes a moment to pull up his pant legs and adjust the straps above his knees. He watches Cal hesitate a moment wondering if he should put on his tactical suit under the seat, but quickly abandons the idea. This meant whatever Caligo sensed; he was preparing to fight.

"We have company," Zero whispers to the pair.

Zero turns to shake Pippa awake, his eyes starting to glow with his Source. Sylas watches with worry as Cal's eyes go black. What did they sense?

"Sy, Pippa, stay in the wagon," the King orders, jumping down from the box. "Zero, come with me," he adds, pulling his curved blades from the back.

Pippa and Sylas watch as Zero grabs a small mace from his belongings and follows Cal, both Keepers ready to take on whatever was lurking in the trees. They could see Zero's hands power up before disappearing into the tree line behind Caligo.

Scanning the trees as the rain pelts the awning above him, Sylas's stomach fills with nerves. The sound of the large drops on the wagon cover made it impossible for him to hear much of anything. He turns to exchange a look of worry with Pippa who was trying to figure out what she had missed. Seeing Cal and Zero were on edge, she begins to dig through the bags and locates her crescent blade. She climbs into the front with Sylas and unsheathes it.

"What's happening?" she whispers.

"I don't know," Sylas admits, climbing down from the wagon himself, pulling a dagger from his belt.

They both pause at the familiar sound of a screech coming from the forest. Had they seriously already run into an obscurum? Did that mean Mercy was nearby? Looking at Pippa again the pair abandon the cart and rush into the trees after the two Keepers. If this was one of those monsters, they were going to need all the help they could get.

Chapter Fifteen

This felt hopeless. Every attack Caligo tried wasn't even making a dent in this thing. The obscurum beast was fast, strong, and Cal's Source was useless against it. It seemed that with every advance he made, it only built the creature stronger. At this point it felt like a waiting game, buy time and hope for Mercy to show up, or accept the inevitable

Looking over to Pippa, Sylas could see she was lying unconscious on the other side of the clearing. The beast had taken quite a swing at her, a large gash bleeding on her forehead. Cal wanted Sylas to go to her, but clearly the obscurum gave little mind to the young woman now that she was down. It had only struck her to get her out of its way, just as it had done with Zero moments before. Sylas glances to the Light Keeper, who lay unconscious only a few feet from Pippa. This beast had its eyes set on Cal, and it wanted blood.

The creature takes another swipe at the Shadow, this time tossing him into a tree. Cal lets off an agonizing scream as he falls to the wet grass. Hitting the trunk sent a surge of pain through him. Putting his hand to his side he sees the blood soaking his fingers. Looking up he notes his blood dripping from a broken branch, the limb now lying beside him. Maybe he should have taken the time to put on the tactical suit that was in the wagon. At least then he would have a little protection from this thing.

Getting to his feet again, he lets out an annoyed growl as he realizes his prosthetic was starting to get loose on his right leg. With no time to fix it, he now risked losing his leg with the next hit. Inconvenient, but he'd work through that if he had to. This thing hit like a hammer, giving him little chance to hold off being thrown. While Mercy built his legs to withstand his fighting style, they weren't meant to survive the brute force of this creature.

Currently, Cal was more of a toy to the obscurum than an actual adversary. He felt like one of the stupid wool balls Soot would bat around Mercy's house. He had never felt this useless in a fight before. His blades did nothing to this monster and any attempt he made at using his Source just seemed to be absorbed. This explained why Mercy ordered him to stop at the cabin, the Light Keeper had noticed what he hadn't.

It was also unsettling how much this beast's energy mirrored Mercy's Shadow Guard, Sander. He hadn't spent much time with the Shadow Keeper, but he recognized the energy. It was strange. While it felt like Sander and was made of spiritum fog, it didn't have his Source connection. This Source was from the woman, it had to be. How was it obscuring Sander's like this though?

Taking a deep breath, Cal takes a moment to call for Mercy again. He had been calling for his Alia for the last ten minutes, but he hadn't heard a response. Mercy must have been too far ahead of them to sense the severity of his call. While their Voca was strong, it was easier to read when they were close. At a distance it may have been no more than a whisper. A whisper the Light Keeper was expecting since he had run off.

Sylas watches as the beast goes toward Cal again, ready to give him another beating. How on Novus Aitus were they going to defeat this thing? It was the perfect battering ram.

"Sy, get Zero and Pippa out of here!" Cal shouts as the beast approaches him.

"I'm getting all of you out of here!" Sylas snaps, picking up one of Cal's blades from the mud and chucking it at the obscurum as hard as he can.

"Sy! Get them and leave!" Cal orders as the creature gives another strike, flinging Cal toward the river's edge.

Landing hard on the muddy bank, the Shadow breathes a sigh of relief as his legs absorb the landing and he lets himself roll forward to a stop. He wasn't sure he was going to be able to stay on his feet much longer. He rests on his hands and knees, the pain in his side rushing through his body. The pain was starting to fog his vision, but he couldn't give up, not with Sylas, Pippa, and Zero right there. He couldn't stop until he knew they could get away from this thing. He needed them to get away.

Sylas sees Cal go down and bolts to try and protect him in whatever way he could. He pauses in front of his comrade as he hears Cal groan on the ground behind him. Each hit from this monster was just pummeling the Shadow Keeper more and more. Without being able to use his spiritum fog, they were almost defenseless.

Looking up to Sylas, Cal closes his eyes. Why was he still here? Why wasn't he running? He admired Sylas's ability to never give up, but this was a situation where he wanted him to. He couldn't handle Sylas getting injured or worse, killed. He needed to know Sylas, Pippa, and Zero made it out of this alive. The longer Sylas stayed here and tried to hold off the creature, the more danger they were in.

"Sy, please go," Cal begs from the ground.

"I'm not leaving you here to die," Sylas barks as the obscurum moves toward them.

Opening his eyes again, feeling the ground shake, Cal begins to call his Source. If Sylas wasn't going to get out of the way on his own, then he was forcing him. He cared about Sylas far too much to let this thing hurt him. With each step the fear in Cal's gut grew. Just as the obscurum was about to strike again, Cal uses his fog to grip Sylas's arm and pull him out of the way.

With a frustrated scream, Sylas is yanked to the ground, rolling to a stop several feet away from the Keeper. Looking back at Cal with fear in his eyes, Sylas's stomach drops as his heart begins to race. He wasn't about to lose Cal. Not like this. He watches as Caligo gets to his feet, the beast now with its eyes set on Sylas.

Clearly the Nota was putting a wrench in this thing's plans. The creature wanted to get him out of the way just as it had done with Pippa and Zero. As Sylas goes to get up, he feels Cal's fog still gripping his ankle, keeping him on the ground. He follows the tendril of spiritum fog with his eyes to Cal's hand. Cal was trying to protect him, and that was just pissing him off. Why was Cal so hell bent on him staying out of this fight?

"Damn it, Caligo," he mumbles to himself.

Cal lets out an angry scream, trying to get the obscurum to focus on him again, which doesn't take long. The clear target for this attack was Cal to begin with. The King lets out another scream as Sylas watches from the ground in terror.

As the obscurum moves closer to Cal a flash of lightning ignites the sky. For just a moment Cal could see the center of the beast. It had a core, and at the core was a person, or at least what was left of one. If this thing had Sander's energy, did it also have Sander? Using his other hand, Cal slinks out more of his fog and grabs one of his blades from the grass and pulls it to his palm. Maybe if he

161

could hit the person at the core of the creature, he could stop it. He just needed a shot.

Darting his eyes between Cal and the obscurum, Sylas tries to come up with a plan. Cal shakily readies his blade in his hand, his sight set on the beast. With his eyes glued to the Shadow Keeper, Sylas watches in panic as the beast squares up to Cal, who was trying to use what energy he had left to take a stand. The obscurum shoots out a heavy stream of fog at the Shadow, hitting him and sending him toward the river with force. Cal flies backward toward the water from the power. With his Source and a blast of purple light, Cal shoots out one last coil of his fog toward the beast, penetrating the core of the monster with his blade before smacking into a fallen over tree and bouncing into the icy water.

As soon as Cal hits the water's surface the beast dissipates before Sylas's eyes and Cal's hold on his ankle releases with a small shock. This causes Sylas to let off a hiss of pain before he could collect himself. Suddenly, the forest felt quiet, the only sound Sylas could hear was the rushing of the rising water and rain hitting the wet grass. Sylas's eyes scan the air where the obscurum had stood, but it was gone. The woman must have called it off once Cal was out of the picture.

"Cal," Sylas whispers to himself.

Scrambling, Sylas rushes to the bank and scans the murky, churning water for the Shadow Keeper. His stomach felt like knots as his eyes lock on a red streak running through the muddy water about midway. The crimson stain sends a chill through him.

"No," Sylas murmurs, beginning to wade into the water.

With the heavy rain, the small river had started to pick up speed and height. The quick flow berates Sylas as he goes deeper, using the fallen tree to stay on his feet. The sound of the water rushing by him was loud, making it impossible for him to hear anything other than the churning. Scanning the water, he finally spots Cal resurfacing in the mess of branches in the tree, midway through. He was gripping the limbs, trying to pull himself out with what strength he had left. Over the raging water Sylas faintly hears Cal gasping to refill his lungs.

"Cal!" Sylas screams. "Cal, hold on!"

Attempting to pull himself up onto the tree, Sylas lets out an irritated scream. With the water pelting him and the pain shooting through his injured hand, he couldn't hoist himself up. Slamming his hand on the trunk in frustration he locks eyes on Caligo again.

"Just hold on!" Sylas begs, trying to figure out a new plan as the water roared.

Taking a deep breath to calm himself, he shakes off the frustration. If he could focus, he could do this. With a steady exhale he grips onto the tree with his right hand and uses his left to push up. Trying to keep his composure, he is able to hoists himself out of the frigid water. Unsteadily getting onto the tree, he takes another moment to collect himself before shuffling forward. Moving as quickly as he could, he begins to crawl on the trunk, his eyes locked on Cal, who's grip on the branches was quickly fading.

"Just stay above water, Cal!" Sylas pleads.

With the adrenaline coursing through him, Sylas continues to move forward. He couldn't lose Caligo. Not after everything they had been through together. Not without finishing the conversation they had started in the wagon. They clearly had some feelings to work through and he was not letting him die before they could do that. After what felt like a lifetime, he reaches the area of the tree where Cal was tangled in the branches.

"I'm right here," he comforts as the Shadow looks up at him, his eyelids heavy. "I'm gonna get you out, okay? You'll be okay."

He sees a light nod from Cal as the water attempts to suck him under. Sylas's breathing becomes ragged as the situation begins to soak in. Straddling the tree trunk, he braces himself. He turns to see if perhaps Pippa or Zero had come to, but both were still lying in the grass completely out. Scanning the bank, he notes another individual unconscious on the shoreline where the obscurum had once stood. He wrinkles his brow in concern, but quickly shakes away the image. He'd figure that out later. Right now, he needed to focus on Cal. He looks back to the Shadow, his stomach feeling like it was in his chest.

"Please, Elders," he begs, going to grab Cal's arm.

He quickly pauses, realizing his left hand wasn't going to be able to do the job. With a frustrated scream he adjusts himself to face the bank and grabs Cal's arm with his right hand instead. He could see Cal's eyes falling shut and lets out a sharp exhale.

"Cal, I need you to grab on," he voices, trying to shout over the rushing water. "I can't do this without you, Cal. Can you hear me?"

While Cal doesn't seem to comprehend his words, to Sylas's surprise, he reaches his hand above the water and grips his arm. With all the power he could muster; Sylas dislodges him from the branches and begins to pull him from the river. With the little strength Cal had left, he uses his other hand to support himself as he gets on top of the tree, coming to a stop in Sylas's arms.

"I got you," Sylas comforts, wrapping his arms around Cal tightly. He feels the tree shift at the additional weight and puts his eyes to the sky. "Elder Rom," Sylas pleads, "Elder Rom, please. I need help here."

With a shuddering breath, he gets Cal into a sitting position, the Keeper now completely limp. He just needed to take this slow and get Cal to shore. Sylas begins to shuffle himself and Cal closer to the bank, each movement feeling like a mile. Keeping his pace slow and steady, he could feel the tree rocking.

"Don't fall. Don't fall. Don't drop him. Don't fall," he mumbles under his breath.

The tree shifts again causing Sylas to let out a gasp, hunkering down for it to break free. Looking toward the wooden bridge he could see that the water was rising more and more with each passing second. It wasn't the weight shifting the branches, it was the rising water with the storm. He feels Cal grab him as the sudden jolt from the shifting tree begins to break it loose from the bank.

"Shit," Sylas mumbles, his eyes darting around.

He feels Cal pull away and quickly locks his eyes on him as Caligo scans the area trying to make sense of what was happening. Cal's eyes fall on Sylas as he begins to power up.

"Don't hate me for this," Cal gets out, placing his hand on Sylas's chest.

"What are you doing?" Sylas questions.

"Saving the damsel in distress," Cal whispers as the tree rocks again beneath them.

"Caligo, don't. I can figure this out," Sylas scolds, realizing what was about to happen.

"You can't always figure everything out and that's okay, Sy," Cal softly replies, scooting away from Sylas.

"Cal, don't" Sylas argues.

"You'll be okay," Cal assures.

Keeping his hand on Sylas's chest, Cal pushes his fog out through his fingertips and casts Sylas back to the bank. The sudden jerk pulls the tree's roots from the shoreline. The Nota slams into the muddy bank as the tree breaks away into the rising river.

"Cal!" he calls as he watches him fall into the water, swept away with the mess of branches. "Caligo!" he screams again getting to his feet.

Bolting back toward the water, Sylas stops himself, scanning the surface. The water was dark and murky from the added mud being flushed into the waterway. This made it impossible to see anything below the churning surface. If Cal was already in rough shape, there was no way he was going to survive the water.

"Caligo!" he shouts again, the pain clear in his voice. "Cal! Don't do this to me you asshole!"

His eyes continue to dart over the rough water. He couldn't be gone. Sylas drops to his knees in shock. This wasn't happening. He couldn't lose him. Not yet. Not like this. He could handle losing his hand, he could handle losing his shield, he could even handle Mercy leaving him behind, but he couldn't handle losing Cal.

Chapter Sixteen

Up the road, Mercy stops. He had been hearing Cal's calls for the last fifteen minutes or so and had chosen to ignore them. He figured Caligo was just trying to get him to abandon his plan and return to Ozra. Suddenly though, a message pleading for help breaks through to him. He turns to look up the path, causing both Maple and Shay to halt with him.

"What is it?" Shay inquires.

"Something's wrong," Mercy mumbles to himself.

"What's wrong?" she questions.

Without prompt, Mercy's feet begin to move back the direction they had come. Cal wasn't too far off, and his Alia was screaming for help through their Voca. Not just screaming but begging. Whatever was happening up the path, Cal was in desperate need of his aid. He was afraid and completely helpless.

Mercy's feet quickly move to a run as he lets go of Maple's reins. He needed to move faster. He needed to move more than fast.

"The horse!" Shay shouts, chasing after him.

Pausing, he registers what she's saying. Why was he running when they had Maple? He turns back and quickly mounts the mare, pulling Shay up swiftly. He urges the horse forward, racing her up the muddy path. He needed to answer the screams in his head.

The blaring in his mind was nearly overwhelming at this point. It was the most distraught he had ever heard Caligo. This was bad. This was very bad. Whatever enemy he was facing, he was afraid of, and that was rare. Cal seldom went into a fight fearful of the opponent, so feeling this come from his Alia was strange and terrifying.

The fear and desperate pleas quickly shift to dread. Cal wasn't just fearful of losing a fight, he was fearful for his life and those around him. It was making Mercy's head pound. Caligo had never called so strongly and as he drew closer the cries grew more and more frantic. The adrenaline surging through Caligo was starting to mirror in Mercy. His eyes begin to blaze with his Light Source, his connection wanting to react to the impending enemy.

Galloping through the rain the calls suddenly go silent as a wave of nausea hits him. It's followed by a dizziness which causes him to release the reins of the horse. Putting his hands to his temples, Mercy begins swaying slightly as an intense pain takes over his body. He felt like he was going to throw up or maybe pass out, he wasn't quite sure yet.

Realizing what was happening, Shay reaches around him for the reins and guides the mare herself. Mercy buries his face in his hands trying to shake the sickness washing over him. He felt queasy and empty inside and his heart was pounding like it was going to explode. Existing felt painful, his skin burned, and he felt like he was breathing fire. Every pump of his heart was excruciating.

"What's happening?" he asks Shay.

The girl brings the horse to a halt to give the Light Keeper a moment to regain himself. She dismounts Maple, bracing him as he falls to the side. Once his feet reached the muddy path he stumbles toward a tree and leans his hand against it, clutching his shirt at his chest. His chest was aching. His stomach was in his feet. What was going on? What was this feeling? Leaning his head on the tree it suddenly hits him. Cal's calls had stopped. In a panic, he quickly tries to access their Voca, but the line felt dead. There was no other end to his connection. His breathing goes ragged at the realization.

"Cal's gone," he mutters to himself.

"What?" Shay asks.

"Cal's gone!" Mercy shouts at her, another panic attack about to take over.

The feeling he was having was his Source reacting to losing his Alia. The pain was it trying to find its parallel connection to the Shadow Source that was now severed. The hot burn in his upper arm returns as terror sets in, his eyes glowing more intensely. Caligo was gone. He lets out a scream, unsure if it was from physical or emotional pain. He slinks down the tree trying to gain his composure, but this hurt. This hurt in a way he couldn't even describe. Suddenly he felt like only half of himself.

Shay quickly moves to him. She remembered this feeling when her Alia was killed. It was unbearable, not just physically but emotionally. Even though she had severed her Alia's connection to the Light Source before taking the life, the loss of her parallel still resonated through her. She could only imagine the pain Mercy was feeling with Cal's connection still there and the bond the two had forged.

"It'll pass," she comforts, crouching down beside him. "This will pass."

He lets out another scream as tears come to his eyes. What had just happened? How had it happened? He grips the wet grass, digging his nails into the mud. How could Cal be gone? He was supposed to be the one to die, not Caligo. This was all wrong.

169

"He's gone!" he shouts. "He's gone!"

"Just give it a moment," Shay eases. "It will pass in a few moments."

The few moments felt like a lifetime as the feeling of losing Cal ricocheted off every cell in his body. For those few moments Shay sat beside him trying to offer some comfort. She knew it wasn't much, but it was something. Being alone in a time like this was more painful than having a stranger sitting beside him.

He looks at her with agony in his eyes. His Alia was gone. One of the two people put on this planet to support him and aid him in this life was gone. His mind shifts to Sylas. The thing he needed to do was find Sylas. He needed to know his best friend was still alive and okay. Surely Sylas was a wreck if he witnessed this.

Unexpectedly he hears a familiar caw. He gasps as Nex lands in the grass in front of him, hopping toward him. The crow's eyes reflected his own pain in an all too real way. He wondered if she felt the same agony he was.

"Nex?" he asks.

She hops to his feet and begins pecking at the laces on his boots. She wanted him to follow her. With a shuddering breath he gets to his feet and without saying a word goes back to Maple. Nex would take him where he needed to go. She probably knew where Cal was, which was hopefully with Sylas somewhere up the path.

"Shay, can you guide Maple?" he asks, scooting back for her.

The girl nods her head and climbs onto the mare in front of him. Having Mercy put trust in her felt strange, but it was a good strange. The Light Keeper looked paler than usual and was in bad shape. He places his hands on her shoulders and rests his forehead on her back trying to gain his composure, breathing in on an eight count and out on a seven. Digging her heels into the mare, they gallop forward, watching Nex in the sky as the rain begins to let up.

After several minutes, a wagon with two horses comes into view on the path just ahead of a bridge. "That's Draven and Ruta," Mercy murmurs, recognizing Cal and Pippa's horses.

As the pair approached the cart, Nex dives into the trees off the path. Shay pulls Maple to a stop and dismounts. She offers Mercy a hand as he jumps down beside her. He gives Maple a pat on the side before moving his eyes to the trees. He felt nauseous and his bones ached, but he needed to focus.

"Ready yourself," he instructs Shay.

Mercy powers up and pulls his Source to his hands as he moves slowly into the trees. His entire body felt like it was on fire, but he needed to be ready to fight. While losing Cal was supposed to weaken him, he didn't feel weaker. Why didn't he feel weaker?

Shay powers up behind him, ready to offer any support she could. The vision from the conference room begins to play in Mercy's head. Was he going to die here too? He hears Nex's calls and continues forward until he spots Pippa lying in the grass.

Powering down, he rushes toward her. Dropping down beside his friend, he checks her pulse. He lets out a sigh of relief. She was alive. Mercy's hands begin to shake as he looks at Pippa. Seeing her like this made him angry. Who would do this to Pippa? He brushes her hair out of her face and could see the faint glowing scar of a newly healed wound. At his touch, her eyes open.

"Mercy?" she questions.

"Don't move," he whispers to her.

She sits up slowly, unable to comprehend what had happened. He wondered how long she had been out as the anger fades and is replaced with worry. He puts a hand on her cheek and studies her face. She nods at him, assuring her friend she was okay. Without hesitation, he wraps his arms around her and holds her tightly for a moment. At least Pippa was okay.

"I already healed her," he hears Zero's voice shout. "About time you showed up."

Pulling away from Pippa, he looks her in the eyes. "Are you okay?"

"I'm fine," she assures.

Giving a nod of the head, he lets out a shaky breath. Scanning the area, he spots Zero walking away from them and toward another person lying in the grass. He could also see Sylas sitting at the edge of the risen river. The water had flooded the area, causing Sylas's spot to be flushed with at least a foot of water.

Looking to Shay, Mercy exchanges a fearful look. "Stay with her, please."

"Of course," she nods, crouching beside Pippa.

Taking a deep breath, Mercy moves and approaches Zero and the person lying in the grass. He could tell this wasn't Caligo, the brown hair indicating someone of stronger human ancestry. He watches as Zero slowly turns the individual over. With a bewildered gasp, Mercy registers this as Sander. He looked nearly human, except for his pointed ears. The drained Keeper appeared thin and weak, but they had found him. He notes the blood seeping from a gash on his chest and spots Cal's blade a few feet away. Zero begins healing the injury as Mercy watches his friend's face carefully. He wasn't waking up, but at least he was alive.

"Go to Sylas," Zero instructs, his voice lacking its usual harsh tone. "Whatever just happened... When I woke up, Cal was gone."

Mercy nods his head, getting to his feet. Apparently Zero wasn't quite sure what happened himself. Mercy walks toward his best friend and crouches down. The cold water quickly begins to flood over his boots, soaking his socks. Sylas was staring out at the water, his face numb. He didn't even seem to register that Mercy was beside him. His eyes were completely void of emotion as he watched the water churn in front of him.

"Sylas, where's Cal?" Mercy questions in a calm tone.

His voice brings Sylas's attention to him. The look in his Nota's eyes said it all. Seeing his best friend, the one person who cared for Cal more than anyone else on this planet look like this, confirmed his fear. Sylas had just lost the person he loved. Emotions quickly take over as the reality of the situation comes to light.

"Sylas, where's Cal?" Mercy repeats, wanting to hear the words come from his mouth.

His best friend shakes his head numbly. Clearly Sylas was in shock, but Mercy needed to hear it. Even though he knew it in his heart, he needed to hear it from someone who was there. He was desperate for Sylas to say something other than what he already knew.

"Where is he!?" Mercy shouts at him, feeling anger wash over him. "Where's Caligo!?"

Sylas continues to shake his head. His best friend couldn't even speak the words himself. Neither of them wanted to admit what they both knew.

"You were supposed to stay in Ozra!" Mercy scolds, the pain from earlier beginning to bubble up again. "I came alone so you'd be safe! Why'd you come after me!?"

"Why'd you leave?" Sylas whispers, wincing at Mercy's tone. "Why'd you leave, Merc?"

"Where is he, Sylas!?" Mercy pleads, grabbing his friends face, trying to focus him.

"You left," Sylas mutters, his voice louder with his next words. "Why'd you leave?"

"You need to tell me where he is now!" Mercy snaps back, hot tears coming to his eyes.

"You left him! You left us!" Sylas continues to berate him, mirroring his best friend's emotions. "We were looking for you!"

"Shut the hell up and tell me where he is!" Mercy screams.

His Nota pulls away and looks out at the water. Mercy follows his gaze as it becomes clear. Cal went into the water. Cal went into the water and didn't come back up. Sylas's eyes come back to Mercy as he begins to shake his head again, a look of disgust in his eyes.

"You did this," Sylas accuses, hatred in his voice. "You left him, Merc. Why?"

Ignoring his friend, Mercy's eyes scan the churning water as the rain begins to pour around them again. How was this happening? He wasn't supposed to lose anyone else. After Spheara his family and friends were supposed to be safe. How had something like this happened?

Getting to his feet with panic in his eyes, Mercy begins to follow the bank, scanning the surface of the water for any sign of Cal. The more steps he took, the quicker his strides became. This wasn't happening. There was no way he was just gone.

"Cal!" he screams down the shore as a crash of thunder rings out. "Caligo!"

Shay and Pippa watch the Light Keeper begin to move frantically down the river to search for their friend. In that moment, Pippa begins to realize something was wrong. Why were Mercy and Sylas arguing and where was the Light Keeper going?

"What happened?" Pippa questions in fear. "Where is he going?"

"I'm not sure," Shay admits. She looks to Pippa whose eyes were buzzing around the area.

"Where's Cal?" she asks, her voice drenched with anxiety. "Shay, where is Caligo?"

Unsure what to say, Shay shakes her head. She knew the friendship Pippa had with Caligo. Though she only studied with Master Novi for a year, it didn't take long for her to see the sibling bond the two had created during Caligo's years with the Drors. How was she supposed to tell this girl that her brother was dead?

Pippa slowly gets to her feet and moves toward Zero who was still crouched next to Sander. She drops down beside him, Shay staying at her side. If Shay wasn't going to give her an answer, someone else would have to.

Up the river, Mercy continues to move down the bank searching for his Alia. He was desperate to locate him, whether it was to find him alive, or maybe to see his body. He didn't care. He just wanted to find Caligo. He finally stops and falls to his knees on the bank, knowing full well that searching for him was pointless.

"You were supposed to stay in Ozra!" he pleads with his Alia, looking down at his hands that were still glowing. "I can't do this without you, Cal! We're supposed to be a team!" He looks up at the water again and lets out another cry. "Caligo!"

His chest felt hollow. While it hurt to lose others in the past, nothing could compare to the level of emptiness he felt inside right now. He suddenly understood why Meera isolated herself for months after losing Trust. This was a painful feeling. One he never wanted to feel again, and now never would. His other half was gone.

"Cal, please," he whimpers.

He hears footsteps rush through the wet grass behind him followed by Pippa wrapping her arms around him from behind. She must have finally realized what was going on. He could feel his entire body begin to shake as she held him tight. Usually, she would bring him comfort, but her being there in that moment felt forced and unwanted. He pulls away from her, getting to his feet. He begins to step into the water, his emotional mind telling him he needed to go after his friend.

"Cal!" he screams again.

"Mercy, stop!" Pippa begs.

As the water hits halfway up his shins, he lets out a heart wrenching scream. Pippa wraps her arms around him again and pulls him down, trying to get him to stop moving forward. He gives in and collapses into the shallow bank with her. He screams again, unable to make sense of the feelings that were going through him.

Chapter Seventeen

With a sharp exhale, Mercy knocks on the door to Princess Tristia's suite. He glances to the Sentry Guard at the entrance and forces a smile to try and appear normal even though he felt anything but. Returning to Ozra without Cal made his entire body feel heavy.

Once word had gotten to the Princess about Cal's passing, she had asked to speak with him privately. He wasn't even sure what he was going to say to her. Facing Tristia after this felt ominous. Looking at the events it was very clear Mercy's role in the demise of their King.

"Come in!" he hears her voice shout from the opposite side.

Pushing the door open he sees the young Princess sitting on the sofa in the sitting room, signing paperwork on the low table in front of her. With Cal gone and no heir to the throne, Tristia was next in line to take over Novus Aitus. She must have been terrified. Caligo felt overwhelmed being 24 and ruling, he could only imagine how Tristia was taking this, having to take over in his place at the age of 19 on top of losing her brother.

"You wanted to talk," he states in a quiet voice.

"Indeed," she nods.

"Okay," he replies.

She gestures for him to take a seat in the chair across from her. He does as instructed, folding his hands in his lap carefully. The interaction reminded him of getting in trouble when he was a child. It was just like being called to Elder Rom's office to discuss a mistake he had made or a fight he had been involved in. Usually, those fights involved Sylas hitting someone for him. This on the other hand was his own doing, and there was no denying that.

"From what I have been told, you forged a document with Caligo's signature and seal to release Shay Tract," she speaks quickly, looking at him with pained eyes.

"Yes," he confirms, the guilt making his face go sour. "Is Shay okay?"

"She is back in her cell where she belongs," Tristia informs him.

She watches him a moment as he falters at the news. It was noticeable Mercy hadn't been sleeping. It had only been two days since the events at the river, and Mercy's Source was still trying to locate Cal's in a desperate way. After speaking with Elder Maior and Master Novi, they were shocked it was still searching. His Source should have settled into things by now, but it was refusing, causing him to constantly feel woozy and on edge, with tinges of his Source caressing his irises at all times. He didn't feel he had any control of his connection since losing Cal, which made him feel like a bomb waiting to explode.

Tris takes a deep breath before speaking. "In the debriefing with Captain Bellator over the incident, he stated that he feels Caligo's death was your doing and the events leading up to it should be viewed as treason." She pauses waiting for a reaction but gets nothing. "You realize those who are deemed traitorous to the crown with your level of power can be placed in level three with an execution trial set?" She states with serious eyes.

"Sylas said that?" he questions, his voice small.

She nods her head and looks down. "In my experience, grief can make you say things you do not truly feel," she comforts. "In light of the circumstances, I do believe what has happened is punishment enough. I do not think anyone is feeling more at fault for my brother's passing than you are."

He looks to the floor, not wanting to say a word. Forging that document and going out on his own was what led to Cal's death. If he hadn't done what he did, then Cal wouldn't have gone after him. Hearing Sylas had called for his punishment made the pain worse. His best friend was refusing to speak to him or even look at him since that day. When he had gone to speak with him after the debriefing, Sylas wouldn't even answer the door of his suite.

"There is something else weighing into this pardon, and I wish for this to stay between us until a decision is made," she continues.

"Okay," he replies quietly.

"With the eloium tomorrow, I will be required to make a public statement within the week about the future of the Tenebris monarchy," she explains. "Unfortunately, ruling Novus Aitus was never something I particularly wanted to do, nor would I excel at. Caligo was the one meant to lead our people and repair the damage our ancestors caused."

He keeps his eyes to the floor. She had called him in here to inform him she was going to announce a new heir in her stead, but who? The line ended with Tristia. She was the last Tenebris that could take over. Could she be handing things over to her father Rexon perhaps? He honestly never asked Cal if he had any other family besides his sister, so perhaps there was a cousin. That didn't explain why she wanted to speak with him though.

"I also fear that another Tenebris taking up the delicate mantle my brother has left behind would be

179

foolish," she adds, getting his attention again. "My brother barely had the favor of the people, and my approval ratings would be simply dismal in comparison."

"You have someone else in mind?" Mercy asks, looking at her.

"Cal did," she nods, taking a deep breath. "I have thought long and hard about this the last couple of days and I feel the future leader of Novus Aitus is sitting right in front of me."

He furrows his brow at the statement. "Me?" he asks completely dumbfounded.

"Yes," she nods again, her voice somber. "The people admire you, Mercy. They respect you and the Validus name. They view you as a hero and your family is that of diplomats. The respect Western Ozra has for the Validus name echoes throughout the world now. Of course, the National Council and I will be there to guide you on larger decisions until you have your footing." She pauses a moment seeing the unease on his face. "Losing my brother has put the fate of our people into an uncertain time. Announcing you, his Alia and closest adviser, will be taking over his position as King of Novus Aitus will undoubtedly alleviate the fear within their minds."

He nods his head in understanding as his eyes dart across the floor trying to make sense of her request. He could hardly handle taking care of Rieka and the girls, how did she expect him to govern an entire planet? That was millions of people relying on him. After what he had just done this seemed outlandish. Caligo was gone because he chose to be selfish instead of working together with his Alia. He wasn't a leader; he was a fool.

"I do not expect you to make a decision today," Tris adds. "In fact, I believe letting you take the remainder of the week to think this over will be best for all involved. We are all still raw from the loss of Cal. He was meant to do more for our people than the last year has allowed."

"Tris, I can't," he breathes, locking his eyes on her. "You can't ask me to do that."

"You can refuse," she informs him. "I would not blame you if you chose to deny the offer, but personally I believe you are meant to succeed my brother. You were created to lead and protect our people. You proved that with your actions during Spheara. You are wise beyond your years and-"

"Saying someone is wise beyond their years is just another way of saying they have childhood trauma," he retorts, irritation coming to his tone.

He closes his eyes at his own outburst. Lately he had no control over his words. How could she ask him to do this? Requesting him to take over the throne was ludicrous. He wasn't qualified for a position like that. If anything, she should be offering the monarchy to Sylas. He was meant to be with Cal, meaning his future undoubtedly aligned him to support in governing their people. That was Sylas's destiny. Then again, his destiny of being with Cal was gone.

"I can assure you that Cal wanted you to take over for him, Mercy," Tristia adds. "He admired you. He saw the capabilities you have."

"No," he snaps, shaking his head.

She lets out a steady exhale as she pulls a folder out from under the paperwork and hands it to him. Hesitantly he takes it from her and opens it. At first glance he could see it was an official document, signed by Caligo himself.

"What is this?" he questions, starting to scan the text.

"Cal's contingency plan," she shares. "These were his wishes in the event he was to succumb to an untimely death. The second line from the bottom. In the chance he was to pass before producing an heir or finding a partner, he named his heir to the monarchy to be-"

"Mercy Validus," he finishes, letting the document go slack in his hands.

"I will accept the responsibility if you refuse," Tristia states, "but I hope you will heed my brother's final wishes if not my own."

He closes his eyes again. Cal had always had faith in his abilities. While he was sometimes crass about it, he knew Mercy would pull through in the long run. He trusted him in every sense of the word, sometimes more than Sylas did. This made him feel even more shameful for disobeying his orders. How could he have thrown Cal's trust to the side so easily that night?

"This is what Cal wanted," Tristia stresses. "Please just think about the offer."

He nods his head in consideration, getting to his feet. He sets the document on the desk and gives her a forced smile as he walks toward the door. There was nothing he wanted to say to her. There wasn't anything else he could say. Caligo was gone.

Closing the door behind him, he begins to walk down the hall, folding his arms to try and keep himself from shaking. He was sweating suddenly as a shiver ran through him. How was he cold? He was never cold. He feels the same sting in his arm and begins to rub away the tinge.

While he had spent seven years with his connection before meeting Cal, he hadn't started to use it until he met his Alia. Caligo was so tied to his life as a Keeper of Light that the idea of him trying to stay the course felt wrong without him. Did he even know how to be a Keeper without Cal? Without his Alia and with Sylas not speaking to him, what did that mean for his future? Could he even continue his training without his Nota?

As he enters his suite, he pauses at the silence. The girls must have been off to study already and Charlyn must have been aiding the kitchen staff. Without a house to keep in order while the girls were doing their schoolwork, the housekeeper tended to find ways to be useful for the estate staff.

Closing the door behind him, he makes his way to his room. He was exhausted and laying down for a few hours felt more tempting than ever before. While he doubted he would get any sleep, the idea of simply lying there was welcoming enough.

Entering his room, he pauses at the sight of Pippa laying on his bed. She was staring numbly at the wall in a white and purple dress, not even noticing Mercy had come in. Why was she here? He watches her a moment with a frown. She was probably just as broken as he was, if not more. While she didn't talk about it much, he knew how much Cal meant to her. They had grown up together.

Carefully sitting on the side of his bed, he gently places his hand on her side. "Pip?" he whispers.

The young woman perks up at the sound of her name and turns over to look at him. The look on her face told him all he needed to know. She had come here to try and find someone to comfort her or maybe distract her. Losing Caligo wasn't just losing a friend, she had lost her big brother and her best friend.

In that moment, he needed to put his own grief aside and try and give the woman who had been there for him through so much the same security. He gently places a hand on her arm and rubs it lightly as she stares at him.

"Hey," he whispers.

"Hi," she replies back.

"Do you need a hug?" he asks her.

She gives him a small nod and sits up to accept his offer of an embrace. Pulling her close he squeezes her tightly as she buries her face in his chest. He closes his eyes, not wanting to react to the aching in his chest. Seeing Pippa like this killed him. Seeing everyone mourn for Cal was something he didn't want to experience. All of his friends were in pain because of his idiocy.

"I'm sorry," he whispers, rubbing her back.

"Please don't talk," she retorts.

"Okay," he nods as he continues to hold her.

He could feel the quiet tears from her. How could he have been this stupid? How was he going to make this up to her and Sylas? At least Pippa was talking to him. He could find a way to survive Sylas's silent treatment if he had Pippa.

Chapter Eighteen

They had just finished the eloium for Caligo, the event leaving the group numb. Sylas sat beside Mercy on the couch, shuffling a small gem in his fingers, having not said a word to Mercy since they left the river's edge. The silence from his best friend left Mercy feeling empty and alone. He had never wished for Sylas to listen to him more than he did right now. While before he welcomed a quiet evening with his childhood friend, now he despised it. With his mind so scrambled, he needed someone stable to try and help him sort things out.

The Light Keeper had his eyes focused on a drop of water rolling down the side of a glass as he rubbed his upper arm with a sigh. Dolus had brought the group water and a few snacks, but no one had touched them. As the drop hit the tablecloth below, it was absorbed into the white fabric. Mercy takes a deep breath. He wished his own emotions could work like that. He wished once they collected on the surface, they would just vanish.

His mind goes to the vision of his body in the forest again. Now that Cal was gone the vision was even more unnerving. If both were dead, who was going to hold their friends and families together? Seeing how torn up Sylas and Pippa were over the loss of Cal made the idea of his life ending even more terrifying. He wasn't scared for himself anymore; he was scared for the heartache he'd be leaving behind. The thought sends a shiver down his spine.

"Mercy?" Tristia questions.

He looks up quickly, realizing everyone was gawking at him. Scanning the room, he sees Pippa, Master Novi, Emidio, Rexon and Tristia had entered the room. Glancing to Charlyn with the girls, he notes the concerned looks. All were dressed in white, the traditional color for an eloium. They would all be wearing the glaring garments for eleven more days. Nearly the entire planet would out of respect for their fallen monarch. He always found it strange that the color for mourning was white. The color was supposed to signify hope and happiness, but the loss of a loved one felt more like darkness and agony.

"Mercy?" Tris repeats.

He clears his throat. "Yeah?"

"Sander has been asking to speak with you," the Princess states.

He looks at her with wide eyes. When they had gotten Sander back to Ozra he was unconscious. In their debriefings, neither Sylas, Zero, nor Pippa could give a clear answer on how Sander had appeared. No one knew how or when the Shadow had gotten there, so Mercy had been waiting for word that his guard had woken up.

"He is refusing to speak with Captain Skerrick," she adds. "I am hoping you will be able to get information from him."

Mercy takes his eyes to his best friend beside him who was now fiddling with his splint, keeping his eyes on the table in front of them. Staring at Sylas's injured hand, a wave of sadness washes over Mercy again. Not only had his friend lost his archery, but he had also lost the person he loved most. No wonder there was no way to comfort him.

Sylas probably had no idea how to comfort himself, the light in his eyes completely gone.

"Mercy!" Tris scolds.

He looks back up to her. "Sorry. Yes. I'll speak with him," he nods in a quiet voice.

The Princess studies him carefully. He looked just as naïve and innocent as he did the day she met him in the throne room. The young man also looked equally as scared. Even though he wasn't being sentenced to death, he looked like he was.

"I will let Captain Skerrick know," the Princess nods.

Tristia leaves the room with her father, Master Novi and Emidio at her side. The three were attempting to help Tris learn to be the leader Cal once was. No one could be as great as Caligo though. He watches them exit and goes back to staring at the water on the table.

Saphie and Ruby keep their eyes glued to their guardian. While the girls were used to seeing Mercy out of sorts, this was different. None of them had seen him this broken since the day Rieka fell. When he had returned to Rieka and agreed to take in Brokkr's girls he had put on a strong facade, just like Cal had always done. He made himself appear resilient. There was no faking to cover this sadness though.

"Let's go upstairs, shall we girls?" Charlyn forces a smile at the children.

Saphie gets up to follow her, but Ruby continues to watch Mercy. The little girl could see how much he was hurting and didn't want to leave him. After all the time Mercy had spent comforting her, she wanted to return the favor. She moves across the room and comes up beside him, wrapping her arms around his torso as he puts an arm around her in return. He didn't even realize he was doing it; he just did. It was a natural reaction to the little girl to try and ease her worries.

"Uncle Cal wouldn't want you to be sad," she whispers to him.

He lets out a small laugh at the comment. If it was the other way around, Cal would surely be going for blood. He wouldn't even have come back to Ozra for the eloium, the tenacious man would have gone straight for Bryer and ended this before losing anyone else. Mercy couldn't do that though. His first attempt at running headfirst into this had failed, he couldn't risk it again.

"Go with Charlyn, Rubes," he encourages, his voice low and void.

The little girl lets out a flustered sigh and releases him. She goes to Charlyn but keeps her eyes on Mercy as she leaves with the housekeeper. He closes his eyes, not wanting to see Ruby's sad face. What was he going to do?

"I will leave you two," Pippa states, moving back toward the door.

Registering her voice, Mercy looks up to her. "Pip, wait," he pleads.

He didn't want her to leave. If she left, he was alone. Even though Sylas was physically there, his best friend's mind wasn't. Sylas had just been going through the motions. He wasn't even sure why Sylas was sitting with him other than the fact it was just involuntary for the pair. Mercy could feel his Nota's pain just as much as his own and it was weighing on him.

"Can you go see Sander with me?" Mercy asks her in a soft voice.

With a small smile, she nods her head as he gets to his feet. He looks down at Sylas who was staring at the gem in his hand again. He wondered where he even got the small stone. It reminded him of the darker stones that were used in the Tenebris jewels, but it would be odd for Sylas to have one. He pauses, wondering if he should even leave his best friend alone. Was it rude to just leave Sylas?

He taps his friend's shoulder but gets nothing in return. With another sigh, Mercy grabs his chin to force his gaze. It throws Sylas off, but he looks at Mercy with a confused expression.

"You can come," Mercy offers, letting go.

Sylas furrows his brow like he was trying to figure out what Mercy was even talking about. After a moment he looks to Pippa and takes a deep breath before shaking his head. He goes back to absent mindedly shuffling the gem in his fingers. Mercy lets out a sigh and gestures to Pippa to walk. The two leave the room and begin to head down the hall toward the infirmary on the other side of the manor.

Pippa takes the Light Keeper's hand and stays close to him as they move down the hall, speaking in a sorrowful voice. "I fear Sylas is blaming himself."

"Or me," Mercy replies flatly.

"I doubt that," she remarks.

With a sharp exhale Mercy shakes his head. While Sylas had voiced Cal's passing being Mercy's fault, he may have just been deflecting his own guilt. He was trying to sort through the situation and figure out what had gone wrong. Mercy was doing the same thing. The fear he felt from Cal and the cries for help had been playing through his mind like a siren. There was no escaping it. He could feel every ounce of fear his Alia felt.

"I wish I knew what happened," Pippa states. "I wish I had been able to help."

"You did what you could," Mercy assures.

"I should have been more insistent on him staying in the capital. I did not listen to you," she admits. "If I had just followed your orders then-"

"A wise Light Keeper once told me that the brave and courageous are the ones who realize they can 'what if,' themselves to the grave," he smiles softly, looking at her.

She takes a shuddering breath and nods at the comment. "I am fearful for the future of Ozra and all of

Novus Aitus with Cal's passing, Mercy. Caligo was holding what little peace we had together, and now he is gone."

He nods his head in agreement looking at her. He knew she didn't sleep well last night, neither of them did. They were both tossing and turning well into the morning. Even when she was exhausted, she still looked lovely. He shakes his head in annoyance taking his eyes to the floor and rubbing his upper arm again. Why was he looking at her like that right now? He needed to focus.

"What is wrong with your arm?" Pippa asks, pulling his hand away from his shoulder as they stop. "Is it bothering you? You have been trying to ease it a lot the last few days."

"Yeah," he sighs. "It's been… I don't know."

She rolls his sleeve up and studies the raised scar on his arm. "Did you heal this?"

He nods, looking at it with her. The scar on his arm was now bright pink and even more raised. He could feel the ache under his skin as she ran her fingers over it. She furrows her brow, the scar hot to the touch. Then again, Mercy skin felt warm in general the last few days. His inability to turn off his Source was weighing on him physically with each passing day.

"It seems to be a bit rough for your healing level," she states, looking at him with worry.

"I was distracted when it happened," he admits. "It was during the break in, so I wasn't exactly focused on my Light Source healing a cut."

"Has Doctor Willa examined it?" she questions.

"It was just a scratch," he reassures her.

"It may be worth having her look at if it is bothering you, dear," she smiles softly.

He shrugs. "It's fine."

She nods her head in understanding, adjusting his sleeve to lay properly. They begin walking again as he

190

places his hand to the scar, rubbing it gently. It had been aching since Cal had died and he wasn't sure why. While it had been a sharp pain before, now it was a dull ache. He did agree with Pippa that it was strange, but there was no reason he could think to be concerned. He takes a deep breath as she takes his hand again and they continue to walk in the numbing silence.

There was so much he needed to think about in the next few days, the biggest being Caligo's contingency plan. The idea of taking over where his Alia had left off felt impossible. Cal did his job with grace and poise. Even when he was stressed, he held it together for his people and his friends. How was he going to live up to that if he took over the monarchy?

"Tris offered me the throne," he states bluntly.

Pippa pulls him to a stop again and looks at him with fierce eyes. "She what?"

"The people were wary putting Cal on the throne," Mercy explains, urging her forward as he spoke. "She thinks putting me in charge, the one who ended the tyrant, could calm the rebellion brewing. With Cal gone the threat of the rebels is higher than ever."

"Are you going to accept?" Pippa questions.

He looks down at her hand in his and shakes his head. It felt foolish for him to take the position. He didn't know the first thing about leading, nor was he confident that his name on the monarchy would help. He also couldn't accept the position because if his vision was true, Novus Aitus would need another heir shortly after. His death was inevitable, and he had no idea how to stop it. How was he going to stop something from happening when he had no idea when or where it was taking place?

"There's a reason I can't," he explains.

She studies his face in concern. "What is that?"

"The vision I had in the conference room," he keeps his voice low. "I..." he begins to chew the inside of his lip and looks down.

Should he even tell Pippa this? It felt cruel to drop this on her right after losing Cal, but he needed someone to know. At least when Cal was alive, someone was aware. His Alia was able to comfort him and try to ease his worries. Now he was alone in his fears.

"What is it?" she asks, uneasiness in her voice.

His eyes meet hers. Looking at her he couldn't bring himself to admit what he saw. Telling her he was going to be leaving her felt harsh. He didn't want her to look at him wondering when his last moment was going to be. He wanted her to continue to look at him with hope. Pippa had always been the one to believe in him. To believe he could make a difference.

With a slow exhale he closes his eyes. If he didn't make up something, she was going to pester him. He had to lie. "I knew what was going to happen to Cal."

"You what?" she gasps.

"That's why I left the way I did. He knew. He saw everything," he states, the guilt hitting him like a ton of bricks.

"Why didn't you two say anything?" Pippa asks, letting his hand go. Her tone switches from calm to angry. "We could have tried to prevent this. I would not have let him follow you, Mercy. I would not have told him where you were going."

He takes a shaking breath, trying to calm himself. What did he expect to happen? He definitely didn't think this all the way through. He couldn't back track now though. If he tried to tell her the truth it would only make things worse, and she might not even believe him.

"Why did you not say anything?" she pleads, tears starting to form.

Staring at her, he begins to panic. Pippa being furious with him was the last thing he needed. Why did he lie? Why did he choose *that* lie?

"Mercy Validus!" she scolds, raising her voice. "Why didn't you tell anyone about this? Did you even tell Sylas? You do not think he deserves to know?"

He shrugs, unsure what to say at that point. He couldn't even tell if she was angry or just upset.

"What happens to Caligo does not just affect you! It affects all of us! It affects me and Sylas and Tristia and my parents, our people and…" her voice trails off as tears begin to run down her cheeks. "How could you keep that to yourself?"

"I'm sorry," he finally speaks, putting a hand toward her to offer some comfort.

She smacks it away, the anger coming back to her expression. She was furious. If he had told her or anyone else about what he had seen, they could have worked together to keep Cal safe. She would have insisted on them not going after Mercy or maybe would have told the group to flee instead of letting him walk into that fight.

Cal wasn't just her friend; he was her best friend, her brother. She had spent nearly every winter and summer with him. He protected her and stood up for her when needed. He was one of the few people on this planet she could trust. They confided in each other on many different things. The fact she was the first person Cal told about his feelings for Sylas was enough to prove that to anyone. Their friendship had always been important to her and now he was gone. Not only was he gone, but the man who was meant to always protect him had known his fate. Mercy had known and he told no one about Caligo's envisioned death.

"All you have to say is you are sorry?" she lectures. "Sorry is not going to bring him back, Mercy. Sorry means nothing now."

"Pip-" he attempts to plead his case.

"No," she snaps. "I trusted you, Mercy. You were supposed to be there for him! To protect him!"

Backing away from Mercy, she turns to head the opposite direction. He could feel the anxiety in his chest begin to rise, but quickly regulates his breathing. He was such an idiot. Right now, he needed Pippa and she needed him. Instead of being there for her, he had put a very painful wall between them. Telling her the real vision may have been less agonizing than this. Then again, maybe pushing her away was what needed to happen. He was a tidal wave at this point. It seemed every time he cared for someone; they were put in harm's way.

Collecting himself he heads toward the infirmary. He needed to speak with Sander. If Sylas wasn't going to tell him what happened, perhaps Sander could. He needed to know what happened to his Alia, his other half, his twin flame. He needed answers.

Taking the time to check in, the nurse at the desk seemed surprised to see him. He doesn't speak as he signs the document and follows her directions. Outside the door to Sander's room was Zero, guarding the entrance. He wondered why they stationed someone to keep watch over the Shadow Sentry and why it would be Zero. Considering Zero's standing with the Royals, it seemed odd to have him watching over a drained Shadow.

"Prissy Princess said you'd be coming by, but I wasn't expecting you already," Zero admits as Mercy approaches.

"Sorry," Mercy sighs with a small shrug.

"No saving the planet today?" Zero mocks.

"No," Mercy retorts, the humor lost on him.

Zero's face softens seeing Mercy's fatigue. Even though he didn't particularly like Mercy, he still had sympathy for him. "Are you sure you want to talk with him right now?"

"Yeah," Mercy nods, taking a deep breath.

He knew Sander. Sander was a friend. He was the man who had fought by his brother's side until the end, the first soldier to stand up against Mala. He was someone he knew he could trust. Even enough to let him watch over his family while they slept.

Mercy nods to Zero again as he opens the door and enters the room. He furrows his brow at the man. Sander was sitting on his bed, staring out the window and fidgeting with what appeared to be an acorn in his hand. He looked thin and frail, his hands shaking. Whatever had happened must have shaken him up quite a bit.

"Hey," Mercy speaks, his voice quiet.

Sander's eyes shoot to him. He looked fearful, but once his eyes locked on Mercy his expression calmed.

"You're alive?" Sander asks in shock.

Mercy nods his head moving further into the room. Had no one told this man anything? Why would he be questioning if Mercy was alive?

"Are the girls okay? What about Charlyn?" he stands up, worry in his voice.

"We're all fine," Mercy assures, gesturing for him to sit down, Sander doing as instructed. "What happened?"

The drained Shadow Keeper looks down at the acorn. The expression on his face indicated he was just as confused about where he had gone those four weeks as the rest of them. Maybe he wouldn't have the answers Mercy was hoping for.

"Why don't you start with what you remember last?" Mercy encourages, trying to comfort his friend while pulling a chair up to the bed.

"I was standing outside your house," Sander states, still looking at the acorn. "I was standing there and the next thing I knew I was here. There're a few snippets I can remember of being with a woman, but I don't like the memories."

The statement causes Mercy's face to falter. While he was trying to remain calm, seeing Sander like this wasn't something he took easily. There wasn't supposed to be any danger in his job, he was simply supposed to ward off any unwanted guests or thieves.

"She cut symbols into me," Sander states, putting his arm out to show him and lowering his shirt collar with the other hand. "I have no idea what they mean, but I'm afraid to show anyone. They've been odd with me. They won't tell me anything. They're worried I've been corrupted, Mercy, but I promise I'm not. Whatever happened in the forest brought me back. I'm not sure where I was before, but I'm here now. I promise."

"I believe you," Mercy assures.

When Shay had tainted Cal and others, there was a clear shift. He could sense Shay in their minds. Even when she tainted a mortal, he could feel it. Sander was clean. His mind was his own.

Mercy studies the rune on his arm carefully. It was another form of an exua rune, that was clear. While Sylas's was a circle in the center, this one had a diamond. It was the same one the woman had tried to put on Cal's arm. This explained what happened to his Source, but the other he had never seen before.

Moving to look at the one on his chest, he cocks his brow. He now wished more than ever that Pippa had come down here with him. This symbol was intricate and strange. It almost reminded him of a musical note. The gash from Cal's blade sliced right through it.

"I'm going to have Pippa or Sylas come by to look at this," Mercy explains, shaking his head. "This one I know," he adds, pointing to the exua rune. "The woman, Iana, marked a similar one on Sylas when he encountered her, and she tried to put this one on Caligo, but the other… I don't know."

"What is it?" Sander questions, looking at his arm.

"An exua rune," Mercy explains. "She took your Source from you, Sander."

The two remain silent as Sander takes in the information, looking at his arm warily. He runs his fingers over the scar and shakes his head.

"I'm sorry," Mercy frowns.

"You have nothing to be sorry for. I was doing my job," Sander assures him, taking his eyes from the markings. "I'm sorry about Cal," he offers, pulling his arm away. "I can't help but feel I was involved in this situation."

"Even if you were, it wasn't you," Mercy comforts him.

"What else has that woman done while I've been away?" Sander questions, seeing the sadness in Mercy's eyes.

"She's gone after Sylas, Meera, and now Cal. She's powerful. She has these…" he trails off.

He looks to Sander with a wrinkled brow. When they fought the beast at Meera's cabin, he felt Sander there. Zero said they were attacked by an obscurum again on the path, and suddenly Sander was found alive. The Sentry Guard showed up just off the water's edge with Cal's blade beside him. Had Cal figured it out before he went into the river? Did he know Sander was in there and that's why the blade was thrown?

"I need Sylas," he mumbles to himself, getting to his feet. "Sander, I'm sorry. I need to go."

Sander watches as Mercy rushes out of the room. He needed to find out what Sylas and Zero saw and figure out what they knew about the beasts. If the obscurum was

Sander, then they had a new problem on their hands. He grabs Zero's arm and pulls him out of the infirmary.

Chapter Nineteen

Rushing into the room he had left Sylas in, Mercy herds Zero in and slams the door behind them. He needed to try and break through to Sylas so they could figure this out. If they could figure out how Iana was creating the obscurums then they stood a chance at stopping her.

"Mind filling me in here, Validus?" Zero asks, looking more confused than irritated.

Moving over to the corner, Zero dials the Sentry from the tablet on his waist to get someone else stationed at Sander's door. Clearly Mercy was onto something, and Zero wanted to observe whatever it was. There was a reason Cal kept him around, and Zero was hoping he might finally figure out why.

Mercy goes to his friend, who hadn't moved from his spot on the sofa, still fidgeting with the small gem in his hand. "Sylas," he pleads, shoving the low table away and crouching in front of his best friend. "Sylas, I need you to check back in here."

His words don't seem to reach his Nota. With a sharp exhale he watches his friend's face. Sylas was thinking long and hard about something, or perhaps he was trying to put his heart back together. Losing Cal shattered him in a very different way than it did Mercy.

"Sylas, come on," Mercy pleads. "I know you're mad at me, but I need my best friend's genius mind right now. Come back to Novus Aitus for me, will you?"

The words were lost again. He could go try and speak to Pippa, but after seeing how upset she was, he doubted she would be willing to help him. Besides, only Sylas could give him a clear indication of what happened on that riverbank. He just needed his best friend to confirm what he already thought.

"Validus, what did you figure out?" Zero tests, putting the device back on his belt.

"Sylas, come on," he continues to beg, trying to move his friend's eyes to his face. "I know you're hurting, Sylas. I can feel how broken you are, but I need you for just a few minutes. Please."

There was still no response. He looks at the gem he was playing with in his hands when it finally comes together. It was some time ago, but he remembered that gemstone. The oval cut and careful polish was from the crown Cal threw from the cliff on Mount Sacris. That was the first real conversation Mercy had with his Alia and probably the most prominent moment he watched Cal go through those first few days together. It was also the moment he realized how alike they truly were and how serious Caligo was about his decision to diverge from his mother. That gem was important to Cal. Why did Sylas have it?

He slowly puts his hand over the stone in Sylas's hand, blocking his focus. Sylas had tunnel vision on the stone just as Mercy had on the water drop earlier. They were both lost without Cal, and he knew that. The two of them were afraid, mournful, and felt alone, but they needed to remember they still had each other.

"Sy, look at me," Mercy pleads again.

With Mercy's porcelain hand over the gemstone, Sylas's gaze finally goes to his face. His fiery eyes looked void and lifeless as he tried to make sense of the man staring back at him.

"I need your help, Sy," Mercy explains in a soft tone. "This is important."

His best friend nods his head lightly, understanding his words. Mercy returns the nod and gets to his feet, Sylas's eyes following him as he sits beside him. Mercy gestures for Zero to come sit with them as he grabs a napkin from the table, the water and snacks still displayed, and pulls a pen from his pocket.

"Are you going to explain why you pulled me away from my post?" Zero continues to question.

Nodding his head, Mercy starts. "Sander had the exua rune on his arm, just like you Sylas, but he also has another. I'm hoping you might recognize it."

He begins to draw the symbol, Zero watching intently. Sylas smacks his hand to stop him and holds up two fingers. Understanding, Mercy nods his head. They didn't know what the rune did, or what implications creating a full symbol could have, so putting it in two pieces was smart. He draws a backward L and swirl and then two diagonal lines to the side. He places the napkin on the table in front of Sylas to study.

"The lines go here," he adds, gesturing to them. "It's on his chest. Have you seen this before?"

The Nota picks up the napkin and moves it around a few times, taking in the angles. While Sylas was smart, this may have been out of his realm of knowledge. After a moment he shakes his head. Mercy frowns as he hands the napkin back.

"Tell me this," Mercy sighs, trying to keep his tone slow, "did Sander come out of that obscurum? Did either of you see that?"

"I was unconscious," Zero reminds him. "I'd like to be unconscious now actually."

"You know what never helps these situations, Zero?" Mercy asks with annoyance.

"Your shit attitude?" Zero asks with a shrug.

"No, your sarcasm," Mercy huffs, going back to his thought. "Sylas, did Sander come out of that thing?"

While that day was probably seared into Sylas's mind, he wasn't sure if he could recall where Sander had come from. There was no doubt Sylas was focused on Caligo in those final moments. After another beat, the Nota opens his mouth and clears his throat to speak. His voice was weak and horse, but at least he was talking.

"Cal threw his blade before he went into the water," he shakes his head. "As soon as he hit the water the obscurum was gone and when I turned around later, I saw Sander. He was where the obscurum was, but I... I don't know if he was inside it."

"I think he was," Mercy explains, speaking quickly. "Cal's blade cut right through the symbol. I think this rune could be how Iana is controlling her beasts. At Meera's cabin, I sensed Sander in that thing, and you said the beast disappeared and Sander was there. What if Sander *was* the obscurum?" Mercy shares, his eyes big, looking between Zero and Sylas.

"How?" Sylas asks, becoming more intrigued by the accusation.

"I don't know," Mercy admits.

"Seems a bit out there, even for you," Zero notes.

"Why would they kill Cal though?" Sylas asks.

Mercy shrugs, his face echoing Sylas's grief. If Iana and Bryer were interested in Mercy's power, then why would they kill his Alia? It was well known that when you killed a Light Keeper's parallel, unless the power was taken by the Keeper, it weakened them. So why kill Caligo and risk making Mercy weaker? It didn't make sense. What was the end game here?

"I want him back, Merc," Sylas whispers, looking to the gem in his hand.

Tears begin to come to the corners of Sylas's eyes as he looks back to Mercy's face. Gazing at Mercy reminded him of the Shadow Keeper. He could see the same kindness and compassion in Mercy's eyes that Cal held in his. He had always seen it. He understood why they were Alias. The two complimented one another in the best ways. While Mercy was calm and quiet, Cal was fierce and dramatic. The athleticism and combat skills Cal possessed, contrasted Mercy's brilliance and ability to outsmart anyone in the room if given the time and resources. It wasn't hard to see that Mercy's timid traits complimented Cal's theatrical flair to perfection.

"I know. I miss him too, Sylas," Mercy whispers in understanding.

Sylas shakes his head. If only he had been a little quicker, or stronger, maybe even a little more assertive, Cal would have still been alive. Maybe he should have let Mercy go alone and not even woken Cal up that night. If he had just thought through the possible consequences, then maybe Cal would be okay.

"Why did you leave?" Sylas mutters.

"What?" Mercy questions.

Mercy sees Zero get up from the couch from the corner of his eye. He glances to the Light Keeper as he goes to the other side of the room. Why was he leaving? As Sylas begins to talk again, his eyes shoot to his best friend.

"If you had stayed in Ozra, or even just waited for Cal to cave, he would still be here," Sylas accuses. "I've played that day over and over again in my mind and if you had just waited… You didn't accomplish anything going off on your own. The only thing you did was get Cal killed."

Hearing his words, Mercy's stomach drops. His eyes dart over Sylas's face seeing his grief turn to anger.

"He was the leader. Cal was the one who saved everyone. Without Cal you're nothing," Sylas states. "You chose to be selfish and act like a child and because of you, Cal is gone. He died because of your idiotic need to prove yourself."

"I wasn't trying to prove anything," Mercy retorts, his voice quiet in shock.

"You went against his word. You disobeyed his direct orders, and for what? You're right back where you were before your little rogue mission and now, we don't have Cal," Sylas lectures. "You are everything you are because of what that man did for you and how did you repay him? By letting him die. All because you couldn't take no for an answer."

"Sylas, stop," Mercy begs, the words feeling like knives in his chest.

"You're selfish, Mercy. You always have been, and you always will be," Sylas blames.

The two lock eyes as Mercy gets to his feet. Was Sylas being serious or was this the grief talking? Even the things he had said to Tristia were filled with hatred. Was his best friend really this angry?

"Everyone we've ever lost is because of your selfishness, Mercy. Every single one," Sylas continues, getting up as well. "Charity, Trust, Berk, my dad, the entire damn village. You only ever focus on yourself and now they're gone!"

Fidgeting a moment, Zero looks between the two in concern. He knew Sylas well enough to know he'd regret this once he collected himself. Powering up, he steps between Sylas and Mercy and focuses his glowing eyes on the Nota as he activates his peritia. Within half a second, Sylas releases a steady exhale, the agitation leaving his body. Sylas's eyes stay on Mercy, who had a pained expression as Zero holds his gaze.

"You're okay, Bellator," Zero eases.

"What are you doing to him?" Mercy asks Zero, watching Sylas close his eyes tightly, trying to regain himself.

"Stopping him from saying anything else stupid," Zero admits as Sylas lets out a deep breath. "You two are supposed to be a united front, not passing the damn blame back and forth until someone breaks."

As Zero powers down, Sylas furrows his brow. He knew what Zero had just done, but why was Zero's Source working on him and not Mercy's? With the exua rune on his arm, shouldn't he have been unable to be affected by any Sources.

"You two have my will to live running on empty lately," Zero snarls, the light leaving his eyes.

Taking a deep breath, Mercy backs away and exits the room. Whatever Zero just did may have calmed Sylas's emotions but it didn't take back what he had said. He felt bad leaving Sylas, but anymore blame put on him was going to make him lose it. First Pippa and now Sylas. He couldn't catch a break.

As Mercy leaves the room, Sylas lets out another steady breath. "Thanks, Zero."

"Don't mention it," he replies, feeling relief wash over him with the exit of the other Light Keeper. "Sophos. He's a damn wave of misery every time. I can't stand it!" he groans.

"I'm sure I'm not much better," Sylas laughs tensely.

While most viewed Zero's sarcasm and cold demeanor as annoying and unapproachable, Sylas knew the real reason he put up the front. It was Zero's way of coping with feeling the emotions of those around him. Zero's ability to influence emotions was the main reason Cal had

205

kept him around and gave him so much respect. The Light Keeper could sense false pretenses or dark intentions before they were acted upon, making him a great ally and aid on assignments. He was also able to keep Cal or anyone else levelheaded when things got intense.

"I need to go," Zero huffs moving toward the door. "I need to go take a nap or throw myself off the roof. I haven't decided yet."

"Can you do me a favor before you go... nap. I really hope it's a nap," Sylas chuckles nervously, raising his left hand in the splint. "Maybe you can fix this?"

Giving the Light Keeper a small smile, Sylas watches him roll his eyes. He takes his attention back to the purple gem in his hand and frowns as Zero unwraps his hand and attempts to heal what was left of it. He winces at the touch as the wave of relief hits him like it had done so many times before. When Zero pulls away, Sylas gives him a forced smile, not even looking at the work he had just done.

"We need to try and keep Validus from losing his shit," Zero shares. "He's a time bomb. We don't need him taking out half the estate with his emotions."

"Maybe that's why Bryer killed Cal," Sylas frowns. "Nothing like setting off his Supra Keeping than with emotional trauma."

"Maybe," Zero sighs. "Just... Stay away from him. If his face pisses you off that much, then don't look at it. Got it?"

"Yeah," Sylas nods.

"Also, maybe go find Miss Pippa," Zero instructs moving to the door. "She's... not taking this well."

"Okay," Sylas nods as Zero leaves the room.

Chapter Twenty

Opening his eyes slowly, Cal tries to register where he was. He hisses in pain as he attempts to move, his entire body aching, and his hands bound behind him. Leaning back, he could feel the pole that had his arms firmly locked around it. He pulls at his wrists trying to free them, but with every yank, the ties only seemed to get tighter.

The last thing he could remember was going into the icy water at the Mors River. The look on Sylas's face as he went under was seared into his mind. The pain and fear in his eyes were all too real as he forced him back to the bank. Sylas was probably livid right now. Then again, Sylas probably thought he was dead. The idea makes his stomach sink. Leaving Sylas thinking the worst was not what he intended, though he was surprised he was alive himself. How had he survived?

Looking around he tries to make sense of where he was. It seemed to be a dimly lit tent. It was tall enough for someone to stand in, but small, only able to sit a few people comfortably. He was the only person there and it didn't seem like anyone was going to be joining him anytime soon. Attempting to adjust his legs he quickly realizes his prosthetics are gone, meaning even if he could think of a way out of here, he wouldn't be able to move fast.

Leaning over to peek out the slit in the tent he notes someone standing just outside with a weapon at the ready. He hisses in pain as he gets into a more comfortable sitting position. He could feel the wound on his side throbbing and his back ached. That obscurum had really done a number on him and neither Mercy nor Zero were there to patch up the injuries.

Tilting back on the post he lets out a heavy exhale. He just needed a moment to collect his thoughts and figure out where he was. Maybe he could call for Mercy? With their Voca he didn't particularly need to know where he was for Mercy to find him. Closing his eyes, he attempts to access it, but the line was dead. There was no connection to his Alia. What did that mean? Had they gotten to Mercy while he was out? Was he dead?

"Do not even try to call for him," a voice chimes as the tent opens.

Opening his eyes, Cal sees a man enter with the woman from the cabin. Iana wore an eye patch now, a little reminder of her brawl with Nex. He couldn't help but smirk at the injury. The man pulls a solis orb to his hand, lighting up the tent with its ghostly luminance. Cal squints his eyes as they try to adapt to the sudden addition of light.

Adjusting to the brightness, he could get a good look at the man. His hair was cut short with a neatly trimmed beard. His eyes were the same steely silver as Mercy's. The man was large, probably taller than Cal, and muscular. Something about the man seemed familiar to him, but he couldn't quite place it. This was someone he must have known from his past, but with all the faces that had been shuffled in front of him, he had no inclination of who.

"Are you lucid this time?" Iana questions. "Four days we've been waiting for you to have a coherent thought."

"Four days?" Cal asks, his voice not even sounding like his own. "Where am I?"

"A Malice compound," the man shares. "Just over the boarder of Vicinia."

"Vicinia?" Cal repeats.

"Yes," the man confirms approaching him.

As he gets closer, Cal attempts to call his Source to him. He lets out a gasp as his connection doesn't come through. The Shadow Source wasn't responding to his calls, and he was clueless as to why. Looking to the bit of his arm he could see from this position; he notes his skin was still it's dark pewter hue, yet his connections to the Shadow Source and Mercy were gone.

"Don't try," the man states. "Iana took it upon herself to block your connection."

"Block my connection?" he repeats back, confusion in his tone.

"You must know about the exua runes at this point, Caligo," Iana retorts. "Look around you."

His eyes get wide as he looks down and sees the large piece of wood under him with an exua rune burned into the surface. This one was similar to the rune that had stripped Sylas of his Light Source protection. He attempts to get a better look but lets out a groan at the pain again. Twisting to look made his body ache even more.

"I would move less," the man instructs.

"I would prefer to be able to move more actually," Cal counters, trying to keep his confidence.

Letting himself seem vulnerable to these people would only let them believe they had an upper hand. He wasn't going to allow them to think that for even a moment. He had gotten out of more than one bad situation on his own, and he had no intention of staying in this tent.

"The King of Novus Aitus," the man states, crouching down in front of him. "Without the use of your Source, you don't seem like much, now do you?"

"Do not underestimate me," Cal growls.

"Let me take care of him, father," Iana asks, seeming to get giddy.

Cal registers the woman's comment. If this girl truly was Iana, that meant her father was Bryer and this was the man who was trying to send Mercy a message. How was Iana alive though? Her records said she was dead. Looking at Bryer, his eyes narrow. He was the one responsible for the attacks on Sylas and Mccra. This Keeper was after the people he cared for, and he needed to make sure he didn't get to them. Whatever their game was in keeping him alive, he wasn't about to play into it.

"Patience, Iana," Bryer lectures, keeping his eyes on the King.

The man pulls a sword from his waist and uses the flat side of the blades to move Cal's face side to side to get a better look at him with a stoic expression. Cal's body tenses at the touch of the cold metal, unsure what to expect. Bryer gives a small shake of the head, almost like he was showing disappointment in the monarch.

"The Prince of Death," Bryer sighs, sheathing his blade. "Or should I say the King of Death?"

"I have rescinded that title," Cal remarks, keeping steely eyes on the Keeper.

"Rescind all you want, that does not undo the things you've done, Caligo," Bryer states, beginning to circle him. "You have killed thousands and continue to fill your people with fear at the very mention of your name. From what I've gathered you have done little to improve the lives of our people since you took power, other than throw the perks of the capital at them and funnel money to your own kind. The Keepers. You have made a vow to restore the balance to Novus Aitus, yet you," he pauses his speech until he comes

210

to the front of Cal again, "you, King Caligo, have done the most damage to the very balance you wish to restore."

Cal's face turns to a scowl as Bryer locks eyes with him. Looking away from the man, Cal puts his gaze on the floor. Was he really going to make him think about his mistakes? He had been trying to improve the state of the planet, but he could only do so much with the National Council denying his requests. While he had the power to go over the NC, he didn't want to rile them up more than they already were. His goal was to have peace and agreeance within the planet, not separation.

"A summer night, just three years ago, you and a troop of 80 Unity Council Guards stormed the village of Satis in Magna Luke killing over 300 citizens," Bryer begins with a steady tone. "You led those UC Guards to slaughter your people. They had committed no crimes, yet you used your Source connection to tear them apart. Some limb from limb, some with your blades, others by simply taking the air from their lungs. You personally executed 178 of the people who perished that night."

"I know what I have done," Cal retorts quietly.

"When you were still a teenager, just 19 years of age, you slaughtered 93 protestors outside the gates of Ozra's capital. You Royals gave no reason for the actions taken on those innocent people that day," Bryer shares, glancing to Iana who looked pained by the words. "Those 93 people were only trying to express their want for freedom from a condemned system your family created."

"You don't understand," Cal tries to defend. "I was not-"

"The attack on the southern border of Ozra!" Bryer snarls, cutting him off. "You slaughtered dozens and showed no remorse in your actions. This included your Alia's father, Orlo Validus, a well-known and respected Keeper of Light, just as his son," Bryer states, studying

Cal's reactions. "Have you told young Validus this or is the shame too much for you to admit what you've done?"

"Stop," Cal mutters, squeezing his eyes shut, the words making his stomach ache.

"The Fall of Doma," Bryer adds, crouching down beside Cal again and pulling a solis orb to his palm. "You showed up and facilitated the complete destruction of that village without batting a single eyelash. You took the lives of hundreds of children that day, tearing families apart. You killed children, Caligo. You destroyed my home and forced us to rebuild with the little resources we had left. Unlike Rieka, we had no aid from you Royals. No number of public apologies will make up for what you've done."

"I said stop!" Cal roars, attempting to tear his hands from the pole again.

With the outburst, Bryer launches his orb at Caligo causing him to pull back at the heat from the orb. He closes his eyes as it dissipates in front of him. The control Bryer had of his Source showed he had many years of training and years of hiding to perfect it. Cal lets out a shaking breath but composes himself before glaring at the Keeper again. He needed to keep it together.

"You will listen to what you have done," Bryer snarls, pulling another orb to his hand.

Cal didn't want to listen. Hearing what he had done was painful. He didn't want to relive those horrors. He had worked hard to leave those nightmares behind and now this man was reciting every horrific act to his face. He didn't need him to convince him that what he did was wrong, he already knew, and he hated himself for it every single day. The fact he was able to move forward at all was astonishing.

"I have done the math, Caligo," Bryer sneers. "Your documented body count is 3,253, and that is withholding the 109 UC Guards you killed in the Fall of Rieka."

Attempting to hide his emotions, Cal keeps his gaze steady. The key word to what Bryer had just said was "documented." There were hundreds more that his mother had not written down in the seven years he was doing her bidding. The number could have been well over 4,000 at this point.

"You have to understand that was not me," Cal pleads, pulling at his hands again.

"Caligo Tenebris, is that not you?" Bryer questions, beginning to pace.

"I'm not that person. I never was," Cal explains.

"People do not change!" Bryer thunders, looking down at him, aiming his glowing palm at the King.

The outburst causes Cal to flinch. He curses himself in his mind at the reaction. He felt weak and vulnerable but was trying not to show it. The reaction brings a small smile to Bryer's face. He was pleased to see his threats were being taken seriously.

"What do you want with me?" Cal finally asks.

"I want you to pay for the things you and your family have done," Bryer replies. "I want you to feel the pain you have inflicted on your people. I want the world to see you for who you truly are."

"The world knows the things I have done," Cal states, regaining his assertive demeanor.

"The world will not see you for who you are until Mercy Validus does," Bryer stresses.

"Leave him be," Cal snaps. "That man has seen enough heartache in his life."

"Yet he still sees you as a trusted ally," Bryer retorts, shaking his head. "Once we are through with him, he will be on the side of Malice, and you will be nothing more than a crushed beetle."

Looking down, Cal closes his eyes. The fact his friends saw him as a good person was the only reason he felt capable of doing good. The people he had befriended

213

like Mercy, Sylas, Pippa, and Zero had showed him that even with his jaded past, he had the ability to improve the lives of his people and those around him. Their words of affirmation and encouragement were one of the few things that got him out of bed in the morning.

"You are nothing more than an executioner," Bryer pressures. "You have the instincts of a killer, and no number of good deeds will change who you are. Try as you might, you will always be the antagonist to those under your ruling. It is time the Tenebris crown falls."

"Then kill me," he tests.

"I don't plan to kill you," he mocks. "I plan to break you down in every aspect of the word until you regret the very life that still runs through your body."

"I already do," Cal retorts.

It wasn't a lie. There had been more than one occasion where he wished death on himself. While he may have never been able to go through with the act, he had hoped others would. His life had been nothing but a never ending series of traumatic events and pain. This man didn't need to prove to him what he already knew.

"Are you ready to relive every mistake you've ever made, nephew?" Bryer asks.

"Nephew?" Cal repeats, looking at Bryer with a wrinkled brow.

It hits him in that moment. He had only met his uncle Voltas once or twice as a child, the man wanting nothing to do with the Royals. When his father joined Mala as a ruler of Novus Aitus, his father's family all but abandoned him. He understood why as he got older and learned how cruel and horrific his mother was. He often wondered what his father would have done if he hadn't passed when he did. Would his father have allowed the abuse his mother put her children through? If this was his uncle, this meant that not only did Cal have Shadow

214

Keeper lineage on his father's side, but he also had Light Keeper.

Cal winces suddenly, trying to regain himself as a sharp pain goes through his side. Bryer looks down at the blood-stained shirt he wore and frowns. The injuries were severe, but not enough for him to risk healing the monarch. He couldn't risk giving Caligo any strength back.

Pulling a dagger from his waist, Bryer uses the blade to cut away the dingy shirt Cal wore. It was caked with mud and silt from the river. He traces his blade over Cal's chest as the Shadow Keeper watches closely. What was he going to do to him? He hisses as the blade pierces his skin and Bryer begins to carve something into the right side of his chest.

"What are you doing?" he asks through gritted teeth.

"An obscurum needs a battery," he mutters to him.

"What?" he questions as he pulls away.

Bryer watches the blood seep down Cal's chest, as his expression falls to a scowl. "What is this?" he asks under his breath.

Cal looks down to see a faint purple light shining from his chest, lighting up the dark tent. The carved marks slowly begin to heal over, leaving smooth skin. Cal glances to Bryer and then to Iana, both of them mirroring each other's shock. The power coming from his wound was mirroring a Light Source connection, but how?

"Try again," Iana orders.

With a deep breath, Bryer attempts to carve the symbol into his nephew's chest once more. This time, as soon as the blade touches him, it is flung from his hand. The familiar feel of the electricity that used to run from Sylas to Cal's touch could be felt in his chest.

"It's the Light Source," Iana snarls.

"You used the exua rune," Bryer reminds her, gesturing to the floor.

215

"I used the exua rune for the Source of Shadows," Iana retorts with irritation in her voice.

"Then use both," Bryer snaps.

"I can't," she informs him. "Using both could void the effects all together or possibly kill him. We were ordered to keep him alive."

The man gets to his feet and picks up his blade. He stands over Cal and watches him a moment as the light from his chest begins to fade. Looking down Cal could see the purple glow still dancing under his skin where the rune once was. What was this?

"Leave him," Bryer snaps, nodding his head toward the door.

As the pair exit the tent, Cal's body relaxes. He keeps his eyes on the light in his chest and watches as it pulses one last time before it begins dissipating. What the hell was this? How was the Light Source protecting him? Why was it healing this rune but not his other injuries? He looks up to the entrance of the tent as his mind begins to race. How was he going to get out of here and why was this man claiming to be his uncle?

His eyes shoot to the floor as a familiar friend sneaks into the tent. A little smirk comes to his face as Nex moves toward him, hopping over the dirt, trying to not be noticed by the man guarding the entrance. With a nod of the head, he gestures behind his back. Listening to her Keeper, Nex moves to his hands as he slips a gold ring from his finger. The crow grabs the ring in her beak and makes her way to the front of him. She drops it in front of him and begins to peck at his pants waiting for instructions.

"Take that to Sylas and Mercy," he whispers, "as fast as you can. Please, girl."

She hears his words and picks up the ring again. She slowly makes her way to the entrance. He watches as she creeps out of the tent and takes to the air. Letting out a steady exhale, he closes his eyes. Hopefully Nex could get that ring to one of his friends and let them know he was alive and needed them.

Chapter Twenty-One

It had been two weeks since Caligo's death. Since then, Bryer and Malice had gone silent. There had been no strange reports or sighting of the beasts since. It seemed Bryer had gotten what he wanted, and that was to take down the King of Novus Aitus. The silence from the rebel group felt ominous after the words spoken by Iana at Meera's cabin. If they were so intent on getting something from Mercy, why had they completely gone silent after that horrific day at the Mors River?

Though Mercy had thought long and hard on Tristia's offer, with it being Cal's wish for Mercy to take over the throne, he couldn't bring himself to do it. Part of him wanted to forget Cal had ever existed, but that was impossible. The man was so intertwined with who he was that the day he went into the water was the day Mercy lost a piece of himself. It didn't seem like the world was going to keep turning, yet here he was, sharpening a blade in his shop as he had done every day before.

He pauses a moment, blinking his eyes a few times. They had been filled with a faint glint since Cal's passing causing his eyes to be bloodshot and sore. This had caused a constant headache and forced him to try to get some sleep several times a day. His joints ached from his Source burning through him consistently too. He had spoken to both Elder Maior and Master Novi about it, but neither of them seemed to have an answer as to why his connection wouldn't power down, no matter how much he willed it. It had become exhausting. The only explanation they had was that his connection hadn't accepted the loss of Cal yet, which made little sense.

"Master Mercy!" he hears Yule, his apprentice, shout from the front desk.

With an eyeroll, Mercy goes back to sharpening the blade in his hands. If he was needed that badly, the apprentice could come find him. While Yule was capable of taking care of things in the shop, he always craved approval before every decision. It drove Mercy crazy some days, especially lately with the unrest his body and mind felt. The human teenager reminded him of himself though. Mercy had always craved Brokkr's approval.

"Master Mercy, Charlyn is looking for you," his other apprentice, Katya, informs him, entering the back room while putting her gloves on.

"What does she need?" he questions, pausing his work.

"She said there's a visitor from the capital here to see you, sir," she enlightens.

"From the capital?" he asks as someone knocks on the entrance to the workshop.

He turns his head, and a small grin comes to his face. Pippa gives him a soft smile and a wave. She wore a thick winter coat and had her long hair bundled in a hat. He hadn't spoken to her since the day of the eloium, but he was happy to see she was doing well. Pippa had kept her distance and rightly so. As far as she was concerned, he could have prevented Cal's death, and honestly, he agreed with her.

"Pip? What are you doing here?" he asks, setting down the blade and moving to hug her, Katya heading to her station in the back of the workshop.

"We need you back in Ozra," she informs him, accepting the embrace. "I wanted to come speak with you myself."

He lets go of her and studies her face. His smile quickly falls as he realizes the worry in her gaze. Whatever they were calling him back for was serious. The fact they sent Pippa to get him spoke volumes to whatever was happening. This meant they were worried he was going to take some convincing or perhaps begin to panic.

He furrows his brow. "Is Bryer back?" he questions. "The obscurums?"

Their conversation is interrupted as Charlyn and the girls walk into the shop. His eyes go to the housekeeper who averts hers to the floor. Ruby abruptly pulls away from Charlyn and runs toward Mercy.

"Ruby, wait!" Saphie scolds.

The little girl races to Mercy and throws her arms around him, holding him tightly. He looks back to his housekeeper with a concerned expression, unsure why Ruby would be acting this way. He glances to Saphie who also had a look of unease. He gives Saphie a nod of the head to assure her that it was okay for Ruby to have an outburst. That was one thing he appreciated about Saphie, she always held herself strong for her sister. Mercy had done the same thing for Charity growing up, and he admired Saphie for her dedication, but at the same time wanted her to express herself as well.

"She's going to ask you to leave again," Ruby informs him. He pulls her away a moment to crouch down to her level. "You can't leave!" She shouts, wrapping her arms around his neck tightly.

Mercy hugs her and looks up to Pippa who gives a soft smile at the pair. The girls had given Mercy a softer side and she enjoyed watching him grow into his new family. The last year he had gotten more confident, and she thanked the girls for that. There was no more thinking only for himself or time to focus on his mistakes, he had to think about the two little girls that depended on him. Pippa had seen him go from worrying about his own future, to the future of the two little girls in his care.

"You can't go!" Ruby pleads. "You can't leave us again!"

"Ruby, it's okay," he comforts as she shoves into him harder, knocking him off balance. He falls back to sit on the dirt floor of the shop with a thud. "We don't even know why Miss Pip is here yet."

"I'm sorry, Mercy," Pippa frowns. "I am afraid I am here to ask you to return with me."

This causes Ruby to squeeze Mercy even tighter, the fear showing in her embrace. This little girl was terrified he was going to end up just like Caligo. She knew his last assignment ended with losing the King of Ozra, and she wasn't about to let Mercy be the next.

"What if you leave and don't come back?" Saphie asks, as Ruby pulls away to look at him for his response.

He opens his mouth to speak but was at a loss for words. What if he left and didn't come back? His vision weeks ago had said that was in his future. Any assignment he went on could leave him alone and dead in the forest just as he saw in that vision. He looks up to Pippa who gives him a pained expression. Somehow, he felt that she knew what he was thinking, but wasn't aware of the severity of the fear Saphie and Ruby had. If they lost Mercy, it was going to be like losing their parents all over again.

Peeling Ruby from him, he gives her a serious look. "I understand you're both scared," he states, taking a deep breath and gesturing for Saphie to come to him. She moves away from Charlyn as Mercy puts a hand on her shoulder and forces a smile. "I'm scared too, every single day, but we can't let fear guide our actions. You both know that."

He sees Saphie nod her head as Mercy takes another deep breath and glances between Charlyn and Pippa. Neither of these women were going to be able to offer the girls comfort. He wasn't going to be able to just hand them off to his housekeeper and hope she could explain his job to them. He needed to suck it up and do it himself.

Turning his attention back to Ruby and Saphie, he studies their faces. Ruby reminded him so much of Brokkr. She had the same dark skin and pale eyes as her father, while her dark hair and features mirrored her mother, Senna. Saphie on the other hand was the spitting image of Senna. Even her mannerisms and expressions reminded him of her. Everything about these two girls was a reminder of the man and woman who offered him their time and kindness. Their father had taught him to master a craft and had every intention of leaving the shop to Mercy upon his retirement. Something Mercy gladly took on after the Fall of Rieka. Reopening Brokkr's Forge was something he was proud of and took seriously upon the rebuilding of their village.

He remembered the day he gave Abtal and the other Elders the confirmation he would take in the girls and how Sylas had to all but convince him. He was so worried about his ability to take on the parenting role, but Sylas didn't doubt him for even a second. His best friend reminded him of how he took care of Charity after his own parent's passing and how no one could guide Brokkr's girls quite like he could. Mala and the UC had taken his parents just as they had taken Ruby and Saphie's. Seeing their fears now wasn't a surprise to him. The idea of losing another parental figure was painful and something he understood well. Losing Elder Rom and their father was a pain he didn't want his girls to live through.

222

The Light Keeper clears his throat and looks between the girls sternly again. "You remember the day you both came to stay with me?" he asks as the girls nod. "I was so scared. You two needed me, and I was in a bad place. I was in a really bad place."

"Because of Spheara," Saphie finishes, remembering those days well.

"Exactly," he nods, looking at the ground thinking back. "I was so scared I was going to let you two down, or your parents, that I let my fear guide me. I gave up my Source because I was scared it was going to take me away from you, but I realized it wasn't just you girls who needed me and that being afraid wasn't right. I lived a long time being afraid of the future, and some days I still am, but we can't let that be what guides us. Do you both understand what I'm saying?"

"Yes," Saphie replies quietly.

Mercy looks at Ruby as the little girl nods her head, taking a step back, grabbing her sister's hand. This felt a little complex for a child to comprehend, but he hoped it would make sense. Saphie studies his face for a moment before dropping her eyes to the ground. To these girls, he was the closest thing to a father they had. Mercy was the man who took care of them, was raising them, would make them feel safe. While they weren't entirely aware of everything he did for their people or who he was in the grand scheme of things, they did know he was important. That didn't matter though, because even if to the world he was a famed hero, to Saphie and Ruby he was simply Mercy. He was the young man their father taught in his shop and their mother made sandwiches for. He was the man that now made them feel safe and secure in their new home.

Scooting back a few feet to his workstation, he digs through a wooden box. He had been working on creating a few items for the girls for their birthdays or holidays, but now felt like a good time to give a small gift. Grabbing a small brass tube, he scoots back to the girls and shows it to them with a small smile. The brass tube had a beautiful display of glass that could be turned at the end. The floral design around the cylinder had been carefully engraved into the metal by Mercy. The item was no bigger than the Light Keeper's hand which made the work that went into it even more impressive.

"What is it?" Saphie asks, looking at the item.

"A kaleidoscope," he informs her. Shuffling it in his hands, he moves the glass pieces by twisting the end lightly and hands it to Ruby who looks through it right away. "You can look through it and see all sorts of colors," he shares. "More colors than either of you could ever dream are right inside that little device."

"You made this?" Saphie asks as Ruby hands it to her so she could see too.

"I did," he confirms. "You see... that little thing takes all the broken pieces, all the good and bad and maybe even the ugly parts and makes them into something beautiful. So, while I'm away, you can look through it and you can think of all the color you brought to my life," he continues as Saphie hands it back to her little sister, knowing Ruby needed the comfort in that moment. "When you're worried, or scared, or maybe you just miss me, you can hold that and think of me."

Ruby takes the device from her face and looks at him with big eyes. He puts his arms out for her to hug him again, which she quickly accepts. Saphie hesitates a moment, knowing Mercy wasn't much for public displays, but he gestures for her to come as well. With a small smile she lets him wrap one of his arms around her and hold her close. He didn't want to leave them. Something about leaving this time felt like the wrong decision, but he had a job to do. Just like Cal, he had to be willing to put it all on the line, even if it meant leaving his girls behind.

He embraces them tightly for a few moments, trying to take it in before pulling away to look up to Pippa. He could see she had a soft smile on her face from the interaction. Getting to his feet, he picks up Ruby and places her on his hip and takes Saphie's hand gently, trying to get back on task. Ruby leans her head on his shoulder as she holds the kaleidoscope tightly in her grasp.

"What do they need?" he finally asks, taking a moment to adjust Ruby.

"I think it would be better if we spoke at your house," Pippa shares, becoming serious again.

"Sure," Mercy agrees. "Yeah... Just give me a minute. Katya!" he shouts, tearing his eyes away from the young woman.

The perky girl winces, Mercy having forgotten she was in the room. "Yes, Master Mercy?" she asks, stopping what she was doing.

He jumps and turns to look at her. "Sorry. I didn't- I'm going to step out for a bit," he informs her. "Can you make sure Yule finishes that order for Master Jerin."

"Of course," she nods, slight worry on her face.

"And check it this time," he instructs. "Jerin was livid with the last shipment."

"Yes, sir," she nods.

"I'll be next door if you need me," he assures.

He gestures for Pippa to follow him and takes the lead with the girls, both Pippa and Charlyn behind him. The group make their way to his house just beside the shop without saying a word. Mercy's mind buzzed as they moved forward, hearing Ruby fiddle with her new toy. He could also feel Saphie's hand shaking in his grasp. It pained him to feel the nerves wracking her. The only reason they would ask him to come back to Ozra was for an update on Bryer or to go after him.

Nodding to the Sentry Guard who was standing on the porch, Mercy lets Saphie open the door and lets Pippa and Charlyn go ahead of them. As they enter the home, Pippa notes the house was more cluttered than she had seen in the past, with books on every surface. Mercy must have been reading everything he could get his hands on to try and make sense of the obscurum beasts and in search of the rune on Sander's chest. Why was Mercy researching on his own though?

"Where's Sylas?" Pippa asks, scanning the books.

"Vermeer," Mercy bluntly retorts. "We haven't really been talking."

Closing the door, Pippa pauses in the living room as Mercy turns to her. He places Ruby on the floor beside him as she and her sister go to the sofa to continue to look through the kaleidoscope as Charlyn joins them. A small meow comes from Mercy's feet as Soot greets him. Bending down, Mercy scoops up the small white cat, cradling her in his arms, and scratches her belly. She seemed happy to have Mercy home early.

"Perhaps we could speak in your office?" Pippa suggests, glancing at the girls.

Mercy nods his head with a look of concern. Why was Pippa being so secretive? The two make their way down the hall as Pippa glances around the house a bit more. Mercy had really grown into the space and created a home here. There were images of Saphie and Ruby on the walls as well as art they had made. There was even a picture of Brokkr and his wife Senna. A few of Cal's drawings were placed throughout the home too, depictions he had drawn of Mercy and his family during his visits. The sketches showed the Shadow Keeper may have been gone, but he was not forgotten.

Along the hall, Mercy had built several cat trees for Soot to climb on, including an intricate system of platforms and walkways along the walls. There were small woolen balls and hand sewn mice strewn across the floor to entertain the feline while the household was away during the day. Pippa couldn't help but smile at the bond Mercy had continued to create with the small white cat he was holding in his arms. She knew he had originally used Soot to help cope with the loss of his village, but now she seemed to be a dear friend to the Keeper.

They pause as Mercy unlocks his office door, Soot climbing onto his shoulders to let him free his hands. They enter the small room, Mercy shutting the door behind them. Putting Soot on the floor, the feline begins to weave between her owner's legs, wanting him to continue to hold her. Pippa goes to sit in a chair as Mercy stares at her, waiting for information.

"What's going on?" he inquires. "You're being very strange, or is this because you're upset with me?"

She lets out a heavy sigh and shakes her head. "Tristia put together a team to try and weed out Bryer and Iana Nitesems. She believes they're hiding at a Malice camp run by Bryer and his rebels," Pippa shares. "I assume you've spoken to Sander these last couple of weeks?"

Mercy nods his head. While they had speculated the events at the river, Sander had started to gain his memory back. He was able to recall the events and paint the gruesome story of Cal's last moments. The Sentry Guard was so distraught over what he had done, he was still in the infirmary under heavy sedation trying to cope. Even with the guilt and painful memories returning, he had taken the time to write Mercy a letter spilling the heavy details of that horrific day and apologizing to the Light Keeper for what he had done.

While the idea of Sander playing a role in the death of Cal was disheartening, Mercy was more upset he had been manipulated the way he was. What Sander had endured during his time with Iana was horrifying and unsettling to read. The letter had made him sick to his stomach.

"Zero and his team believe that Iana has been behind some recent abductions as well," she enlightens. "There have been reports of Shadow Keepers going missing the last four weeks and with the theory we have from you and the confirmation from Sander we have a fairly good idea as to why."

"You think they're trying to create more of those monsters?" Mercy asks with a raised brow. Pippa nods her head. "What does Tris need me to do?" he asks.

"Shay is refusing to help any further unless we bring you in," Pippa explains with sadness in her eyes.

Looking at her, Mercy could tell how exhausted she was. He couldn't tell if it was from lack of sleep, the several days of travel, or the stress of the last two weeks weighing on the young woman. She clearly had been working very close with the Sentry Guard and National Council on this operation, which was out of the ordinary for Pippa. While she often was a consultant on these types of Source related ordeals due to her friendship with Cal, seeing her speak like an official worried him.

Pippa takes a deep breath. "Have they attempted anything here that you haven't reported?"

"No," Mercy replies, shaking his head. "Bryer's left me out of things. Besides, he'd be stupid to try. With Meera and Velia here, I had Tris station multiple Shadow Guards, and three Light Keepers for night watch," Mercy explains. "Other than the estate, this house is the most heavily guarded spot in Ozra. Tristia and I-"

He stops speaking as his ears begin to resound the all too familiar ringing. He lets out an annoyed groan, putting his fingers to his temple, the light resounding through the vessels in his forehead. What did the Elder's want from him now? Why did these visions always come at inconvenient times?

"Are you alright?" Pippa questions, getting to her feet to aid him.

He shakes his head and shoos her away as his head begins to pound. With a gasp, he is pulled from his office and forced back into the forest. His stomach drops as he looks around at the image he was seeing. Why was he back in the woods? Scanning the area, he could see a thick layer of snow on the ground as the same blackness from his last vision obscured his sight past the first few lines of trees again.

Taking a few steps, he hears a shrill scream. He jumps and turns quickly as it echoes around him, trying to locate where it came from, but he sees nothing. Why were the Elders sending him another vision like this? The scream cries out again, this time feeling recognizable. Was it Ruby? Rushing through the trees he searches.

It was difficult to make much sense of where he was with the darkness taking over just 20 feet in front of him. Looking around the forest floor his eyes stop on Pippa. He feels his heart race at the sight of the young woman, lying in the snow. She was alive, but she was covered in blood, the snow around her stained the same crimson. The look on her face proved how terrified she was as she held her hands to her face.

She looks up to him, seeming to lock eyes on his form. He furrows his brow at the interaction. None of his past visions had been able to see him before. He shivers as something rushes past him toward Pippa. She lets out another scream as the vision goes black and he's pushed back to reality.

Stumbling backwards, he falls into his desk. His eyes dart around until he locks them on Pippa who was staring at him with worry just a few feet away. Moving swiftly, he wraps his arms around her, holding her tightly. She was there, and she was okay. The vision felt real but also felt tainted by something he couldn't quite place.

Holding her in his arms sent a wave of relief through him. He lets out a trembling breath, not wanting to let her go. He needed her to be safe, even if it was from the unknown.

"It's okay," he whispers to Pippa. "You're okay."

"I am fine, Mercy," she assures him, thrown off by the sudden affection from the Keeper.

He pulls away and studies her face carefully between his hands. Whatever he had just seen was something he didn't want to happen. He looks to her injured eye and shakes his head.

"What did you see?" she asks him.

"I-I don't even know," he admits, taking a deep breath as he continues to hold her face. "You- I don't- My visions have been strange."

"Strange?" she questions.

He pulls his hands away from her and shakes his head, his hand going to his upper arm again. A sharp pain shoots through him as his Source comes to his eyes, reacting to his worry. Squeezing them shut, he takes a deep breath, feeling another round of panic rushing toward the surface. He needed to tell her. If he kept the truth from her, he'd regret it.

"I saw myself die, Pip," he blurts out, keeping his eyes tightly shut. "It wasn't Cal who I saw dead, it was me. I lied to you."

"What are you talking about, Mercy?" she asks, confusion clear on her face.

"In the conference room," he mutters, finally looking at her. "I saw my dead body in the forest, not Cal's."

"Why would you-" She cuts herself off.

Looking into his eyes she understood why he would lie. Telling others about that vision would only unnerve those around him. They had just lost Caligo, and he didn't want to worry them more. Mercy's death would no doubt shake Novus Aitus just as much. If word got out of his soon

230

to be untimely demise, then they would have even more chaos on their hands.

"When? How?" she begs.

"I don't know," he admits in defeat, taking a seat in his office chair. "None of my visions are making sense right now. The one I just had of you... I couldn't even tell where you were, but you were scared and-"

"If the Elders are sending you visions, they are trying to help you prevent those outcomes," she informs him. "There must be something in them to aid in that."

He shakes his head. Of course he wanted to prevent the things he was seeing, but how? His body was sitting in a forest, completely unmarked. There was no one near him, not a single person or sign. It was the same with the vision of Pippa. They were both alone and defenseless.

"What are you thinking, my dear?" she questions.

"What if they're a warning?" he replies, thinking out loud.

"Of course they are. The Elders send you these visions to help you prevent horrific events," she adds as he looks down in thought.

Trying to focus, his mind begins to wander again. There was almost like a haze as he tried to make sense of the visions. His attention wasn't there, and his thoughts were scattered. Why couldn't he focus? Suddenly he wished Sylas was there. If he was hearing this, he would no doubt be able to put the pieces together.

"Mercy?" Pippa chimes in worry.

"I don't know," he admits with a nervous laugh, getting up again. "Honestly nothing is making sense, Pip. I can't even try to figure this out. My mind is just..."

"Just what?" she interrogates.

"I don't know," he shrugs, putting his fingers to his temples again. "I can't even think straight right now. I'm sorry."

"You are just shaken up," she eases. "Losing Caligo has affected you in ways we do not understand."

He shakes his head and closes his eyes. Maybe that was it. Maybe the loss of his Alia was simply causing his mind to feel fogged. Combined with the lack of sleep and his Source connection being antsy like it was, he was probably close to his body just shutting down from exhaustion. Trying to make sense of the vision right now wasn't going to help anyone if he couldn't think.

"Grief is the price of love, is it not?" she questions, wrapping her arms around him, trying to offer him solace from the events in his mind.

"Yeah," he sighs, weakly returning the embrace.

"Caligo was strong, resilient, and believed with the right people there to support him, anything was possible," Pippa states, happy to have Mercy in her arms again. "We need to continue to be that support in any way we can, even in his death."

He lets her hold him for a moment as his hands begin to shake with anger. The things Cal could have done if given the time would have been amazing. In the short period of fourteen months, he had already made a mark on Novus Aitus. There was no telling what another 100 plus years could have brought to their people. With Bryer and Malice wreaking havoc on their planet, they had no idea what else they could rob their people of. Mercy needed to stop trying to live a normal life in Rieka and be the man Cal always knew he could be.

"I won't let grief hold me back," he announces, pulling away from her.

He walks over to the cabinet in the corner and pulls out the Pura Blade from its case. He looks at the knapped dagger, the sharp edge of the stone familiar to him. Looking to his father's sword hanging above his desk, he removes it from the mount. While his heart and mind ached for the loss of his Alia, he had to get himself together for their people. He had a job to do. If their King was gone, then they needed their hero and hope restored once again.

"What are you doing?" Pippa asks, following him with her eyes.

"Someone needs to stop Bryer and his rebels," he announces. "Vision or not, someone needs to stand up to him before anyone else gets hurt."

"Mercy, think this through," she cautions.

"If it were the other way around... If I had died that day, Cal would have stopped at nothing to bring down Malice," he states, looking at the hilt of his blade. "I need to stop being Mercy Validus and start acting more like Caligo Tenebris."

Chapter Twenty-Two

Back at the shop, Mercy was beginning to prep for his impending absence as Pippa follows him. The sudden shift into hero mode made her uneasy. While she trusted his heart, some moments needed logic. She kept at his heels as he moved around the shop.

"What about the shop?" she questions as he hides an eyeroll.

"Simple," he sighs, glancing at Pippa. "Katya, you're in charge," he instructs his apprentice, who was watching him closely as well. "I'm trusting you to get all the orders you can finished on time and make sure nothing gets forgotten. Remember to explain we are short staffed to any new orders that come in, especially blades. If anyone requests my work specifically, tell them they will be logged as back orders," he continues.

"Yes, sir," she nods.

"Yule, make sure you double check every horseshoe and tool you make," he lectures. "I'm not going to be around to remake them when they're sent back."

"Yes, Master Mercy," Yule laughs with a small bow, his thumb to his palm.

"Don't burn the place down while I'm gone," he finishes. He gives Pippa a soft smile and heads back toward the house with a leather bag full of gear.

"What about the girls?" Pippa questions.

"Charlyn is more than capable of taking care of Saph and Rubes. Plus, she has Meera here to help," he reminds her. "The Sentry Guard will be in full force. It's not like I haven't left before."

She grabs his arm and brings him to a stop. "You know what I am talking about."

He presses his lips into a line and looks down. She wasn't talking about going to the capital, she was talking about the idea of him never coming back.

"Could you stay here with them?" he asks, turning to look at her.

"Mercy Validus, don't you dare ask me to stay behind on this," she rebukes.

"You owe me, Pip," he reminds her. "I told you to keep Cal in the capital and you didn't listen to me. If you had just listened to me then-"

Her face grows angry. "Are you trying to say losing Cal was my fault?"

"No, I'm- Sophos! I don't have time for this right now," he breathes shakily, starting to walk again, wanting to avoid the conversation.

"And when will you have time?" she asks, keeping in pace with him.

"When my life doesn't involve putting out one fire after the other," he suggests.

"So never," she laughs in annoyance.

He stops in his tracks. Ever since Spheara he was going from one fight to the next, using his presence and Source to calm the storm that was post Spheara Novus Aitus. The Light Keeper's life had become more and more hectic, and with Cal gone, it felt like keeping the peace was solely on his shoulders. Combining that with the fact he

236

could feel the metaphorical clock ticking to his own demise, his stress was at an all-time high.

"I'm sorry," he admits, angry with himself for saying something like that. "I shouldn't have- Cal wasn't your fault. It's just...I care about you, Pip," he sighs, looking at her with pained eyes. "I *need* you to stay out of this. I *need* you to listen this time. Please."

The last time she didn't heed his words they lost Cal, and she couldn't negate that. He was hurting, and the thought of losing anyone else was terrifying to him. Seeing the sincerity in his eyes, Pippa gives a forced smile and nods her head in understanding.

Mercy looks to her with tired eyes and places his bag on the ground. He moves to give her a hug, which she reluctantly accepts. From the day he had met Pippa she had been a support system he desperately needed. When he met her, she saw the fighter he was capable of being. After everything he had been through with her, he couldn't imagine opening himself up to the possible heartache that came with losing her. Until things calmed down with Bryer, he needed her to stay on the sidelines.

"I worry without someone there to keep you levelheaded you will lose yourself," she whispers.

"I'll lose myself if I lose you," he murmurs back, giving her a tighter squeeze.

Pulling away, she nods her head again. "What about Sylas?"

"I'm still debating on that one," he huffs, picking up the bag with one hand and taking hers with the other.

"Why?" she asks.

"He hasn't exactly been all there since..." Mercy explains, starting to walk again. "Did you know he slept in Cal's room the night I left?"

"I figured as much," she confesses, remembering the comment he had made to the guards that night. "How did you know?"

"Voca," he shrugs. "After me and Cal figured it out, sometimes we couldn't turn it off. Well... Mostly Cal. Especially when he got flustered, and trust me, Cal was *very* flustered," he laughs nervously. "Yes, it was annoying, and yes, I miss it." He sighs at the thought as they approach the house. "Those two cared for each other," he states, pausing to look at her, sadness in his eyes. "More than either of them wanted to admit."

He looks down thinking back to when the two had split up. While Cal and Sylas had assured him that it wasn't due to him taking his Source back, he knew deep down it played a key role in their choice. Cal and Sylas made sense to him, and they cared for each other deeply. They may have been very different people, but they were exactly what the other needed.

While Sylas was eccentric and hopeful, Cal tended to be more serious and analytical. Even with their personalities being opposites, they still found common ground in their interests. They both loved reading and history. Sylas loved art and Cal loved making it. They both had an appreciation for music, Sylas playing his guitar often for the pair. They also enjoyed training together. No one understood Sylas's bond with Mercy quite like Caligo did and vice versa. He could remember the countless times the pair sat in silence while Cal drew and Sylas worked on his writing, whether it was in the tomes or for his own personal enjoyment. They laughed constantly, even when trying to be professional. The pair had a love for each other, one that Mercy envied. He could feel that love from Sylas and he could hear it from Cal. They brought out the best parts of each other, and that was clear to anyone who was around them.

"They were stubborn," Mercy adds. "Stubborn to the point it was too late."

He looks at Pippa and frowns. Maybe he was being stubborn too. His entire life he had always been the one to just hope people would understand he cared for them through his actions. Voicing his feelings and sharing his thoughts was never something he was good at. He couldn't even remember the last time he told the girls or even Sylas he cared for them out loud. The interaction at the shop with the girls was the first time he had hugged Saphie in months. He was sure she needed his comfort just as much as Ruby did this last year, but since she didn't ask, he never gave it. Maybe he needed to start making sure the people around him knew how he felt.

Clearing his throat, he looks back to the ground to avoid Pippa's gaze. "I'm worried Sylas might see this as a way to get revenge. I can't let him do that. His heart is good, but it's broken."

"You need him," she pressures.

"Yeah," he nods with a small smile. "If I'm gonna die, I guess I should take Sylas with me."

"I could not see it any other way." She forces a laugh in response.

The two approach the wagon, Mercy throwing the gear into the back. He lets out a heavy sigh and turns to look at Pippa again. She was happy to see him accepting his role as a leader for their people, but she worried for him. Even though he hadn't officially taken up Cal's mantle, she knew in some form he was going to try once he got to Ozra. With how he had been acting lately, there was no predicting what could set him into a series of questionable actions.

Keeping her gaze on him, she could feel her eyes begin to well up. If he died on this assignment, then where did that leave her? Even though he had gotten stronger over the last year, he was still emotionally broken. The panic attacks he had frequently, his clear lack of sleep and focus, and the grief of losing Caligo were proof of that. While she was livid with him over keeping secrets from her, she couldn't just let him go. Not only was he emotionally vulnerable, but so was she.

He pauses seeing the tears dancing in her eyes. "What is it?" he asks.

"Your heart and your mind are in two different places. I'm begging you to not do anything you'll regret," she lectures, her words littered with emotions.

"I can handle this, Pip," he assures her with a confident nod of the head.

Looking at him she could see he had lost the innocence she once knew so well. The last year and a half had hardened him. She was starting to see the same look of boldness that used to dance in Cal's eyes. He had even started to form the same steely gaze that demanded the attention of any room. He was growing into the Keeper she always knew he could be, but something in her worried. Deep down she could feel a nagging that something wasn't right.

"What's wrong?" he questions, furrowing his brow at her silence.

"What if I can't handle it?" she adds, the tears finally coming to her.

He lets out a heavy sigh. "Pip…"

The day she met him; she knew Mercy was something special. He was stronger and braver than he thought he was. He had passion burning within him. Though Mercy was his own biggest critic, that's what she loved about him the most. He analyzed his mistakes to avoid making them again and was constantly trying to figure out how he could improve himself, just as he did with the blades he forged and items he created. When Cal had brought him into her home, she saw a warrior in the making. She saw someone who was strong willed and brave but afraid of that part of himself.

"Out with it, Pip," he states, folding his arms.

She pulls back and looks to the ground. Admitting her feelings now was only going to make this harder on him. If she told him how she felt, it would only cause a bigger distraction and make him question his actions more than before. The pressure of having others depend on him was Mercy's biggest stressor in life. She shakes her head and takes a step back.

"Pippa?" he asks again.

"Uh…" she looks to the guard in the driver's box and back to Mercy, wiping away the tears. "Make sure to pack warm clothes."

He stifles a laugh. "Really?"

"Just that," she shrugs, forcing a small smile. "They are predicting snow soon."

"Come on, Pip," he teases. "You're the worst at keeping secrets."

Knowing Mercy could possibly lose his life made this harder. Seeing him get into that wagon to head back to Ozra was going to tear her apart. He had been the first person to realize her path in life was one she didn't want to follow. While she was still sticking to her studies and acolyte duties for the sake of her family and aiding the Royals, she had comfort in knowing Mercy saw through her façade. Losing Mercy meant she was losing her comfort. She would be missing the last person on Novus Aitus who understood her and made her feel safe. After losing Cal, she wasn't sure she'd be able to handle losing Mercy.

"I can't lose you too," she gets out, a tear escaping her eyes. "Mercy, I care for you. I love you dearly, you know this. I love you with everything in me. I cannot lose you right now."

His eyes dart over her face as his expression begins to reflect his nerves. While Pippa had expressed her adoration for him on multiple occasions, she had never used the word love. Is this why she was being so persistent?

Was that why she got so mad at him? Was Sylas right? Who was he kidding? Sylas was always right, and he was just in denial.

His face shows his panic. "Pip, I-"

She stops him. "My heart cannot take losing you too, Mercy. Not you."

He attempts to speak again. "Pippa, we should-"

"Mercy, I am not-"

"Let me talk, please," he interrupts her, placing his hands on her shoulders and giving her serious eyes with a small smile. She nods her head lightly as he takes a deep breath. He needed to word this carefully. "My emotions confuse me, now more than ever, but you're important to me, Pip," he confides, "I care about you and that terrifies me. The idea of caring about or loving anyone, especially you, is the scariest thing to me and I can't even explain why. It's not because you don't deserve love, because you do, but… It's not fair for me to do that to you. To continue to disregard your feelings because I'm too afraid to admit my own."

She relaxes and furrows her brow at his words. Where was this going? "Mercy, I-" she mutters, as his eyes go to the ground, and he continues to speak.

"You are kind and compassionate and thoughtful, and for some unknown reason you care about me," he adds, with a deep breath. "When everything goes wrong, even when you're livid with me, you're still there. You still comfort me." He looks up to her, keeping his composure. "Even when I don't deserve your approval, you still give it and I wish I knew how you could do that. You look at me and see the person I want to be. You look at me and you see through every mask I put on and just see me for me and-"

She puts a hand on his cheek as he takes a pause. Admitting this was hard for him, and she knew that. Saying how he felt out loud was opening him up to the fear of more loss, but he was willing to break down his walls for her. He needed her to understand why he couldn't do this. He needed her to understand that he cared for her but couldn't be what she needed him to be right now.

"You deserve someone who will love you," he states to her, studying her face. "Someone who will do anything for you. Who will move mountains to give you what you need, and I can't be that for you right now, Pip. I can't even be that for myself."

"Then I will be that for both of us," she whispers.

"No, Pip," he sighs with a pained expression. "That's not your burden to bear."

Nodding her head, she looks to the ground. After a moment, she embraces him again, holding him tightly to show he didn't need to continue. What he had said was enough for her.

"You're important to me, Pip," he whispers in her ear. "That's why I need you to stay here, okay?" He feels her shake her head.

"I am coming to the capital with you," she sighs, pulling away. "We were both alone in your visions, so let's make sure we stay together."

With a shaking breath, he wipes away the small tear that was escaping her eye and gives her a soft smile. When it came to Pippa, there was no telling her what to do. If she felt she needed to do something, there was no changing her mind. She was persistent when she wanted to be, and that was what Mercy needed.

"Okay," he agrees.

"We will get Sylas first," she assures with a sniffle. "You need your Nota right now."

"Okay," he concurs, pulling away and nodding his head.

Chapter Twenty-Three

Looking back at Pippa in the wagon, Mercy lets out a steady breath. Being back at the cabin in Vermeer felt strange. Even though Sylas had been living here off and on for several months, Mercy hadn't been here since the events leading up to Spheara. Sylas always came to Rieka or met him in Ozra so there was never a reason for him to come out to the cabin, until today.

Walking onto the porch he turns to look out at the tree line. The last time he had sat on this porch was when he learned Sylas was his Nota. That he was more than just his best friend, but a person who was meant to guide him through his journey as a Keeper of Light. Thinking back on that night, it felt like the day their friendship started its slow decline. Nothing had really been the same between the two of them since that day and it made his chest ache. There had been a feeling of doubt regarding his best friend every step of the way after that. Was Sylas there because he wanted to be, or because he had to be?

Taking another deep breath, he knocks on the door. There was never a time he felt he had to knock on the door of a Bellator. They were his family and had treated him like a son since the day he was born. His father was close with

Sylas's father, Ezra. Their friendship was one of the reason Sylas and Mercy had forged such a strong bond in their early years. This made the sentiment of needing to knock on his best friend's door feel foreign and wrong.

As he waits for an answer, he looks back to Pippa again. Why was he nervous to face Sylas? He had known this man his entire life. They grew up together. The learned everything they could together. They defended each other on more than one occasion. Every waking moment he knew Sylas, until this last year, he was just a short walk down the road. Now it felt like he was about to face a stranger.

He jumps as the door opens and Sylas appears. He looks at his friend's face, his eyes getting wide at how out of sorts he appeared. He hadn't shaved in days and his eyes were bloodshot and red. He frowns seeing that Sylas had cut off his long curls, the sudden absence alarming to him. He had those curls since they were kids and now, they were gone and replaced with a short buzz cut. Seeing him without his shaggy locks made this encounter feel even more like seeing a stranger. Those curls were Sylas's symbol of deviation from his chosen career. They were part of who he was. This man standing in front of him didn't even look like Sylas.

"Hi," Mercy finally speaks.

"What do you want?" Sylas asks, leaning on the door frame, rubbing his eyes.

"They summoned me back to Ozra and…" Mercy trails off, as the smell of alcohol hits him.

"And?" Sylas snaps, raising a brow.

"Have you been drinking?" he blurts out in shock.

"Yes," Sylas sighs.

"It's not even noon," Mercy notes.

"This is my house. I can drink if I want," Sylas explains, annoyance in his voice.

"Sorry," Mercy mutters.

245

Looking back over his shoulder, Mercy notes Pippa had ducked back inside the wagon to give them some privacy. He didn't want the privacy though, he wanted reinforcements. Facing Sylas felt like a death sentence, especially if he had been drinking. Sylas tended to lose his filter when he drank, which meant there was no telling what he was going to say. Taking a deep breath, Mercy closes his eyes for just a moment, feeling the heat from his Source on the back of his lids. If Cal were here, he'd be yelling at him to get his shit together. This was just Sylas. This was his best friend.

Looking back at his friend, he straightens up. "I need you."

"You need me?" Sylas questions, folding his arms. "The Sentry Guard who is on leave for a hand injury and counseling?"

"Yes," Mercy nods, questioning his own decisions in that moment. Shaking in place, he speaks again, talking much quicker than he intended. "I'm sorry for everything, Sylas. You were right. I was being selfish, and I'm an idiot and I shouldn't have gone off on my own. It was a dumb decision and now we are all living with the consequences of my stupid actions and-"

"Slow down," Sylas warns, putting his hand out. "Take a breath, Merc."

Taking a steady inhale, Mercy forces a pained smile. "Sorry."

He looks at Sylas's hand that was outstretched toward him and could see that the wound on his hand was now healed. He furrows his brow knowing it should have been several more weeks before the remnants had healed over that well. They were hardly even showing scars.

"Stop saying sorry. You have nothing to be sorry for," Sylas lectures.

"I'm sorry," Mercy replies, looking down at his own use of the word again. "Sorry."

Studying Mercy, Sylas lets out a heavy sigh. He could see how afraid he was to face him after their last encounter, and he didn't blame him. What Sylas had said was harsh.

"Come in," he announces, pushing away from the door and walking into the cabin.

Nodding his head, Mercy follows his friend through the doorway. Glancing around, he could see that Sylas had remodeled the place. He had replaced most of his father's furniture and storage crates with things that fit his needs and style. Many of the hunting supplies and tools were removed and replaced with homey, soft and wooden furniture, creating a welcoming feeling within the space. He had a neatly folded stack of blankets on the couch and one wall was now lined entirely with shelves fill with books of all sizes and genre. He had even replaced the outdated kitchen appliances with newer ones.

On top of the fireplace were two framed sketches from Cal as well. It was common for Cal to gift his artwork when he filled a book. Now that he didn't feel the urge to hide his talent, he was open to sharing his works with those he cared for. One of the images was of him and Sylas together during one of their trips. There were hardly any signs left that this place had belonged to Ezra.

The smell of meat cooking hits him as his friend goes to the stove and pokes around something in a pan. Mercy walks over to the counter and watches him nudge what appeared to be chicken. Glancing to the trashcan in the corner he could see quite a few whisky bottles piling up with a few half drank bottles on the counter. While it wasn't uncommon for Sylas to drink, it was uncommon for it to be alone.

"Sylas, I'm sor-" his friend glares at him through his brow as Mercy shuts his mouth. "I'm just trying to say... Cal and I were better as a team, not... alone. I was an idiot and if I hadn't-"

"They wanted him dead," Sylas replies, cutting him off, his tone numb. "I don't think it would of mattered if you were there or not. Those things are ruthless, and I think it would of killed him regardless."

Nodding his head, Mercy looks to the floor and takes another shaky breath. "I shouldn't have let you sit with this by yourself either," he adds to the conversation. "The last two weeks... I should have been here for you."

"I needed space," Sylas shrugs, turning the heat off on the stove. "When it comes to Cal, sometimes I just need... time."

"Leaving someone alone with their thoughts can be cruel though," Mercy replies.

"Letting someone be your distraction can be just as bad," Sylas retorts with an irritated laugh.

"I guess," Mercy huffs, watching Sylas move the meal to a plate.

"So, you want me in Ozra?" Sylas enquires, trying to change the subject.

"Yeah," Mercy nods.

"Fine... I'll go," Sylas agrees, moving away from the stove to the area of the counter Mercy stood by.

"Just like that?" Mercy asks, watching him as he sets his plate down.

His friend lets out a heavy sigh and takes a bite of his food. Even though Sylas was still livid about the situation, what choice did he have? This was his best friend, and he knew deep down that if Mercy had any idea what was going to happen that day, he would have done everything in his power to prevent it. While Sylas loved Caligo, Mercy was Cal's Alia. Losing Cal was just as brutal for the Light Keeper as it was for him.

"You're all I have, Merc," Sylas explains. "My family is gone, Cal's gone, my job's gone... The only thing I have left is you."

"That doesn't sound like a good enough reason to move on from this," Mercy responds.

"But it's the only one I need," Sylas stresses with a small, forced smile. "You're my Keeper and I can't do my spiritual obligation if I'm pissed at you. As your Nota I need to move past things so I can keep you moving on the path you're meant to be on."

"Sylas, no," Mercy lets out a frustrated sigh.

They had gone over this a dozen times. Sylas making his choices based on being Mercy's Nota was unfair. The job the Elder's had given him shouldn't have been influencing his decisions like this. He wasn't an animal like Nex, he was a person. He had complex thoughts and emotions and a thinking process.

"I know what we agreed on," Sylas affirms, "but at the end of the day, that's what I am. We're bonded, Merc, meaning I can't hold a grudge."

"I don't want you to have a grudge in the first place," Mercy states.

"Good because I don't have one," Sylas enlightens. "Cal is gone, and I might never get over that, but trying to move past it sounds a hell of a lot better than losing you too." He gives Mercy a pained smile as he looks at the plate in front of him with a heavy exhale. "You're my best friend, Merc. You're all I have left on this screwed up post Spheara planet, and I can't let myself lose you too."

"I messed up," Mercy replies in a small voice.

"We all mess up," he remarks, gesturing with his hands. "I mess shit up all the time, but you never hold that over me. Look at my hand, that was a pretty big screw up if you ask me."

"This is different," Mercy argues, glancing to his friend's hand and shaking his head. "Cal is-"

"Gone," Sylas finishes. "He's gone and there isn't a damn thing either of us can do about it. So… let's stop trying to change the things we can't and start focusing on what we can."

The two are quiet for a few moments. Looking at his friend, Mercy wasn't even sure if bringing him along for this was a good idea. Sylas looked rough. His best friend usually made a point to look somewhat put together, but now he was worse than ever. He had never seen Sylas this shaken up by anything.

"Are you up for this?" Mercy questions, an air of compassion coming over him.

"Of course," Sylas nods.

Even with how broken he felt, he knew standing by Mercy was his first step to healing.

Chapter Twenty-Four

No one was brave enough to touch the screen in the table of the conference room for fear they wouldn't be able to handle it as smoothly as Cal once did. While all of them were familiar with the Aitian technology the capital provided, none were confident with it.

For this meeting Tristia had gotten together Mercy, Zero, Novi, Sylas, and a woman named Silika who would be leading the assignment. Silika was from Denali and had apparently been working on infiltrating Malice the last few weeks. She was an Aitian Shadow Keeper, with a lower canine that jutted out over her top lip. She was brawny to the point it was intimidating, and she spoke with an angry tone much of the time.

They all sat in silence waiting for the Sentry Guard to bring Shay into the room. Part of Mercy was looking forward to seeing her again. She offered him comfort in the forest all those weeks ago and had proven to be more than the evil girl Mala had turned her into. She had a kind side, and he was hoping he could prove that to Tristia.

"Mercy, I am optimistic you can get this stubborn girl to tell us what she knows," Tristia shares. "She is keeping information from us; Zero has confirmed this."

"Stubborn?" he asks with a raised brow.

"Yes," Tris nods. "She has started to refuse cooperation and I would like to know why."

He nods his head, furrowing his brow. That didn't sound like the Shay he had worked with. During their brief time together, she had done nothing but help. She was even willing to fight by his side and prodded to get him to speak about his choices. Why would she suddenly switch her behavior when her freedom was on the line?

"Perhaps Master Validus should put a shield up?" Silika suggests, interrupting his thoughts.

"Sure," he agrees, his eyes lighting up brighter.

Scanning the room, he places one of his shields over everyone at the table, apart from Zero. Mercy's ability to call shields so easily and precise was something that actually annoyed Zero, but he was willing to admit when his skills weren't good enough. It honestly felt like Zero had been spending much of their training trying to one up Mercy. While he was meant to be testing Mercy, it seemed like most days it was the other way around.

As soon as the shields go up, there is a knock on the door. Zero gets to his feet and opens it to reveal the guard who knocked and Shay. The sight of the girl causes Mercy's eyes to grow wide. Her cheek was bruised, and her right eye was swollen shut. She had a contraption over her mouth and her hands were so tightly bound there was blood oozing from her wrists. She spots him and her eyes automatically begin to plead for his help. She wasn't refusing to work with Tristia because she was being stubborn, it was because she was scared.

"What'd you do to her?" Mercy blurts out, his gaze going to Tristia.

Every eye in the room shoots to him as he gets to his feet and drops the shields. Locking eyes with Shay again, he could see she was begging with him to help. This

253

was why she wanted him on this assignment. They had been treating her like a monster, not a person.

"Get rid of the shackles and, by the Elders, take that off her face," he orders the Sentry Guard holding her in place as he walks over to her.

"She is a threat, Mercy," Tristia stresses.

"She's a child!" he snarls, glaring at the Princess, the light in his eyes flaring.

None of them had seen what she had done in the forest that day, not even Sylas. Shay had comforted him and took him to where his friends were. She went to the river with him ready to fight. She stayed with Pippa while he tended to Sander and Sylas. It didn't matter what she had done during Spheara, she had been at his side as an ally in the forest the day of Cal's attack. He had even stated that in his debriefing after the incident.

"You want my help, then you treat this girl with some dignity," he snaps, glaring at the Princess.

"That would be unwise," she warns him.

Sylas speaks up. "Cal would never treat a prisoner like this. Not even Shay."

Mercy looks to his friend with big eyes, surprised to hear his voice. The young man had cleaned himself up for the formal meeting, but his eyes still showed his grief. Mercy nods a "thank you" to him and looks back to Tris. Both Mercy and the Princess lock eyes, his glowing with rage at what he was seeing. Tris scowls for a few moments and shifts her eyes to the guard holding onto Shay. She gives him a small nod to do as Mercy ordered. The guard quickly removes the shackles and snaps the contraption from her mouth.

Taking a deep breath, Shay begins to rub her wrists and flex her jaw. Seeing the pain on her face, Mercy grabs her hands and begins to heal where the metal had dug into her skin. This was horrific. He could only imagine the state other prisoners could be in on level three. At least when Cal was on the throne they were treated like people and not animals.

"Are you okay?" Mercy questions in a whisper, moving his hand to her face to heal her swollen eye. She gives a small nod.

"Mercy," Tris snaps.

He ignores Tristia until he finishes healing the girl. He could feel his hands shaking with anger as Shay takes a step to stand behind him. The young woman knew the only person in the room willing to protect her was him.

"Is this how you're treating all our prisoners now?" he asks the Princess. "I won't stand for this. They're our people too."

"They are prisoners," Silika retorts in annoyance.

As a pain shoots through his arm, Mercy brings his Source to his hand and aims his palm at Silika. He wasn't talking to her; he was talking to Tristia. The rest of the room needed to remain silent. The anger that was washing over him felt strong and uncontrollable, but also made him feel powerful.

"Your Grace, answer my question," Mercy demands with fiery eyes.

She looks from his face to his hand. Unexpectedly, she looked fearful of him too. While Mercy was normally quiet and spaced out during these meetings, he was now demanding the attention of the room. The shift in his behavior was sudden and jarring to the group. It was like they were looking at Cal again. Mercy was fierce and ready to take on whoever disobeyed him, just as Cal would have done in this situation.

"If this is how we're going to handle the inmates helping us, we need to reevaluate our system," Mercy adds, his eyes looking over the room, his irises ablaze. "Even someone who aided Mala in Spheara shouldn't be treated like this. We are here to set an example, to show our people we are better than Mala, not that we're the same. As the rightful heir to this monarchy, I'm disgusted," he eyes Tris with a raised brow for her reaction.

Sylas looks to Mercy with confusion. He hadn't heard this news yet and was shocked by the statement. The Princess on the other hand takes a deep inhale and nods her head. Even though Mercy initially denied Cal's request, she knew the document could be used to hand the throne over to him at any time. If he was going to make demands, she needed to do as he said. She turns to look at Zero for input, unsure what to say to appease the angry Light Keeper glaring at her. She could see his eyes were ablaze as well, on edge by Mercy's outburst no doubt.

"I'll set up a review of the prison for you, Validus," Zero suggests, as Mercy drops his hand.

"Thank you," he nods, taking a steady breath. He needed to calm down. "Shay will be *my* responsibility from here on out. Do I make myself clear, Tristia?"

"Crystal," she concedes.

"I'm *allowing* you to act in my stead. Don't forget that," he reminds the young woman.

"I apologize," she adds, looking to Novi.

The Penumbra had a smug look on her face. She knew that Mercy had just as much aptitude and nerve as Caligo did, he just needed to find it. Seeing him take a step toward using his full authority was something she was happy to see.

"Now let's progress with this meeting, shall we?" Mercy states, keeping his voice and mannerisms assertive. He gestures for Tristia to sit down, she hesitantly does as instructed. "I want details," he states. "Pippa filled me in on what information Shay has provided so far, but I want to know the plan here. Zero and Silika?"

Clearing his throat, Zero speaks. "We were hoping to get approval to put together a team to search the Malice camps we've been able to locate. We're assuming Bryer and Iana are hiding in one of them."

256

"Is the goal to find Bryer and Iana?" he questions with a raised brow.

"To eradicate them, sir," Silika informs.

"Eradicate?" Mercy questions.

"Kill them," Sylas elaborates, his voice sounding strained.

"No," Mercy replies harshly. "The monarchy is no longer a killing machine. Caligo made that very clear while he was here, so we will move forward with his vision for the monarchy in mind."

"They are directly responsible for the death of our King," Silika scoffs. "We can't just let them go."

"Then we capture them," Mercy redirects, scanning the table. "We find them, detain them, give them a trial and punishment. We live in a world with both Source Keepers now. As Light Keepers we are meant to protect all living things on this planet. We pass judgement for a crime and let the Shadows enact punishment. That's how things are supposed to be. That's how our ancestors on Aitus did it, and that is how we will too."

"They are criminals, Your Grace," Silika retorts.

"They are our people!" Mercy snaps back, his eyes glowing more intensely again. "No one in this room is angrier about losing Cal than I am. I was his Alia. I had a connection with him that no one in this room will ever comprehend, but that doesn't change the fact that the people who took him from me, from us, are still our people. Their actions were guided by their disapproval of the monarchy's decisions, and with that in mind we will set things right. We will not give them an excuse to see us as the enemy. Am I clear?"

"Yes, sir," Silika yields.

"Now… I want a new plan," he barks, smacking his hand on the table. "I want someone in this room to come up with a tactic that will get us into those camps, secure Bryer and Iana, and get out any Shadow Keepers they may have

257

taken before they get a chance to do anything to them. Understood?"

"Yes," the room echoes.

"With that being said, I will lead this assignment," Mercy instructs looking at Novi. "I trust that you will make sure Cal's wishes are seen through while I'm away?"

"Certainly," Novi nods.

Mercy looks around the room again, his eyes stern and still glowing strongly. "Meeting adjourned!" he growls. Looking to Shay his face softens. "You're sure you're okay?"

"Yes," she whispers.

The men and women in the room get to their feet and begin to shuffle out, Sylas noting the agitation on Zero's face as he exits. Novi gives Mercy a reassuring pat on the shoulder before her exit, showing her approval of what he had just done. They leave Shay, Sylas, Mercy, and Tristia alone, the Princess looking cross.

"How dare you," Tris sneers at Mercy.

"How dare I?" he laughs. "How dare you!"

"Need I remind you that you are the one who declined Caligo's contingency plan," she iterates to him. "You said you did not want this."

"I was wrong," he retorts. "I was wrong to believe anyone could fulfill Cal's wishes but me."

"So what?" she scoffs. "You want the throne now?"

Looking between Shay and Tristia he thinks a moment. Was he willing to uproot his life based on the treatment of Shay? If he took up this mantle it meant he had to move his family to Ozra. He'd have to either move his shop, or let Yule and Katya run it while he was in the capital, which would be a majority of the time. Seeing Shay treated like this made him livid though. Cal would have never treated a prisoner like this, not even the girl who had manipulated him like she had.

"Yes," he shudders, locking his eyes on the Princess. "I'll send word to the National Council tonight."

"You are insane," she snaps.

"This is what Cal wanted," Mercy reminds her. "Insane or not, I'm the person he wanted to take his place as the leader of Novus Aitus, not you."

"Merc," Sylas warns, seeing his Keeper getting fired up.

"You are changing your mind based on the treatment of a criminal," she scolds, gesturing to Shay.

"I'm changing my mind based on the treatment of a child!" he screams at her. "A child who was there the day Cal was attacked and was willing to risk her life to defend her King," he enlightens her. "She was there, Tristia. Where were you?"

His last words render the Princess speechless. With that, Mercy turns and opens the door to the conference room, Shay and Sylas following his lead. As soon as the door closes behind him, he feels his knees buckle. The confidence he had was replaced by exhaustion. The rage that had fueled his actions swiftly is overcome with nerves, and it made him feel sick. His emotions were rattled, and he didn't feel like himself in that moment.

Chapter Twenty-Five

"I'm an idiot," Mercy mumbles to himself, scratching his arm, pacing back and forth in Cal's office. "Why'd I do that?"

After he had sent the notice to the National Council he had started to fall apart. Taking on the leadership position of King of Novus Aitus was a big deal, and he was hoping he made the right decision. He knew Caligo, and he wouldn't have written his name on that document without knowing he could do the job. Mercy just needed to take a breath and compose himself. He needed to calm down. Calming down had felt impossible the last two months though. There was no calm.

He finally sits down in the chair behind the desk and buries his face in his hands. Taking a few deep breaths, he looks up and locks eyes with Sylas who was watching him with a raised brow from across the room.

"You good?" his Nota asks.

"No," Mercy laughs tensely. "I don't think I've been good since I was ten."

Sylas nods with a small laugh and looks down. His mind was racing just as much as his friend's was.

"Why didn't you tell me about being the heir?" Sylas asks, looking at him again.

"I'm sorry," Mercy sighs. "I should have."

Of course he should have told Sylas. There were a lot of things he should have confided in his best friend. After Sylas got back from his trip, the two had agreed to no longer keep secrets from each other, yet Mercy was keeping several. It didn't help that they hadn't spoken much since losing Cal. When was he even supposed to tell him?

"Did you think I'd be mad about it?" Sylas asks, wanting to get an answer. "Or jealous?"

"No," Mercy huffs. "It's complicated."

"Well, uncomplicate it," his best friend urges, moving to the chair in front of the desk.

"We haven't exactly been on the best terms since..." Mercy trails off and looks down.

They both go silent. The words Sylas had shouted at Mercy after the eloium still echoed through him. Blaming him for the loss of Cal stung. Blaming him for the loss of everyone they loved was agony, but was Sylas wrong? Had he really caused all that heartache for the two of them because he was being selfish?

Sylas watches Mercy closely, knowing he hadn't even given his friend a chance to confide in him. He had pushed his best friend away and that was his own fault. Maybe Mercy would have told him about the contingency plan if he had been there to hear about it. There was no doubt Mercy was scared of the idea when it was originally brought to him and having no one to discuss it with certainly didn't help. At least he was putting on a brave face now.

"I'm sorry," Sylas whispers. "You just have to understand that the moment he went into the water..."

"I know," Mercy sighs, not sure he wanted to relive that tragic day.

Sylas shakes his head and looks to the floor. "My heart stopped that day, and I don't know if it ever started back up again," he admits, his tone wavering.

Registering the emotion in his voice, Mercy gets up and moves around the desk. He gestures for Sylas to get up, the young man listening, and hugs him. Mercy begins to rub his back wondering how he was seeming so composed compared to how he found him at the cabin. This was the first bit of normalcy the pair had since the riverbank. While it was nice to see Sylas attempting to open up, it also broke Mercy's heart.

"You've kept your head above water this long, don't give up just yet," Mercy comforts.

He feels Sylas squeeze him tighter. "I don't think I can do this without him, Merc," he mutters.

"I know," Mercy nods.

While he wanted to tell his best friend everything was going to be okay he knew the words would be lost. To Sylas, he was never going to be okay again. Even though they were on separate paths, Sylas's world still revolved around Caligo. The stolen glances and hidden smiles were seen by Mercy many times in the last year, Cal doing the same in return. Neither of them wanted to admit they hadn't moved on, but Mercy knew.

"I loved him," Sylas adds, his voice quiet. "How can someone so powerful and strong just be gone?"

"I don't know," Mercy states, pulling away from his friend who seemed close to tears.

The pair stand silently as Mercy glances around the room awkwardly. This was Cal's office. This was the room he had spent nearly every day in for the last fourteen months of his life, signing documents, having meetings, and making decisions on how to run his monarchy. Now it felt empty. Without Cal in the room, it felt drained of life. Looking around the office a sketch hanging with a series of pieces Cal had framed catches Mercy's eye.

"You're on the wall," Mercy gestures.

Moving his eyes to the sketches, Sylas walks over and looks at it. It was a sketch of Sylas sitting in tall grass, taking in the sun. He could tell it was a day the pair had gone off on one of their hiking trips, the flowy shirt depicted proved he was dressed for a relaxed walk somewhere outside of the city.

"Yeah," Sylas laughs. "I remember this," he informs Mercy, taking a steady breath. "It was about two months after Spheara. Right before you moved back to Rieka. Cal had given the sentencing on Mala and people were angry. He wasn't upset though... He was emotional, sure, but that was because he was finally done with Mala. He didn't have to look at her or think about her anymore... The things she did to him, Merc..."

Mercy joins him by the artwork. He studies the sketch and frowns. "Everyone thought Mala was cruel to her people... They had no idea the person she was cruelest to was living under her roof."

Giving a small nod, Sylas looks down at the floor as he continues his story. "I invited him out for a walk after the sentencing," Sylas shares. "I packed a lunch; we left the city and found a quiet place so he could have some time to himself and draw. He always told me he drew to get a new perspective. It was his way of trying to make sense of the things happening around him and how he was feeling... I just sat there and let him sketch for hours that day. We were there until well after sundown... We probably would have slept out there if I wasn't spoiled with luxury sheets by that point," he laughs to himself. He quickly becomes serious again. "Mala really did a number on him," he adds, shaking his head. "His father though... the few years he had with him kept his heart good."

"Did he ever talk to you about Emrys?" Mercy asks, looking at Sylas, who still had his gaze on the floor.

263

"A little," Sylas shrugs. "Emrys tried to keep Mala in line. He didn't want her to kill the Keepers or the humans," he shares, finally looking at Mercy. "Cal thinks... well... thought the only reason Mala was able to go through with the genocide was because of Emrys's assassination. Not out of spite, but because no one was there to hold her back. If the rebels hadn't killed him, Spheara may have never happened. Which after hearing Cal talk about it, it sounds like Mala planned his assassination. The rebels knew Emrys was on their side, so why would they kill him?"

"Why am I not surprised?" Mercy mumbles.

"Cal was only four when he died, but that man left a lasting impression," Sylas elaborates, looking back at the artwork. "A good father can do that, and that's what he had. I just wish he had gotten to grow up with a parent who cared for him. I wish he had grown up with any family who cared. I mean the Drors did what they could, but by that point the damage had been done. He deserved all the love a true family could offer."

"You were his family," Mercy replies.

"*We* were his family. He had a chosen family that he loved," Sylas corrects, taking his eyes from the sketch to Mercy again. "Right before the attack we were talking about getting back together," he adds, looking down again. "We didn't get to finish the conversation."

"He wanted to," Mercy confirms.

"How do you know that?" Sylas asks, his eyes shooting to his friend.

"Voca."

"Right," Sylas laughs, looking back to the picture. "I thought you guys could turn that off?"

"We could, but when he got flustered, and let me tell you... you flustered the hell out of him, he'd slip up," Mercy smiles with a shrug. "He slipped up a lot."

264

"Please tell me you didn't hear *everything* he thought about me," Sylas winces with an amused smile.

Mercy grimaces and chuckles with a nod. "Oh, I heard things I wish I never did."

"Oh no," Sylas giggles.

"If I had to hear him think about your eyes or your ass or anything beyond that one more time, I may have given up my Source again," Mercy smirks, folding his arms. "He also liked your incessant enthusiasm and somehow, your horrible sense of humor... I don't know who could like those puns, but he did."

"I'm so sorry you had to hear that," Sylas laughs, giving the first genuine smile Mercy had seen in weeks. "I'm sure you needed a good *brain washing* after."

The Keeper gives a small chuckle at the joke. "You two made sense," he shares, putting an arm around Sylas's shoulder. "You always did. Even when I was too stupid to realize what was happening."

"In your defense, I was also too stupid to realize what was happening. I mean... until I decided to kiss him in a bathroom," Sylas admits as Mercy pulls away and heads back to the desk.

"So, Caligo was right all along... We're both idiots," Mercy teases, sitting in the chair.

"Mostly you..." Sylas trails off, sitting down, the tone getting serious again. "So, the heir?"

Giving a small nod, Mercy lets out a deep breath. Did he even want to have this conversation with Sylas? Was this even a good idea to talk about? How much could Sylas even take in his current state?

"I want you to understand that I know I can't rule like he did," Mercy explains, picking up a folder and handing it to Sylas. "This is just what he wanted. Apparently, you get to take care of Nex," he informs him with a broken smile. "I haven't seen her... but she's yours."

Sylas opens the document and scans the contingency plan. Reading the words brings a frown to his face. He understood why the document existed, but seeing it made his stomach hurt. The fact Cal even had to think about his own death was painful. Too his surprise, Cal had left many of his belongings to Sylas, including his sketchbooks and many of his family heirlooms that he assumed Tristia, or the Drors wouldn't be interested in.

"You'll do great," Sylas reassures. "I can't see you as a King though," he admits.

"Me either," Mercy sighs. "I can't leave this to Tristia though. Not after what she did to Shay."

Sylas nods his head and lets out a steady exhale as he finishes reading the document. He was shaking slightly from his emotions but collects himself slowly. While he wanted to leave the room, he knew this was going to be where Mercy spent most of his days in the capital.

He hands the folder back to his Keeper as he furrows his brow. Cal had left Nex to him. Where was she? Getting up from his chair he goes over to a window and moves the curtain. He scans the outside windowsill as Mercy watches him. Moving away from one window he goes to the next and pushes the curtain out of the way.

Coming to another window, Sylas smiles and opens it. He picks up a few items and brings them back to Mercy's desk. Even though Nex hadn't been seen, she was leaving gifts as usual. When Cal was around, he always left a window open for his crow, but with him gone, the office had been closed off. This meant instead of the objects ending up on the desk, the Nota was leaving them on the windowsill hoping someone would spot them.

"Look," Sylas smirks, placing four small items onto the desk.

"Trash?" Mercy asks.

"No," Sylas chuckles, moving around the desk. "Nex always brought Cal presents. She would go out and bring him things she liked."

Leaning down, Sylas opens the bottom drawer of the late King's desk to reveal it was full of random odds and ends. There were metal rings, bolts, screws, and small stones. There were even some random bits of plastic and a few tree nuts. Every item in the drawer had been something Nex had brought Cal since he took over the office. Closing the drawer, Sylas looks at the four items on the desk.

Scanning the objects, Mercy takes note of them. There was an acorn, a piece of painted metal, a small pinecone, and a gold ring. Mercy picks up the ring and studies it. It was a thick gold, loosely braided band, a raw ruby set in it with gold peaking around the edges of the stone like roots. He knew this ring, because he had been commissioned to make it himself nearly a year ago. He flips it around to read the inside of the band to see Sylas's initials inside to confirm it. This was a ring Mercy had made for Cal to give Sylas on their six-month anniversary. An anniversary the pair were just a week shy of before they broke up. Cal had started to wear the ring instead, not wanting Mercy's hard work to be forgotten.

"So, she's still around?" Mercy questions, handing the ring to Sylas with hopes he would slide it onto his own finger.

"Yeah, but staying away for some reason," Sylas adds, taking the ring. "This looks like Cal's."

"It is," Mercy nods. "I made it for him." Mercy's eyes fall to the painted metal on the desk, and he furrows his brow. "This is part of his prosthetics," he shares, picking it up to look at it closer. "Titanium, coated in purple enamel paint. Did he break one?"

"Wouldn't be surprised if something snapped at the Mors River. That obscurum was throwing him around like a child's toy," Sylas shrugs. "Mementos I guess," he sighs, taking the metal from Mercy's hand.

Mercy moves his gaze to the acorn and small pinecone. Why would Nex bring this stuff to them? The ring he understood. If she found Cal's ring, she'd want it to be kept safe, but the other items seemed odd. He glances up to Sylas who's hurt expression was all too clear as he studied the ring in his hand.

"Are you going to be okay helping me with this?" Mercy asks, eyeing his best friend. "If you don't want to do this then-"

"I can do it," Sylas assures, setting the metal piece down. "If anyone can bring Bryer and Iana in and get Cal some justice it's us."

"Good," Mercy smiles, a hint of reluctance in his eyes.

"But don't keep things from me anymore," Sylas pleads with a heavy exhale. "I can't take you keeping shit from me on top of all of this. I'm not a child."

"I should've known better," Mercy admits. "I've just been stressed and-"

"You can talk to me, Merc," Sylas emphasizes. "Right now, we need each other more than ever. So, you can talk to me about anything. Whether as your Nota or best friend is up for debate."

"Best friend," Mercy smiles softly. "I always need you as my best friend."

They both go quiet for a moment, staring at the items Nex left behind. This was a big deal. Mercy accepting the crown was going to shake things up and no doubt cause chaos. There was already an upset after Cal's death. Having him take the Tenebris crown and turn it into the Validus reign was going to be an interesting experience.

The Light Keeper watches as Sylas slides the gold ring onto his finger. Mercy gives a small nod, happy to see the item where it belonged. Sylas flexes his right hand a few times with pain in his eyes. The ring was a perfect fit as expected, its original home meant to be on Sylas's finger.

"What about your hand?" Mercy asks, watching him closely. "You sure you can *handle* this."

Sylas laughs, happy to see his humor rubbing off on someone. He puts up his left hand, showing the injury and waves at Mercy.

"I have the best inventor in Ozra looking at me," he shrugs. "I bet he can think of something."

"I have a few ideas," Mercy confesses with a sly grin.

Chapter Twenty-Six

"Your concern is that without part of your hand and fingers, you can't hold things," Mercy explains, leading Sylas down the hall. The Nota had his bow and quiver at his side, nodding as Mercy spoke. "Holding the string of your bow, grabbing a sword, things like that are more difficult now. I've noticed you're resorting to smaller weapons you can use with your right hand, like daggers, which I guess you didn't have a choice in until Zero... Your left-handed though, so that can't be easy for you."

"Right," Sylas nods as they enter Mercy's suite.

"So... we fix that," Mercy shrugs, heading toward the couch and pointing to it.

Sylas sits as Mercy disappears into his room. He sets his bow down and leans it against the table and waits. Whatever Mercy had up his sleeve he had been thinking about for a while. His friend walks back out of his room with a leather bag and drops it on the low table in front of Sylas. He sits on the floor by Sylas's feet and begins to dig through it, pulling out four separate things.

"I've been thinking about this," Mercy informs. "I can fashion a prosthetic that can mimic finger movement when you bend your wrist. It'll use the natural movement and tension to grasp things and you'll be able to lock the grip, so you don't have to strain yourself. So, it'll curl over whatever you need and give you some stability," he explains, pulling out a prototype.

"Okay," Sylas nods, with a raised brow, taking the item from him.

"Let me show you," Mercy encourages, scooting over and yanking his friend's hand without warning.

Sylas lets out a surprised yelp then smiles. Taking the prototype, Mercy slips it onto Sylas's hand and makes a few adjustments. A strap secured it around his wrist and the other around the base of his thumb. A system of complex pieces of steel ran from mid hand to the padded prosthetic fingertips to create a truly genius design.

Mercy looks at the bow and wrinkles his brow. He wanted something lighter. Getting to his feet he walks around the room until he looks at his waist. He pulls the Pura Blade from its sheath and walks back over to Sylas, placing the dagger in his new hand, he nods.

"Bend your wrist," he instructs.

With some uncertainty, Sylas does as he's told and to his surprise the strange item does as Mercy explained. The prosthetic fingers react to his movement, gripping the hilt of the blade with ease. While it wasn't the most comfortable device, he had no doubt Mercy would fix that. His friend quickly grabs his hand again and hits a few small buttons on the first knuckle of each prosthetic finger, locking them around the blade and letting Sylas relax his wrist.

"See," Mercy smiles, proud of his work.

Moving his hand around, Sylas watches it. He was able to hold the dagger with no effort. He couldn't help but laugh in shock at what his friend had made. He certainly wouldn't be as quick to ready a weapon for a while, but it was a step in the right direction.

"I'll need to make some adjustments and get some better measurements and probably cast your hand to get a perfect fit, but I can make you something even better. I'll do with you what I did with Cal. We'll work on it until we find something you're comfortable with," he shares, as Sylas hits one of the small buttons, his finger snapping out straight again at the touch.

"A total genius," Sylas admits, giving his hand back to Mercy.

The Keeper quickly removes the device and sits on the floor again, setting it to the side before moving to the next item. "I also modified a bow release for you. Pip said you were trying to practice without an aid, and since a normal trigger release uses your index finger, which you don't have anymore," he notes, handing him the bow release. "The release on this will lay flat to your palm and the trigger is- Let me show you," he gestures, grabbing his wrist, and putting on the release. "You should be able to reach the trigger with your thumb. Again, I'll need to make some tweaks, but it shouldn't take me long. A bow release is simple enough mechanics, you really just needed something custom. Honestly, once you get the hang of it, you'll have way better stability since you're using your whole arm on the drawback. At least in my opinion. I really have no idea what goes into what you do, I just know how to make things."

Speechless, Sylas looks at the trigger release in his hand and smiles. Why hadn't he thought of using a bow release? Why hadn't he come to Mercy sooner? He should have known his best friend would come up with a way to make this easier for him.

"That's not all," Mercy informs, undoing the wrist strap and resting the release on the table.

He scoots back to the table, being in his element. One of his favorite things was coming up with new gadgets and finding ways to improve things. While he liked forging

273

blades, his real passion was coming up with new and exciting creations. It was how he spent much of his free time. As soon as he realized how serious Sylas's injury was, he started thinking. He had spoken with Doctor Willa and Cal about how he could improve his best friend's predicament. Doctor Willa knew the anatomical side of things, while Cal knew how to shoot an arrow and fight.

His next item appeared to be a spin on a leather bracer. Mercy puts it on his own arm and turns his body to Sylas to show him what he had made.

"You'll like this one," the Keeper smiles.

He makes a few adjustments to the straps and turns his arm over for Sylas to study. He watches as Mercy angles his hand forward and hits a hidden button on his palm with his two middle fingers. Suddenly a blade pops from the bracer on Mercy's forearm, extending about eight inches past his closed fist. The area over the back of his hand and palm were concealed by a partial glove and protected with steel plates and a thick synthetic material to protect it from the blade.

"Did you just give yourself a knife arm?" Sylas laughs, looking at the device.

"I did," Mercy chuckles, still smiling. "I gave Cal a set a while ago," he informs, entranced with what he was doing. "They look like a regular bracer to other people. It makes it easy for you to get a sneak attack in. You can reload them by using any protected part of your hand to push the blade in. It's all springs and latches. You have to be careful though, they aren't idiot proof, but I think it could work for you. The fact it's attached to your arm means you don't have to worry about trying to pull out a sword or dagger. Plus, it's cool."

"You really thought this through, didn't you?" Sylas asks as Mercy reloads the bracer and begins to take it off.

"When Cal said we'd get your perfect shot back, he meant it," he replies with sincerity.

274

With a small nod of approval and a smile, Sylas couldn't help but be proud. Seeing Mercy enjoying his work made him happy. He hadn't seen his best friend smile or get excited in a long time. The last couple of months Mercy seemed plagued with anger, fear, and grief, so this was a nice change.

Looking to the table Sylas sees one last item concealed in a small pouch. "What's that?" he asks.

"Oh." Mercy's smile falls as he grabs it. "You mentioned on the way here you were worried about losing the gem Cal gave you so…"

He gestures with the small bag toward Sylas who furrows his brow. Reaching into his shirt pocket he realizes the gem was gone. His heart drops and his eyes widen as he looks at Mercy. His best friend nods toward the bag, knowing full well Sylas was panicking at the idea of losing the last keepsake from Cal.

"Put your hand out," Mercy encourages.

With a heavy sigh, Sylas opens his palm. Mercy upends the bag, dropping the item into Sylas's hand. As soon as Sylas registers what he was holding his eyes begin to well up. He bites his mouth shut trying to keep himself from showing emotion as he studies it. Mercy had taken the gemstone and set it into a dark leather. He also decorated around the stone with silver wire, shaped into intricate swirls. The pendant was strung on a leather cord to match.

"The leather… It's from the armor he wore when we left Sintus… before Spheara," Mercy explains. "That's when you said you-"

"Thank you," Sylas whispers under his breath, cutting off his friend.

He watches Sylas stare at the pendant trying to collect himself. Letting out a sigh, Mercy grabs it and reaches to drape it around his neck. "I know I don't say it enough, but I do love you, Sylas."

Sylas nods his head. "I know you do, Merc."

"We both need to get better about telling others how we feel, don't we?" Mercy laughs softly from the floor.

"Mostly you," Sylas teases, tucking the pendant into his shirt. Mercy eyes him for a moment before Sylas lets out a small laugh. "I love you too," he whines.

"That's what I thought," Mercy smiles softly.

Speaking in general was something Mercy had done very little of until this last year. It took losing everything for him to gain his voice. Now that he had it, he didn't even know how to use it.

"I've been keeping something else from you," Mercy speaks, starting to chew his lip.

"Okay?" Sylas replies with concern, scooting off the sofa and onto the floor with his friend.

"The Elders sent me a vision," he explains, taking a deep breath and a slight pause before his next words. "I'm going to die."

"You're what?" Sylas asks, his eyes going wide.

"Yeah," Mercy nods, looking down. "It didn't make much sense, but I saw my body in the forest. I was drenched in water. My head was bleeding and so was my side." His friend goes silent taking in the new information as Mercy continues to explain what he saw. "There was nothing around me but trees and a river. It was the strangest vision I've ever had…"

"A river?" Sylas questions, perking up.

Mercy nods looking over to Sylas. He could see the cogs in his friend's mind turning as he thought over the words Mercy had said.

"A river and you were drenched?" Sylas asks, wanting clarification.

"Yes," he replies.

"A river… you were drenched…" Sylas mumbles to himself.

What Mercy was describing lined up with the injuries Cal had at the river. The tree had ripped open Cal's

276

side and when he went into the river, he had hit his head. It sounded like and elaborate coincidence, but that was something Sylas didn't believe in anymore.

"What if you weren't seeing yourself?" Sylas suggests. "What if you were seeing Cal?"

"It was me," Mercy replies, shaking his head. "I saw my face and-"

"Cal dying is a form of you dying," Sylas explains to him. "You said you were in the forest and there was a river…"

Thinking back to the vision, Mercy begins to see where Sylas was coming from. Comparing the scenery at the river to his vision he could see the similarities. That would make no sense though. Mercy's visions had always been straight forward.

"But Cal died *in* the river," Mercy argues. "I was dead on land."

"You were on land when he died," Sylas stresses. "The injuries and the scenery your describing was Caligo. That was what I saw. Him going into that river killed a part of you that day and-"

"Why wouldn't the Elders just show me Cal dying then?" Mercy questions. "Why give me some vague metaphor that I couldn't decipher to prevent it?"

Sylas looks away, trying to make sense of it himself. In the past it seemed the Elders sent very clear visions to his Keeper. They were giving clear indications of how and where things would happen. It made no sense they would suddenly send metaphors to Mercy like this.

"What if it wasn't the Elders?" Sylas asks.

Shaking his head, Mercy sighs. "What are you talking about?"

"You know how Novi gets snippets of information from her future self?" Sylas asks, as Mercy nods his head. "What if that's what this was? What if someone was trying to send you a message?"

277

"You think I can get visions from myself now?" Mercy inquires with a raised brow.

"Not necessarily," Sylas clarifies. "What I'm trying to say is, what if another Keeper has a peritia that can put images into someone's mind. What if they were trying to send you a warning about Cal's death that day? Or maybe trying to stop you from seeing it?"

Furrowing his brow, Mercy considers the statement. The last two visions he had made little sense and felt very different than those he had before. His visions from the Elders appeared like blurred images of events, while these were clear, and almost seemed cloaked in darkness. Perhaps Sylas was onto something.

"Shadow Source mind manipulation doesn't work on me," Mercy states, shaking his head.

"But another Light Keeper's could," Sylas edits, gesturing to Mercy's head.

"Light Keeper's don't manipulate minds," Mercy sighs, batting Sylas's hand away.

"Zero can," his friend continues.

"He can?" Mercy questions with a raised brow.

Sylas nods. "He can alter your emotions. That's what he did after the eloium... He calmed me down. Besides, we're still learning about the peritias Light Keepers can have. Maybe this is one we haven't come across yet. Maybe they can manipulate minds, or maybe it's a Penumbra like Master Novi."

"That doesn't make sense, Sylas," Mercy groans, putting his head down on the table. "Nothing makes sense anymore."

"What are the odds of you and Cal dying from the same injuries?" Sylas questions.

"Slim, I guess," Mercy concedes, keeping his head down. "You're making my brain hurt."

"That's not hard," Sylas pokes. "Keepers have only been on Novus Aitus for 100 years, we have more to discover! This could be possible."

"Or," Mercy turns his head to rest his cheek on the table and look at Sylas, "or, hear me out, I'm *actually* going to die."

"I refuse to believe that," Sylas shrugs smugly, folding his arms.

They both look to the door as Pippa clears her throat. Beside her was Shay, who had been cleaned up and given a fresh set of clothes. Pippa had made sure to find her something suitable to wear which was solid black from head to toe with a dark green vest.

"Hi," Mercy greets from the floor.

"Shay was informing me you are taking the crown," Pippa states, entering the room. "I wanted to come by and see for myself."

He gestures to himself, full of sarcasm and annoyance at the situation. "King Mercy, ruler of the soon to be Validus monarchy at your service."

Both young women stifle a laugh, knowing full well he wasn't trying to be funny. Seeing him sitting on the floor making such a statement was humorous though. Sylas gives Shay a small wave, the nerves clear in his expression.

"I have some information you may want to hear," Shay adds, looking between the two of them. "Something I was worried to tell Tristia."

"What is it?" Mercy asks, perking up at the statement and collecting himself.

"There are rumors in some of the Malice minds that Bryer is related to Cal somehow. They are upset, stating this was familial, not simply wanting to take out a Tenebris," Shay announces to the room.

"What?" Sylas looks at her with wide eyes.

"I could hear it in the minds of the few members we had tracked down last week," she continues, folding her arms, speaking softly. "I feared telling Tristia would incite anger in the girl or maybe another beating thinking I was being dishonest. Bryer is related to the Tenebris monarchy in some way by blood."

"Anything else?" Mercy asks, getting to his feet at the statement.

"Yes. He's targeting you next, Mercy," she informs them. "Not to unlock your powers, but to kill you. If he's a relative, then perhaps he wants the crown himself. Maybe he knew about the contingency plan."

They needed to come up with a plan quicker than they thought. They needed to find Bryer and end this before he could get to Mercy. While they could flush the camps with the Sentry Guard, that would only put an image into the people's minds that Mercy was ruthless as well. With who knew how many abducted Shadow Keepers at their disposal, they had to think this through. There was no room for a mistake.

"There also may be someone above Bryer, but no one seems to know who," she adds.

"Sophos," Mercy sighs, folding his arms. "Have you been able to get into Bryer or Iana's heads directly?" he asks, approaching Shay.

She shakes her head with a disheartened look. Though she had been able to find a few Malice members during the last couple of weeks, Tristia hadn't allowed her to get close enough to any of the compounds to search for the leaders. The Princess was still wary of her abilities and fearful what the girl could do if she got her hands on the people who killed the King of Novus Aitus.

"Think out loud, please," Sylas pleads.

Nodding his head, Mercy looks around the room at the three of them. "Silika wants to throw everything we have at Malice, but I think that's the wrong move."

"Agreed," Pippa nods.

"What do the three of you think about doing this on our own?" he suggests.

"Why do that when we have the entire military at our disposal?" Sylas tests.

"Because we need to be smart about this," Mercy states. "Malice is going to expect us to come at them with everything we've got. I also don't feel comfortable trusting Silika's teams on this."

"So, we send in Zero's," Sylas suggests.

"I know you trust Zero, but I don't," Mercy admits. "What I do have is three people I trust in this room." He glances to Shay who furrows her brow. "I know it's risky, but I think this is our best shot. With mine and Shay's Sources and your two's brains, this should be easy."

"Pippa and I don't have protection like you two do," Sylas reminds him.

"I can put shields on every single one of you," Mercy shrugs. "I'll run this by... well I guess myself..." Putting his finger to his chin, Mercy furrows his brow. "I guess I approve the assignment."

Chapter Twenty-Seven

Drifting in and out of consciousness, Cal couldn't help but focus on what led up to this moment. Not the day at the Mors River, but the years that created the Prince of Death. When he was just twelve, he began training to refine his combat skills. Working with the finest military men and women Ozra had to offer, his mother and Captain Atrox fashioned him to be the deadliest weapon they could muster out of a teenager. By the time he was sixteen he hardly remembered a time before he was a trained killer. The reflex to kill had been so engrained in his mind by that age, he didn't know much else.

Day in and day out he would train. He could probably kill a person in a hundred different ways by the time he was fourteen. His ability to learn quickly and memorize techniques made him an easy choice for the symbol his mother was hoping to create. Adding the fear of a beating from her or Atrox pushed him further than he knew he could go. Though sometimes the beatings were given to help strengthen him, or so they said.

For four years he underwent the grueling abuse, exhausting exercises, bloodied knuckles, unending bruises, and psychological manipulation to create the weapon Mala saw him capable of becoming. She conditioned him to see no other life than the life of a murderer. There was no option for him. It was to kill or be killed. Having a son destined to wield the Shadow Source made him valuable in ways he didn't even understand at the time.

At the age of fifteen she ordered him to kill his first victim. That was the day he was handed his scythe blades and was told they would symbolize who he was to their people. It was a teenager from Detritus, a city in the Southern Quarter, who had been responsible for a series of thefts in their small market. A trivial offence in the grand scheme of things, but the message it would send Mala's people was important. Having Caligo take the boy's life showed she was a force to be reckoned with, and even the pettiest of crimes would not be tolerated. From that day on, he would be known as the Prince of Death. It took him a matter of seconds to end the teenager's life and he didn't think twice about it. As far as he was concerned, punishing a criminal was his duty and he did it well.

As soon as the boy stopped breathing, he felt guilt wash over him. The boy had done nothing deserving of death. Stealing a few loaves of bread and fruit to feed himself was not a crime deserving of his life, but Cal had taken it. He could remember looking up at the cameras, the execution broadcasted all over Novus Aitus, and being unable to mask his disgust in what he had just done. After the slaughter, his mother called him into her office and reviewed the footage with him. She wanted him to understand the waiver in his expression was a sign of weakness and his disloyalty to the Tenebris monarchy. The beating from Captain Atrox that followed was one of the worst he had ever experienced. Unfortunately, this was just the beginning of the bodies that would soon pile up.

When he came into his Source was when Mala sent him to Master Novi. At that point he had become cold and numb to the physical abuse he endured during his time with

Atrox and expected the same treatment from his new mentor. Novi, on the other hand, showed him compassion and kindness. For the first time in his life, he wasn't training to survive, he was training to understand. Master Novi was caring and genuine with him. She helped him learn to master his Source in a very different way than he mastered any weapon before. For once in his life, he was being nurtured in his craft, not forced. She was patient, kind, and gave him the encouragement he needed to thrive.

The first day he felt his calling to Mercy was on a training expedition to the Western Quarter with Master Novi. He was visiting the sector with her to gain his bearings in the mountainous environment. Maneuvering his spiritum fog within the dense trees and rocky terrain was much more difficult than the wide arenas Master Novi had started his training in. She had brought him there to perfect his Keeping, or so he thought. When he had wandered off, the urge to follow the calling in his mind was undeniable.

He found his Alia for the first time walking in the forest outside of Rieka with his sister. While Charity spoke with enthusiasm, Mercy just nodded his head and gave the occasional response as Cal kept his distance. At the time he didn't quite understand why he had been drawn to the Riekan mutt, but now he did. Upon his return, he expected a beating from his mentor, but instead was met with understanding and encouragement to venture out on his own again. Novi wanted him to cultivate the connection he had to Mercy, for reasons unknown at the time.

His mind stops wandering as he hears voices outside the tent. His entire body was shaking as the entrance opened in front of him. Cal wasn't sure if he was trembling from the cold or perhaps from how weak he felt.

Finding himself awake, he looks up. The last two weeks had been torture, and Cal was hoping they'd just kill him already. This was worse than his time training with

Atrox. What was the point in keeping him alive if they couldn't use him in their little scheme anyway?

"We believe they are finally making a move against us," Iana announces as she walks up to him, an apple in one hand and a burlap sack in the other. "The capital summoned that Light Keeper of yours."

Moving his eyes down, Cal says nothing. Bryer had been waiting for them to call Mercy into their investigation of Malice. They probably would have forced Mercy's action themselves if the Sentry Guard hadn't been in full force in Rieka since his murder. Of course, Bryer and Iana were all too happy to inform him that the capital had held his eloium and that many people were celebrating in the streets that the King of Death was dead. He didn't blame his people for being happy he was gone. He was a symbol of their oppression for more years than he wasn't.

"Word was also sent to the National Council that Mercy Validus will be taking your place as governing leader," Iana continues, sitting down in front of him, making sure to avoid the rune. "What do you think of that, Caligo? Your closest friend and advisor is attempting to replace you."

"He is not replacing me," Cal mumbles, his voice feeling distant. "He is just following orders."

"You did have a plan then?" she questions, pulling a blade from her pocket and slicing into the fruit. "So, you realized you're not immortal?"

"No one is immortal," he speaks in a whisper.

She nods her head, eating a piece of the apple and cutting another. He looks at her with a scowl as she offers him a slice. Taking his eyes away, he looks to the ground again. He had hardly eaten anything they gave him. At this point he had become numb to the hunger. They even tried sending in a young Light Keeper named Liliya who seemed to have some type of calming peritia to coax him to eat something, but even that didn't work.

"At least you're staying hydrated," she shrugs eating the piece herself. "Be a pity if you let yourself die."

He had contemplated just refusing anything they offered him, but if he stopped trying, that meant he had given up. He couldn't give up, no matter how much his body wanted him to. Leaving behind those he cared about without trying would only haunt him in the afterlife, especially leaving Sylas the way he did. He could only imagine the guilt he was carrying with him. If he ever made it back to Sylas, he was sure a scolding would be in his future for his actions at the river. He had to save Sylas though. If that was his last interaction with the man he loved, he could die knowing he saved his life.

"We're still trying to figure out what to do with you," Iana sighs, looking to the inflamed wound on his side. "We should clean you up, shouldn't we? People would be very displeased if I allowed you to die due to an infection."

"Death doesn't sound too bad right now," he adds, looking at her again.

He takes a deep breath, wincing at the pain from the wound. He was still covered in mud, the temperatures had only gotten colder, and his body was fighting to keep itself alive. The pain in his back had started to subside, but he was sure it was only due to the fact he had hardly moved in what felt like weeks.

"You're shivering," she notes, getting to her feet and grabbing a blanket. She tosses it over his shoulders before going back to sitting in front of him.

"Too kind," he adds, staring at her shoes.

At least it was Iana talking to him and not Bryer. Every time that man came into the tent, he just recited more of the horrors Cal had done in his past. He'd then leave him to sit in silence as he replayed those haunting memories repeatedly. It was the worst kind of torture. Being forced to relive all the things he had tried so hard to forget was

286

agonizing. He was starting to wonder why he hadn't just killed himself years ago. At least if he had ended his own life, thousands wouldn't have had to perish at his hands.

"I like you, Caligo," Iana smiles at him. "You see, they were discussing killing you, but Lili and I stood up for you. We told them you were useful."

He clears his head and lets out an annoyed sigh. "I have no interest in being used in whatever you have planned for Mercy," he mumbles with a cold gaze. "I would rather sit here and continue to waste away before I help you."

"Putting the pieces together I see," she laughs. "A Supra Keeper of the Sources," she shrugs. "I never thought we'd have one on Novus Aitus, yet here he is. How does it feel to be the weaker of the two? Were you even aware of how weak you really were, Caligo? Everyone is weak compared to Mercy Validus. His power is limitless. He isn't tethered by the same rules you and I are."

"Mercy has his own rules," Cal retorts. "He has morals and a steady mind."

"A good heart can be easily swayed, and a steady mind can be destroyed," she continues. "Especially with someone you care for on the line."

"You clearly know nothing about him," Cal chuckles at the words. "The woman who took everything from him, he refused to kill."

"But the man who gave him everything... he may be willing to change his methods for," she points out. "Caligo Tenebris, King of Novus Aitus, the ruler who brought Keepers out of hiding, the man who protected Mercy and his village from the Unity Council and made sure he succeeded in his destiny. You even gave up the love of your life to watch Mercy prosper while you let yourself fall deeper into your own misery."

He takes his eyes from her again and closes them. Letting Sylas walk away from him was the biggest mistake he had ever made. Letting him go all those months ago was thoughtless and refusing to reconcile with him was tearing him apart. Sylas was sitting somewhere thinking he was dead and probably felt more alone than ever before.

"I shouldn't mention Bellator then?" Iana snickers, taking a bite of the apple. "Did he forget about the fact you killed his family yet? Or is that still fresh in his mind?"

"Please stop," he begs, squeezing his eyes shut.

"Ezra and Berk Bellator were reported to be among the UC Guards lost in the Fall of Rieka, am I wrong?" she questions with a snake like grin. "Reports can be wrong you know…"

"What are you talking about?" Cal looks at her with fire in his eyes.

"You can't trust a single person you have working for you," Iana notes. "You should know that by now. Half of the people working for you want to see you fail. Adding any fuel to the fire that could be used against you is in their best interest."

"What?" Cal questions.

"I'll leave you with that thought," she states, getting to her feet finally. "You of all people should know that no one is ever truly gone, and minds can be easily manipulated, Caligo. Or is it Cal? I hear your friends call you Cal. I want to be your friend, Cal."

"I am not in the market for any new friends right now," he snarls at her.

"Shame," she sighs. "I think you and I could get along under the right circumstances."

"Untie me and maybe we can talk about it," he suggests, trying to move his hands again.

"I'm no idiot, Cal," she sighs, her tone sounding sweet. "I know that even without your Source or your legs, you're capable of doing some damage."

"You are right about that," he confirms.

While he did have an escape plan, he needed to wait until the right moment to enact it. Mercy's innovative mind had left him with one last trick up his sleeve, but he was being patient. If he attempted to escape without the right circumstances he was screwed. Without his prosthetics he was going to be slower and a bit clumsier, but it wasn't something that was going to stop him. Losing his legs had never been a limitation before.

"Then again, would your weak body even allow you to take a shot at me," she inquires. "Oh! One last thing before I go."

She crouches down again and sets her bag on the ground. Cal watches her closely as she pulls something from the bag, his eyes getting wide. He watches in horror as the body of a black crow is tossed in front of him. A surge of anger and grief hits him as he attempts to hold back the tears in his eyes.

"Nex…" he mutters to himself.

"Just a taste of the pain you've caused millions," she announces, her perky face going to a scowl as he stares at his Nota with pained eyes. "How does it feel to have your Nota taken from you, just as your mother did to thousands of Keepers before you. Doesn't seem fair that her precious son was allowed to keep his while so many others mourned their spiritual guide."

Iana stares at him waiting for a response, but Cal was too dazed to speak. His heart felt shattered as he stared at her dark feathers. Nex had been his constant over the years. Ever since he came into his Source, she had been there. She had protected him, gave him comfort, and watched over him for the last eight years. She had even tried to attack his mother on various occasions, but after a very real threat from Mala, he instructed her to back down. The unspoken agreement was for the crow to stay out of his fights unless it was life or death.

"I just wish I could remove you from that exua rune so you can feel the pain I felt when Mala slaughtered my Nota," she scowls. "It hurts me that you will never feel that level of emptiness."

He shakes his head as the shock continues to go through him. How could they do this? How could they just kill Nex like this? How had they even done it? Nex was clever and had a knack for hiding. She knew to stay out of sight when things were going wrong.

"I'll leave you to say your goodbyes," Iana smiles. "A curtesy your mother never gave me."

His eyes finally go to Iana as he begins to tremble. Shaking his head, he speaks, "You are a monster."

"Am I?" she laughs. "Take a look at yourself, King Caligo."

"I am not my mother!" he screams at her. "Nex did nothing to deserve this!"

"Oh, but she did," Iana sneers. "Serving the Prince of Death is enough reason."

With that she exits the tent, leaving Cal to sit with his Nota's corpse. His eyes go back to the familiar black feathers. He could feel his face get hot from the anger and grief bubbling up inside him. His Nota was dead. His spiritual connection was severed. His best friend was gone forever.

Chapter Twenty-Eight

The group was making their way along a trail within a forest. Shay had been able to pinpoint the location of a Malice camp base from within the city of Lues that was just up the road. Her abilities were honestly something to behold. She barely had to power up to activate her peritia and she seemed to be able to keep it going for extended periods of time. Then again, Mercy didn't have to be powered up to use his gifts either, so maybe it wasn't as surprising as he thought.

The group had armored up for this assignment. Mercy stayed in his combat suit while Sylas wore his Sentry Guard armor. Pippa and Shay both wore light synthetic and leather to offer some protection. Mercy made a note in his mind to get Pippa's measurements to get a better set of armor made for her. Going into a mission like this without enough protection for her made him a bit nervous, but he knew she could hold her own. The young woman could have a deadly impact when the time called.

Pippa watched Mercy closely as he walked in pace with Sylas, his face stern. Seeing him like this was off putting. Losing his timid demeanor meant he was going to be bolder in his actions and the fear of his grief taking over the logical part of his mind was very much a risk. It seemed his emotions had become stronger and leading his behavior more than before. While he had always been one to let his heart lead his decisions, this was different.

Before they departed the capital, she left a note for her mother explaining what they were doing in fear that they would go on this expedition and never be heard from again. Someone needed to be aware of their movements. The last thing her mother needed was the loss of another child. While Novi would never admit her true grief for the loss of Caligo, Pippa could see it in her eyes. Losing Cal wasn't just losing her mentee, it was losing her son. Her mother had always seen Cal as another child since he came into her care at sixteen. They all saw him as family.

Coming up beside Mercy, Pippa entwines her arm with his and pulls him away from the group slightly. Sylas sees the interaction, and in turn slows his pace to give them a moment. Seeing Pippa's sudden urgency to speak with Mercy meant it was going to be important.

"There is a war waging in your head again, Mercy," Pippa whispers. "Would you mind sharing?"

"No war," he shrugs at her remark. "Just trying to fill some very big shoes."

"Do not become someone you are not out of fear," she cautions.

"Isn't fear what got us this far?" he retorts.

"Perhaps, but fear is a dangerous entity to play with," she reprimands.

"Fears we don't face, are the ones that become our limits, Pip," he bluntly replies. "You said my power is limitless, so why let my fears hold me back?"

"Your power may be limitless, but you are not," she states, keeping her voice low.

"When you get as good at nearly dying as I am, maybe you stop being scared?" he smirks.

The comment throws her off. Was this Mercy talking or Cal? Was his ambition to keep his Alia's memory alive causing him to become a new person? Perhaps he was simply growing into himself, and this was his true persona.

"You could have stayed in Ozra," he adds in response to her reaction, taking his voice out of the whisper.

"And let you have all the fun? Never," she retorts, the concern clear in her tone.

While he understood Pippa's worries, they didn't have time. If they decided they needed backup once they arrived at the camp, they'd simply need to find a call post in Lues and get the Sentry there. There was no reason to be fearful of this situation getting out of hand. The four of them could handle it.

The group goes back to silence as they continue to walk, none wanting to risk giving themselves away. They all pause as Shay puts her hand out and points forward with the other. She turns to Mercy as her eyes return to their normal form.

"We're about 50 yards out," Shay whispers. "It's just ahead."

"Anything on Bryer or Iana?" Mercy asks, in a hushed tone.

He watches Shay's expression shift. She had to have heard or seen something. "No, but there is buzz about the Sentry Guard," she states, looking around the group. "Just as Mercy said, they're expecting a full raid of the camps."

"Then good thing we aren't giving them that," Sylas assures, looking to Mercy.

The Light Keeper takes a deep breath. "No sign of Bryer?" Mercy clarifies, looking at Shay, rubbing his arm again.

She shakes her head as Mercy looks down the trail. If Cal were here, he'd probably charge forward and demand to speak with someone in charge, but he wasn't. This was Mercy's assignment to direct, but he honestly had no idea what his next step was. What was he expecting to happen at the first camp? Was he hoping they would find what they were looking for on the first try?

He looks to Sylas. "What do you think, Captain?" he smiles faintly.

"You know what I think," Sylas replies, pulling his bow from his back.

"We are grossly outnumbered," Shay warns, shocked at Sylas's suggestion.

"We were at Spheara too," Sylas reminds her, getting his bow ready to go, securing the bow release around his wrist. "Still took you down."

The Shadow gives a sour look in response.

"Mercy, think this through," Pippa advises, giving him cautious eyes as Shay looks to him.

Scanning the group, he begins to feel anxious. Sylas wanted to fight, and Pippa wanted to back down. This was up to him. Did he stick to his pacifism, or did he let Sylas make the call? Now that he was taking on Cal's mantle, did he even have the option to make safe choices anymore?

"Merc, we can handle them," Sylas pressures. "We owe this to Cal."

"They can and will kill us," Pippa shoots back.

"We have these two," Sylas shrugs, gesturing toward Shay and Mercy. "A Shadow who can manipulate people and a Supra Light Keeper. We're practically unstoppable," he pokes.

"Don't get overconfident," Shay scolds.

"Me? Overconfident? Never," Sylas laughs, dripping with sarcasm. "I see an opportunity to shut down a rebel camp, and we'd be stupid not to take it."

"Cal was not worried about Malice," Pippa informs the group. "They are harmless. He wanted to keep peace with the rebels, not start another war."

"Harmless my ass," Sylas retorts. "If those obscurums are working for them, they are the farthest thing from harmless."

"We go into a fight, and we could risk handing Mercy over to the enemy," Pippa argues. "They wanted to draw him out and here he is."

"Come on, Pip," Sylas scoffs.

Sylas goes to take a step forward, but Shay moves in front of him, her eyes dark. "Wait."

Caught off guard, he pauses, waiting to see what she was about to say. She turns to look at an area to their right as spiritum fog begins to drip from her hands.

"Someone is watching us," she warns the group.

As the words leave Shay's lips, Mercy's hair begins to stand on end. Another Keeper was nearby. He urges Pippa behind him, the need to protect her taking over as he powers up. They were ready to go on the defense if needed. Even if Cal thought the group was harmless before, Sylas was right. They weren't. They wanted something from Mercy, and he needed to make sure he didn't give them ammunition to get it.

As someone emerges from the tree line, both Mercy and Sylas go slack as their eyes get wide. They both knew this person, and they knew him well. Mercy begins to power down as Shay and Pippa look at him in confusion. From the trees emerged someone from their past they didn't expect.

"Berk?" Sylas questions, relaxing at the sight of his older brother.

The man was just a few years older than Sylas and looked exactly as he did the last time they saw him. The military cut their father had tried to force on Sylas more than once was still clean cut and slicked back. His skin was a few shades lighter than Mercy's best friend, and he was dressed in black and dark blue armor. They had every reason to believe this was Berk, but one thing didn't sit right. Why was Mercy sensing another Shadow Keeper?

"You're supposed to be dead," Sylas speaks as the man approaches the group. "I saw the reports."

296

"You saw what they wanted you to see," his brother states, the same cold tone coming through that both Mercy and Sylas remembered. "What are you doing here?"

Mercy looks to Shay who shakes her head lightly. Even if this was Berk, they needed to play it safe. Whatever was in this man's head, Shay was heeding them to keep their guard up.

"Don't say anything, Sylas," Mercy orders. "What are *you* doing here, Berk?"

Berk's eyes dart to Mercy. "I should have kept you away from my brother from the beginning. Look what you've done."

"He's done nothing," Pippa remarks.

"You've turned my brother into a pet of the Tenebris monarchy," Berk growls, pulling a mace from his back. "Orlo was stupid to trust you would follow in his footsteps."

Keeping his mouth shut, Mercy looks to Shay. She was waiting for instruction from him on what to do. He knew she could easily disarm Berk, but what would that do to Sylas? In the off chance this was Sylas's brother, they needed to be careful.

Looking to his best friend, he could see the complete shock on his face. The idea of Berk being alive wasn't something he had ever thought about. Cal had killed Berk and their father. Of the 109 military members that Cal's Source took, his father and brother were included. While he had been too shaken up to say his goodbyes by identifying the bodies, he trusted Abtal. Abbey grew up with them. He was in Berk's class. There was no way in his mind that Abtal could misidentify his family.

Swinging his mace, Berk suddenly advances on Mercy. In return, the Light Keeper powers up and shoots a solis orb at the mace to deflect it. Berk's face fills with rage as he attempts another swing at Mercy, this time Mercy flashing his palm in Berk's face, disrupting his eyesight.

The Light Keeper turns and uses a wave of energy from each palm to push Pippa and Shay away from him, both girls stumbling to keep their footing. If Berk was looking for a fight, then he was going to get one.

"What do you want me to do?" Shay asks, getting ready to back up the Light Keeper.

"Nothing," Mercy grunts, pulling more Source to his hands.

The light danced through his veins nearly up to his shoulders. He could feel the stinging in his arm again but needed to focus. He was ready to give Berk, or whoever this was, all he had. All he needed to do was get an opening. If he could render him unconscious or just disarm him, they could collect themselves and move forward. After all his training with Cal, this should be simple.

Using another surge of energy, Mercy knocks Berk back into the tree line, causing him to drop his mace. The Light Keeper pulls a solis orb to his hand and launches it, burning Berk's hand before he could collect his mace. The man lets out a scream of irritation and looks at Mercy with angry eyes. Something wasn't right. Something about this version of Berk didn't feel like the man Mercy grew up with.

"What?" Sylas asks, looking to Shay who had her eyes locked on him.

Glancing to Sylas who had backed away some, he sees his friend ready to charge. As Berk advances on Mercy again, Sylas shoots his bow, skimming Berk's arm. Sylas lets out an irritated groan, dropping his bow and rushing forward, tackling his brother to the ground.

The Light Keeper looks to Shay who appeared to be panicking. What was going on? What was she putting into Sylas's head right now? As Berk squirms, trying to break free, Sylas punches him as hard as he can. The blow causes blood to spew from the man's nose and mouth as Sylas continues to punch him. They all pause as the Nota continues to beat on the man, rendering him unconscious within seconds. Mercy quickly realizes that his friend was showing no signs of stopping and watches as Sylas pulls a dagger from his belt.

"Sylas, stop!" Mercy shouts, rushing toward the pair and wrapping his arms around his friend.

Mercy attempts to pull him off as he feels the blade slice his forearm. Backing away, he watches as Sylas puts the dagger to the man's throat. While this wasn't the first time he had seen Sylas use deadly force, this felt wrong. The man was disarmed and was being dealt with accordingly. Why was Sylas doing this?

He jumps as Pippa rushes toward him and gives a hard kick to Sylas's chest, stunning him for a moment. In addition, Shay snakes her fog around the Nota and pulls him away as hard as she can, causing him to fling backward onto the trail. He hits the dirt path with a thud as Pippa moves toward him, her crescent blade in her hand.

Suddenly the image of Berk's face fades revealing a woman behind the miraged mask. The entire group gawks at the woman who was breathing raggedly. Sylas pants as he gets to his feet, trying to collect himself as he realizes what he just did.

"Sylas, what the hell?" Mercy scowls, looking between his friend and the woman on the ground.

"Sophos... I didn't mean... I lost it," he admits with a tense laugh, looking at his bloodied knuckles on his right hand. "Sorry," he apologizes.

Moving to the woman, Mercy places his hands over her face to heal the injuries his Nota had caused. After a moment the ragged breathing subsides, but she remained unconscious. Mercy looks to Sylas with worry in his eyes. What had he just done? He more than lost it.

"You knew it wasn't Berk?" Pippa questions, looking at Sylas while sheathing her blade.

"First off, my brother was *for* the Tenebris crown, not against it. He'd be celebrating that I screwed Mala's son. Secondly, Shay told me what was going on," Sylas explains, picking up his bow. "This is just a Shadow Keeper with a very nifty set of skills."

"She was sweeping the perimeter," Shay informs them, giving Mercy an apologetic look. "I'm sure they'll realize she's gone soon."

Sylas stares at the woman on the ground with a concerned face. He wasn't sure what had come over him. Part of him felt bad for beating the woman, but the other part felt accomplished. Taking out one member of Malice was some sort of justice for Caligo, but then again, he couldn't place where the emotions really came from.

Tearing his eyes from the unconscious Shadow he looks to Mercy who was studying him with unease. They lock eyes for a few moments as Sylas shifts back into his childish manner.

"You keep giving me that longing gaze, you're going to give Pippa the wrong idea," Sylas winks.

Mercy forces a small laugh and looks from his best friend to Pippa. He glances down to see his Source healing the cut on his arm, Sylas seeming not to worry that he had cut him. Mercy was honestly in shock at what he just saw. He could have handled the woman. He was showing no signs of struggling, yet Sylas intervened. Sure, he was angry, maybe even furious, but he gave Sylas no inclination that he needed to step in.

He shakes the thought trying not to overthink it. Sylas was probably just worried about losing Mercy. Sylas was his Nota and sworn to protect him. He knew about the vision and they both knew that if he lost Mercy, he wasn't going to be able to cope. This meant he was bound to make some moves without thinking them through.

"Let's get out of here before they realize she's missing," Mercy states, locking eyes with Pippa who mirrored his worry.

"The next camp is south," Shay informs them, as they begin to walk.

"We'll grab the horses and get some distance between us before making camp. We can take it on foot in the morning," Mercy instructs. "Give the horses a break and us some time to regroup."

Chapter Twenty-Nine

Sitting in camp, Mercy keeps his eyes on Sylas. While his best friend was no rookie in a fight, seeing him lose control like that was alarming. Sylas was usually the one who calmed Mercy down, not the other way around. If he started to slip, then that put them both in a bad place. Not only because it would worry Mercy, but because of how much he depended on his Nota. With his mind so scattered lately, he needed Sylas to keep him grounded.

Taking his attention to the girls, Mercy notes Pippa bundled up in a blanket sipping some hot tea while Shay was staring at the fire, unsure what to do while they rested. Though they had a strong group, they all seemed to be in their own worlds. Pip still looked upset with Mercy's choice to go on this mission while Shay was just the odd man out. Sylas on the other hand had motives here. Finding Bryer meant finding the person responsible for Cal's death.

"Sylas, check the perimeter with me?" Mercy asks as his best friend looks up.

Sylas nods his head, putting down what he was working on and getting to his feet. "Sure."

"We'll be back in a bit," Mercy states to the women and gestures for Sylas to follow.

The two of them walk in silence for a few minutes, Mercy trying to figure out what he was going to say. He needed to know what Shay put into his friend's head to get the response Sylas had given. Maybe what she had said to him deserved the reaction he gave, or perhaps Shay influenced him. With Mercy's shield gone, Sylas was vulnerable to her peritia.

"Your eyes are still glowing," Sylas states, glancing to Mercy's ghostly irises in the night.

"I know," Mercy sighs. "What happened back there?" he finally asks, folding his arms.

It was getting quite chilly now that the sun had gone down. The autumn air was starting to shift to winter making this venture a cold one. He could tell Sylas ached to turn back to sit by the fire, but they couldn't, not without resolving whatever had happened.

"What do you mean?" Sylas asks.

"You know exactly what I mean," Mercy laughs nervously, coming to a stop. "The woman."

"Shay told me it wasn't Berk, so I took care of it," he explains, pausing beside his friend.

"I had it under control," Mercy stresses, looking at his Nota. "There was no reason for you to step in. She couldn't lay a finger on me."

"You didn't know," Sylas defends.

"I didn't need to," he replies, keeping his tone even. "I had it covered. I disarmed her."

"She was a Keeper of Shadows, Merc. They're never disarmed," Sylas cautions.

"But the only person who injured me in that fight was you," Mercy notes.

"What're you talking about?" Sylas asks, completely dumbfounded by the statement.

Mercy shakes his head in disbelief. Sylas hadn't even realized he cut him. The Nota was usually hyper aware of where Mercy was at all times. The fact he didn't realize he physically injured him was astounding.

"What you did back there... That wasn't okay. That was... I don't know what that was," Mercy speaks.

"They killed Cal," Sylas reminds him.

"That woman had nothing to do with Cal," Mercy clarifies. "This is between me and Bryer, not those rebels. I said I wanted to leave Malice out of this, and you didn't listen to-"

"Stop trying to act like a leader, Merc," Sylas retorts, starting to walk again.

A wave of rage hits Mercy as he grabs Sylas's arm, pulling him to a halt. "Right now, I am," he snaps, his eyes glowing brighter with his anger. "I am your Keeper and the heir to Novus Aitus. With that in mind, I'm telling you what you did back there wasn't okay."

"Are you really pulling rank on me again?" Sylas asks, a shocked smile on his face.

Mercy nods his head. Sylas needed to listen to him. For once, Mercy was the one in charge and Sylas needed to respect that. This wasn't how he was planning to run this assignment, but it seemed no matter what he did no one ever listened to him. Cal, Sylas, and Pippa disregarded him on several occasions since Spheara and he was sick of it.

"Sophos! I miss when you didn't talk," Sylas barks, anger in his eyes.

"And I miss when you weren't such an asshole," Mercy retorts.

His friend laughs in astonishment. Was Mercy really trying to do this right now? "I saved your ass. I always save your ass."

"My ass didn't need to be saved!" Mercy shouts, losing his calm manner. "I don't know what is going on with you but-"

"What's going on with me? What's going on with you? You've been on your high horse since Spheara and

304

now this King shit is going to your head. You're not a leader, Mercy. You never were," Sylas snarls.

"What's wrong with you?" Mercy pleads. "This isn't you, Sylas."

"This is me, Merc!" Sylas retorts, putting his arms out. "Sylas Bellator, the man whose sole purpose in life is to keep you alive. Not just because you're my Keeper but now because you're the damn King of this place, right?"

"By the Elders… Real mature," Mercy snaps, eyeing Sylas. "I'm starting to understand-"

"Understand what?" Sylas asks, folding his arms.

"Never mind," Mercy mumbles.

"That's what I thought," Sylas laughs. "Acting all high and mighty until real shit comes up. You want to talk about someone not acting like themselves, take a look in the mirror, Merc."

"I'm not the one who just tried to kill an innocent person!" Mercy sneers.

"She wasn't innocent!" Sylas yells back.

Mercy was starting to lose his calm again. He couldn't tell where his emotions were in that moment, but they were strong and spiraling. "I get that you're upset over Cal, but that is no reason to-"

"They murdered him!" Sylas reminds him.

"Can you take a breath?" Mercy pleads, trying to lower his voice. "You're acting insane."

"I loved him!" Sylas screams. He pauses a moment glaring at his Keeper. "They didn't just take Cal; they took my future away! They took everything I had left away from me! I loved him, Mercy!"

Taking a deep breath, Mercy tries to cool Sylas down, but his friend had no interest in hearing his words. "I know you did, but-"

"No! That's something you don't understand!" Sylas shouts, frustration flooding his tone and mannerisms. "You never will, Mercy!"

"I do understand," Mercy reasons.

"No, you don't!" Sylas snarls. "You've never been in love in your damn life, Merc. Not once!"

"You can't disregard someone else's life experiences because they aren't the same as yours," Mercy replies, his voice steady.

"Save it," Sylas growls, starting to walk again.

Feeling the rage fuel him, Mercy prods further. "If you loved him then why'd you leave?"

Stopping in his tracks, Sylas's face shifts from anger to grief as he turns to look at Mercy. His expression fills with sadness as he bites the inside of his lip to try and hide his emotions. There was no pulling back now. Mercy had said what he said, and he couldn't take it back.

"If you loved him so damn much, why'd you walk out on him, Sylas?" Mercy asks. "The last conversation I had with him, he wished he were dead. Did you know that?"

"Stop talking," Sylas begs, hatred in his voice.

"I know you, Sylas," Mercy pushes. "I know you were scared that you'd end up disappointing Cal because you think you'll never be good enough for anyone. You've always been like that because that's how you're wired. I guess we can thank your dad for that, huh? For pushing you to be the perfect son. For forcing you to hide behind that bow and arrow and to swallow down your feelings, because being yourself? You'd never be good enough for Ezra."

"Mercy, stop," Sylas warns.

"I get that," Mercy continues. "Cal didn't want you to be perfect though. He loved you just the way you are, Sylas. You don't need your dad's approval anymore. You don't need anyone's approval. Cal loved you for you." As Mercy keeps going, Sylas just looks more and more angry. "You said you needed to work on yourself but in reality, you were just afraid of the life *you* wanted. You were scared of committing to something you wanted for once in your damn life, Sylas. You were the quitter for once."

Seeing the tears dancing in Sylas's eyes, Mercy shakes the anger from his head. What had just come over him? Why did he say that?

"I'm sorry," Mercy pulls back. "I didn't-"

Sylas's eyes shift back to angry at the apology. "You don't know a damn thing you're talking about," he scorns, shaking his head.

Mercy says nothing, but keeps his eyes locked on Sylas. He was starting to think he had made a mistake bringing his friend on this assignment. Everything with Cal was still too fresh and too raw. He was hurting and wasn't thinking rationally. Neither of them were.

"You should go home," Mercy finally speaks.

"What?" Sylas's eyes go big as his expression shows he was upset by the sudden shift.

"Go home," Mercy repeats, keeping his tone confident.

Sylas shakes his head. "You can't-"

"I can. I want you to go home," he reiterates, keeping a firm gaze. "You're off this assignment. You're off all assignments. You can go back to Vermeer, or you can go to Rieka, I don't care, but you need to leave."

"Mercy-"

"Go," he stresses. "Take Maple and go."

"You need me," Sylas stresses, trying to stand his ground.

"I need my best friend, not whoever this is," Mercy clarifies. "Go home."

"You're really doing this?" Sylas asks again.

"Go home!" Mercy repeats, anger seeping into his voice as his irises flare with light.

Sylas keeps his gaze on him for another moment before walking back toward camp. As Sylas turns his back to him, Mercy drops his poise. He closes his eyes and takes a deep breath trying to keep himself calm. He could feel the tinge of another panic attack coming but he needed to swallow it. He takes a deep breath on an eight count and exhales on a seven.

After another moment he heads back into camp to see Sylas already packing his bag as Shay and Pippa watch. Sitting down by the fire, Mercy keeps his head down. The group turns to look at him unsure of the interaction they had just missed. The tension between the Keeper and his Nota was painfully obvious though. After another few minutes, Sylas unties Maple and gets into the saddle.

"You gonna say anything else?" Sylas asks, his tone cold as he glares at his Keeper.

Mercy shakes his head, staring at the fire. He felt bad sending Sylas home, but he needed to. His best friend's mind wasn't where he needed it to be. Then again, neither was his own. As Sylas digs his heels in and gallops away, Mercy closes his eyes. He could only hope Sylas was going home and not trying to take things into his own hands.

The group was quiet for a few more minutes as Mercy sat with his eyes shut, trying to keep himself composed. He could feel his breathing get ragged and his heart begin pounding. Another pain shoots through him, this time rendering a hiss of pain as he rubs his arm. He opens his eyes as Pippa comes up beside him and wraps her blanket over his shoulder to share it with him. He pulls the half over his shoulder and gives her a small smile, blinking away the intense Source gleaming in his eyes to a dull glow.

"You made the right choice," she comforts.

"Doesn't feel like it," Mercy mumbles.

"Sometimes you have to care about someone from a distance," Pippa adds.

"I know," he breathes, closing his eyes again.

"I feel this is my doing," Shay adds, looking from the fire to the pair.

"Sane Sylas wouldn't have reacted like that," Mercy states, shaking his head. "I was stupid for thinking he could handle this. He's too close on this one."

"And you're not?" Shay questions with a raised brow.

"I am, but I can handle my world falling apart a little better than most people. It's kind of been a shit show since I was born," Mercy smirks.

"I fear you are not giving yourself space to grieve," Pippa adds. "Grief is part of mending yourself."

"And you are?" he prods back.

This prompts Pippa to take a sharp breath and look away from him. Grief had never been Mercy's strong suit. He tended to put off his pain until it built to the point of no return, and he could feel that happening again. Maybe that was why his thoughts had been so jumbled lately. Perhaps it was because of his Nota being so out of sorts. This meant there was no one to guide him.

His mind goes to Nex, wondering where she was. Reaching into his pocket he pulls out the small tokens he had from the bird. While Sylas had the ring, he still had the small pinecone, the acorn, and the piece of Cal's prosthetic. Moving them around in his hand, he furrows his brow. He pulls the acorn from the pile and studies it.

"Sander..." he mumbles to himself.

"What about him?" Pippa questions, looking at the items in Mercy's hand.

"He was playing with an acorn in the infirmary when I saw him," Mercy states. "I don't know where he got it from... but he had it." He shows her the items from Nex. "Sylas found these on the windowsill of Cal's office along with a ring... What if she was leaving clues?"

"An acorn and a shortleaf pinecone," Pippa announces, thinking a moment as she takes the pinecone from his hand. "Both of those trees would grow in and around Vicinia." Looking between the two of her comrades, Pippa speaks again. "I know we wanted to run reconnaissance on the Malice camps before making any big moves, but maybe we should head toward Vicinia? If it was Nex leaving these items, perhaps she was trying to guide you there."

"Why though?" Mercy asks, his brow furrowed.

The young woman frowns. If this was Nex leaving clues, what was the birds motive? "Perhaps she wants justice for her Keeper."

"Maybe," he admits. "So, we change our course."

"Is it a good idea to get that close to Malice's center though?" Shay heeds. "Surely if these people are hiding in Vicinia, they would be keeping their strongest Keepers there to ward off any threats from the Sentry Guard. We could be walking Mercy into a bloodbath."

"Why do they want me dead if they want someone who isn't a Tenebris on the throne?" Mercy sighs, looking to her.

"You've been at the side of a Tenebris since you emerged from hiding, they fear you're immoral as well," Shay clarifies.

"Cal wasn't immoral," Mercy defends.

"But they believe he was," Shay adds, gesturing slightly with her hands. "When people look at someone like Mala Tenebris, they see a blazing fire, an inferno that has left nothing but destruction in its wake. While Caligo was on the inside trying to put the blaze out, the smoke was shrouding him. He appeared to become part of the fuel that powered the firestorm in their eyes. As far as Novus Aitus is concerned, he aided in making the fire burn brighter. The blaze that was Mala is over, but they still see the disasters she caused. Being focused on the glowing embers and ash is making it difficult for them to see that Caligo is the one who extinguished the blaze."

"And they think I'm going to be another fire," Mercy nods in understanding.

"You won't be," Pippa comforts, nudging him softly with a smile.

"Mala Tenebris ruled her people by instilling fear into their hearts, not just of her, but of her name," Shay explains. "That name holds meaning, and not a good one for most. Think back to before you met Caligo. You feared his ruling just as much as Mala, am I correct?"

Mercy lightly nods his head. He didn't realize how truly good Cal was until he got the opportunity to know him. The compassion and loyalty Cal had for those he cared for, and their people was so clear to him, that the idea of others not seeing it seemed strange. Before they had spoken on the edge of the Source Temple grounds, he was afraid of Cal. He was more than afraid. Not because of the fact he was a Shadow Keeper, but because he was a Tenebris.

"In time, he may have been able to prove his divergence from the name, but now, Tenebris is still tainted. You need to show the people you are different," Shay instructs. "Show them that you weren't close to the Tenebris name because Caligo was your Alia, but because he was a good person."

"How though?" Mercy asks.

"By doing exactly as Cal wanted," Pippa states. "Ending the bloodshed without adding to it."

Chapter Thirty

Mercy wasn't sure what he was expecting, but it certainly wasn't to be halted at the Vicinian border crossing. Then again, he did have a criminal with him and had abruptly left the capital after sending word of him taking over the monarchy. This surely left a sour taste in the mouth of the National Council.

A man leaves Mercy to wait in a small room. They had separated him from the others, and it was making him anxious. The longer they sat at the border, the bigger the threat they had of Malice catching onto them. He jumps as the door opens again and a woman enters. She was older than him but still young. Her hair was pulled up into a bun and she looked tired. He nods to her as she moves across the room to the table in front of him with a tablet in her hands. She was an Aitian, but due to her brown eyes, was most likely a mutt.

"Mercy Validus," she smiles. He nods, unsure what the interaction was going to be. "My name is Nuwa. My daughter is a big fan, an aspiring young Light Keeper herself," she gleams, giving him a small bow with her thumb to her palm. He nods again in response with a soft smile. "I heard you don't speak much, so I'll do the talking."

"Okay," he agrees, folding his arms.

"The National Council was happy to hear you showed up at our border station," she shares, taking a seat across from him at the table. "I hear you're going to be our new monarch."

"Uh, yeah," he confirms.

"That's exciting," she smiles again. "Novus Aitus is truly blessed by the Elders for your decision." She waits for a response but gets nothing in return. "You're probably wondering why we're detaining you, Your Grace."

"Please, just call me Mercy," he instructs, trying to keep his tone light.

"Yes," she laughs. "Right. Mercy. You're probably wondering why we're detaining you, *Mercy*."

"I'm assuming it's because I have Shay Tract," he admits. "I have the proper documents and-"

"Actually no," she informs him as he raises a brow. "The National Council put a Missing Persons Alert out on you, sir. They've been searching for you for days."

"An MPA? Really?" he asks with a furrowed brow.

She nods with a regretful expression. "They are sending a Captain Skerrick to collect you. He was heading the team searching near our border station. He should be here within the hour."

"Collect me?" he questions.

She nods her head again as he lets out a sigh. Why was he even surprised? The National Council was strict with Cal, why would they be any different with him? On the other hand, he was going to be the King soon, so couldn't he just refuse to stay and wait for Zero?

"Can't you just let us go?" he asks.

"I apologize, Mercy," she admits, getting to her feet. "Unfortunately, since you aren't officially King of Novus Aitus, my hands are tied. I can't go against the

National Council. This would be an entirely different discussion if you were already crowned."

He lets out another heavy sigh. This was stupid. They were so close to Vicinia and finding Bryer. Nuwa heads toward the door and pauses to look at him.

"Again, I'm very sorry," she reiterates.

As soon as she leaves the room, he lets out a frustrated scream. He was about to lose his cool again and he could feel it. He gets to his feet and kicks over his chair and lets out another shout. They were so close to finding Bryer, yet so far. He begins to pace trying to come up with another plan. As soon as Zero got there they were going to be ushered back to the capital and lose any chance they had of sneaking up on Malice.

Knowing he needed to calm down, he takes a deep breath and picks the chair back up. He sits at the table again, leaning his head on the top of it, trying to steady his breathing. If Zero was going to be there within the hour, he wasn't sure what else he could do.

After sitting at the table for nearly 45 minutes, there's another knock at the door. Mercy doesn't react, keeping his head down as someone enters the room.

"Validus," he hears Zero's voice as the chair in front of him moves and the man takes a seat.

With a heavy exhale, Mercy lifts his head and looks at the other Light Keeper with tired eyes. For once the intimidating man seemed somewhat relaxed. While he was still in all black, his dark shirt had the Light Keeper rune embroidered on right side of his chest. Since Spheara, Keepers proudly wore their symbols whenever they could. Well, everyone except Mercy.

"How are you?" Mercy questions, trying to make small talk.

"Doing a hell of a lot worse now that I'm talking to you," Zero retorts, taking in Mercy for a moment. "Accepting the crown and then running off with a war

314

criminal and Master Novi's daughter. That's ballsy of you, Validus," he smirks. "Honestly, I didn't think you had it in you."

"I'm full of surprises," Mercy mumbles, sarcasm coming through.

"What's your angle anyway?" Zero asks, leaning forward. "You're not the kind to veer off a set path."

"I have my reasoning," he states, folding his arms.

"A death wish maybe?" Zero prods, mirroring the gesture. "Well, the NC isn't exactly happy with their new leader's behavior."

"Yeah," Mercy nods.

"Novus Aitus saw you taking over the crown as a step up from Cal," Zero continues. "If I were them, I probably would too. Cal isn't the most likeable of people I've come across."

"If you didn't like Cal, then why did you work for him?" Mercy pries with a raised brow.

"I want the system to change," Zero shrugs, "and usually to change the infrastructure of a government you have to become a part of it."

The two lock eyes as a small smile comes to Zero's face. While most would describe Mercy as quiet and timid, he was seeming to be anything but. He studies Mercy another moment as an awkward silence takes over and a staring contest ensues. Zero holds his smirk as he stares Mercy down, Mercy beginning to fidget.

There was always something about Zero that Mercy disliked. He wasn't sure if it was his overall unapproachable demeanor or maybe a nagging from the Elders, but the man in front of him put him on edge. Though Sylas and Cal seemed to have faith in him, it was difficult for Mercy to see anything other than a snarky asshole.

315

"I have it in my right mind to take you back to Ozra and have you face the National Council," Zero finally speaks, getting to his feet.

"You do that, and Malice will kill me," Mercy warns. "They already killed Cal; they'll take me out next."

"Damn, and here I was hoping I'd be next on their hit list," Zero shoots back, leaning his hands on the table. "Lucky for you, I don't have my right mind today," he admits with a smile. "At first, I was a bit surprised when Cal went over the contingency plan with me. I didn't see you as the type to take the lead. You're a hot mess, Validus."

"You knew about it?" Mercy asks, his brows raised.

"I did," Zero nods. "Caligo and I were closer than he let on."

"How so?" Mercy questions.

"Doesn't matter," Zero deflects. "What do you say I let you cross into Vicinia and play out whatever little plan you have with Miss Dror and Shay, on one condition."

Not sure what Zero could want, skepticism shows through Mercy's expression. What could this Light Keeper want out of him in exchange for a passage over the border? Did Zero even have the power to make that choice to begin with?

"What's that?" Mercy asks.

"I supervise," Zero suggests.

Furrowing his brow, Mercy thinks over the statement. The idea of having Zero along for this mission wasn't one he was a fan of. He didn't know if he could trust him. Cal was worried about who he could and couldn't trust after he took over, so the fact Zero had his faith made him open to the idea. The man looking back at him also had enough regard from Cal to watch over the one person his Alia valued the most. Sylas.

"If you're going after Bryer, and from what I gather you are, the Light Source works much better against those

316

obscurums than the Shadow. Sure, you have Shay to help you, but another Light Keeper, one who *knows* what he's doing and has faced these things before, could be useful," Zero adds to his offer with a sly smirk.

"You were pretty useless at the Mors River," Mercy prompts him.

"But now we know how to kill these bastards thanks to you and Cal," he reminds.

"Zero-"

"I'm not done," he snaps. "I might have a death wish, Validus, but not before I prove myself," Zero adds. "I owe something to every single Keeper killed by Mala. I even owe you and your brother."

"You don't owe me anything," Mercy disagrees.

"But I do," Zero corrects. "I rotted in that prison for twelve years. I was used as a lab rat and my family thought I was dead. If it weren't for you, I'd be in a very different place right now. I can help you."

If they went head on with an obscurum, Mercy would be on his own until Shay could get into Iana's head, if she even could. Zero also knew Mercy hadn't mastered his Source. While Novi and Zero had been working with him to help learn his magic, he still lacked the skills needed to win a true battle. He was sloppy and inexperienced, and it showed when he was under pressure.

"I know you're going after Malice," Zero informs. "Whether that's to avenge Cal or save your own ass... I'm in this."

"You'd go into this blind?" Mercy asks.

"For you? Sure," Zero assures.

"What if I don't trust you?" Mercy tests.

"That's fine," Zero admits, "but Caligo and Sylas do. Maybe your Nota and I don't always see eye to eye, but he trusts me with his life."

"And if I don't agree to this?" Mercy continues.

"Then I walk out of this room, call Ozra, and escort you and your friends back to the capital," he states with confidence. "Or you can suck it up, let me second you on this, and I walk out of this room and call Ozra saying you escaped your detention and I'm pursuing you into Vicinia. Adding that I don't need back up, because I can handle a novice Light Keeper just fine on my own."

Taking a sharp breath, Mercy pauses a moment to think this through. They were down a man after he sent Sylas home and having another Light Keeper could be beneficial. He also didn't have much of a choice. Either he allowed Zero to join them, or the assignment was off.

"What's it gonna be, Validus?" Zero tests. "I don't have all day."

Mercy nods his head. "Fine."

Chapter Thirty-One

Standing outside the camp, Mercy pauses for Shay to scan the Malice member's minds. The four of them were hiding within the trees just outside the camp waiting for the right time. Examining the area, there had to be at least fifty people moving around the camp with various tents and wooden structures of all shapes and sizes. In that moment it was clear that the colors of Malice were a dark blue and a pale yellow. It seemed every building and member were sporting the colors in some fashion.

"Bryer and Iana are in there," Shay confirms, her eyes going back to their normal slate hue. "I found Iana no problem. Bad news though, Bryer has been touched by the Light Source."

"Well, that makes this a little more difficult," Zero admits with a groan. "I didn't sign up to fight another Light Keeper."

"You didn't need to come," Mercy retorts.

Glancing to Zero, Mercy notes the faint glow in his eyes. The Keeper must have been on edge and his Source was reacting to the danger they were about to go into. Mercy's own eyes would probably be showing his anxiety if they hadn't been glowing every day since losing Cal to begin with.

"They also have prisoners here," Shay adds, her eyes showing hurt. "What they are planning to do with them doesn't seem clear to anyone here. In fact, most of Malice's intentions are shrouded. Bryer seems to be keeping his plans close to the cuff. This is not good."

"What's our move?" Zero asks, his hand going to the handle of his mace.

"I want to talk to them," Mercy admits.

"You're joking," Zero states in shock. "Are we just planning to walk in there and ask them how their day's going? Maybe get a cup of coffee? See if they'd be up for a game of cards?"

"Something like that," Mercy nods, his face serious.

Pippa, Zero, and Shay all look at him in confusion. Did he really want to speak with these people? With their combined abilities they could easily get the abducted Shadows out and flee back to Ozra, but he wanted to speak with them?

"You really do have a death wish," Zero laughs.

"My father was one to use his words before force," Mercy justifies. "These people already know we have power so let's show them we know how to negotiate too. We go in attempting to reason with them, we may have a better chance of shutting this whole thing down."

"I don't think they're interested in sitting around a fire singing folk songs, Validus," Zero snaps. "They're holding people hostage."

"We don't know that," Mercy glares. "These people aren't looking to start a war, Zero. They're looking to end one, just like we are."

With that, Mercy breaks through the trees and enters the camp. His comrades pause a moment in shock before moving forward with him. Zero, Shay, and Pippa all keep their weapons at the ready, Zero's eyes lighting up even more as Shay's go dark. Having a fully realized Shadow Keeper, a Master Light Keeper, and a Supra meant they had the fire power to show themselves here.

As they move forward, it doesn't take long for them to gain attention. Not only because a pair of Light Keepers were walking through the camp, but the most famous one was leading the pack. Mercy's face was one of the most recognizable ones on the planet at this point. Every single person in that camp knew exactly who he was.

Within the camp, Cal still sat in his tent, tied to his post. He was breathing shallow and shivering. He had been wracked with chills off and on for the last two days while sweating profusely. The gash on his side had no doubt become infected and it was making staying awake almost impossible. He wasn't even sure how much longer he was going to be able to hold on and his captors didn't seem to care.

Sitting up slightly, he adjusts his hands. He still wore the bracers Mercy had made him, both fashioned to conceal a blade. He was thankful Bryer hadn't taken a closer look at them before tying him up. He should have used them to try and escape weeks ago, but the opportunity never arose. How long had he even been here anyway?

He perks up at a commotion outside as someone rushes in. He looks up, his neck aching, as the guard that was stationed outside his tent readies himself. Trying to look around him through the small opening, Cal quickly gives up. Leaning over made his entire body ache and his chest feel tight.

Letting his neck go slack, he closes his eyes when he hears someone scream a familiar name. "Validus is here!"

His eyes shoot to the entrance again. Was Mercy actually here? Had his Alia found him?

"Ready for the Sentry!" another voice screams from outside.

321

Hearing the shuffling behind him, the guard turns to Cal and scowls. He keeps his body limp, trying not to show his interest in what was happening. If Mercy was out there, he had a chance. All he had to do was get Mercy to realize where he was.

Adjusting his hands, he caresses his thumb over the blade's trigger. He only had one shot at this. If he didn't cut the ties and disarm this guard, he was dead, whether Mercy was here or not. Taking a deep breath, he feels his heart begin to race. It didn't even matter if he lived through today, the odds of him dying were likely regardless. These people didn't care about what happened to him. If he died in this camp no one would be any the wiser.

He closes his eyes and listens carefully as the commotion outside continues. It was now or never. Looking up to the man with determination, he hits the bracer's trigger, the blade quickly coming out and cutting his opposite hand. He stays silent through the pain as the guard looks to him in concern at the sound, unsure what it was. Moving his hands carefully Cal cuts the ties between his wrists and waits for the guard to turn back around.

With a deep breath, his adrenaline kicking in, Caligo gets to his knees and throws himself into the man's legs. Cal lets out a groan as he falls to the ground, the sudden movement sending shooting pains through his body. He quickly collects himself through the aching and gets back on task. He launches the other blade out and quickly punches the man in the back, the blade piercing through his body as blood began to soak the floor.

Pausing to catch his breath, Cal moves to the opening of the tent on all fours, his knees echoing the same ache as the rest of his body. There was never a moment he wished he had his legs more than he did right now, not that he'd even be able to stand at this point. Nevertheless, he was a force to be reckoned with and he wasn't about to let the inconvenience stop him from getting Mercy's attention.

It didn't take him long to spot Mercy and Zero's snowy hair in the crowd heading through the camp with Iana and Bryer leading the way. Mercy's Light Keeper suit gleamed in the sunlight with Zero, Pippa, and Shay right at his heels. While he had left the exue rune, his Source still wasn't coming to him. It felt like the more he attempted to call his Source the further away it became.

"Mercy!" he finally screams.

Hearing his name, Mercy stops in his tracks and turns quickly to scan the camp. He knew that voice. His eyes begin to blaze at the familiar sensation of Caligo's Source. The hole in his chest that had been there for weeks quickly began to fill as he lets out a shocked gasp. What was this? Though it felt weak and distant, Cal's Source was there. Suddenly the hallow feeling he had been so focused on the last month or so was starting to ease.

"Mercy!" the voice cries out again.

Hearing his name, the rest of the group comes to a halt, all recognizing the voice. Examining the camp, they see a few people moving toward a specific tent quickly, most likely to silence the prisoner who had escaped.

"Cal," Mercy mumbles, his feet moving the direction of the calls.

"Validus!" Bryer shouts, trying to regain the Light Keeper's attention.

Ignoring Bryer and powering up, Mercy walks forward and aims his palm at the group surrounding the escapee. Without saying a word, he shoots a blast of energy toward them, the wave of light tossing the Malice members back with force. This gains the attention of more members but causes most to flee the scene once they saw who was causing the ruckus.

As the crowd clears, Mercy spots him. He sees Cal. The reveal causes the rest of his group to get their feet moving toward him as Bryer and Iana begin to panic. A large part of the plan hung on Mercy believing the King of Novus Aitus was dead.

"By the Elders..." Mercy mutters, his walk quickly turning to a run.

"Shit," Zero mumbles, his pace also shifting to a run at the sight of the King.

Mercy throws a shield up over Cal to protect him from the rebels coming toward him. He grows it from a few inches above him to several feet, forcing the remaining members away from his dear friend. He watches as Cal collapses from his knees to the ground.

Caligo looked bad. Mercy could tell his friend had been hurt at some point and was given no medical care causing him to deteriorate over the last several weeks. He was thin and looked horrific. He hardly even looked like himself. Though he still seemed to have a connection to his Shadow Source, it was weak. Mercy wasn't sure why though. He had never felt such a dull energy from his Alia before.

Approaching Cal, Mercy drops to his knees beside him. It doesn't take him long to register the intense trembling. As soon as he touches him, he feels the fever wracking Cal's body. He gets his Alia to a sitting position and looks him over. This was Cal, but he was close to death. Caked in mud from weeks ago with an inflamed and clearly infected wound on his side, Cal was in bad shape. They needed to get him out of here. Mercy looks up as the rest of the group rushes over, dropping a portion of the shield to let them in.

"Help me," Cal begs, his voice small.

"That's why I'm here," Mercy whispers, looking to Zero with worry.

Hearing Caligo plead for help was painful. Cal was strong and fierce and could take down any enemy, yet here he was weak and unable to defend himself. Anger comes through the Light Keeper as searing pain shoots through

324

him. Zero puts his hand over the inflamed wound on Cal's side and quickly heals it. While healing took care of the source of infection, it wasn't going to stop the aftermath. The act does little to ease the trembling or fever.

"He needs a medic," Pippa announces.

Cal clutches Mercy's arm as tightly as he can, bringing his attention to the blood seeping from his hand. "Where's Sy?" Cal asks in a soft voice.

"He's safe," Mercy assures. "He's at home. He's alright. I promise."

Cal gives a small nod of the head, dropping his hand from Mercy. Reaching out, Zero heals the cut and begins to unlatch the bracers on Cal's arms to free him of the blades. Having Zero there suddenly felt like a blessing. Mercy was in shock and without Zero he wasn't sure Cal would have been taken care of this quickly.

"What did they do to you?" Mercy asks, trying to keep himself together.

He watches his Alia shake his head and close his eyes slowly. With Mercy and Zero there, Cal could finally let his guard down. Mercy exchanges a look with Pippa who appeared close to tears herself. They couldn't even be happy they found Cal because of the condition he was in. Even though he was breathing, he was right on death's door. Taking his eyes back to Cal, Mercy shudders. He could see how shallow Caligo's breathing was, the adrenaline from whatever he had just done wearing off quickly.

"Hey, Cal," Mercy mutters, lightly tapping his face. "I need you to stay awake. Sylas is gonna kill both of us if you die twice."

With no response, Mercy begins to shake with anger. Had they really found Cal just for him to die again?

"How did he escape?" Bryer shouts, approaching Mercy and his friends as a Malice member comes out of the tent behind the group.

"The guard is dead," the member announces, squeezing past Mercy's shield.

The fact Cal was able to get this far in the shape he was in was impressive. At least he hadn't lost his fighting spirit. Taking his eyes from Cal to Bryer, Mercy suddenly couldn't control his rage. Compared to this, killing Cal at the river looked humane.

He shifts Cal over to Pippa and Zero and gets to his feet. Keeping the shield on his comrades he leaves the protection and moves toward Bryer. With every step his Source grew more and more within him. He was angry and this time he knew why. These people didn't deserve a negotiation nor to have their voices heard. As he told Pippa weeks ago, people who hurt his family couldn't be reasoned with.

"What did you do to him!?" he screams at Bryer. "What did you do!?"

This causes Bryer to pause and take a few steps back. While Malice had been looking to get Mercy's full power to show, he was afraid of it. Having the Light Keeper use it on him was not part of his plan.

"I was simply dealing with a murderer how they are meant to be dealt with," Bryer explains with a small smirk. "King Caligo has committed acts against the balance and needs to be punished. He is a monster."

The words cause Mercy to halt. The power surging through him was causing the wind around him to pick up and his hair to blow back. He couldn't remember the last time he was this furious. He may have never been this angry in his life. This man let him believe Caligo was dead for weeks and during that time was slowly letting him waste away. This man had forced a wall between him and his best friend. This man had made Sylas believe the love of his life was gone forever. This man caused Pippa to believe her best friend was gone forever.

"The only monster I see here is you," Mercy snarls, raising his palm to Bryer.

"Mercy, don't!" he hears Pippa scream from behind him.

His expression falters at her words. Every part of him was willing to give up his Source to kill this man, but he wasn't sure why. Out of everything that had happened to him, why was he suddenly feeling pushed to take a life? Looking back at Cal, he sours his face. What Bryer had done to his Alia was horrific. It was a crime against the balance he was meant to be protecting.

"The Tenebris reign needs to end," Bryer states. "It will end with him."

"Caligo is not Mala!" Mercy barks, trying to regulate his breathing. "Cal is not his mistakes. He is not Mala's or Prima's terrible acts. What he is, is the reason you can stand here today a free man. He's the reason I'm free. He saved every single Keeper, human, and mutt and you still want to punish him based on a last name! A name that he hates just as much as you do!"

Bryer looks at him, not saying a word with a sly grin. Mercy's eyes go to Iana who was beginning to power up. Letting out an annoyed growl he aims his palm to her and shoots a solis orb into her chest. She flings back into the tent behind her, disappearing within the fabric. He refocuses on Bryer and scowls.

"I came here today to reason with you. I didn't bring an army. In fact, the National Council has no idea where I am right now. I did that to keep you and your rebels safe, but I'm starting to see that was stupid," Mercy addresses. "You people want me to prove I'm not a Tenebris, yet you're doing exactly what Mala Tenebris did all her years reigning over this planet. You are torturing someone based on something they can NOT control."

"The Tenebris reign is over," Bryer announces again, cockiness in his tone.

327

"Then welcome to Mercy's reign," he snarls. "Maybe Cal didn't see you as a threat, but I do, and I will end you, Bryer. I will end you and this entire organization."

"Mercy, let's go!" Shay shouts.

"Cal has done nothing but try and help you and our people since he took the throne, and this is how you repay him?" Mercy continues. "You're no better than that tyrant. Actually, you're worse than her. I'm willing to kill you for what you did to him. Do you understand that?"

"Mercy!" Pippa shouts.

Keeping his palm aimed at Bryer, Mercy begins to back away toward his comrades. He glances back to see Zero had gotten Cal on his back, his Alia completely unconscious. Mercy takes one last shuddering breath before dropping his hand and entering his shield. Morphing the structure with his group into a cloak, they quickly leave the camp with Cal in tow. They would have to send the Sentry to raid the camp for any other captives later. Right now, their goal was to get Cal the medical attention he needed.

Chapter Thirty-Two

Moving away from the small stable at the side of Mercy's house, Sylas walks to the porch holding a large bag close to his side and his bow on his back. He had been at his cabin in Vermeer for the last couple of weeks and the quietness was starting to wear on him. He honestly welcomed the summons to Rieka. He had to admit he was surprised to hear Mercy wanted him for an assignment this soon and was even more surprised the summons was to Rieka and not the capital.

He pauses on the porch for a moment. Was he ready to face Mercy again? The last time they had spoken had gotten intense. His best friend had said some hurtful things, but perhaps it was time to move past being friends with Mercy and to accept his role as his Nota. Maybe friendship wasn't what he was meant to have with his Keeper anymore. He couldn't simply walk away from him though. The call to Mercy had only gotten stronger since his friend began to unlock his true abilities.

He looks down at the pendant Mercy had made for him. He hadn't taken it off since he had been gifted it. Even if Mercy had said those hurtful things, it was clear he still cared. If he didn't, he wouldn't have made such a kind gesture. At the end of the day, he knew he wasn't ready to go on that mission. Losing Cal was too fresh. What he had done was out of line and his best friend was only trying to look out for him. Mercy didn't want him to do anything he was going to regret.

With a heavy sigh he pushes the door open and enters the house. Closing the door behind him, he turns to see someone sitting on the couch writing in a book. He freezes at the sight.

"Cal?" he whispers, his brow wrinkled in confusion.

The young man looks up at him and gives a small wave. Sylas laughs in disbelief as Cal closes his sketchbook and gives a broken smile. He was sitting with his legs pulled up on the couch and was wearing a pair of pajamas, looking like he had been there for the night. The Shadow looked thinner and frailer than usual and something about him echoed the broken pieces Sylas had worked so hard to put back together.

"Are you really Cal?" Sylas asks in shock. "This isn't Shay's Shadow magic, is it?"

Cal shakes his head and speaks, his voice sounding weak. "Mercy figured you would not be here for at least another day or so."

Dropping his bag and bow to the floor, Sylas rushes toward him. Hearing his voice was enough to confirm it was really him. He stumbles over the low table in front of the couch, but kicks it out of the way and falls to his knees, wrapping his arms around Cal. The enthusiasm in the embrace catches Caligo off guard, but he welcomes it, tightly wrapping his arms around Sylas in return. Sylas holds him for several minutes, afraid that if he let him go, he'd disappear again. Cal was alive and he was right in front of him.

Finally pulling away, Sylas takes Cal's face between his hands and studies his features carefully. He looked exhausted and thin, his undercut had started to grow out as well, but this was Cal. He was alive and he was sitting in Mercy's living room, drawing in his sketchbook like he had seen him do dozens of times.

"But how? The river- I saw-" Sylas stammers in complete disbelief.

Seeing Sylas's face causes Cal to well up. The last few weeks all he had thought about was Sylas and how he had been affected by his presumed death. His heart ached at the idea of Sylas mourning him. One of the only things that kept him going was the idea of getting to see Sylas again. If it wasn't for him, he wasn't sure he would have made it to the rescue. He might have given up.

"Hello," Cal smiles softly, trying to hold back the tears even as they were already escaping. "Where'd all your hair go?" he asks, running his fingers over the buzz cut.

"I can grow it back. It'll all grow it all back. Is this really you?" Sylas questions, brushing Cal's curls away.

As Cal nods his head, Sylas goes in and hugs him again. Caligo was supposed to be dead. They had an eloium for him. They mourned him. Mercy's coronation date was announced just days ago. Yet here Cal was sitting on Mercy's couch, drawing in his sketchbook like he had never left. How was this possible?

"How?" Sylas asks pulling away again. "Actually, I don't care. I really don't care," he laughs, kissing him.

Cal welcomes the kiss, tears still flowing. He lets himself take a moment to just be content. It had never been clearer to him than it was in that moment that Sylas was his safe place. Being with him again made him feel at ease. As long as Sylas was in that room, he could let his guard down. Pulling away, Sylas continues to keep his hands on Cal's cheeks and studies his features once more.

"I am never letting you go ever again," Sylas warns, wiping the tears from Caligo's face. "Never. Not once. You are stuck with me until you actually die. In fact, we're dying together."

"Okay," Cal nods, letting a small laugh escape.

"It's really you," Sylas breathes, wrapping his arms around him again. "By the Elders, it's really you. But how?"

"I have told you all I am too stubborn to die," Cal retorts.

"And Mercy?" Sylas asks, pulling away, but keeping a gentle hand on Caligo's chin.

"He is trying to get me some better legs," Cal shares with a defeated smile.

"As he should be, giving you a leg to stand on and all that," Sylas nods falling into his puns, taking his hands from Cal's face to grab his hand. "Do you need anything? I can get Charlyn, or I can get it myself. Whatever you want-"

"I'm fine now, Sy," Cal assures.

"I am so confused right now, but I don't even care," Sylas laughs, moving his hands back to Cal's face. "I thought you were gone, Cal."

Cal begins to shake, his face quickly going from joyful tears to sad. Sylas shouldn't even have been happy to see him, he had killed his family. Worry hits Sylas as Cal reaches for another embrace. While seeing Sylas filled him with hatred for himself, he also knew he was the only one who could give him comfort.

Readily giving into the hug, Sylas feels sobs wrack Cal. Shushing him, the Nota realizes the tears weren't because he was reunited with him, but from something else. Cal was uneasy or maybe afraid. He feels Caligo grip him tightly, trying to get every ounce of comfort he could from him.

He was terrified in that tent and even seeing Mercy didn't feel like a rescue. When he saw Mercy's face, he was thankful he'd survive to see Sylas, but not that he'd continue to live. All he could think about was the pain he had caused so many and how his existence still filled people with fear. The image of him slaughtering their friends and family was still engrained in their minds. No matter what he did he was always going to be the Prince of Death.

"I got you," Sylas comforts. "You're safe. What can I do?"

He feels Cal shake his head as he buries his face in Sylas's shirt. The Shadow felt like he had been through 100 wars and lost every single one. His whole body ached, he felt scared and vulnerable. Even though Mercy and Doctor Willa had tried to heal him, there was still an ache in his joints that was going to require months of therapy and patience. It also seemed like the infection was still wracking his body, even though he had undergone the intense antibiotics for over a week to treat it. Not to mention the fact that his Source still hadn't returned to him. He didn't even want his Source back. With his Source came a bigger emptiness about losing Nex than he already felt.

The only reason he was in Rieka was to keep him protected and out of Bryer's hands until they could figure things out. He wasn't going to take his place as ruler again, nor was he going to be involved in any battles. He was useless and now considered himself dead weight going into the war with Malice.

Keeping Cal in his arms, Sylas maneuvers himself onto the sofa beside him. He keeps his arms wrapped around him as Cal keeps his face buried in his chest. What had they done to him? Caligo had been through a lot, but Sylas had never seen him like this. He was completely shattered, and his spirit was broken. No matter what he had been through in the past, Cal had always stayed strong, even if he was just putting on a mask to appear that way. Now though, his entire persona felt different.

"I got you," Sylas whispers, giving him a soft kiss on the head. "Just try to breathe. Can you do that?"

He shudders with sympathy as Cal lets out a scream into his chest. He could feel the pain resonate through his entire body as Cal continued to break down in his arms. This was pain Sylas had never seen before. This was years of agony built up.

"Breathe, love," he instructs.

"I can't," Cal gasps into his chest.

Holding him tighter, Sylas squeezes his eyes shut. He felt helpless in that moment. What could he even do?

The two sit on the couch as Cal continues to break down. Even Charlyn peaked in from the other room to check on the pair, Sylas shooing her away. At this point, Sylas didn't even feel like he was comforting him, he was just there. There was no comforting this.

As Cal begins to calm down and his gasps slow, Sylas kisses his head again. "Try to breathe," he repeats, his voice soft. "Just try to breathe."

He feels Cal nod as he pulls away taking a few ragged breaths. He looks at Sylas's face and frowns. Looking at him, Cal begins to break again. After everything he had done to Sylas, this man was still sitting here trying to offer him some kind of security.

"I killed your family," Cal gets out.

"Don't worry about it," Sylas whispers, wiping the tears from Cal's eyes.

"I hurt you," he stresses.

"No, you didn't," Sylas denies.

"I did," Cal insists. "You said you hated me. That day we broke up, you said-"

"I lied," Sylas admits. "I say stupid shit when I'm upset, you know that. I could never hate you. If you hurt me in a way that was unforgivable, I wouldn't be sitting here right now," Sylas explains, pulling him back to his chest.

Cal closes his eyes, letting his head rest on Sylas's chest. He didn't believe him, but right now he just wanted to sit there. He just wanted to be held by the person he knew cared for him; no strings attached. Sylas had always seen him as a good person, no matter what he had done in the past. From the day he met Sylas all he saw was good.

Chapter Thirty-Three

Closing the door behind him, Mercy scans the living room. The girls were still at school, so the house felt quiet. He carried a new pair of Cal's prosthetics in his arms, ready to get his Alia back on his feet. With the amount of prosthetics he and Cal went through, he always had custom sockets on hand at the shop. He had thought about throwing them out weeks ago but was now relieved he hadn't.

Looking into the room, he frowns. Cal wasn't on the couch anymore. Where had he gone? His stomach drops as he looks around. He had to still be in the house, the Sentry Guard were outside with no indication anyone had entered his home that wasn't supposed to be there.

"Char!" he shouts, hoping his housekeeper would have an answer.

Moving forward, he trips over something. Steadying himself, he looks down and recognizes the large leather bag and bow at his feet as Sylas's. It was the bag his best friend used every time he had come to Rieka for a visit. This meant he must have gotten the message and left much quicker than anticipated. Picking up the bow, Mercy places it by the door and shoves the bag to the side with his foot.

The summons to Rieka didn't give any reason why, the National Council wanting to keep Cal's survival and whereabouts unknown. The only people aware the monarch was alive were the members of the NC, a few medical personnel, and those who were with him when he was located. He wasn't sure why the Council wanted to keep this under wraps, but he wasn't about to question them after his last escapade.

He sees Charlyn peak in from the kitchen. She puts a finger to her lips and points down the hall toward one of the guest rooms. Mercy nods his head as she goes back into the kitchen. Moving slowly down the hall, he walks past his office as Soot runs up behind him and begins to weave between his legs. He lightly scoots her out of the way with his foot and watches her jump onto a cat tree and scale to walk above him on the catwalk. Looking to the downstairs guest room, he could see the door was slightly ajar.

Approaching it, he pushes it open lightly and spots both Sylas and Cal lying in bed under the blankets. He breathes a sigh of relief seeing the pair. Looking at the two he notes both had their eyes closed. Cal was curled up against Sylas, his arm wrapped around him. Mercy smiles softly, happy to see their reunion went well. Setting the prosthetics against the wall by the door he turns to leave.

"Merc," he hears Sylas whisper.

Pausing, he looks back into the room as Sylas gestures for him to come closer. Mercy was a bit nervous to talk to him again, but that seemed to be the theme for the pair the last six weeks or so.

"You got him to sleep," Mercy mutters, walking over to the bed. "I don't think he's slept much since we found him."

"Took some time, but I did," Sylas whispers back. "What happened? Where was he?"

"A Malice camp in Vicinia," Mercy explains. "He was in rough shape when we found him. He was

338

unconscious by the time we got him to the border to call for emergency medical back to Ozra."

"By the Elders…" Sylas mumbles.

"We decided I should bring him here. Malice won't expect him to be anywhere other than the capital," Mercy continues.

"You think they're looking for him?" Sylas questions.

Mercy shrugs. "We're going after them in full force. We've already raided the camp he was in and rescued about a dozen Shadow Keepers, all of them with the same rune on their chest that Sander had."

"So what? They're making an obscurum army?" Sylas interrogates, keeping his voice low.

"Maybe," Mercy sighs, folding his arms and going to lean on the wall. "They had one on Cal too."

"What?" Sylas asks, his eyes darting to Caligo.

"For whatever reason, it didn't work," Mercy assures. "Willa couldn't find anything pointing to him being used to fuel one like Sander and Cal isn't talking."

"Sophos," Sylas breathes.

"Has he said anything to you?" Mercy questions with a raised brow, rubbing his shoulder.

"In all honesty… He's mostly just cried," his friend explains with a heavy exhale, looking back at Mercy. "I've never seen him like this."

Mercy nods in understanding and looks to the floor in defeat. "I don't know what they did to him, Sylas, but he needs you right now."

"Well, I'm not going anywhere," Sylas replies with a soft smile, furrowing his brow at Mercy's incessant rubbing of his shoulder. "What happened to your arm?"

"Just irritated. Everything's still sore from my Source being powered up while Cal was gone," he admits, shaking his head and dropping his hand from it.

"You're okay though?" Sylas questions.

"Yeah," Mercy assures. "I can't stay long. I need to head back to Ozra in the next couple of days, but Meera and Char'll be around if you need someone to talk to or help with anything."

"Okay," Sylas replies with a frown. "Why didn't you tell me you found him when you summoned me?"

"I wanted to, but the NC didn't want to risk the message getting intercepted," Mercy clarifies. "They want to keep the people in the dark on this until we can get a handle on the situation. Clearly Malice is a much larger threat than we originally thought."

"Clearly," Sylas agrees, looking at Cal again.

They go silent for a few beats as Mercy looks at his Alia. A pained expression comes to his face. Seeing Cal like this was scary. He had hardly spoken since they got him out of that camp. It seemed he was just going through the motions and doing as he was told. He could only imagine what was going through his head. Not only had he seemed to have lost his Source, something that was a core to who he was as a person, but he had been a prisoner. Even Pippa couldn't explain his lack of powers.

"I'm sorry for what I said the last time we talked," Mercy sighs, looking at Sylas. "I was out of line."

"I deserved it," Sylas replies.

"No, you didn't," Mercy differs. "You were hurting, and I just made it worse."

They both pause as Cal readjusts, neither of them wanting to wake him. He quickly fades back out as Sylas gently rubs his shoulder. He waits another moment to be sure he was still asleep before looking back at Mercy.

"He never gave up on you," Mercy shares with a small smile. "In fact, I'm pretty sure 90% of what he's said the last two weeks was asking when he could see you."

"You kept him from me for two whole weeks?" Sylas chuckles at the realization. "Was that punishment for being an asshole?"

"I didn't have a choice," Mercy frowns, not seeing the humor. "I'm at the mercy of the National Council. I'm starting to understand how Cal got nothing done. They're relentless. You get the title of King, but none of the authority."

They go quiet again as Sylas watches Cal's face. Looking to the floor, Mercy lets out a sigh. Was Sylas even listening to him? While he wanted to talk to Sylas about this, clearly Cal needed his attention more. He'd have to give them some space and figure this out on his own.

"Is he gonna be okay?" Sylas asks, shifting his gaze to Mercy.

"I think so," Mercy sighs, watching Cal. How was it that even asleep, he looked exhausted? "It'll take some time for him to get back into a fight, but you two can work at it together." Mercy takes a pause and fidgets a moment. "His Source is gone, Sy. I have no idea why, but it is."

"He's still marked," Sylas retorts in confusion.

"I know," Mercy acknowledges. "It's strange… When we found him, I could feel my Source connect to him and finally calm down, but it was so weak. He mentioned exposure to the exua rune, but it's not on his body like yours is."

"Guess I have some reading to do," Sylas huffs, looking to the ceiling. "Pip or Maior have any theories?"

"No," Mercy sighs, "and Master Novi hasn't exactly been easy to reach with Caligo related issues."

"She's not happy he was found?" Sylas questions with an air of worry.

"I dunno," Mercy replies, giving a small shrug.

The Light Keeper looks to the floor again. It made sense that exposure would work differently than a direct mark on the skin. Cal had said they had him sitting on an exua rune for nearly the entirety of his time in the camp so perhaps it was just a delayed reconnection. His eyes shoot up as Cal rearranges again, this time taking a deep breath and clutching onto Sylas's shirt.

"I should go," Mercy states, pushing away from the wall. "I'm just disturbing you guys, and he needs to sleep. His prosthetics are here," he shares, pointing to them. "They might not fit right since he's lost some weight, but it'll do for now. Get him on his feet when you can."

With a nod from Sylas, Mercy backs out of the room and closes the door softly. If he could trust anyone to keep Cal away from Malice, he knew it was Sylas. His best friend wasn't going to risk losing his partner again and while Mercy knew he needed his Nota, Cal needed him more.

Walking back down the hall he jumps as Meera appears at the bottom of the steps. "How es he?" she asks, her accent throwing him off guard for a moment as she nods toward the guest room.

"Asleep," Mercy sighs, moving passed her. "Sylas worked his magic."

"He feels safe wit' 'im," Meera explains, following Mercy.

"Yeah," he nods in agreement, heading into the living room. "I hope it's not too much to ask for you to keep an eye on them. I'm sure Sylas'll get it together for Cal, but I need someone with a sane mind in this house."

"Yew think Charlyn innit sane?" she chuckles.

"Charlyn is chasing kids around all day," Mercy laughs. "She has limited sanity left."

"N' yew think I do?" Meera retorts with a raised brow.

"True," he smirks, remembering Velia was upstairs sleeping.

"I'll write up uh raport ev'ry night," she states. "Will that ease ya worries?"

"Yes, please," Mercy chuckles.

"Kin do," she nods. "Are yew headin' back to Ozra?"

"Unfortunately," Mercy admits, adjusting the low table by the sofa. "I have to figure out a plan here. The National Council is pressuring me to go through with some kind of coronation, but Cal's alive. He's still the King of Novus Aitus."

"Don' give in tuh tha pressa," Meera instructs him with worried eyes. She studies him a moment as he thinks. She could tell there was something he knew that he wasn't sharing. "Wha' es it?"

He looks at her with a furrowed brow. "I've been spending the last week or so reviewing the NC meeting notes and... These people. I don't think I can handle this."

"Wha' do' Cal say?" she asks as Mercy begins to head toward the kitchen.

He shrugs. "I tried to talk to him, but he didn't seem like he cared. Whatever Bryer did or said to him has him shaken up so I'm not going to push anything. I know what it's like to be afraid like this. When I look at him right now, I see myself. He's afraid of something, maybe himself, I'm not sure yet."

"Wha' do' Tristia say?" Meera continues to question, following behind him.

"I didn't ask her," Mercy laughs at the idea, walking into the backyard to get some fresh air. "After what she did to Shay, I don't care what she thinks."

After they rescued Cal, he made sure to keep Shay surrounded by people he trusted to keep her out of trouble. Those people being Novi and Pippa. Master Novi allowed Shay to return to her studies with her and he was fairly sure the Penumbra was just happy to have the distraction. She had been awfully strange since hearing Cal was alive, and it was unsettling for everyone.

"Why er ya watchin' ou' for tha girl?" Meera asks, pulling him to a stop as she closes the back door.

"She has a good heart," Mercy explains. "I can see that in her, just like I saw it in Cal. She was a child that was manipulated by Mala, just like he was."

"Wha' if she's playin' yew?" Meera tests.

"I don't think she is," Mercy admits. "She's had a dozen opportunities to use her gifts. She could have used them on Tris to get the beatings to stop, but she didn't. She wants to prove herself."

"Or she es playin' tha long game," Meera differs, trying to get him to think this through.

"So could half the people we have working for the monarchy," he shrugs. "I'm honestly not sure who I can trust outside of this house right now, but I can tell in my gut that Shay is one of them."

She pauses a beat and nods her head. Whatever was going through his head, he was trying to stay rational. After losing Cal she feared he was going to revert back to his old ways. He had gotten quiet and timid again, but it seemed after that trip to the capital he was finding himself once more. Now that he had found Cal, he would hopefully stay levelheaded.

"Yew get more like Trust e'ery day," she smiles at him softly.

"Is that a compliment?" he laughs with a raised brow, knowing she wasn't one to voice her praise.

"It es," she confirms. "I wish yew got tuh know 'im betta. Ya time was too short."

He nods his head and looks down. The two of them hadn't really discussed Trust. Talking about his brother with her always made him nervous. He wished he could speak to his brother again, if not for himself then for Meera. It seemed the spirits had little interest in speaking with him lately.

"I wish Velia got some time with him," Mercy states, keeping his eyes to the floor.

"She gets time wit 'im through yew," Meera assures, keeping her small grin.

Looking up from the floor, Mercy's eyes meet Meera's as he nods his head. Her words did bring him some comfort. It had been nice having her at the house with him. For a long time, he dreaded getting to know Meera but now he was starting to see why Trust had fallen for her. Even with her tough exterior, she was kind and gentle. Watching her with Velia and the girls brought that out even more. If the only thing he could do for his brother was protect the woman he loved and help raise his daughter, then that was what he was going to do.

"Wha' es ya plan wit' tha National Council then?" Meera questions.

"Probably something stupid," Mercy shrugs, folding his arms.

Chapter Thirty-Four

Sitting at Cal's old desk, Mercy stares out the window. He glances to the perch that had been there for Nex, no one having seen the bird since that day at the river. He hoped she was still out there somewhere, since she had left the small tokens at the window for Mercy and Sylas to find. The clever crow had been leaving them clues and they were too stupid to figure that out at first. He had tried to ask Cal about her, but his Alia didn't seem to care to answer the questions. With a heavy sigh, he takes his focus to the papers in front of him and begins to look them over.

In one stack were the reports from the Malice camp raids and in another were the reports from Caligo's time working for the Unity Council and his mother. Part of him wanted to see everything that Cal had done in his past. He felt he needed to see the documents to make sense of why Malice had done what they did to Cal but was honestly afraid. The stack of Cal's UC reports was much taller than the ones from the Malice raids which wasn't too surprising considering what he already knew about Cal's time working for Mala. With a sigh, he moves Cal's reports to the side. Right now, he needed to focus on going through the reports from the camps.

A light knock brings his attention to the door as Zero enters the room with a tablet in his hands. Since returning to Ozra, Zero had made a point to work closely with Mercy just as he had done with Cal. The Light Keeper had been useful in helping distinguish who Mercy could and couldn't trust and knew the processes of the government much better than he did. It seemed he had been Cal's righthand man when Mercy wasn't around. It was odd that Cal hadn't really spoken on the friendship with Zero in the past, but he appreciated his assistance. Someone having some idea of what they were doing, no matter how annoying they were, was helpful.

"I love to interrupt your private time, Validus. We have a situation," Zero begins, walking into the room, automatically wincing at the energy from Mercy. "You know it takes a lot for me to call it a situation."

"What kind of situation?" Mercy asks with a raised brow.

He hands the tablet to Mercy and taps the screen to play a video. Mercy's brow furrows at what he was seeing. On the screen was one of the worst riots he had seen since before Spheara. Countless citizens, Aitian and mutt alike, were attacking the Sentry Guards that had been sent to their city to try and calm the storm with the political upset. Just as Cal had predicted before his presumed death, with the fall of Caligo Tenebris came a power struggle within the various countries and sectors of Novus Aitus.

"They killed four Sentries and injured another seven before we could get a handle on the rioters," Zero explains, sitting across from him at the desk.

"Where is this?" Mercy questions as he watches a citizen throw a large rock and hit a Sentry Guard. The soldier falls from his feet as another attempts to pull him from the crowd. "Sophos…"

"Magna Luke," Zero clarifies. "There's been a large upset there and it's only getting worse. It started off as

347

peaceful, but as usual, a few aggressors started a domino effect. They caught a few shops on fire, so the Sentry Guard was called in. Once the military stepped in, things only got more intense."

"What are they protesting?" he questions.

"They want emancipation from the monarchy, and they aren't the only ones asking for it," Zero explains as Mercy hands the tablet back, not wanting to see any more of the video. "I'm all for sticking it to the man, but these people are being idiots."

"Cal was right," Mercy sighs.

"Right about what?" Zero asks, pausing the video and resting the tablet on the desk.

"Before everything, he told me he couldn't step down as King because it would cause Novus Aitus to break apart. That they would attempt to create their own governing systems and that the National Council wasn't going to be enough. I don't think they realize how little power their governing monarch actually has," he clarifies.

"Cal wanted to step down?" Zero pries.

"Yeah," Mercy nods with a frown. "He was... unhappy." He glances up to Zero who was staring at him intently. "Not that it's any of your business."

"Right," Zero laughs, clearing his throat and getting back on topic. "Anyway, I think we need to shift our focus from Malice to the emancipation riots," Zero suggests. "We can't-"

"These riots aren't something we can just fix overnight," Mercy argues, shaking his head and looking to the desk to think. "Besides, Malice can and will do more harm than these rioters."

"Malice has been pulling back," Zero shares, his eyes beginning to tinge with light as he argues his case. "We have proof of that across Ozra and Vicinia. If we-"

"I," Mercy snaps in annoyance, narrowing his eyes. "If I, not we. You're an advisor, Zero. Remember that."

The people were upset because they were worried that Mercy was going to be another Tenebris. While he had hoped his actions at Spheara would have been enough to ease their minds, he was sadly mistaken. Just as Shay had told him, the people feared he was going to follow in the footsteps of the Tenebris rulers. It didn't matter that it had been thrust into his control, he was too close to Cal, and that closeness was a threat. While Caligo had been wary to try and argue his authority, Mercy wasn't. At least he wasn't anymore.

"I want a meeting with the National Council," Mercy states, staring at the tablet. "I want it as soon as possible. Can you send out the summons?"

"What's the NC going to do?" Zero asks, intrigued by the sudden request.

"Novus Aitus wants me to prove that I'm on their side," he thinks out loud. "The reason Cal couldn't get anything done was because of the NC. I'm not going to give them a chance to let me fail."

Zero shakes his head in disagreement. "If you think talking to them is going to-"

"I don't plan on talking to them," he shoots back. "I plan on showing them."

"Showing them what?" Zero asks, with a raised brow. "That you're a Light Keeper with questionable politics? Get in line, Validus."

"That I'm not going to take their shit," he stresses. "Believe it or not I was once just as afraid of Caligo as they are. I'm sure you were too." Nodding his head, Zero looks down. "I'm going to show them I'm not going to let them treat me how they treated Cal."

"And how do you plan on doing that?" Zero asks, his eyes shooting to Mercy.

"I have a few ideas," Mercy announces, looking to the pile of paperwork. "Summon the Council and..." he reaches over his desk and slides Zero Cal's reports. "Put these back in the archive for me. Have someone pull the archives for the National Council meetings again and can you page Pippa?"

"Sure," Zero nods, taking the stack and getting to his feet.

As he heads toward the door, he pauses. He looks back at Mercy who was squeezing his eyes shut and rubbing his temples. Zero shakes his head in annoyance before exiting the room.

Chapter Thirty- Five

There were 20 people around the table staring at Mercy as he stood and watched them carefully. Every single one was there to give the opinion of 20 very different areas of their planet. It was clear the divide between the parts of the world based on the attire of everyone. The cultures were different in every place, some adopting human cultures while others keeping strong to their Aitian roots. Elder Maior was there to represent Ozra alongside Mercy. The old man's face gave him some peace, knowing that perhaps he had someone on his side.

The nerves in his stomach were growing with each passing minute. Being in charge was never his strong suit and now he had to take the lead. He just needed to stick to his plan. Clearing his throat, he stands up straight and takes a moment to lock eyes with each person in the room. Behind him, Zero stood at the door with his arms folded, keeping his eyes to the floor. The sarcastic Light Keeper was so adamant on attending the meeting that Mercy finally gave into his persistence. There was no harm in having another mind there to review the meeting with later.

Taking a deep breath, Mercy speaks. "Over the last several weeks riots have broken out all over Novus Aitus with demands of emancipation from the monarchy. With Cal's presumed death, the governments are attempting to gain independence from a broken system, and I don't blame them. The state of this government is dismal." The men and women looking at him in this room were responsible for the unrest that came with Cal's ruling, and he was going to make them see that. "How many of you know about the events in Magna Luke?" Mercy questions, raising his hand.

Scanning the room, he sees every hand go up. He nods his head in approval. He was happy to see this Council was aware of the events happening. A group of leaders in the dark was one he didn't want.

"How many of you are having similar issues within your sectors?" he follows up, putting his hand up again.

All but two raise their hands. Mercy nods again, taking a deep breath. He had a plan here. He simply needed the National Council to see the problem and understand that he was the solution.

"Emancipation from a broken system is reasonable, but these protests and riots started long before Caligo's alleged death. What I have come to realize is the system is broken because of the people in this room," he states, setting his hand on a stack of folders on the table. "I have gone over every National Council meeting, and it is obvious within these documents that nearly every single person in this room wanted to see our last monarch fail and I will *not* allow that to happen to me."

A woman raises her hand to speak. This was Adella, a woman from the sector that just bordered his own. In order for the National Council to work, they had to break up each of the land masses within the planet. Adella oversaw the sector of Tunc while Ozra was part of Semel. Semel held about seven different countries within it, their representatives being the King and Elder Maior from Ozra.

352

"If I may speak, Your Grace," she offers. Mercy nods his head, staying on his feet. "I fail to see how the Council kept King Caligo from preforming his duties."

Giving a small laugh, Mercy opens the first folder in front of him. "The Equal Trades Act," he begins, reading from the document. "The ETA was presented to the National Council three months before Caligo Tenebris's coronation. The act was meant to aid the smaller outlying villages of each country by creating trade routes, funded by the governing Councils, to bring food and supplies to the villages that struggled to gain access to them. This included things like produce, meats, winter clothes, and more. A truly genius proclamation that would give minimal pay cuts to our already wealthy representatives but… this was voted against seventeen to four. The discussion following the vote states, and I quote, 'the majority of the room feared Prince Caligo did not have the aptitude or means to put forth such an audacious goal nor had he thought through the affects it could have on the structure of each village and city.'" He looks up to the room. "Would any of you care to elaborate on that comment?"

Keeping his eyes stern, he studies the room as a man named Fen raises his hand to speak. This representative came from Aacla, which contained the country of Magna Luke. With a firm gaze, Mercy nods his head for the man to speak.

"Your Highness, that was just after the fall of Mala. We were wary to let him start off his ruling with such a large and delicate act, especially before his coronation," Fen explains.

"Okay," Mercy nods, taking a deep breath, and grabbing another folder, "but two months ago, Caligo Tenebris brought another suggestion. This was what he titled the Roving Hospice Act. An act that would give our people access to the appropriate care needed for their sector at any given time. He wanted to create a team, with the help of Ozra's Doctor Willa, with the main goal being to travel from country to country and offer high quality care to our citizens. Care that could aid any country in the event of a natural disaster or widespread illness." He locks eyes on another NC member named Talay. "In fact, this act was inspired by the earthquake that led to the deaths of thousands in Aegar last year. Thousands of deaths that could have been avoided if proper treatment was available quicker. Looking at this though I can see, yet again, this was voted against at eighteen to three. One of the votes against it being the very representative in charge of the country of Aegar. Would you like to speak on that, Talay?" Mercy questions, keeping his eyes on the representative.

The man shakes his head and looks to the floor. Closing the folder Mercy picks up the remaining and slams them down on the table with force to emphasize his point. The more he read these notes the angrier he became. The sabotage of the National Council was glaring, and he couldn't understand how Cal let it get to this point.

"I looked at the numbers, I did the math, and I scoured the archives. Countless lives could have been saved this past year if Caligo had your support," he snaps, his emotions switching to anger. "You people wanted him to fail. You people wanted your citizens to see him as a tyrant, like his mother. Why? Maybe to get an upper hand? Maybe to try and solidify an image of him you already had in your minds? Regardless, you put roadblock after roadblock in his way, and for what? For our people to suffer. Well, I won't let you do that to me." He glares at them, resentment in his eyes. "Caligo may have feared you, but I don't. Do you understand that?"

No one speaks. He wasn't sure if they were afraid of him or simply listening to his words. What could they say to change his mind anyway? He had read each of the files. With each one he grew more and more frustrated. While he had sat in on his fair share of National Council meetings, he had never truly observed what was happening. Once he saw it in writing though, it pained him. Shuffling through the folders he pulls out one last document.

"Source Keepers Directive," he adds, opening the folder. "Presented by Princess Tristia Tenebris, Miss Pippa Dror, and Caligo Tenebris nearly six months ago. This would give Keepers of both the Shadow and Light Source regulations to follow and would require the Keepers to take a licensing exam at the age of 20. This states that from the time of coming into their Source to the age of 20 they would be required to attend schooling to learn the history of the Sources and master their connection. Something our Keepers desperately need, especially our Light Keepers. This would also give us grounds to arrest and penalize those who use their Source in an unregulated way. Yet another brilliant idea by the best minds Ozra has to offer, but this one was flat out denied with a vote of nineteen to two. The two votes in favor coming from Elder Maior and Caligo himself. When asked about the denial the Council said, and I quote, 'Keepers are a dangerous group of individuals that we do not quite understand as a society, therefore allowing a Shadow Keeper to regulate their actions is unjust.'" He looks up at the room again. "Unjust? Do you know what's unjust? An unknown Shadow Keeper running rampant in Semel, my sector, using her Source to turn Shadow Keepers into her own personal spiritum puppets."

He slides his hand over the touch screen in the table and brings up a projection of the obscurum that was rendered. The room goes silent as he spins the beast around so they could get a good look at it. Seeing the beast makes his stomach hurt. Knowing that what he had seen that day was Sander was heartbreaking.

"This right here would have never been allowed under the Source Keepers Directive, but all of you in this room, every single one of you, chose to disregard the very

355

real threat a rogue Keeper could have if given the resources," he explains, tapping his index finger on the table. "Licensing them, giving them the ability to be nurtured in their craft, would do nothing but benefit. In fact, nearly every single proclamation, act, and directive I have in front of me would have aided our people, but the representatives in this room chose to weaponize their authority against an ally."

Fen tries to speak again. "Your Grace, we-"

"I'm still talking," Mercy interrupts, putting a hand up, feeling the sting as his eyes ignite. "I grew up in the village of Rieka, Ozra. My family and village were slaughtered by Mala Tenebris and the Unity Council. You don't think I was afraid of the Tenebris name? You don't think I saw Caligo as the enemy? For 23 years I saw him as an extension of Mala, but I gave him a chance. I was given the opportunity to get to know him, to learn his politics, to call him my friend. Caligo is not his mother. He is not a tyrant or a murderer. He is a compassionate ruler who cares deeply for his people, and I'm disgusted that the people in this room didn't give him the chance to try and show what a great ruler he could be. I will not allow you to take that opportunity from me too."

"Did you call us here for a lecture or to actually speak on a matter?" a representative named Calix finally asks, folding his arms.

"It's only a lecture if you see it that way," Mercy shrugs, removing the image of the obscurum from the table. "Caligo is still alive, but you as a Council have chosen to let me take his place as regent. Though I think you chose that with the impression I'd be too naïve to catch onto what you were doing. I'm afraid you're wrong about that"

Fen attempts to speak again. "Your Grace, please-"

"I'm not here today to speak on any matters," Mercy glares, "because based on the hierarchy of this government, I am above each and every one of you. With that being said, the National Council is disbanded until further notice. All rulings from here on out will be royal decrees, put into effect immediately."

"That would make this a d-" Fen goes to protest but is quickly cut off.

"A dictatorship? Perhaps," Mercy admits, standing up straight.

He takes a shuddering breath, nerves filling his stomach, and lets the chaos ensue. This hadn't gone exactly how he planned, and he definitely got a little carried away, but he needed to do this. It felt foolish, but what choice did he have?

He turns to look at Zero who's eyes were glowing as he scanned the room himself. The other Light Keeper looked on edge but gives Mercy a small nod of approval. At least he had someone on his side.

"This meeting is over," Mercy states, exiting the room with a fiery air about him.

Chapter Thirty-Six

What he had just done was madness, but Mercy didn't regret his decision in the least. Seeing how broken Cal was and now understanding what the National Council had been doing all along was enough fuel. There was no solving these issues with the NC right now, he had to do this on his own. Showing the people he cared would be easy without them breathing down his neck.

"You made the right choice," Zero assures him, standing watch by the door.

"Did I?" Mercy scoffs.

Going through the folders, Mercy's eyes rest on the Source Keepers Directive. This was one he wished had been enacted when brought to the Council. Not only due to what Iana and Bryer were doing, but because it would have given those who were younger, just coming into their Source, some solace in these unsettling times. He had wished he had someone to show him how his connection worked when he came into it. Perhaps then he wouldn't have been so fearful of his own Source for so long. There was no denying that his uncertainty with his connection played a key role in him suppressing it.

He sighs as he begins to reread it. While he wanted this to be the first order he gave, he knew it couldn't be. He needed to be careful with his first choice. It was going to set the pace for the next several months.

He jumps at the sound of a knock on his door. Looking up, he watches as Zero slowly opens the door, but is quickly shoved aside. They are greeted by Novi with Pippa trailing behind her looking worried. Novi's expression showed she was cross with him while Pippa was simply rambling to get her mother to calm down.

"What you have done is unreasonable, Mercy," Master Novi barks. "Dissolving the National Council like this? In the times we are in?"

"You didn't explain this to her, did you?" Mercy questions, looking at Pippa.

"I don't even think I understand it myself," Pippa retorts, annoyance in her voice.

He lets out a sigh and closes the document. "I know it seems like a rash decision, but I promise I'm not going crazy."

"Prove that to me," Novi snaps.

"Yes," Pippa nods. "Prove that, please."

"The only way to get the people on my side was to remove the last roadblock in my way, and that was the National Council," Mercy rationalizes. "With them taking leave, I can enact all the rulings I need to and give them no say in the outcome."

"He's trying to show the people that the National Council is the enemy, not Cal," Zero clarifies, making his presence known. "On all of these orders will be Caligo's name and they won't even realize. While they'll think it's Mercy giving them refuge, it will actually be Cal."

"You are showing your inexperience," Novi scolds glancing between the two Light Keepers. "That Council was created to give our citizens equal access to their governing monarch and-"

359

"It failed," Mercy glares, his eyes stern. "Have you sat in on any NC meetings lately? Every single ruling Cal wanted to move forward on, they blocked. They wanted him to fail, just like everyone else."

The woman pauses, her face growing calmer. While she still felt Mercy was being reckless, she could see his heart was in the right place. He wasn't trying to take over Cal's monarchy, he was trying to give their true King a leg to stand on when he was well enough to return. Something still felt strange though. She couldn't quite place it, but the young Light Keeper didn't seem to be himself.

"It's going to take time to flush out Bryer again," which gives me time to focus on restoring Cal's name," Mercy explains to her.

"You are being thoughtless," Novi differs, watching him closely.

"I honestly don't care what you think, Novi," he states firmly.

"Mercy!" Pippa scolds.

Keeping his eyes on Novi, Mercy shakes his head in annoyance. "Cal gave me everything I have. He gave me my freedom, my home, my family, he saved what was left of my village… He gave me a life. I owe this to him."

"You do not owe him anything," Novi retorts.

Mercy disagrees. "I do."

"You are smarter than this," Master Novi argues.

"Save me the lecture," he snaps. "Unlike you, I've seen Cal after his rescue. You haven't tried to see him period."

"Mercy Validus, you do not disrespect my mother in such a way," Pippa addresses.

"Maybe she shouldn't disrespect me," he retorts, glaring at Novi.

They all hear a small snicker from Zero in the corner. Pippa's eyes shoot to him with a glare. "Do you have something you wish to say, Captain Skerrick?"

360

"Nope," Zero laughs, collecting himself. "Just happy to see someone put Master Novi in her place."

"Shut up, Zero," Mercy snaps, continuing to keep his gaze on Master Novi.

The Penumbra's face falters. Caligo was like a son to her and seeing him in any state but healthy was something she was afraid of. She had hardly been able to handle when his mother had taken his legs, there was no way she could handle seeing him the way he had been described when he returned. While she was relieved he was alive, she knew he wasn't well. Visibly seeing what her daughter had explained to her would no doubt cause her maternal instincts to kick in. It was better for her to remain neutral for everyone's sake on this matter.

"You are right," she yields. "I apologize."

"I promise my connection to Cal isn't the only thing fueling this," he assures her. "I have our people's best interest at heart. Without the National Council, I can make a difference. Honestly, if Zero and I had listened to them we wouldn't even have figured out Cal was alive," he informs her. "They were trying to keep me out of Vicinia." He pauses at his own words. "They were trying to keep me out of Vicinia..." he mumbles to himself, looking to the floor as he thinks a moment.

Why were they trying to keep him out? Of course, they were worried their new monarch was in trouble, but they had never told Caligo he couldn't go on an assignment, even a reckless one. The cogs begin turning in his head as he begins to open another folder. Why would the NC be so determined to keep Mercy away from Malice? What did they know that he didn't?

"Were there any meetings about Malice the National Council were involved in?" Mercy asks the room, scanning through another proposal.

"Cal kept Malice out of NC meetings," Zero states, watching him closely. "He saw them as harmless and didn't want to worry the Council with a rebel group unless they were getting out of hand. What are you thinking?" he asks, moving to the desk as Mercy opens another folder and scans it.

"I need the Malice files," he mumbles to himself, getting to his feet and moving toward the door.

"I will come with you," Pippa assures, grabbing his hand and nodding to her mother.

"Sorry, Novi," Mercy sighs, leaving the room with Pippa in tow.

The two move down the hall in silence as Mercy's mind continues to work through the possibilities. Maybe he was just being paranoid, but it seemed too coincidental that they were already searching for him near the border and then wanted to deny him access. The fact they even put a Missing Persons Alert on him alone was strange. They also seemed less than concerned about the obscurum.

As they enter the archives room, Mercy smiles at the girl at the desk. She ignores the two as they head through the shelves. He had been in here quite a lot the last couple of weeks and was starting to know the system by heart. He reads the codes at the top of the stacks carefully, mumbling the letters and numbers to himself until he reaches a shelf that read R701.

"Here," he whispers, pulling Pippa down the aisle with him, her hand still in his.

He moves his free hand over the shelves reading the numbers, pulling Pippa along until he comes to a stop on a box labeled with the number 8039. He lets go of Pippa's hand and pulls the box out, placing it on the floor. He sits beside it and begins to dig through the files meticulously.

Watching him a moment, Pippa frowns. Something wasn't right with Mercy, but she couldn't place it. He was acting frantic and scattered since the return of Cal. Perhaps he was still reeling from his emotions, but usually the young man was much more reserved. She takes a deep breath and kneels beside him. With Sylas and Cal no longer nearby to help guide him, there was no telling what he could do. The connections to his Nota and Alia were fading with each passing day.

"Sitting on the floor is not very royal of you," Pippa teases.

"I'm just a kid from Rieka with an important title," he shrugs, opening a folder.

"What are we looking for?" Pippa asks, grabbing a folder herself to humor him, watching his eyes dart over the pages.

"Anything that might tie the National Council to Malice," he explains, his voice quiet.

"Your mind is hard at work I see," she smiles softly, looking down at the paper.

"It hasn't stopped since they went after Cal," he mumbles. He tosses the file in his hand to the side and grabs another. "If I learned anything from growing up in the Western Quarter, it's that rebellion will always end in blood. Either your own or someone you care for."

Going back into the box, his hand pauses over a folder that didn't quite match the rest. While the other files were marked with orange, this one was marked in yellow. He furrows his brow pulling the file from the box and opening it. As he scans the pages, he gets more confused.

"What is it?" Pippa asks.

"Information on Bryer Nitesems," he mumbles, beginning to chew his lip. "I guess the recruitment center found it."

"What?" Pippa questions. "I thought they didn't have anything on him?"

"No way," he murmurs, turning the page.

This couldn't be real. This information didn't make any sense. Why hadn't anyone said anything to him about this? Seeing the panic in his eyes, Pippa attempts to read over his shoulder. In shock, he hands the folder to her and runs his fingers through his hair. This wasn't possible. There was no way this was correct.

"What are you seeing?" Pippa questions.

"He's dead," Mercy states, looking to her. "Cal said he was dead. He knew he was dead. There's no way."

"Whatever you are thinking, it is just a speculation," Pippa adds, shaking her head and reading the file trying to see what he was talking about.

"Bryer Nitesems. Bryer Nitesems…" he mumbles to himself. "That can't be right…"

"What is it, Mercy?" Pippa presses.

Pulling the file from Pippa's hand he takes out a pen and begins to write on the bottom of the page. He mumbles to himself as he begins to compare the letters in Bryer's name to another, crossing them out as he went. With each letter he marked off, his stomach became more nauseous. After a moment he gawks at the paper and goes through the letters again.

"It's an anagram," he mutters, redoing it.

"What is?" Pippa asks, as he turns the paper to her.

"Bryer Nitesems is an anagram for Emrys Tenebris," he states, pointing to the letters.

"Caligo would recognize his own father," Pippa argues, taking the file from his hands to look at it again. "He saw Bryer. We know this."

"He was four when he died," Mercy differs. "How good can a four year old's memory be? I was older than that when my father and mother died, and I hardly remember their faces."

"He would know his father," Pippa glares.

Being as close to Cal as she was, Pippa was sure Cal would remember that face. There were photos of the fallen King in the archives as well as in a frame kept in his bedroom. While Emrys had been gone for much of Cal's life, he left a lasting impression. Cal had held onto the idea of his father his entire life. Mercy didn't understand the emotional hold King Emrys had on his son and she wasn't about to try and explain that to him. Mercy was wrong.

"Bryer was discharged the same day as Emrys's assassination," he continues. "Look at the date his birth records were added to the system, Pip. Bryer Nitesems isn't real."

Pippa argues back. "You are going out on a limb here, darling."

"Sounds like the theme of the last few months," he laughs to himself, trying to collect his thoughts. "I need you to ask me questions or give me ideas."

"What do you mean?" Pippa asks, thrown off by the request.

"That's what Sylas does when my mind gets scattered," he explains. "He helps me figure things out. Gets me back on track. I need to figure this out."

She looks at him as he continues to think, his leg shaking. She hadn't really thought about how the pair had worked together. With Sylas being Mercy's Nota, he tended to help guide his Keeper's thoughts when Mercy couldn't do it himself. Without Sylas, Spheara wouldn't have happened. While Mercy was clever, Sylas was the one to decipher the puzzles and come up with the plans. Perhaps that was why Mercy was making such outlandish decisions. He was on his own without Sylas, and he was scrambling.

"Why would Emrys capture and torture his son?" Pippa asks, giving in to his request.

Trying to think, Mercy lets out an annoyed groan. Suddenly he wished more than anything that Sylas was here. He always helped figure this stuff out. His best friend was the perfect match of genius and crazy to come up with at least some theory that made sense.

Getting to his feet, Mercy picks up the box. Pippa follows in silence as he hauls the Malice files out of the archives and toward his suite.

"Where are we going with them?" Pippa asks, trying to keep the questions going.

"I need Sylas," he explains.

"You can't rely on him that much," Pippa disagrees. "You are your own person after all."

"We didn't become our own persons until Spheara," Mercy laughs in embarrassment. "We can see how well that's going. Sylas had a mental breakdown, I nearly got Cal killed... Somehow, I'm ruling an entire planet. I need Sylas to keep me on the right path. That's his job, right?"

"Job aside, you are your own people," Pippa adds. As the box begins to slip, she helps him steady it.

"Sylas and I have always been a package deal," Mercy shrugs. "We're connected."

"You and Cal are also connected, but live separate lives," Pippa explains as Mercy regains his grip on the awkward box. "What are you going to do? Haul this box all the way to Rieka?"

He pauses and looks at the box in his hands. What was he even doing? Letting out a flustered laugh he looks between Pippa and the box. They could figure this out without Sylas. There had to be a way to figure this out without Sylas.

Chapter Thirty-Seven

Sitting on a bench facing Mercy's backyard, Cal was wrapped in a blanket staring at the snow coating the grass. His expression was blank as he watched it drift over the stark lawn. The backyard was fairly large with a few toys for the girls placed in a bin beside the door. Though Mercy and his family had grown into the house, the backyard lacked the same homey feel. It didn't seem like it was used for much more than letting the girls run around. Cal keeps his eyes forward as the door from the kitchen opens and Sylas walks out with two mugs awkwardly held, one in his hand and the other hugged between his chest and arm.

"Here," he says in a quiet voice, handing one of them to Caligo. "Mint and chamomile," he states, "might help ease your mind a bit."

"Thank you," Cal says, taking the mug and helping Sylas adjust the other.

While Cal didn't particularly like tea, he did enjoy the smell of it. Tea had always been something Sylas drank after a long day, but Cal usually passed on the offer. Today though, he welcomed the warm mug. It meant Sylas was going to sit with him while he drank his own, which was always nice. He moves over slightly as Sylas sits down beside him on the bench. They both stay silent as Sylas drinks his tea and Cal stares at his.

"I thought I was supposed to be the one who kept things to himself," Sylas pokes after a few minutes.

"Yeah," Cal nods, taking a drink. He grimaces at the taste and lets out a steady exhale.

"It's been over a week," Sylas adds, offering to take the mug but Cal ignoring the gesture, "and you've hardly said a word to me."

"I know," Cal admits, looking down at the cup.

What was he supposed to say? Sylas had already worked through his trauma with him, he certainly wouldn't want to hear about it again. They had spent months getting to know his painful past, Sylas putting his optimistic mentality to good use every time. He always made him feel like he could move past the things that haunted him.

Sylas takes a deep breath and takes another sip of his tea. Though he was happy to have Cal back, this silence was agony. No matter how hard he tried, Caligo was keeping whatever happened to himself. His responses to anything were short and tended to lack any emotion since that first day. There were a few breaks in the numb façade, but for the most part they were in limbo. What was Sylas supposed to do with him? The routine of sitting in silence and waiting for Cal to open up was getting tiring.

"I have killed 4,365 people," Cal states in a quiet voice.

"You counted?" Sylas asks, surprised by the sudden choice of topic. Caligo nods his head and lets out a small shaky breath. "That isn't who you are anymore," Sylas reminds him.

"But I can't forget the things I have done, Sy. The world will not allow that," Cal replies blankly.

"Forget what the world thinks," Sylas retorts. "Those people don't get to tell you what kind of person you want to be. You do."

With a small, flustered laugh, Cal shakes his head. How could he do that? How could he just forget what the world saw him as? They saw a monster. It didn't matter what his friends or Sylas saw. How could he focus on what those he cared for thought when the world was screaming at him about how horrible he was?

"My people are happy I am dead," Cal informs him, his voice quiet. "Millions celebrated. Millions more will with Mercy taking the crown. The Tenebris name is truly gone with me out of the picture."

"Those people didn't get to see the real you," Sylas lectures him.

"The real me slaughtered 4,365 people," Cal stresses, looking at Sylas with pained eyes.

"You did what was needed to survive," Sylas corrects, getting aggravated. He takes a breath to calm himself before continuing. "Your mother manipulated you, Cal. She forced you to do those things. She didn't give you a choice."

"I killed Orlo," Cal states bluntly, looking back down at his mug.

The comment catches Sylas off guard, causing him to choke on his tea. He goes into a coughing fit before collecting himself. "You did what?"

"You heard me," Cal sulks, looking out at the yard again. "That battle at the southern border I told you about, when the veins began to show... I killed Mercy's father that day. I looked at Orlo Validus and I killed him."

"No, he killed himself," Sylas differs.

Cal shakes his head in disagreement. "He faced me without his Source. A suicide for anyone."

"How do you know it was him?" Sylas questions in concern.

"I know because…" he pauses a moment and looks to Sylas. "I know because Mercy has Orlo's sword. I knew that sword long before it was given to Mercy because I'm the one who used my Source to rip it from Orlo's hand and then tear him to pieces. I was so out of sorts at Spheara I didn't even notice he had it." He takes his eyes to the mug in his hands again. "I didn't realize it was the same sword until months later when I came here, and I saw it hanging on the wall in the office."

Sylas shakes his head. "A lot of swords look-"

"None are like Orlo's," Cal argues, a spark of resentment in his voice. "The hilt is unique, and that stone set in the pummel is a channeling stone. An ipdum that he must have put in the blade knowing Mercy would also be able to wield it. A channeling stone chooses a Keeper and that one chose Mercy, or he would not be able to hold the hilt in his hand."

The sword was mounted in Mercy's office not long after the house was finished being built. Pippa had suggested he hang it since he was wary to use the blade in battle. He had said it had too much sentimental value to use in a fight, which was understandable. It was one of the reasons Mercy kept his father's dagger boxed up as well as the Pura Blade until recently. Cal had seen it hanging in there at least a dozen times since it was mounted. Sylas wondered why he hadn't said anything before.

"You're afraid to tell him?" Sylas asks, keeping his eyes locked on Caligo.

A small nod comes from Cal. "I looked at Orlo and I didn't even think for a moment. It was quick and thoughtless, and done in a fit of rage. I wanted that day to be over with so badly, I didn't even give myself a moment to contemplate what I was doing."

"We've gone over this, Cal," Sylas whispers, trying to wrap his head around it all. "You're not the monster your mother created."

"Yes, I am," Cal snaps.

Taking a deep breath, Sylas speaks calmly. "No, you're not. You want to know what I see when I look at you? I see strength, loyalty, power, dramatic for sure, you're definitely short tempered, and maybe a little hardheaded, but above all of that, I see your compassion. From the moment I met you, I never saw a monster. I saw you, Cal."

"Who am I?" Cal asks, a frown coming to his face.

"You're Caligo Emilian Tenebris," Sylas states with confidence. "The man who saw all the pain and suffering his ancestors put on this world and chose to diverge from their path and forge his own. Only someone with a lot of strength could look at the path laid out for him and choose to turn the other way. You risked everything you had to change the course your mother put you on and you never let them break your spirit, Cal. Why let someone break it now?"

"I don't see me that way," Cal differs. "I see someone who should have been tried and executed for his crimes." The two lock eyes for a moment before Cal looks away. "The sooner I'm dead-"

"Don't you dare finish that sentence," Sylas pleads, using his hand to nudge Cal's cheek to look at him. "I need you. Do you hear me, Caligo? I was stupid to ever think I didn't or that I could get through this shitty life on my own because I need you, Cal. Please don't finish that sentence."

Glancing to the hand on his cheek, Cal could feel the change in touch with Sylas's fingers missing. Somehow it even felt like that day in Orior was his fault too. If it wasn't for him, would they even be targeting Mercy? If Malice wasn't targeting Mercy, then Sylas would have been fine that day. Sylas would have his fingers and his archery, and he wouldn't be tucking his laces in his boots or barely be able to write his own name. Sylas needed his hand, and now he didn't have it.

"Sy, I cannot-"

"Stop it," Sylas orders, his tone growing flustered, taking his hand away. "I'll be damned if I let you look at your life and not see all the good you've done. Just look at Rieka," he adds, gesturing to the yard. "My village would be gone if you hadn't stepped in. Mercy and I would be dead if it weren't for you. Those little girls in the house behind us are alive because of your sacrifices. I don't give a shit what they told you in that camp. You are a hero, Cal. You're my hero. You saw the damsel in distress, and you saved his ass more than once. Now get over your damn pity party, put your big boy pants on, and move past this. You're worse than Mercy. He's supposed to be the one whining about how shitty his life is, not you."

"I suppose he does whine a lot," Cal agrees.

"Exactly," Sylas nods. "You're sitting here thinking about how horrible your life is while Mercy got his shit together and is doing your job. I hate to say it, but I think he might be the stable one for the first time in his life."

"That is a bit scary to think about," Cal admits, furrowing his brow.

"It is!" Sylas concurs. "So maybe it's time to forget what other people think and get your fighting spirit back. This whole depressed, self-loathing bullshit," he continues gesturing to Cal's whole person, "does *not* look good on you."

"What about my Source?" Cal asks, taking another sip of the tea and souring his face.

"Screw the Shadow Source!" Sylas argues, getting to his feet and setting his mug on the bench. "Millions of people on this planet get by just fine without shooting magic from their hands. You don't need it." He puts his hand out and gestures for Cal to get up. "Come on. Let's go."

"Go where?" Cal asks, setting the tea down and letting Sylas pull him to his feet.

372

"You'll see. Let's go," Sylas urges, putting his arm around him and leading him back inside.

After stopping in the house to put on some more appropriate clothing for the chilly air and for Cal to put a mask around his nose and mouth, the pair exit the front door and move down the street. Cal follows, keeping at Sylas's side as they walk through the snow. With each step, Cal could feel the pain of his ill fitted prosthetics. He wondered when he'd have the time to get new sockets. He watches Sylas as they exit the village to try and figure out his motives here. Where was he taking him?

After about 15 or 20 minutes they come to a stop on one of the steep and rocky hills outside of Rieka. Cal pulls his mask down as the cold air fills his lungs. He glances to Sylas who offers a hand and pulls him to stand next to him on the edge of a steep incline.

"Whittington Point," Sylas states. "Merc, Charity, my brother, and I used to come up here to talk or sometimes just sit in silence," he explains. "There was a little fox that used to have a burrow right over there." He points to an old tree with dried grass around it.

From where they stood, there was a clear view of Rieka down below. Cal could somewhat see in the architecture where the expansions were within the small township. There was even a view of Brokkr's Forge from where they stood, the sign that hung outside sticking out over the road. They had made quick work of removing the burned remains from the attack a year and half ago, leaving very few damaged buildings still standing. Seeing Rieka from here made it look much quainter than it felt being within it.

"Sometimes I forget you grew up here," Cal admits, watching the people buzz through the streets down below.

"Born and raised," Sylas laughs with a shiver. "I can point to every spot where I kicked someone's ass for Mercy too," he smirks.

"I can't see you being a brawler," Cal discloses.

"You've seen me kill someone point blank with an arrow, but you don't see me as a brawler?" Sylas asks with a raised brow and a smirk.

"I never thought of it that way," Cal confesses with a small shrug.

He began to wonder just how well he knew Sylas. They never spoke about Sylas's childhood or really any part of his past. The fact he had seen Sylas kill people never sat with the image of the man he saw before him. In fact, Sylas's entire career in the military made little sense to him. He was a scholar, he loved books, he had more in common with Pippa than anyone in the Sentry Guard.

"May I ask you something?" Cal prompts, keeping his eyes on the village.

"Always," Sylas nods, moving to sit on the boulder behind him, intrigued by the clear turn. Usually, Sylas was the one asking questions.

"Why did you never formally join the Royal Guard?" Cal queries, turning to look at Sylas. "When we met, you were almost 22 and still in training. Why?"

"You of all people know I have commitment issues," Sylas states with a laugh.

"To your job though?" Cal asks.

Nodding his head, Sylas takes a deep breath. So, this was what Cal wanted to talk about. Sylas had been thinking over what Mercy had said about his need for approval, and he was starting to see the truth in his friend's words. He made most of his decisions based on what his father wanted, not what he did.

Seeing his apprehension, Cal backpedals. "It's fine if you don't-"

"No," Sylas interrupts. "We can talk about it," he assures, taking another deep breath before speaking. "When I signed up for the UC Guard, I did it because I thought that was what I was supposed to do. My grandfather was in the

Guard, my father, my brother… As far back as I can remember the Bellators were soldiers. So of course, I thought that was what I was supposed to do too… It's what my dad wanted anyway. My dad was happy when I got the offer to join the Royal Guard. He supported Mala and the UC with everything he had," he looks to the ground as he continues to speak, "but for me taking that offer meant something different. While my dad and Berk saw joining the Royal Guard as an honor, I saw it as a way out of Rieka."

"Well, why did you want out of Rieka?" Cal asks, folding his arms, interested to see Sylas speak about himself for once.

"I knew I wanted more than what this little village had to offer," Sylas acknowledges, looking at Cal. He pauses a moment before continuing. "Can I tell you something and you not get weird about it?"

"Of course," Cal urges.

"When I was a kid, there was a girl… Her name was Lili. We had plans. We had a lot of plans," he admits with a shrug.

Cal furrows his brow at the statement. He had never thought about the life Sylas would have had if they never met. Was he saying that he had a relationship with someone? It wasn't completely obscene of an idea. With Sylas's good looks and charisma, he was surprised he was single when they met. More than surprised. Then again, with a sense of humor like his, maybe it wasn't shocking at all.

"Don't get weird," Sylas smirks, watching Cal think through the statement.

"I'm not," he assures. "Did you have feelings for her?"

"If you mean 'did I love her?' Then, no. I don't think I really knew what love was at the time," Sylas discloses, looking down. "We were both kids who wanted to see the world, and I could give her that. I had promised her I'd get her out of Rieka one day. I was going to join the UC Guard and when I finished my training, we were going to see the world," he adds with a small smile looking at Cal. "It wasn't love though. I didn't know what that was until I met you. It was just kids making promises to each other, but I keep my promises. I figured she was out there somewhere, so I kept it. She was like a sister to me, but who knows where that future could've gone."

"Did she pass during the last attack on Rieka?" Cal asks, unsure where this was going.

"No, not the Fall of Ricka," he clarifies. "She was a Light Keeper. Lili Clarus," he explains. "Mala… When she came for Mercy's family, the Clarus family fled. No one saw or heard from them after the attack…"

The statement causes Cal to look to the ground. The Clarus and Validus Keepers of Light were both well known in the Western Quarter. While Mercy had mentioned the Clarus Keepers being from Rieka when they met, Cal had somewhat forgotten about it. It was another family his mother no doubt destroyed. It was just another thing for Cal to feel guilty about when it came to Sylas. Taking a deep breath, he looks back up to him.

"Are you certain she is…?" he trails off.

"I looked up her file as soon as you gave me the clearance," Sylas admits with a pained smile. "Deceased."

"I am so sorry, Sy," Cal replies in understanding.

"Yeah," Sylas sighs. They go silent for a moment before Sylas clears his throat to get back on topic. "When I actually got faced with finishing my training though, I got scared," Sylas confesses. "As soon as I signed that paperwork, I was going to be Mala's puppet and I… I couldn't do it," he reveals, with a shrug. "Committing to something I didn't believe in and serving the Tenebris crown… Knowing what Mala did to Mercy and Lili's families and to so many others… I didn't want any part of

that. I didn't want to be forced to kill innocent people. So…
I put it off, and just kept training. How was I supposed to
tell my dad I didn't want to follow in his footsteps? He was
so proud of me… I wanted to make him proud, but I
couldn't do it. They couldn't force me to sign on."

"What about your mother?" Cal continues.

"She left," Sylas laughs tensely, shaking his head.
"As soon as I said I was joining the UC she walked. She
was so against me and Berk joining. She said we had too
much kindness in our hearts to live the life of a soldier. I
always felt like her leaving was my fault…"

Seeing the pain on Sylas's face when speaking
about his mother was hard for Cal to see. This was the most
he heard Sylas talk about his parents and he didn't want to
dive too far into it if he wasn't ready. He knew the subject
of his mother was a hard one from what Mercy had told
him, so maybe it was time to move on from the topic.

"So why join the Sentry Guard then?" Cal inquires,
changing the subject.

"You have a lot of questions today," Sylas laughs.

"You are talking for once and I want to
understand," Cal shrugs.

Nodding his head, Sylas lets off a nervous laugh. "I
thought it was what I was supposed to do," he adds. "I'm
good at what I do, and it felt useless letting all those years
of training go to waste. I guess I do a lot of things because I
think it's what's expected of me."

Cal pauses a moment before speaking again. "If I
always did what was expected of me, we would not be here
right now. You will never discover how far you can
possibly go if you are not willing to take the risk," Cal
shares, with a small smile.

"True," Sylas nods, looking to the ground again. "I
do know something now though. Something I want to the
take the risk on."

"What is that?" Cal asks.

"The one thing I'm sure *I* want is standing right in front of me," he admits, locking his eyes on Cal. "Care to finish that conversation we started in the wagon?"

Keeping his gaze locked with Sylas, Cal lets a small smile escape. They had never finished that conversation, and Cal certainly didn't forget. Sylas smiles, patting the boulder for Cal to sit beside him. As Cal goes to join him, Sylas offers him his hand and he takes it without hesitation, intertwining their fingers together. They sit for a moment, both looking down at the village trying to figure out their next words.

Clearing his throat, Sylas lets out a steady breath. "You've come a long way since I met you, and seeing you lose your spark… It scares me."

"Scares you?" Cal questions, raising a brow and looking at Sylas.

"Yeah," he nods, "you told me the worst mistake I could make was looking at my hand as something that was going to hold me back, but here you are doing that with your Source and whatever the hell happened in that camp. I listened to you, and I've been putting in the work, now you need to put in yours. Unlike you though, I'm here to help you and not fall into a river and make you think I'm dead for a month," he smirks.

"Alright," Cal nods with a small laugh.

"What were you gonna say?" Sylas tests.

"When?" Cal questions, looking down at Rieka.

"In the wagon," Sylas clarifies.

As Cal watches the small village, his gaze goes to Mercy's house beside the shop. His eyes get wide as he registers the commotion happening in front of the home and the Sentry Guard scrambling to get inside.

"Something is wrong," Cal states. "Look at the house."

Moving his eyes to Mercy's home, Sylas sees the same thing. They both rush back down the rocky hill toward the village as fast as they can, Cal stumbling a few times, but Sylas quickly helping him steady his feet. If the Sentry Guard was stirred up, whatever was happening couldn't be good.

As soon as they enter the village, they could hear the shouting from Mercy's house. Moving swiftly, they come to a stop in front of the home. They could see the spiritum fog seeping out of the front door meaning there were Shadows active inside. Sylas looks to one of the Sentry Guards who was holding people back, the citizens trying to figure out what drama was playing out at the Validus home yet again. He spots Meera, clutching Velia to her chest several feet away with a Sentry aiding her. He rushes over to her, a look of fear on her face.

"Meera!" he shouts, grabbing her shoulders as Velia cries in her arms. He looks her over quickly. "You okay?"

"I'm fine," she breathes.

"Where's Ruby and Saph?" Sylas questions.

Clearly shaken up, Meera shakes her head in response. Turning around he spots Cal walking toward the house. What was he doing? He needed to stay out of this. If something happened to Mercy's family or Cal on his watch his best friend would never forgive him.

"Finnick, where're the girls?" Sylas shouts, moving toward one of the Light Keepers trying to signal the nosey citizens to get back.

"I don't know, Captain," the man responds.

"Shit," Sylas retorts, taking off in a run for Mercy's house after Cal.

As he gets to the door, Cal feels Sylas's hand fall on his shoulder and pull him back. There was no way Cal was ready to face anyone, let alone a Shadow Keeper.

"Stay outside and stay out of the way," Sylas orders, moving past him.

Frustration on his face, Cal lets off a low growl. No better time to try and activate his Source than a fight. Not

379

listening to Sylas, he goes in anyway. As they enter the living room, they could both hear a commotion upstairs. The spiritum fog was trailing down the stairs, showing there was someone letting off a lot of Source power on the second floor. Running down the steps was Charlyn, who quickly bolts to Sylas in fear.

"She has the girls," she gasps.

"Who has the girls?" Sylas questions as Cal grabs Sylas's sword by the door and runs up the steps in the direction of the commotion. "Damn it, Cal! Come back here!"

As Caligo reaches the second floor, he hears shouting coming from the girls' bedroom. Barging in he sees two Shadow Guards disarmed on the floor by the entrance. He pauses a moment, fog completely filling the room, putting a chill in his bones.

Squinting his eyes, he finally locks them with Iana. She gives him a smile as she shoots her fog at the last Sentry in the room who was guarding Saphie behind him. She yanks him across the space as the man gasps for air, her pulling it from his lungs, letting him go motionless before dropping him to the floor.

Iana takes her attention to Cal as her fog dissipates. He had a sword in his hand and was ready to fight. He pulls the mask down around his neck and lets his coat drop to the floor to give him better motion.

"I wondered where they were hiding you," she laughs as he realizes she was holding Ruby in her smokey tendrils.

"Uncle Cal!" the little girl cries.

"It'll be okay," he assures her, keeping his voice even and calm, not wanting to scare her. "Let her go, and I will go with you willingly."

"Unfortunately, you aren't my target today, Cal," she frowns, turning her attention to Saphie.

Iana puts her hand out toward the older of the girls, who was cowering in place, paralyzed with fear. Not giving himself time to think, Cal drops the sword and bolts to the girl to shield her. Waiting for the fog to hit him, he squeezes his eyes shut. He feels the fog grab him and begin to slink around his body. Trying to stay calm, he opens his eyes to look at Saphie and grits his teeth trying not to react. Being on the receiving end of a spiritum fog attack was something he hadn't experienced in a long time, and it was just as excruciating as he remembered. While solis orbs burned with heat, spiritum fog felt more like an acid.

As the fog begins to creep toward his face, the blood in his ears begins to pound as a burning sensation fills his eyes and vessels. Suddenly it felt like time was moving at half speed as the fog pulls away from his face. He knew this feeling a little too well from his time as a Penumbra. There was no way this was possible.

He feels Saphie pull away from him abruptly as the fog completely releases him and Iana screams. Looking to the wall, he sees a pale purple luminance reflecting off the surfaces around him. Looking at his hands, he realizes it's coming from him. He locks eyes on Saphie who's shirt was singed from his heated grasp but appeared to be okay. He turns to Iana and looks at his hands again in shock. Just like Mercy, his veins were illuminated with light. It wasn't white like Mercy's but an ominous purple glow that was replacing his coal filled veins. Even the black tips of his fingers were resonating the ghostly hue.

Remembering his short time with the Light Source, he stands in front of Saphie and aims his palm at the woman. His vessels full of light, he stands his ground and glares at Iana.

"What is this?" Iana snarls.

He feels Saphie grip onto him from behind, knowing he was her protection in that moment. As long as she avoided his hands, she would be safe with him. Fear and adrenaline coursing through him, Cal looks at Ruby. The small girl was terrified and unable to move in Iana's grasp.

"Let her go!" Cal snaps, not able to move much with Saphie clinging to his waist.

He watches as an arrow flies through the doorway and strikes the woman in the shoulder. She lets out a scream, Ruby attempting to take the moment to squirm away but unable. Sylas enters the room, his hands shaking slightly with his bow release holding the string taut. He had been aiming for her heart, but his shot was a bit off. The Nota hadn't been keeping up with practicing with the release, and he was regretting it now.

"Get Saph out of here," Sylas orders.

Looking to the door, Cal sees another Sentry Guard come into view. He shuffles Saphie through the door, the Sentry taking the girl and heading down the stairs with her in tow.

"Ruby!" Saphie cries before being taken out of sight.

Iana keeps her focus on Sylas. Cal comes up beside him, keeping his hands aimed at the Shadow Keeper in case she tried to counter another attack. He wasn't sure how he was doing it, but the Light Source was still emanating from his hands.

"What the hell?" Sylas gawks, realizing what he was seeing, but quickly going back to Iana.

"I can't grab Ruby," Cal warns. "I don't know how to control this."

The woman takes the pause from the pair to adjust her grip on the girl. She lets out a scream as Iana pulls her to her chest, using the girl as a shield.

"Let her go, or I'll shoot and he'll... Cal'll do whatever he's doing," Sylas stumbles out.

"Smooth," Cal mumbles.

They watch as Iana pulls her fog up behind her. She gives them a small smirk and backs into the cloud of spiritum fog. Cal realizes Sylas was about to shoot, his thumb tensing on the trigger. Wary of his aim, Cal grabs Sylas's arm and jolts his shot to the wall as the fog dissipates within the room. In response to the touch, Sylas drops the bow and lets out a hiss of pain. Caligo's hand was hot, burning a hole in Sylas's long sleeved cotton shirt.

"What the hell was that!?" Sylas snaps, brushing the burned sleeve. "I could have had her!"

"You also could have hit Ruby," Cal scolds, his eyes wide as he looks around the room, the fog clearing. "Oh no… Ruby…"

Cal's shift to panic brings Sylas's attention to the situation. The room was empty. Iana and Ruby were gone. The two exchange a look, Sylas furrowing his brow at what he was seeing. Cal's eyes were glowing, his irises giving off a purple gleam. He could see the vessels around his face glowing faintly as well. What was this?

Chapter Thirty-Eight

Walking into the switchboard room of the estate, Mercy's eyes were filled with panic. He had been working on a few documents in the office when Zero came to find him. An emergency in Rieka was not something he wanted to hear right now, especially with Cal there. He enters the room swiftly with Zero at his heels.

"I was paged?" Mercy asks the woman at the switchboard.

"Your Grace, you have a call from Elder Abtal in the village of Rieka," she shares, grabbing one of the headsets beside her and handing it to him.

He puts it on and nods his head. "Put him through, please." He waits a moment until the line beeps. "Abtal?" he asks, nerves showing in his voice.

"Sylas," he hears his best friend's voice.

He breathes a sigh of relief, but it was quickly lost. Why would Sylas be calling? He puts his hand to the headset to try and make sure he could hear him clearly and glances to Zero.

"What's going on?" Mercy inquires.

"There was a situation at the house," Sylas explains as Mercy listens. "I already have Abbey and Yule packing up a wagon, but can you have a transport meet us? Iana and Bryer know Cal's here now and... Sophos, I don't want to tell you."

"Don't want to tell me what?" Mercy demands.

After a long pause he hears Sylas hand the call off to someone else. "Mercy?" he hears Cal's voice.

"By the Elders. What the hell is going on?" Mercy asks, eased hearing his Alia's voice.

"I want you to understand we did everything we could. Sylas got a shot in, and I even tried to bargain with her," Cal begins.

"Where's Velia?" Mercy interrogates.

"She is fine. Meera and the baby are fine," Cal assures him. "It's Ruby. They took Ruby."

As soon as the words come through, Mercy drops his hand from the headset. His entire body freezes as his breathing begins to quicken and his Source comes to his irises. What did he mean they took Ruby? Why the hell would anyone take Ruby? He pulls the headset off as panic begins to fill him. Zero grabs it and puts it on to finish the call as Mercy backs toward the wall, his heart racing. He could feel pains shooting through his body as his Source began to ignite his vessels.

After seeing what they did to Cal he could only imagine what they had in store for Ruby. She was a child. Who would take a child? Who would take *his* child? He backs into the wall and begins to slide down it knowing he was going into another panic attack.

"Page Miss Pippa," he hears Zero order the woman at the board, continuing to speak with Cal.

This wasn't happening. There was no way this was happening. Ruby was supposed to be safe. They had several Sentry Guards stationed at the house and Sylas and Cal were there. The two people he trusted the most on Novus Aitus were in that house. How did someone just walk in and take his child?

He puts his hand to his chest, making sure his heart was staying inside it. He needed to try and calm himself, but he didn't know how. There wasn't even anyone in the room who knew how to handle him when this happened. He didn't even know how to handle himself.

As terror continues to wrack his body, he could feel his Source burning brighter and more painful than ever before. Of course he was powering up. He was panicking and his Source was trying to protect him as usual. He looks down at his hands and sees the light filling his veins as he continues to gasp for air.

He jumps as Pippa enters the room and drops to the floor beside him. He looks at her with horror in his eyes, unable to even comprehend her words as she looks from him to Zero. She moves to block his view of the switchboard and puts her hands on his face to redirect him and keep his focus on her. Instead of speaking, she just begins to take slow and steady breaths, trying to get him to mimic her. After a few moments he begins to copy her actions, nodding his head as his heart begins to slow and he is able to finally breathe.

"Keep breathing," he hears her say to him. "Deep breath in, steady exhale out."

Continuing to follow her breathing, he feels himself calm, his Source leaving his body. It was smart for Zero to call someone Mercy knew to try and calm him, but even with the attack subsiding, he was terrified. Malice now had his little girl. They had Brokkr's daughter.

"They have Ruby," he mutters to her in panic. "They took Ruby."

"I know," Pippa nods.

He looks to Zero who's eyes were lit up as he stared intently at Mercy. "Zero?"

"I'm already sending a transport to meet them," he informs. "They should be here by morning."

"Are you using your peritia on me?" Mercy asks, looking at the Light Keeper.

"Yeah. Sorry. You were making me nauseous," Zero admits, blinking his Source away. "I already have a transport prepping to meet them. The Riekan Elder Council will have a full report from the Sentry Guard before nightfall. I'll have someone bring it to your office as soon as it's patched through."

Mercy nods his head as he gets to his feet, his heart still fluttering. Why hadn't Zero used his peritia sooner? Why did he use it at all? He felt a little violated with the Keeper toying with his emotions, but at the same time he was grateful.

Pippa clings to his side as he continues to think about what he just learned. Ruby was now in the hands of Malice. They needed to act on this fast. They didn't have time to form a plan with Ruby on the line. The anger begins to creep in as he feels Pippa hold his arm. Unexpectedly her touching him made him irritated.

"Get off me," Mercy orders, pushing Pippa away in annoyance.

"We should wait for Caligo and Sylas to get here," she states, watching him with concern. "We need to know the full story before you go rushing into this."

"Listen to the rich girl," Zero agrees as the phones begin to ring again.

Hearing the shrill ring, Mercy winces and exits the switchboard, both Pippa and Zero staying close behind. Mercy needed to leave the call station to try and get his thoughts together. Moving to a bench outside the room, he sits to try and collect himself. He squeezes his eyes shut feeling the brain fog take over again. His leg begins to shake as his mind continues to feel like static. He couldn't focus here. He couldn't focus anywhere. The ringing of the phones sounded like fog horns and even his clothes were making his skin crawl. What was this?

"I know this is Ruby, but you need to think this through instead of doing something impulsive," Pippa warns. "Going after them will only play into the hands of your enemy. You must understand that."

"Shut up for two seconds, Pip," he whispers, still trying to catch his breath.

"Promise me you will wait for Cal and Sylas," she pleads, looking him in the eye. "Promise me."

He shakes his head, looking to Zero, the other Keepers eyes ringed with light. Most likely in case Mercy had another melt down.

"Can I meet them with the transport?" Mercy asks.

"If you hurry," Zero sighs, exchanging a concerned look with Pippa.

"Are you listening to me? Your actions influence millions now, not just yourself," Pippa continues, folding her arms in irritation.

"We're taking two," Mercy states to Zero, ignoring his friend. "One to bring my family here, the other to get my kid back."

Pippa's eyes dart to him. "Mercy, I do not think that is a good-"

"I don't care what you think," he snaps, getting to his feet.

"Mercy Validus," she scolds.

"Pippa Dror," he mocks, switching his gaze back to Zero again. "Zero, there's a stack of documents on my desk that need to be sent through processing. Can you do that for me while I'm gone? Tris can help."

Zero laughs, shaking his head. "With how you're acting lately, I think it would be a better idea for me to go with you to babysit your chaotic ass."

"I'm not asking, I'm ordering," Mercy edits, glaring at the Light Keeper. "I want as many of those orders put through processing as possible before I come back. If you get any backlash, I don't care. I give no shits about what

388

anyone has to say. I'm done letting other people run my life. Do you hear me?"

"You're insane. I can literally feel the insanity emanating off you," Zero informs him with a shocked smile. "Elders give me strength," he mumbles.

"I'll make a formal broadcast when I get back," he assures, beginning to head down the hall.

Pippa pauses beside Zero and watches him in disbelief. She could see the agitation in Mercy's gait as he moved forward. She wasn't sure how she felt about the person Mercy was becoming. While she hoped it was just the stress of the situation, she couldn't help but recognize the mask he was putting on. It was one she had seen Cal wear for years, one that Cal had finally taken off.

"Guess I'll call the port and tell them to hold for him," Zero sighs, turning toward the switchboard.

"Tell them I will be joining," she announces, causing him to pause.

"Master Novi ordered for you to stay on the estate grounds," Zero advises her.

"Good thing I am an adult and not a child then," she smiles, following in Mercy's footsteps.

"I'm not dealing with your mom for you!" he shouts after her, rolling his eyes. "This isn't my problem!" She ignores him and continues forward. "Pippa!"

Zero lets out a disgruntled growl as she turns the corner and disappears from his sight. This was not going to be good.

Chapter Thirty-Nine

They had left Rieka within thirty minutes of the incident and were being herded toward Ozra as quickly as possible. Abtal was leading the wagon with a Light Sentry, making sure to give the group an escort Mercy would trust. In the darkness of the night, Cal feels the wagon begin to slow to a crawl.

Everyone was asleep except for Cal. Sylas was beside him, his head in Cal's lap while he slept. Meera had been up not long before trying to comfort Velia, but the pair had drifted off again. Charlyn had Saphie held tightly to her as they rested. Cal honestly wasn't sure how any of them were asleep. His mind had been racing since they left trying to come up with a way to get Ruby back and to make sense of the Light Source he was currently carrying. As the wagon comes to a complete stop, he nudges Sylas awake. The Nota looks up at him with a furrowed brow.

"Your eyes are still glowing," Sylas notes with a yawn as someone taps on the back of the wagon.

Sitting up and moving to the back, Sylas unzips the cover. His eyes lock on Mercy as a feeling of relief washes over him. Jumping from the back of the wagon he nearly tackles his best friend to the ground, happy to be reunited with his Keeper.

"I'm sorry!" he shouts in his ear. "I'm so sorry! I'm an awful babysitter."

Mercy shushes him as he peels him off, seeing that the rest in the wagon were still asleep. The seriousness in Mercy's eyes casted an intimidating mood and force Sylas to calm down almost immediately in response. Cal emerges, his eyes glowing faintly. They catch Mercy's attention right away, but he quickly moves on not wanting to waste time on the odd anomaly.

"You two are coming with me, the rest are going to Ozra," he explains.

"What? Why?" Cal questions.

"I'll explain in the transport," Mercy states, looking into the back of the wagon as Meera begins to stir.

The mother looks to Mercy and gives him a smile as she pulls Velia to her chest. He reaches in and shakes Charlyn awake. His housekeeper nods to him and gets to her feet. She picks up Saphie carefully, not wanting to wake her and hands her to Mercy slowly. He takes her and heads toward the two vehicles stopped on the path ahead. Cal and Sylas grab their bags and follow him, this was not what they had discussed with Zero.

"You two get in, I'll be there in a minute," Mercy orders, pointing to one transport while taking Saphie to the opposite.

Both Sylas and Cal listen, moving to the vehicle he pointed at. They open the door to the back and see Pippa was inside dressed in a purple and white Sentry tactical suit. She looked somber and lost in her own thoughts. Both her and Mercy felt off.

"Good evening," she smiles at them as they climb into the back.

"What's going on?" Sylas asks, sitting down beside Cal across from her.

391

"We are going after Iana," Cal informs him. "I can already tell by the look in Mercy's eyes."

"Speaking of eyes..." Pippa gawks, moving to crouch down in front of him. "Why are yours glowing?"

"Your guess is as good as mine," he declares. "I lit up when Iana tried to use her fog on me. My eyes have not stopped glowing since."

"This is strange," she announces. "You have not been able to access your Shadow Source since being exposed to the exua rune but now you are accessing the Light Source?"

"I already have a theory," Sylas states, as she begins to turn Cal's head side to side. "Been thinking about it the whole ride."

"A theory?" Pippa remarks.

"You were asleep," Cal points out.

"Stop it," Sylas scolds his partner, keeping his eyes on Pip. "What if he's a Supra too and the exua rune only works on the primary Source? I know my exua rune is different than the Shadow Source exua but Zero could heal me. He shouldn't be able to do that."

"That is a little farfetched," Pippa differs, going back to her seat.

"So is an obscurum," Sylas reminds her. "You said yourself Cal's more powerful than he should be."

"I also said it would be unheard of for both-" she begins.

He laughs and cuts her off. "Mercy's eyes glow when he gets scared, we've seen Cal literally dismember people just by thinking about it, my pain tolerance is somehow connected to my best friend in some screwed up way, Sander was used to power a fog monster, but Cal being a Supra is a little too hard for you to grasp?"

"I see your point," Pippa yields.

"If Mercy's a Supra, couldn't Cal be one too?" Sylas suggests. "You said a Supra can manipulate both the

Light and Shadow Sources in some way. Cal did that in Rieka. He still is. That's why his eyes are glowing. He might have gotten a handle on Mercy's Source a year ago, but he never learned to use his own. Maybe that's why Mercy's Source didn't feel right to him. He already had his own."

"You think I am a Keeper of Light?" Cal laughs at the idea, rubbing his burning eyes.

"I've seen weirder things," Sylas shrugs.

"Like that damn woman opening a literal portal to hell in the girls' bedroom," Cal notes as Mercy climbs into the transport and closes the door.

"Cal's a Light Keeper," Sylas announces to his friend as Mercy pounds his fist on the steel between the back and the driver.

"What?" Mercy questions, looking to his Alia.

"He used the Light Source," Sylas explains. "Look at his eyes."

"I doubt that," Mercy bluntly retorts, sitting down beside Pippa and rubbing his arm. "I have Cal's polearm under the seat and both of your Sentry armor," he shares, grabbing a tablet out from under him. "I figured you'd have your bow, Sylas, but I packed a tactical one just in case."

"You could at least act interested in the fact that a Shadow Keeper used a Source he shouldn't have," Sylas adds, watching his friend closely.

"Sure. Exciting stuff," Mercy nods, seeming to ignore the statement.

Feeling the awkward tension between Sylas and Mercy begin, Cal interjects. "Where are we going?" he asks, watching Mercy begin to run his finger over the tablet.

"You really think I didn't put one of those stupid tracking devices into my kid's clothes?" Mercy asks with a raised brow, looking at his friend. "I might hate Aitian tech, but I know when it's useful."

393

"You seriously put a tracker in her clothes?" Sylas asks with wide eyes.

Mercy nods, studying the screen as the transport begins to move. "After what happened with Sander, I wasn't taking any chances. I even put one in Meera's shoes. Charlyn has one in the apron she wears around the house; she knows about hers. The girls I put a pouch in each of their shirts and dresses and showed Char how to move it from outfit to outfit. I even have one in your pendant, Sylas."

"That's creepy," Sylas adds, pulling the gem out from inside his shirt and studying it.

"It's behind the stone," Mercy informs.

Cal puts his hand out to look at the pendant. Sylas takes it from his neck and hands it to him. During this exchange, Cal spots the gold, red gemmed ring on Sylas's finger. He ignores the pendant and grabs his hand to look at the ring closer, Sylas nearly dropping the pendant at the interaction.

"Where did you find this?" Cal asks.

"Nex I think," Sylas shrugs.

"Nex…" Cal breathes, pain in his eyes.

"Yeah," Sylas confirms. "She left it outside your office window."

He hadn't thought about his crow much since his return. The pain of losing his Nota was something he hadn't even shared with Sylas yet. The emotions still felt too raw and bringing it up now risked fueling Mercy's anger.

"Have you seen her?" Sylas asks as Cal flips his hand back over and takes his attention to the pendant.

"No," Cal replies numbly. He takes the pendant and studies the piece, happy for the change of subject. "Did Mercy make this?"

"I did," his Alia confirms.

How had Cal not noticed the pendant until now? How had he not noticed the ring? He honestly hadn't thought about what Sylas had done with the gem he had given him, and he thought the ring had been lost with his Nota. He turns the pendant over in his hands a few times pleased to see that Sylas was still holding onto it.

"You can have them back if you want," Sylas urges, watching him.

"No," Cal smiles softly, returning the pendant. "I would rather you hold onto them for me."

"I can do that," Sylas assures, putting the gem back around his neck and tucking it into his shirt.

Pippa gives the two a soft smile, happy to see the pair were getting comfortable together. There was no doubt in her mind that the reason Cal was being talkative and acting more himself was due to Sylas. Mercy's suggestion of summoning him to Rieka was the best thing they could have done for Cal. Letting him spend time with the person who put him the most at ease was a genius move.

"The signal was dropped just across the border in Summa," Mercy states, tucking the tablet back under the seat. "We're getting my daughter back."

Sylas cocks his brow. This was the first time he had heard Mercy refer to either of the girls as his daughters. Until that moment he had always referred to them as "the girls" or by their names, but never his daughters.

The tablet begins to alarm at Mercy's feet. He picks it up again and scrolls his hand over the screen. He turns to show Pippa who gives a concerned nod.

"What now?" Sylas asks.

"The Source Keepers Directive got set into motion today as well as the Equal Trades Act," Mercy shares with them, typing on the tablet. "Zero and Tristia are working to get things moving while I'm gone, and I'm happy to see they're not wasting any time."

"What about the National Council?" Cal questions, exchanging a look with Pippa.

Looking at the young woman he could see she was troubled. Pippa was being oddly quiet now that he thought about it. Considering everything that had been going on he was expecting her to be Mercy's voice of reason and more active in the strategy he was concocting. Instead, she was silent and letting him disregard her. This was certainly an odd shift in dynamic between the pair and something Cal did not like.

"What Council?" Mercy laughs condescendingly, sending a response and putting the tablet beside him. "I need to catch you two up, don't I? I said to hell with the National Council. Welcome to my dictatorship."

"Have you gone mad?" Cal snaps at him in shock.

"If I did, I learned it from you," Mercy shrugs. "I wasn't going to let them do to me what they've been doing to you, but unlike you, Cal, I'm not afraid of them."

"Excuse me?" Cal scoffs.

"You were the King, Caligo," Mercy explains. "Those meetings should have been a curtesy, not how you made decisions for the people."

"You get my crown for a month and suddenly you are reworking my entire system?" he barks. "Do you understand how hard I worked to create that?"

"It was failing," Mercy differs with a patronizing tone. "I fixed it. I looked at every single file from those National Council meetings. They didn't want you to succeed. They wanted to keep power over you. In fact, I'm pretty sure they were working with Malice. I have a good load of proof I'd be happy to show you when we get back to Ozra."

"Proof?" Cal asks, skeptic of his words.

"Yes," Mercy confirms. "At least two members of the NC are associated with members who are considered high up in Malice. At least according to the files *your* team

396

made up. I honestly regret not having Shay in that final meeting with them. It would have been nice to have her there to figure things out for me, then I wouldn't have had to spend the last three days scouring the archives."

This sets Cal aback. While he knew Mercy could handle the job, this wasn't what he was expecting. His friend had taken the monarchy into his own hands and was doing things in a way that seemed rash and not thought through. He glances to Pippa who was keeping her eyes to the floor of the transport. What was going on with her? How was she not correcting this madness?

"I'm going to fix things," Mercy assures Cal. "I'm going to make things right."

"Forcing proclamations and new laws on our people like this is *not* going to fix anything," Cal argues. "It is only going to make things worse."

"Not if I do it right," Mercy explains. "The acts that I'm starting now will take months before they show any progress. That'll give us time to work out the kinks in the system and test run it in the local governments. I'm not going into this with blind rage or a need to prove anything. Well, maybe prove the National Council is a load of shit, but that's about it."

"I don't know if I should be proud of you or call you completely stupid," Sylas finally adds with a shocked smile on his face.

"Maybe a little bit of both," Mercy smirks. "I'm just channeling my inner Cal."

"Oh! So that's where all the cockiness went," Sylas pokes, wrapping an arm around Cal and gesturing to his best friend. "Mercy stole it."

"Just borrowing," Mercy corrects. "I don't think I can keep up this charade for too long."

"I hope not," Pippa adds, looking at Mercy with hurt eyes. "I'm not a fan of this version of you."

"Oh…" his smile falls to a frown.

Both Cal and Sylas exchange a look not sure what to say as Mercy and Pippa keep their eyes locked. This is the Pippa Cal knew. He was pleased to see she was finally speaking up. She had been spending much more time with the Light Keeper recently, neither Cal nor Sylas could really gauge his actions quite like her.

"I don't see confidence or cockiness when I look at you. I see a reckless, arrogant child," she shares.

"Pip," Sylas tries to interrupt, but Cal nudges him.

The Nota looks to Cal who shakes his head lightly, signally to let Pippa finish. She could hold her own and whatever she had to say, Mercy needed to hear. No one knew Mercy's mind like Pippa did and Cal understood that. Letting her say what she needed to was going to benefit all of them. At least he hoped.

"You are moving too quickly and making decisions without properly thinking them through," she addresses. "You are acting like water, rushing with the weight of gravity, and taking out everything in your path. You are being just like water, trying to carve a path through stone, disregarding and disrespecting the soil around you that built your foundation. That path will not open within a day, and it will not open kindly. It takes time to erode enough earth so the water can flow freely and with ease. Are you giving yourself time to erode the wall between yourself and the enemy? No. You are not."

"I don't have time for your metaphors, Pippa," he glares at her.

"Fine. Then allow me to be blunt, Your Grace," she glowers. "You are putting everyone in this vehicle in danger. You could be marching every single one of us to our deaths. Did you even think of that? Caligo can't access his Source properly, Sylas is still trying to remaster his combat and bow proficiencies, and while I can fight, I would be rather useless against Iana and her obscurums. You have a transport full of individuals who are not suited for this mission. The only one suited to go into this fight may be you, Mercy, and even that I am skeptical of. You have been reckless, arrogant, demeaning, and downright unbearable and I will not allow you to put my friends in danger. I already lost my brother once and I will not lose him again because of your idiocy."

She glances to Cal as he gives her a small nod of the head to show his support for her words. She keeps her serious face and looks back to Mercy. The two lock eyes as the Light Keeper waits for her to continue. Once he realizes she's done, he looks to the other two.

"Do you agree with her?" he questions.

Pulling away from Cal, Sylas lets out a heavy sigh. "I'll agree you don't seem like yourself, Merc," he admits. "Forging the document to release Shay, the outburst with Tristia, the shit you've said to me lately, running after Malice and lying to the NC and-"

"If I hadn't gone after Malice, Cal would be dead," Mercy argues, glaring at his Nota.

"Doesn't matter. It wasn't you," Sylas adds, grabbing Cal's hand to apologize.

"Sophos," Mercy scoffs. "You haven't even been around for this. Neither of you have. You've been playing house and letting my daughter get kidnapped."

"You think Iana taking Ruby was our fault?" Cal scoffs at him, anger clear in his voice. "You little-"

"Cal, stop," Sylas mutters to him, knowing he was about to be set off.

"Mercy, you stop that this instant," Pippa remarks, grabbing his face and forcing his gaze. "You are a smart man, but you have never been this arrogant."

"All I'm trying to do is keep you safe," he snaps at her, pulling away as his eyes power up. "Don't you see that? Everything I've done for months has been to keep all of you safe. To try and keep my kids safe. Meera safe. My niece safe. I just want to keep everyone I care about safe and clearly the old me couldn't do that, but you know who can? This version of Mercy can."

The all go quiet, as he looks around the group waiting for a response. Sylas looks down, wanting to avoid the interaction while Cal stays silent, keeping a firm gaze on his Alia. Cal knew if he spoke, it wouldn't be kind words.

Mercy had never been put in a position of having this many people dependent on him. After his family was taken by the Unity Council, he kept to himself. Suddenly being forced into all these important relationships must have been difficult for him, but he needed to try and get used to it. None of them were going anywhere anytime soon.

"But you cannot keep everyone safe," Cal finally adds with a frown. "Pippa is right. If you had done what you had every time in the past, which is put your trust in any single person in this transport, then none of this would have happened. Sylas would not have lost his hand because you would have been on that assignment with him. I would not have gone into that river, because you would have been there to ward off Iana's obscurum. Ruby would not have been taken, because you would have been there to make sure she was protected. This new version of Mercy would have killed Mala without a second thought. This one is losing sight of the bigger picture."

"Sylas?" Mercy looks to his best friend, wanting him to give words of encouragement or defend him, but hears nothing. In fact, Sylas wouldn't even look at him.

Trying to tune into the Elders, Sylas keeps quiet another moment. When Mercy was straying from his path, they let him know and right now he could sense something was wrong. The group needed to hold off. Not just because Pippa and Cal were wary, but because the Elders were too. They sensed something was wrong with Sylas's Keeper and he needed to take time to tend to him.

Taking a deep breath, Sylas leans forward to finally speak. "We're not saying we shouldn't go after Malice, but we need to come up with a plan here... as a team," he states, looking to his Keeper, hoping he was doing the right thing. "Going into this without proper planning will kill us and you know that."

Mercy shakes his head in disbelief that Sylas would contradict him, taking a shuddering breath. "I need to get my daughter back."

"We will get her back," Sylas assures him. "I will give my life before I let Iana or Bryer or anyone on Novus Aitus harm that little girl." He pauses seeing the fear in Mercy's eyes. "I know you're scared right now, but I will not let the Elder Spirits take anyone else from you, especially your child. I am just as sworn to protect her as I am you, alright?"

Mercy nods his head again in understanding. He didn't realize it until Sylas spoke up, but he did need his Nota right now. He didn't need his optimistic best friend; he needed his guide's reassuring words and level head. Sylas was there to help him on his journey as a Keeper of Light and he would not let anything happen that would cause him to veer off his path. If Sylas was saying they needed to take a step back, then they truly did.

Sylas turns around and knocks on the steel wall. After a moment the small window opens. "Change of plans. Take us to the nearest city for the night. We're going to get some rest."

"Vermeer?" the driver asks.

"Sure," Sylas nods as the window shuts.

Chapter Forty

The group had stopped at Sylas's cabin for the remainder of the night. They needed somewhere to rest and try to forge a plan before Mercy got any more frantic. Cal and Sylas were in his room trying to get some rest, but neither could. The day had their minds racing and Cal's eyes were still burning with the Light Source, making keeping his eyes closed uncomfortable.

Sitting in bed, Cal worked in his sketchbook to try and pass the time. He had been watching Sylas attempt to doze off but could tell he was struggling. The tossing and turning was only adding to the inability to get some rest.

"I can't sleep," Sylas announces, turning over to realize Cal was up working.

"You don't say?" Cal sighs, staring down at him.

"I very much say," Sylas laughs, sitting up himself and kissing him.

Cal knew what this was going to lead to. Sylas takes his shirt off and goes in for another kiss as Cal places his sketchbook on the side table. Readjusting himself, Cal lets out a hiss of pain and pushes Sylas away, before laying back on the bed with a grimace.

Pulling back, Sylas looks at him with wide eyes. "What'd I do?"

"It's fine," Cal hisses, squeezing his eyes shut and sitting up slowly. "My back's been..."

"I'm sorry," Sylas states, watching Cal try to stretch it out a bit. "Are your new prosthetics off? Mercy said the fit could be wrong. I can get him," Sylas offers.

Cal shakes his head. "I was tied to a pole for a month... Not great for the back. Not that my back was any better before, but-" He looks at Sylas who had concern on his face. "I'm sorry."

"It's fine," Sylas reassures him.

"Eight years as a living weapon is not great for...well anything," he admits with a shrug.

They both go quiet as a small knock on the door gets their attention. Cal hears Sylas give off an annoyed groan as he gets off the bed, angry that someone was interrupting them. Cal couldn't help but laugh at the aggravation on his face. Maybe it was good they were interrupted.

Opening it, he expected to see Mercy, but instead Sylas locks eyes on Pippa. He quickly folds his arms over his chest and laughs nervously. For some reason he felt uncomfortable with her seeing him without his shirt on. He could hear Cal stifle a laugh from the bed as Sylas becomes awkward in Pippa's presence. At least one of them was amused by this.

"Can-Can I help you?" Sylas asks, clearing his throat.

"May I speak with you both for a moment?" she asks, holding a book in her hands.

"Uh... Sure," Sylas nods, moving so she could come into the room.

He glances into the main room of the cabin and spots Mercy placing a log on the fire. Knowing Mercy, he was letting his mind wander. He was either feeling guilty or trying to come up with an answer as to why Iana took Ruby. It didn't matter that they had Cal back, Mercy was going to take charge regardless.

"Go to sleep, Merc," he pokes, getting his Keepers attention.

"You first," Mercy shoots back.

"Seriously," Sylas eyes him. "I don't want to deal with your sassy, sleep deprived attitude in the morning."

With a heavy sigh, Mercy rolls his eyes and plops down on the sofa. He had made up a small bed on the couch, presumably giving Pippa the guest bed in the loft. With an amused smile, Sylas closes the door and quickly finds his shirt. Trying to act casual he resorts to sorting through his duffle bag at the foot of the bed. If they were going on an assignment, he needed more than just a few sets of lounge clothes. Pippa stands beside him, looking back and forth between the two. She could tell she interrupted them, but she didn't care.

"I know I am usually giving you two information from books about the Sources but…" she starts, placing the book on the bed.

Leaning forward, Cal reads the cover. "A psychology book?" he questions, looking at her.

"I have been watching Mercy very carefully, it is no surprise he is troubled," she explains.

"No shit," Sylas scoffs, keeping his eyes on what he was doing.

"Anxiety, depression, PTSD," she lists. "He needs to talk to someone."

"I'm pretty sure everyone in this cabin needs therapy, Pippa," Sylas notes, looking at her with another laugh. "Cal admits he wants to off himself frequently, you definitely have some serious fixer syndrome, and I'll attest that I've been a total mess since Spheara," he explains. They both glare at him as Sylas scans over the two. "I'm just being honest."

"This is not a joke, Sylas," Pippa scolds.

"I'm not saying it is," he retorts. "I'm saying you aren't telling us anything new."

"Has he spoken to either of you about anything personal recently?" Pippa asks, looking between them. "Has he reached out? Has he talked to you about how he has felt or is feeling?"

Both Cal and Sylas exchange a look. Neither of them had really thought about it. While Cal and Mercy had gotten close, it seemed it was mostly Cal opening up and Sylas had just grown used to Mercy walling himself off. His best friend was silent, and he respected that. Sylas didn't like being forced to speak, so why make Mercy?

"He's fine. He always says he's fine," Sylas shrugs, putting away the few sets of clothes.

"Did you ever think that maybe 'I'm fine,' is his way of asking for help?" Pippa lectures.

The two young men exchange another look. The pair had been so caught up in their own lives, maybe they had started to let Mercy fall to the side. Cal was running a planet; he didn't have time. The pressure and stress that came with the job made it impossible for him to focus on anything, even himself. Sylas on the other hand was so busy trying to find his independence from the Keeper that he was neglecting his role as Mercy's Nota and best friend. They couldn't deny that Pippa was right. They were both letting Mercy slip through the cracks.

Clearing his throat, Cal speaks up. "Do you two know about the vision?"

"The one where he dies?" Sylas questions, seeing a small nod from Cal. "Yeah, he's mentioned it."

This makes Pippa go quiet. Hearing that Mercy had confided in the two about the vision made this more upsetting. The fact the two of them were aware their friend was facing the idea of his own death made their separation from him infuriating. Mercy needed them right now, but instead they were too focused on their own issues to see the glaring one in front of them. How had they not showed any worry about Mercy's vision?

"He opened up to me briefly when he had it, but I think it was because he didn't have a choice," Cal states, looking back at the book. "He said he couldn't breathe and sounded troubled, but I simply thought it was due to the vision and stress…"

"He has not had a good night's rest in nearly a year due to nightmares," Pippa explains to them. "Did either of you take interest in his panic attacks? Do you even know how to bring him out of one?"

"His panic attacks?" Sylas asks, with a raised brow.

"Going boneless," Cal states, feeling shameful for not realizing sooner. "I am sorry, Pip. You have been dealing with this by yourself…"

"Yes, I have," she confirms, folding her arms. "You two think me sleeping in his room is cute, but I only do it so he can sleep at all. Just like you are doing with Sylas, Caligo. The only reason you are well rested and becoming yourself after that camp is because you have been using Sylas as a safe haven."

"What panic attacks?" Sylas asks again, going to sit on the bed beside Cal.

"You haven't seen them?" Cal questions with a cocked brow. "He freezes up. He looks like he is about to die. He can't breathe or speak or move or anything. It is like what he used to do in a fight, but worse."

"The one he had when you called about Ruby is the worst I have ever witnessed," she explains to them. "I have tried to get him to open up about it, but he claims it is just how he is, which apparently is what you two think as well. I cannot keep doing this alone. I know you are both going through some difficult things yourselves, but your friend needs you. I need you to step up if you are able."

"I'm sorry, Pip," Cal repeats. "You should not have to deal with this."

"What happened with you, Cal... That changed him," she shares, her voice wavering. "He came back to Ozra a completely different person, and I have been afraid ever since. My mother is uneasy as well. She is not hearing good things in Mercy's future."

"What did Master Novi say?" Sylas asks, his brows furrowed in concern.

"The path he is on right now may be a dark one," she enlightens them, looking down, tears dancing in her eyes. "I fear we may lose him once Bryer causes him to force his hand." She locks eyes with Sylas. "The brighter the light, the bigger the darkness."

"Master Novi thinks what's happening with Ruby will cause him to unlock his Supra Keeping," Sylas nods in understanding.

"It will," she confirms. "And unlocked under dark pretenses may be enough to sway him down a malevolent path," Pippa states, trying to hold herself together. "Mercy is a good person, with a good heart. We cannot let him lose that. The only reason I left the estate with him was to try and keep him from doing anything he will regret. My mother will be livid once she has found I left."

"Livid? Why?" Cal asks, alarm in his voice.

She shakes her head. If Master Novi told her to stay out of this, that meant she heard something gruesome in her daughter's future. Cal's stomach drops as he looks to Sylas with worry. If anything happened to Pippa, he wouldn't be able to forgive himself. The young woman in front of him was like a sister. The last eight years Cal had become a part of the Dror home. In his first year of training with his Shadow Source under Master Novi, he had spent nearly every day with Pippa studying the Sources.

"We won't let anything happen," Sylas assures her. "We won't let Bryer get to him."

"There is something else," Pippa adds, reaching into the pocket of her dress and handing a piece of paper to Sylas. "Mercy found something in the Malice files that is concerning," she states, looking at him. "I think it would be best for you two to discuss this alone. I will be just outside if you need me."

"Way to be ominous, Pip," Sylas mutters, taking the paper from her hand.

"Just remember who the enemy is," she stresses, backing toward the door.

She exits the room as Sylas hesitantly unfolds the paper. He begins to read what was written, realizing quickly it was Mercy's scrambled handwriting. His brow furrows, showing his confusion with each word. Caligo watches him carefully not sure what to take of the interaction but was fearful. After a few minutes of reading, Sylas refolds the paper and looks to Cal.

"What is it?" Cal questions.

"Don't freak out," Sylas stresses.

"Why would I freak out?" Cal asks.

Taking a deep breath, Sylas hands Cal the paper. "Mercy thinks Bryer is Emrys," he shares.

"No, Bryer is his brother, Voltas," Cal laughs in shock, taking the paper and reading it himself.

"He's what?" Sylas questions.

The sheet of paper explained in detail what Mercy had found in the archives. The more he read the more shocked he became. His father was documented as having Light Keeper lineage, but the records had been altered shortly before his Unity to Mala. Mercy had even written down the file locations and numbers so he could reference them when they got back to the capital. At the bottom of the page was both his father's and Bryer's names written out with the word "anagram" beside them.

"This cannot be right," Cal mutters, panic filling his voice. "Bryer told me himself. He is Voltas."

"Mercy is pretty thorough when he researches," Sylas adds, taking the paper.

"My father is dead," Cal snaps. "My mother killed him. I know she did. We had an eloium for him."

"We thought Trust was dead," Sylas adds, keeping his voice low, trying to stay calm. "We thought you were dead too."

"My father *is* dead," Cal bites again, glaring at his partner. "My father would never do to me what Bryer did. Voltas? Yes. My father? No."

Seeing the fear and anxiety that was filling Cal causes Sylas to shiver. He could see the Light Source beginning to burn brighter in Cal's eyes casting a purple hue in his irises. While he wanted to comfort Caligo, it seemed more in his best interest to rationalize what they had just read. He knew Mercy, and Mercy wouldn't drop something like this unless he was sure.

"What do you know about Voltas?" Sylas questions, trying to figure this out.

"Uncle Voltas…" Cal begins, speaking quickly. "I only met him once when I was a child. I was young when my father died, and his family gave little care in my upbringing after his passing. I was the son of a tyrant and any association with me was fuel for the rebels. Mala did not speak of them, and she rarely spoke of my father."

"That was 20 years ago," Sylas states quietly. "People change in 20 years."

"Not my father," Cal adds, shaking his head.

"This is some compelling evidence," Sylas differs, picking up the paper again.

"I would know my father," Cal snaps, the light growing brighter in his irises, mirroring his anger. "He told me himself, Sy. I am telling you the truth. That man is Voltas."

"Okay, so Mercy's wrong," Sylas edits.

"My father would not say the things Bryer said to me," Cal continues. "King Emrys is dead, and I will not allow Mercy to spew this lie. I can accept Bryer being my uncle, but not my father."

"I can tell this is bothering you," Sylas notes.

"Of course it is!" Cal snaps. "I will not let Mercy try to convince me my father said those unbearable things."

They go quiet a moment as Cal glares at Sylas. The look in his eyes painted a clear picture. Whatever Bryer had said to him was the cause of this shift back into his old ways and Sylas needed to figure out why. Cal was strong and resilient. How had Bryer broken him down?

"What did he say?" Sylas asks. "I can't help you if you don't tell me. Remember what you told me? Robbing yourself of the ability-"

"Please don't," Cal begs, looking at the paper in Sylas's hand. "Please ..." he closes his eyes, taking a deep breath.

"Cal, you need to tell me," Sylas pleads. "I can't help you through this if you don't tell me what he said."

Taking another deep breath, Cal gives a small nod. He wanted Sylas to help rationalize this. He needed him to. The only way to do that was to talk.

Locking eyes on Sylas, he speaks in a quiet voice. "Every wrong decision, every killing, every foul word that left my mouth, he recited it all to me like it was poetry, like he enjoyed watching me crumble. I deserve to suffer in his mind. He wanted to make sure I felt the pain of my people..."

Hearing Cal's words, Sylas nods his head. This felt like déjà vu, but at the same time deeper. While Cal had opened up to him about the things Mala had said and done to him before, he rarely spoke about the actual effects doing her dirty work had. Even hearing Cal's body count was terrifying. While Sylas had killed in the past, his number was just at a few dozen. Being a Junior Guard for five years had forced his hand on a few occasions, as did protecting Mercy on assignments.

Taking a deep breath, Sylas moves to sit closer to Cal and puts at arm around him. "So clearly, Bryer, or whoever the hell this whack job is, doesn't know you," Sylas comforts. "As far as I'm concerned, he has no idea what the hell he's talking about, so you shouldn't listen to a single word that asshole has to say. He's insane. Probably crazier than Mercy."

"Crazier than you?" Cal asks, with a small smile.

"Oh definitely," Sylas nods. "He kidnapped my boyfriend and my niece, which makes him certifiably insane."

Nodding his head, Cal looks at the book in front of them. He and Sylas had been through this. Sylas had sat with him countless times during their six months together to try and sort through his trauma. Bringing it back up again and having him give the same pep talk felt foolish.

With a deep breath Cal opts to change the subject. "Do you think Bryer is going to kill that little girl?"

"We won't let him. I also don't think Mercy will ever let us babysit his kids again," Sylas adds jokingly. "We did a horrible job. Worst babysitters on Novus Aitus. I hope he fires both of us."

Cal nods his head with a small laugh looking down at the book again. Sylas grabs his chin and forces him to look him in the eye. His face was serious, but the playful glint was still in his gaze.

"Now that we've figured out Mercy is mentally ill and your uncle is a psychopath, I think it's time we figure out why the hell your eyes are glowing," Sylas states, looking back and forth between Cal's irises. "We've been acting like this is normal for too long, and your eyes are starting to go bloodshot."

"It's not pleasant," Cal admits rubbing his eyes. "I don't know how Mercy handles this."

411

"The Shadow Source doesn't irritate your eyes?" Sylas questions, releasing his chin.

"Not like this," Cal states, blinking a few times. "My Shadow Source is more of a sudden, sharp pain that quickly dissipates once I'm powered up. This though... This is a constant burning, like when you open your eyes under water. You get used to it, but it's still there."

"Are you nervous about something? Mercy's will stay with him if he's anxious or afraid sometimes," Sylas explains as Cal continues to rub his eyes.

"Perhaps," Cal informs. Closing his eyes, he could feel the dull heat on his lids. "I don't think I can sleep like this."

"The things I'd do for that genti Source Tome right now," Sylas laughs, getting to his feet and moving to the bookshelf in the corner. "Mercy should have brought it. He knows I like reading material on road trips."

"My Source still being gone," Cal begins, watching Sylas, "do you have any theories on that?"

"I do," Sylas states, scanning the books for another few seconds before turning to Cal. "This would be easier to figure out with the books Pippa has in Ozra though," Sylas scoffs at the inconvenience. "Nothing is ever easy with you and Merc, is it? We're going to try and solve this the same way Merc does. Up for some target practice?"

"Target practice?" Cal questions.

Sylas grabs Cal's prosthetics and sets them on the bed. "When Mercy's used to act up, he'd have to blow off some steam. We're trying that."

Chapter Forty-One

The group was exhausted, the sun starting to peak over the horizon, but Mercy was determined to help Cal get this under control. Even if that meant using Cal as a target. The two of them had been going at it for nearly two hours, Mercy finally just throwing everything he had at his Alia. The Source in Cal reacted occasionally, but it was sporadic, making Caligo more frustrated with every passing moment. He basically had to stand there and let Mercy beat him, and with Mercy having more control than ever over his Source, it was not a pleasant experience.

Sylas and Pippa sit on the edge of the porch and watch Mercy and Cal in the yard. Even though Cal had experience with the Light Source, this seemed to be entirely different. It was like the Light Source he held was simply reacting and not letting him control it.

"This is painful to watch," Pippa remarks.

"They're just getting in some *light* training before bed," Sylas smirks.

She smiles at the joke. "I have been wracking my mind trying to make sense of this. If Cal has the Light Source, then you should have been able to interact with him even when you had Mercy's shield. Had you two interacted since he returned Mercy's Source?"

Thinking back, Sylas furrows his brow. He couldn't think of a time the two had tried to physically touch each other since their breakup. They had said their final goodbyes on Cal's balcony that night and then for the most part avoided each other. They went months without seeing one another, and when Sylas decided to return to the military, the two tended to keep distance between them.

"I don't think so," he admits. "Cal was cautious. He stayed aware of where I was and made a point to avoid me. Not just because of personal boundaries, but because of the shield. He didn't want to get burned or shocked."

"So, you do not even know if he could still interact with you?" Pippa continues to question as Mercy shoots a blast of energy at Cal, throwing him back a few feet.

Sylas winces at the sight and shakes his head again. "What are you thinking?"

"I am wondering if he still has some of Mercy's Source in him," she suggests. "Or perhaps he has a shield like you once did. Perhaps Mercy or even my mother could be protecting him without realizing."

"My shield didn't give me Source magic though," Sylas differs. "It just protected me. He was drawing the Source to him back at the house. His eyes are glowing, and his vessels were lighting up, and his hands were hot, just like Merc. He said he healed himself in that camp too. He healed the rune on his chest. This is different..." He rolls up his sleeve to show the burn mark on his arm from Cal's heated grasp the day before.

"Yet he is not marked with the Light Source, and it did not heal his major injuries," she notes. "What if he had started to unlock this well before this week and that was why you were able to touch during your time as a squire? What if it had nothing to do with Mercy's Source?"

"I was also able to carry him to your parent's house that night he got hurt," Sylas remembers. "Mercy put Rom's robe over my arms, but still…"

"Perhaps, like most Source abilities, he had to unlock it. Being so in tune with the Shadow Source may have delayed it, unlike Mercy who had suppressed his connection to the point he could access both when he decided to accept his gifts," she adds.

Sylas nods. "A weakened or severed connection to the Shadow Source could give the Light Source an opportunity to show itself."

They both go quiet for a moment as Mercy walks up to Cal and grabs his face to study his eyes. Cal had reacted to a few of Mercy's advances, but not much. They watch as the two talk to each other for a moment while Mercy heals the burns before going back to their training.

"You said Zero could heal you?" Pippa prods, looking at the burn again.

"Yeah," Sylas confirms, showing her his hand, where his fingers once were. "He used his peritia on me after the eloium too."

"Perhaps your theory is correct then, and the exua rune only strips the primary Source associated with the individual," Pippa suggests.

"Why would Bryer want to strip my protection?" Sylas asks.

"They could know something we do not," she frowns. "The effects of the exua rune on a Nota is not in the Aitian Source Tome. Maybe the rune is what is keeping Nex at bay for Caligo as well."

"Maybe," Sylas sighs, looking at the rune on his arm. "I hate not knowing. It creeps me out that it's on my body and I don't know what it does."

"You could read every book in the Great Library of the Source Temple and still not know everything," Pippa comforts. "On another note, I am glad to see you and Cal have reconciled," she adds, watching as Mercy takes a few steps away from Cal. "He is more himself with you."

"He's a pain in my ass," Sylas laughs, "but you can't help the things your heart has a longing for."

"Very true," Pippa nods with a smile.

Sylas watches her a moment as she keeps her eyes on the pair. He leans over toward her, putting on his playful smile. "And what is your heart longing for, Pip?"

She snickers at the remark and gives a shrug. "I am not sure, if I am being honest with you."

"I think it's a Riekan blacksmith turned ruler of the world," Sylas states, raising his brows at her teasingly.

"I am trying not to let myself fall into that," she admits with a heavy exhale. "I have learned that caring for Mercy Validus is a dangerous game."

"What makes it dangerous?" he asks, losing his joking manner.

"You cannot love someone who does not love themselves," she explains. "Mercy... He does not like who or what he is. He is constantly at war with himself. Caring for someone like that is treacherous."

"I guess I can agree with that," he nods, looking to Cal as the two pause their training again.

Even though Mercy had gained confidence and found his voice, he still was wary about himself. He had some certainty in his actions, but not in who he was. This made him a complicated person to be around, and Sylas knew that. Being afraid of things was just part of who his best friend was. Though, now that he thought of it, perhaps that jumpiness was deeper than just a personality trait. Hiding his Source for seven years had to have taken a toll on him. Living every day with a fear for his life and his secret being discovered had undoubtably taken levy on his mind. He had been despised for so long, and even now people were scared of him.

"Do you think Cal loves himself?" Pippa questions, interrupting his thoughts.

Letting out a deep breath, Sylas looks to the ground. He thought he had gotten Cal to a point where he had learned to accept himself, but now he wasn't sure. Self love was something Cal had struggled with since they met. No matter how hard he tried, it seemed Cal would never see himself as anything other than the weapon he believed Mala forged in him. Every time he took a step away from the notion, it seemed someone or something thrust him back.

"I think he wants to love himself," Sylas finally answers, looking at the Shadow Keeper.

"And you? Do you love yourself?" she pries.

He laughs a moment, then shakes his head. "I don't know," he confesses, taking his eyes back to the ground. "Being a Nota...Nex exists to serve Caligo. Her entire world revolves around her Keeper... Shouldn't mine too?" He looks to Pippa. "When I realized what I was to Mercy, it was like I was suddenly tied to him in a way I can't quite explain." He pauses and thinks a moment. "Sometimes listening to him makes me so angry, Pip. I can't stand it when he tells me what to do, but because of what I am, I have to listen. It's like I'm wired to do whatever he says... One moment I'm his best friend and the next I'm valued no more than an animal."

"I can see that being a difficult position to be in," Pippa empathizes.

"Pushing Merc away when I thought Cal was dead... It was a mistake. It made things worse. It was why I gave in so fast when he came to ask me to Ozra. As soon as I saw him at my door, I felt less empty. I think it was one of the reasons I spiraled the way I did after Spheara too. Even without his Source, I was still tied to him in a nonphysical way. I was away from my Keeper for months and I knew what was happening and just fought it," he explains. "The longer I stayed away, the more the Elder Spirits pushed me toward him. It's like a nagging, hollow feeling. I hate it. I despise it."

"Did you feel that way before?" Pippa questions.

He shakes his head. "No." He pauses a moment to think through his next words. "Until then... Being his best friend, protecting him, that was my choice. I chose to be there for him, to help him, to build him up. Now I don't feel like I get a choice. He kept me away from Cal." He lets out a sigh and shakes his head a moment before locking eyes with Pippa. "I'm afraid once we figure this out, he'll keep me away from him again."

"I will not allow Mercy to come between you and the person you love," Pippa comforts, intertwining her arm around his and leaning her head onto his shoulder. "Cal will not stand for it either."

"Thank you," he smiles softly.

They both watch as Mercy and Cal walk back toward them. Caligo was shaking his arms out, his face serious. The two of them looked exhausted. As he gets closer, Sylas could see the faint purple glow had dissipated from Cal's eyes. Blowing off some steam was exactly what he needed.

The two of them approach the porch, Mercy going inside without saying a word to anyone. They weren't sure if he was tired, worried, or angry. He had been relatively silent since they had gotten to the cabin. He had said a few words to the driver upon arrival, but that was about it. Though silence was something they were all used to, this felt very different. This was an unnerving silence.

"What's he moping about?" Sylas asks, as Cal sits down next to him on the edge of the porch.

"Your guess is as good as mine," Cal admits. "I can't get in his head anymore."

"Really?" Sylas asks in surprise, looking back at the door. "Damn..."

419

"We should all get some rest," Pippa announces, getting to her feet. "Goodnight, boys."

"Goodnight," Cal nods at her.

"Night, Pip," Sylas chimes watching her go inside.

The two of them sit in silence for a few beats. Sylas stares at the sunrise peaking over the horizon trying to think through what he had just shared with Pippa. He wondered if he was going to be struggling with being Mercy's Nota for the rest of his life. Was this metaphysical tie to Mercy going to affect everything he did?

After Spheara, Mercy had mentioned that his father had been Orlo's Nota. That there was maybe some link between the Bellators and Validus Keepers of Light that they didn't know about. While their fathers were close when they were children, he had always sensed the tension between the pair as they grew older. The arguments he had heard between their fathers leading up to the night Mercy's mother was killed still ran through his mind at times. His father became rather cold when Orlo was taken by the Unity Council all those years ago, yet still cared for Mercy and Charity. Ezra probably knew Sylas was going to be Mercy's Nota. That meant he didn't have a choice but to nurture the children Orlo left behind or his own son was going to suffer the consequences.

"Are you okay?" Cal asks, staring at Sylas who appeared lost in thought.

"Uh, yeah, I'm okay," Sylas laughs nervously, coming back to reality. "We can go inside."

"You are worried about something," Cal notes as Sylas goes to get up. Cal pulls him back to a sitting position on the edge of the porch. "Is it Mercy?"

"Not entirely," Sylas admits.

"If you need to talk, I will listen," Cal reassures.

The two keep their eyes locked a moment. He could see in Cal's gaze that he was ready to listen, the man giving him a soft nod to speak. Letting out a heavy sigh, Sylas looks to the ground.

"I was thinking about mine and Mercy's fathers," he shares.

"I see," Cal nods in understanding.

Certainly, Sylas wasn't going to want to speak about their fathers with him. Cal was the reason they were both gone. He stares at the tree line waiting for Sylas to get to his feet again but to his surprise, Sylas clears his throat and begins to talk.

"I'm trying to make sense of why my dad didn't care what happened to Orlo after the raid on Rieka when we were kids," Sylas shares. "My dad was Orlo's Nota and for me, being away from Mercy is difficult... I don't exactly know how to explain it."

"Like Nex and I being apart," Cal nods in support, his face showing pain in his words. "It is a different kind of lonely."

"Exactly," Sylas agrees with a heavy sigh. "It's just making me wonder... Why did my father not care when the UC took Orlo?"

"I wish I had an answer for you," Cal replies, offering his hand, showing sorrow in his eyes.

"I'm worried that maybe he started to hate Orlo," Sylas expresses, slipping his hand into Cal's. "I mean... sometimes I don't like Mercy because of our connection to each other. What if my dad felt the same way? What if I start to act like my dad? What if I make the same choice, and turn my back on my Keeper?"

"You won't," Cal reassures, squeezing his hand.

"What makes you so sure?" Sylas questions, his eyes serious.

Cal nods his head in understanding, thinking through the statement before taking a deep breath. "Because we are not the sum of our parent's mistakes."

He looks at Sylas who gives a small smile. "You remembered that?"

"I have not let it leave my mind since you said it," Cal discloses. "Sometimes I say it to myself multiple times per day. It helps me separate myself from Mala." They go silent a moment before Cal continues. "The things Orlo did for Novus Aitus may have been valiant, but at what cost?"

Cal watches Sylas furrow his brow at the statement. Letting out a heavy exhale, Cal squeezes his hand before speaking again.

"We can assume Orlo Validus knew the fate of our current world," Cal clarifies, looking down to collect his thoughts. "He knew putting Mercy on the path of a hero would kill his daughter. He chose to let his eldest son sit in a prison for ten years before giving his life. He willingly let Mercy's mother die. He predicted all of the bloodshed and the loss you and Mercy would experience, yet still chose to create that family, while at the same time did nothing to prevent the outcome." He pauses a moment, before looking at Sylas. "Perhaps your father saw this and chose to see the cruelty in Orlo's actions instead of a selfless martyr."

Taking a shaking breath, Sylas contemplates his words. Orlo knew everything that needed to happen to give the outcome of Spheara. He knew Aalin and Charity would die, he knew the loss Mercy was going to experience in the fight, perhaps he even knew Rieka would fall. Odds were, he confided in his Nota and because of Ezra's duty, he simply had to watch it happen. He couldn't say anything, or he would be defying his Keeper's direct orders, something that was difficult to do.

Now that he thought of it, his father's coldness didn't even begin until Orlo's disappearance. While he was always a stoic and intimidating man, he hadn't begun to show a hateful side until that day. Until he had to look at Orlo's children and begin raising them to do what his Keeper wanted.

"He watched Charity grow up to be killed," Sylas voices in shock.

"And he watched you and your brother, his sons, grow to care for a girl, a sister, who would be taken from them," Cal adds.

"Shit…" Sylas breathes in shock.

"Knowing what he did could break even the strongest of men," Cal continues. "Orlo's choice to let Mercy enact the Spheara vision was allowing your family to suffer too, Sy. He may have even known he and your brother would die as well. You lost your family just as much as Mercy did over Orlo's choices."

After a long pause and fidgeting with Cal's hand, Sylas speaks. "I never thought of my dad that way. I guess I'll never get the chance to ask him either."

"I'm sorry," Cal states, pulling his hand away. "I wish I had been more aware of my actions that day."

Sylas shakes his head, grabbing his hand again, holding it tightly. "You did what you needed to do. Like any good military man, you looked at the situation and did what was best for the majority. You removed your emotions from the equation."

"I suppose," Cal nods, studying Sylas's face closely.

While he was relieved to see Sylas becoming more vulnerable, part of him was wary. The fear of saying the wrong thing and making Sylas upset was not something he enjoyed. Why was this something he wanted in the first place? Seeing Sylas letting his guard down and be emotional was painful to watch.

"Maybe if I had removed my emotions from the equation, Trust would still be alive," Sylas adds, looking numbly at the lawn.

"Sy, no…" Cal whispers, holding his hand tighter.

"I wanted to help you and Merc," he confides. "I defied Mercy's orders and Trust's warnings. I let my emotions get the best of me and I put myself into that fight." He looks to Cal with pained eyes. "Trust was pushing me out of the way, Cal. The only reason he was there, at that moment, was to protect me."

"Trust made his choice," Cal defends. "Of all the people there that day, he knew what was going to happen and he chose to still do it anyway."

"But I chose to leave that wall," Sylas deflects, shaking his head and averting his eyes to the ground again. "I made a choice and it cost someone their life. Not just anyone, but someone I cared about. How am I supposed to live with that?"

"Sadly, I don't think I am the best person to ask," Cal admits, looking down at the grass himself.

"How are you coping with it?" Sylas questions, looking back at him with a serious gaze. He nudges him softly to get him to lock eyes.

"I'm not," Cal bluntly replies. "I am simply trying to forget that day ever happened." He shakes his head. "Some days I can hardly even look at Mercy."

Nodding his head in response, Sylas goes quiet again. That day had affected him in more ways than he was willing to admit. Sylas genuinely thought that day was the end. Every part of him believed he was going to die in that courtyard. He was ready to say goodbye. While at the time he was content, knowing he was dying for a good cause, now he was terrified. Before that day he wasn't afraid of death, but now it was his greatest fear.

"How do you keep living when you always feel like you're about to die?" Sylas whispers.

"You just do, Sy," Cal replies squeezing his hand.

They go silent for another moment, both staring numbly at the front lawn with the others hand held tightly. With the childhood Sylas had compared to Cal, he felt bad for complaining. Comparing his life to either Cal or Mercy

424

made him feel bad. The worst thing to happen to him before Spheara was his parents splitting up.

"Sorry for ranting," Sylas finally states.

"Do not apologize. Your thoughts are always valued here, my love," Cal retorts, pulling Sylas's hand to his face and kissing it before getting to his feet.

The comment brings a small smile to Sylas's face. Just because someone's life seemed a little easier, didn't make it any less difficult to handle. Pulling Sylas to his feet, Cal gives him a small nod and smile.

"Alright. Enough moping," Sylas states, a hint of humor coming back to him. He moves up the steps, with Cal's hand still in his. "Inside. Get in my bedroom right now. I know exactly what we both want to be doing right now."

Pausing, Cal pulls back and shakes his head. "Sy, I'm tired. Now is not-"

"Sleeping," Sylas laughs, looking at Cal playfully. "I was going to say sleeping. I need some decent sleep before Mercy takes us on another suicide mission. Let's go."

"Sophos, I hate you," Cal smiles with a shake of the head.

"What'd you think I was gonna say?" Sylas teases, putting an arm around him and kissing his cheek.

Giving a huff of annoyance, Cal shakes his head again. As much as he outwardly showed his disapproval of Sylas's jokes, he did appreciate them. Sylas always had a way of lightening the air when stress was high.

Chapter Forty-Two

Mercy was the first to wake up an hour or so ago and it was already well passed noon. They had all been awake into the early morning hours, so he decided to just let the group sleep. He had already sent the driver to town to be taken back to the capital. With Cal here, they didn't really need the driver anymore.

Sitting in the grass in front of the cabin, Mercy closes his eyes and takes in the afternoon sun. It was chilly, but he didn't mind. Being alone gave him some time to think over what Pippa had said. Was he really acting that out of character? All he was trying to do was fix things. The state of the government and the rescue of Ruby were important things to act on. Thinking of Ruby makes his heart sink. Why was he just sitting here? He should go wake them up and drag them to go look for her.

Slouching forward, he begins to pick at the grass. With the cold weather coming in, the grass was starting to die off, but it was still early enough in the season that it was trying to keep going. He never thought he'd relate to grass, but here he was. He envied its strength. It could be killed off every winter and come back stronger the following spring. Every plant around him followed that cycle, why couldn't he?

He glances up as the door to the cabin opens and Pippa exits. She gives him a small wave as he nods his head and begins to pull a few long pieces of grass from the ground. The young woman walks over and sits down beside him as he focuses on the strands in his hands and begins to fidget with them.

"Hello, dear," she smiles at him. "We were wondering where you wandered to."

"I'm right here," he sighs.

"I see that," she chuckles, watching him fiddle with the strands of grass. "Sylas is making lunch if you are hungry," she informs him.

"I already ate," he shrugs.

"But was it Sylas's cooking?" she teases.

He lets out a small laugh and shakes his head. She made a valid point. Sylas was a fantastic cook. His best friend used to cook with his mother all the time and after she left, Sylas picked up the slack in the meal department for the Bellator home. The home cooked meals Sylas made were always delicious and comforting. Today though, the thought of taking a moment to eat anything felt wrong. His focus needed to be on Ruby, not lunch.

Observing Mercy, Pippa sees him continue to focus on twisting the grass in his hands. It becomes clear he wasn't just playing with it, but he was weaving the strands meticulously.

"What are you making?" she asks.

"Not sure yet," he admits. He glances to her and sees her interest in what he was doing. "Uh… When Charity and I would go foraging in the spring and summer, we would stop for lunch and she would always pick the grass and make it into different things," he explains as he works. "Crowns, bracelets, necklaces, one time she even made a belt," he continues. "Sometimes when I miss her, I try to do something she liked to maybe get her spirit to show up."

"Does that work?" she questions.

"No," he bluntly replies, keeping his concentration on the grass.

"Have you been able to access your peritias on command yet?" she prods as he works.

He shakes his head. "They're pretty useless."

"No, they are not," she differs.

"What use have my visions been, Pip?" he questions with frustration. "The last two have been nonsense. I can't protect anyone."

"That's not true," she differs.

"I can't," he shrugs. "I couldn't protect Sylas, or Cal, or Ruby... I can't even protect myself. I'm a lousy Keeper and an even worse ruler."

"That is a lie," she proclaims.

He shakes his head again. "No, it's not," he laughs. "If I lose Ruby..."

"You won't lose Ruby," she adds. "This will all work out and everything will be okay. Have hope."

"Stop trying to make me feel better," he sighs.

"I am not saying that to make you feel better," she clarifies. "I'm saying it because life still has the opportunity to turn this around."

"You're starting to sound like Sylas," he mumbles.

"That is because Sylas and I speak the same language and that is the language of faith," she informs him.

"I'm out of faith," he retorts.

"Don't say that," she pleads.

"What have the Elder Spirits ever done for me?" he asks, glancing to her. "After this, I'm done, Pip. Once we get Ruby back, I quit. I'm resigning from the Ozran and Elder Councils, I'm turning in my Sentry uniform, and I'm focusing on my family and my shop and my apprentices. I can't be there for them if I'm off trying to save the world every other day."

"I do not-" she begins, but he cuts her off.

"Please don't argue me on this," he begs. "I don't want to fight anymore, Pip. My mind and my body can't take any more of this. I don't even feel like myself these days... I just want time to heal."

"Okay," she nods in understanding.

They sit in silence as he lets out a steady exhale. He abruptly grabs Pippa's hand and wraps the woven grass around the base of one of her fingers. She watches him with a furrowed brow as he takes it back and begins to finish up the small item. While he could sit here and absent mindedly play with the grass for hours, he knew Pippa came out here to bring him inside. There was no doubt that Sylas and Cal wanted to start forming a plan and they needed Mercy to do that. He weaves the last few loose pieces back in and holds his palm out to Pippa to show an intricately woven ring.

"For you," he offers.

She lets out a small laugh and puts her hand out for him to place it on her finger.

"You say I'm like water, well you're like the earth," he informs her, placing it on her finger. "You support the life and foundation around you, you're resilient, and you don't know when to give up."

Letting out another chuckle she nods her head and looks at the ring. His ability to work with small and delicate items never ceased to amaze her. Even though it was just strands of grass, he had created something lovely. It was nice to see him finally acting somewhat himself. Perhaps the storm in his head was finally subsiding.

"We should get inside," Mercy huffs, getting to his feet and offering her his hand.

She accepts and lets him pull her to her feet. They walk back to the cabin together. When Mercy grabs the door and lets Pippa in, the blast of whatever Sylas was cooking hits them both. They see Sylas who was seeming in his element with a few pots and pans on the stove. Cal leans on the counter to help when needed while also working on a sketch.

"Hey! You found him," Sylas praises.

"I wasn't lost," Mercy notes, going to sit on a stool at the counter, Pippa joining him.

"Well, we didn't know where you went, hence you needed to be found," Sylas pokes. "So, what's the plan?" he asks, keeping his attention on the lunch he was preparing.

"Find Ruby," Mercy states, watching Sylas.

"Getting Ruby isn't exactly a thought-out strategy there, sunshine," Sylas replies, pointing at him with a spatula in his hand.

Mercy rolls his eyes and folds his arms. "We need to get my daughter back."

"And I understand that," Sylas assures, taking his eyes back to the stove. "Unfortunately, we need a plan before we go waltzing into a death trap."

"Well, we know Iana took her," Cal inserts, working on his drawing.

"Very observant, Cal," Mercy scoffs.

"Lose the 'tude, star bright," Sylas snaps, pointing at his best friend again. "We're here to help you, so you're going to play nice."

"I am nice," Mercy argues.

"We've already established you've been a grade A asshole lately," Sylas eyes him. "Be nice or take a walk and come back when you can be civil."

"Okay. Okay. Sorry, momma bear," Mercy huffs. "Then what do you think we should do?"

Taking a beat, Sylas gives a small laugh and nods his head. "Alright, this is what's gonna happen," he begins, using his spatula to point at his comrades as he speaks. "Cal will come up with a fairly decent plan. Mercy, you'll plan to execute that plan and probably screw it up forcing a plan B. Then plan B will go horribly wrong. I'll in turn make a new plan B. I will execute that plan. I save all your asses as usual and then we go home."

Giving another eyeroll, Mercy shakes his head. "Ruby wouldn't even be gone if it wasn't for-"

"You?" Cal finishes, his tone crass as he slams his sketchbook shut, setting it down, and glaring at Mercy. "Last I checked everything that has gone wrong the last couple of months has been on you, Mercy."

"Harsh, but I see your point," Sylas admits, trying to play mediator.

"How's that?" Mercy asks with an annoyed scoff, returning the scowl to Cal. "Last *I* checked you and Sylas let that woman walk out of my house with my kid."

"That is not what happened, and you know that," Cal snaps.

"Well, it's what it looks like," Mercy growls.

"I am not doing this," Cal flatly remarks, grabbing his sketchbook and leaving the kitchenette to sit on the sofa across the room. "I did not come back from the dead to deal with your shit attitude."

Seeing the clear tension happening, Sylas tries to refocus Mercy. None of them had slept much and it was about to be a long day. There was no time for bickering or arrogance. Though it seemed since they reunited with Mercy, he had been nothing but arrogant. Cal eyes Sylas waiting for him to say something, but all he gets in turn is an apologetic look from his partner. Forcing an apology from his Keeper wasn't going to solve this.

"Any updates on the tracker?" Sylas asks, pulling plates out of a cabinet.

Mercy shakes his head. He had checked it multiple times throughout the night, but the tracker still showed the last signal pinging near the border of Summa. Bryer had changed his tactic and was abandoning the compound in Vicinia altogether it seemed.

"Surely they will try to get Mercy to follow them wherever they took her," Pippa adds. "If they are wanting to get Mercy at full power, they will need to make themselves known. We need to be patient with this."

"Ruby might not have time for us to be patient," Mercy warns her.

"I agree with Merc," Sylas states. "Clearly, they wanted to use Cal too, but they weren't exactly making sure he stayed alive. We can't let them traumatize an eight-year-old because we're trying to play it safe."

"This is a child though," Pippa stresses. "Certainly, they will not treat her-"

"They have little regard for their prisoners. I doubt they will care she is a child," Cal notes, getting comfortable on the sofa and putting his feet up on the table.

"Fake legs off the oak, Tenebris!" Sylas scolds, staring at him. "My grandfather built that table, and I don't need you scratching it up."

"I apologize," Cal yields.

Caligo quickly takes his legs off the table and readjusts. For some reason he hadn't really thought about the fact he was in Sylas's house. The only home Cal ever knew Sylas to have, had been with him.

"Did they mention any plans they had for you, Cal?" Pippa questions, turning her attention to her friend.

"They wanted me to power an obscurum, but my new Light Source said no," he shrugs. "They got livid and seemed to be stalling, trying to come up with a new strategy. Not sure I would have made it much longer though if you had not showed up."

Sylas frowns. He regretted not being there for the rescue, but it may have been better that he hadn't. He would have probably tried to kill Iana and Bryer himself if given the opening. Seeing how Cal had been described

432

would have been horrific. He still looked thin and had complained even more about the lingering pain in his back and joints when they tried to sleep that morning. He wasn't going to be the same for a while.

"I think we should call for reinforcements" Pippa admits. "We are going into this outnumbered and much weaker than we are used to."

"You're right," Sylas agrees, with a small nod.

"I can send a page to Zero," Mercy suggests. "See if he could step away, or maybe Shay?"

"Since when did you get all smug with Zero?" Sylas asks, his brows raised.

"Since he got us across the border to Vicinia to find your boyfriend," Mercy snarkily remarks.

"The NC would not let you pass over?" Cal asks.

"No," Mercy explains. "I think they knew you were in Vicinia, which is why they tried to keep us from getting over. We lucked out having Zero be the Sentry Captain they sent. I didn't realize the two of you were such good friends either. You didn't act like it."

"Right," Cal nods, looking to the floor.

Watching Cal, Sylas notes the awkward change in demeanor, but keeps his attention on the conversation. As much as he hated to admit it, it wouldn't be a bad idea to have Zero and Shay on this assignment. With Mercy acting off, having Zero there to calm him made it an even better idea.

"Let's get Zero here then," Sylas nods. "He can bring Shay back in to try and track Ruby down and Zero has an eye for details. If we're missing something, he can figure it out. We already have a good lead with the tracking ping in Summa."

"I'll send a summons then," Mercy states, moving away from the group and toward the tablet that was charging across the room.

433

As he gets to his device, he refreshes Zero's contact and suddenly is bombarded with messages. He unlocks the tablet with a face scan and quickly begins to shuffle through them. All the messages were from Zero and they were panicked. Maybe he should have been checking his messages throughout the night and not just checking the tracker.

"Novi wants us to bring Pippa back," Mercy states with a void tone. "Not just wanting but demanding."

"Why?" Pippa asks, moving toward him to read over his shoulder.

"Doesn't say," Mercy shares, shaking his head. "Never mind. Zero said they were on their way here last night. I ignored his messages thinking they were just updates on the paperwork I left him."

"That cannot be good," Cal adds, getting to his feet. "Master Novi must have heard something from herself."

They all jump as someone pounds on the door.

"That was quick," Sylas notes.

Opening the door of the cabin, Cal is met with a worry eyed Novi. She quickly moves past him and grabs her daughter. She pushes Mercy away and pulls Pippa several feet back, conjuring a dark solis orb to her palm. Mercy looks at her in shock as he drops the tablet, and his Source comes to his eyes in response to the threat.

"Whoa! Whoa! Master Novi!" Sylas snaps, dropping what he was doing and rushing to the situation.

"I am taking my daughter home," she snaps, keeping a stern eye on the Light Keeper.

They look to the door as Zero enters behind her, dressed in a black tactical suit, his hands in his pockets. He observes the scene in front of him, nods his head, and steps off to the side to let it play out. Clearly, he knew what this was about. He had told Pippa not to leave with Mercy and now she was going to deal with the consequences.

"What's going on?" Sylas asks, getting between Mercy and Novi. "You can take her home but explain yourself first."

"Him," she glares at Mercy.

Seeing this reaction from the Master Penumbra was alarming and only solidifying the severity of Pippa's words the night before. If Novi was this worried about Pippa, that meant the path she saw Mercy on was bad.

"Mercy?" Sylas asks, turning to look at his best friend. "What did he do?"

"Not what he did but what he will," she snarls.

"Mother, Mercy is our friend," Pippa scolds, pulling away from her.

Her mother grabs her wrist and holds on tightly, shaking her head, the orb still in her palm. "He will betray you. All of you!" she barks.

"Master Novi, this is Mercy we are talking about," Cal argues, moving into the conflict himself. "He is afraid of the dark."

Her eyes go to Cal. Seeing the sternness in her gaze he drops his joking words. Whatever she had heard was enough to put her on edge and waiver her trust in the Light Keeper and that was all Cal needed to see. Novi was right, Pippa wasn't safe here.

"I will be taking my daughter back to Sintus," Novi barks at them, relaxing her stance.

"Mother, I am an adult," Pippa reasons, tearing her wrist away. "If I am needed on an assignment then I will go on the assignment."

"What did you hear from yourself?" Cal asks, giving her a worried look.

"Whatever you were told isn't set in stone and you know that," Sylas adds. "I wouldn't be standing here if a seer's vision was the only possible outcome."

Hearing his words, she calms slightly. Her and Sylas both knew about the true vision Orlo had of Spheara.

435

Sylas had asked her after the events. The way Trust had insisted he stay out of the way and had pushed him, taking the blade himself, led him to believe the worst. He was supposed to be the one who died in that battle, not Mercy's brother. He knew that and he had been sitting on it for over a year. The conversation about his guilt with Cal was just the tip of the iceberg.

Novi glances to Mercy who still had a hint of his Source in his eyes, but seeing his relaxed demeanor was enough to let her guard down. What she had been told was clearly not going to happen today. The young man in front of her still held himself with fear in his eyes.

"What did you hear?" Cal asks again, looking at his mentor.

"A dark path awaits this Light Keeper," she mutters, looking to her mentee. "One that I will not allow my student or my daughter to be a part of. It would be best for you to return with me as well, Caligo."

"Elaborate," Sylas begs, gesturing to his Keeper.

Pippa's words the night before echo through his mind. Clearly Novi's fears were becoming more real from what the Penumbra was hearing. If Novi had shared her worries with Pippa already, what had been said to prompt her to pull her daughter from this mission all together and attempt to pull Cal? Or was she already told not to come, and she deliberately disobeyed her mother's wishes?

"Your enemy has taken away his guidance," she states, keeping her eyes on Cal. "A weakened connection to those meant to keep him in balance was part of their plan all along. Taking the girl was their way of accelerating the process I fear."

"Novi, I would never hurt Pip," Mercy adds, blinking his Source from his eyes. "I care about her. You know that. I would never hurt someone I-"

436

"But you will!" she snarls, turning her eyes to him, moving in front of her daughter. "I will not allow your tactics to harm another one of my children!"

This comment catches Cal's attention. Taking a deep breath, he moves toward her and gets in her line of sight. Perhaps he could calm her down. Novi knew as well as he did that they needed Pippa.

"Master Novi," he begins in a calm tone, "I will not let him harm her. You can trust me to protect her. You have always trusted me to protect her."

Her expression waivers looking at him. She had yet to see him since he was found. Looking him over she notes the weak Source energy emanating from him. She could see the spark had left his eyes; his confidence faded. If she had known this would be his fate, she may have listened to Orlo's instructions more carefully. Cal had lost part of himself because of the actions of his Alia.

"Sylas and I will protect her," he reassures, reaching for Pippa's hand. "I promise you."

"You cannot protect her from what is already seen," Novi warns, moving to the side as Pippa grabs his hand. "I fear we are too far into Malice's games to reverse what has been done, Caligo."

"What do I do?" Mercy asks, his voice reverting back to his timid tone.

As Cal pulls Pippa away from her mother, Novi looks back to Mercy. She relaxes her face as a calmness takes over, recognizing the young man she had come to know. This was Orlo's son, not a villain. This was the young man who ended the tyrant. Her future self had to be mistaken. He would never harm Pippa nor purposely put his comrades in danger.

"I apologize," she breathes, looking to the ground. "I fear I overreacted."

"You're a mother, sometimes an overreaction is needed," Sylas affirms, with a small nod.

437

Novi shakes her head and looks to Pippa again. Sylas was proof that the path could be changed. Trust had shown that by sacrificing himself. Surely the future she had heard was interpreted wrong.

"I'll stay with them," Zero suggest from the back of the room. The group looks to him having forgotten he was there. "I'll keep them out of trouble."

With a small nod, Novi looks to Caligo again. She gives him a painful smile, putting her hand to his cheek. Seeing him like this, powerless and vulnerable, broke her heart. While he was strong willed, much of his confidence came from his abilities as a Shadow Keeper. His Source protected him in more ways than just physically, it gave him an inner strength as well. For years her mentee used his Source to hide behind while he attempted to diverge from his mother. His Source was what gave him the strength to go out on his own and gave him his chosen family.

"My sweet Caligo...By the Elders," she whispers shaking her head.

He grabs her hand on his cheek and gives her a small smile to assure her that he was okay. While he was upset she had avoided him after his return, he understood why. She hated seeing him in pain. She only ever wanted to see him thrive and reach his potential. She was one of the few people in his life who sought for him to succeed for himself, not for her own selfish reasoning.

"I want you to understand something, Caligo," she begins. "You are not defined by a single attribute or skill. Your purpose in life does not lie in your ability to excel at a single talent. You must rely on more than that."

"I know," he nods.

"Exposure to the exua runes is not something that should be taken lightly," she shares, glancing to Sylas then back to her mentee. "It is a powerful force, one of the most frightening from our past. This is why when the knowledge of the runes became known, the Elders of Novus Aitus buried them. The runes falling into the wrong hands could be detrimental to our Keepers as you have already seen."

"Sy and Pippa already told me this," Cal states in a quiet voice.

"I fear they do not know the severity of the rune," she adds, taking a deep breath.

He studies her face, noting the pain in her eyes. What she was about to tell him she feared would hurt him.

"What is it?" Cal questions.

After a long pause, and taking her hand away from his face, she finally says it. "The effects of the exua rune cannot be reversed."

Her words hit him like a ton of bricks. It was like a wall came crashing down on him. The effects being irreversible meant he was never getting his Source back. The Source of Shadows was who he was. Being able to control his connection was part of him. Did that mean this emptiness he felt was never going to go away? He looks to Sylas who was shaking his head, trying to encourage Cal not to panic in that moment.

"We don't know that for sure," the Nota differs.

"Do not fill yourselves with false hope," Novi lectures the pair. "Your connections to Mercy will only continue to deteriorate over time."

This wasn't happening. Cal could handle being vulnerable for a few weeks, but not his entire life. What was the point? How could he possibly keep going like this? Looking down at his hands, they suddenly felt like foreign objects. He feels Novi attempt to pull him to her, but he didn't want comfort, he wanted his Source back. Shoving her away he looks around the room. Why did the room suddenly feel so small?

Sylas looks to Mercy for help. He had been quiet for the most part but was paying attention to the conversation. Mercy avoids his friend's eyes, unsure what he wanted him to say. Wasn't this what the pair wanted?

Sylas wanted to be free of Mercy, and now his wish was being granted by that rune on his arm.

Taking his eyes back to Cal, Sylas could see he had his gaze to the floor, trying to keep himself composed. He recognized the face he had on in that moment. Caligo was on the verge of tears but didn't want to show his emotions to the people in the room.

"This means Mercy may grow weaker," Novi adds, taking her eyes to the Light Keeper. "You need to end things with Bryer before your connection to your Alia and Nota deteriorates more."

Mercy looks at her and nods his head. He wasn't planning on wasting much more time before heading toward the ping in Summa. Looking to Zero, Novi gives him a small nod as he exits the cabin.

"I need some air," Cal shares, moving his feet and following Zero out the door, slamming it behind him.

Fidgeting a moment, Sylas gives a small gesture of apology and heads toward the door to follow Cal.

"Sylas, where are you going?" Mercy pleads, wanting his friend to stay.

Pausing, Sylas locks eyes on Mercy and shrugs. While he wanted to listen to what Master Novi had to say, he wasn't about to let Cal take this news on his own.

"I'm sorry," Sylas apologizes, exiting the cabin.

Going out the door, he glances to a transport to see Zero watching him. The Light Keeper points to the side of the cabin knowing exactly why Sylas had come out there. Moving around to the back of his home, he spots Cal walking toward the far end of the clearing, his head down, his hands clearly shaking. Jogging toward him, his footsteps get Cal's attention. Cal turns quickly, but his face softens at the sight of Sylas.

"Cal, wait," Sylas begins, but pauses and comes to a halt.

He could see the tears in Caligo's eyes. Cal shakes his head and moves his gaze back to the trees. The only reason he hadn't been concerned about his Source not responding before was because he was still marked. The fact he was marked meant his Source had the ability to return to him, but hearing what Novi said meant it was hopeless. His last bit of security was gone.

His Source was his reassurance. For years he had used his connection to the Shadow Source to cope with the hand he had been dealt. His Source brought him to Nex. It was what put him in Master Novi and Emidio's care, the only nurturing parental figures he had. His connection had brought him to Mercy, the first person he met who was equally as afraid of their abilities. His Source was the one thing his mother couldn't take away from him, and the knowledge in the back of his mind all those years that he could end her life whenever he pleased, was comforting. Without his Source or Nex, he had lost his protection and his support system.

"I can't do this, Sy," Cal mumbles.

"Cal, I know-" he tries starting again but is swiftly cut off.

"Nex is gone," Cal states.

"What do you mean gone?" Sylas asks, concerned.

"They killed her," he shudders. "At the camp… She was watching over me and they killed her. They left her corpse with me for days before…" he couldn't even finish the sentence. He didn't want to have another breakdown, not with everyone just inside.

Sylas automatically wraps his arms around him, trying to stop the tears. "Hey, it's gonna be okay. I'm right here. I'm not going anywhere."

"Nex is gone. My Source is gone. What's the point?" Cal asks, accepting the hug. "I don't want to do this anymore. I can't do this anymore. I don't want to try anymore, Sy."

441

"Well, I need you to try," Sylas whispers, closing his eyes tightly. "Can you do that for me? Can we try one more time?"

Hearing nothing in return, Sylas takes a deep breath. Realizing he wasn't going to be able to say anything that could help, he stays silent. There was no use trying to come up with a silver lining or cracking a joke right now because it wouldn't change how Cal felt. Taking another deep breath, Sylas keeps his arms wrapped around Cal. If all he could do was sit there and hold him while he worked through this, that was what he was going to do.

Back inside the cabin, Zero returns with Shay in tow. The girl looked much more spirited than the last time Mercy had seen her and was in a Sentry tactical suit similar to Zero's. It was refreshing to see Zero had made sure she was prepared for the mission.

"Shay can help you find the kid," Zero instructs.

"Just like that?" Mercy asks, looking at Shay.

"Have you met her?" Zero scoffs, folding his arms.

"Pippa, I do want to stress that returning home with me will ease my mind," Novi adds, looking at her daughter with worried eyes.

"I am needed here," Pippa replies, glancing to Mercy. "If what you have told me is true, then I feel I am best suited to stay on this assignment."

"Please, sweet," Novi pleads.

Shaking her head, Pippa stands her ground. She had been watching Mercy closely since they had met. They had forged a close friendship. She felt staying with him would aid in keeping him on a good path, unlike what her mother worried for. The darkness she had warned of felt misplaced. There was no way Mercy was going down a dark path as she was stating.

"So be it," Novi sighs, looking to Zero. "Zero will stay with you to try and alleviate any issues." She glares at

442

Mercy. "You harm my daughter; it will be the last thing you do in this life."

Everyone in the room looks to Mercy who reluctantly nods his head. Whatever Novi had seen, he needed to try and avoid. Could he though?

Chapter Forty-Three

The group was piled into a transport. In the front sat Cal and Sylas, a steel wall with a small door in it separated the pair from the rest of the group. This gave them some silence as Cal kept his eyes on the path ahead. While Cal was dressed for a battle, Sylas opted for more travel friendly attire planning to change if needed. Since he was on leave, he wanted to avoid wearing the uniform. In fact, being out of the Sentry Guard attire made him feel lighter somehow. Not to mention the amount of effort that went into putting on the uniform and his new lack of a dominant hand just making it harder.

Being in a transport was still odd to Sylas. While it was faster and much more efficient, it made little sense to him. The Sentry had let him drive one a couple of times, but overall, the mechanics of it made him uncomfortable. The number of buttons and knobs was overwhelming. Though he could see the benefit of Aitian technology, not growing up with it made it more difficult to learn. After this he planned to dive further into the tech with help from Cal now that they were on good terms again.

He watches Cal use one hand to adjust the speed of the vehicle while he steered with the other. They had crossed the border stop into Summa about thirty minutes prior and Cal was still speeding up with each passing moment. Caligo had a serious look on his face as they continued down the road, having been mostly silent the last couple of hours. The path they were on was one that wasn't traveled often, giving them a bumpy ride.

"Anything you want to talk about?" Sylas questions, breaking the silence.

"If you are asking if I have accepted I am never getting my Source connection back or that my Nota is dead, the answer is still no," Cal states, his tone flat, "but I can confirm that I am not going to kill myself at the idea of my own dreadful existence at this current moment."

"Not exactly what I meant, but I'll take it," Sylas shrugs with a deep breath.

"If it eases your mind, I plan to speak with Willa when we get back to Ozra," he informs. "What you said last night was true. I am miserable half the time, and I should speak to someone about it. Not that talking to you doesn't help, but I need more than that."

"Good," Sylas nods with a small smile. "That does ease my mind."

"Maybe you should talk to her as well?" Cal suggests with a raised brow, glancing over to him. "Like you said, we all need therapy."

"I need to focus on Merc right now," he sighs, shaking the comment off. "Do you think we should be worried about him?" he follows up, not wanting to be alone with his thoughts.

Letting out a small sigh, Cal glances to him again. Sylas was internalizing, and he could see it. With everything that was going on, there was no way he was this composed. They'd have to have a more detailed discussion later, since now wasn't the time.

"I haven't been around Mercy much, if I am being honest," Cal finally replies. "Are you worried?"

"I don't know," Sylas answers, looking out at the trees buzzing past them.

"I do appreciate him trying to restore my name, but he could be going about it in a better way," Cal states. "While I am enjoying being dead, it would be nice to return to the land of the living with my name not striking fear into the hearts of my people."

"Dissolving the National Council was…" Sylas shakes his head, folding his arms. "You can't be okay with that."

"I'm not," Cal retorts. "I understand his reasoning, but I think it was a poor choice. As soon as I take back the crown, I will restore the NC with a new set of regulations," he explains. "Hopefully Mercy can't do much damage before we can reinstate me as King."

"So, you *are* taking it back?" Sylas asks.

"Many celebrated my death, but I am not done leaving my mark on Novus Aitus," he clarifies, looking at Sylas again with a smirk. "Plus, I'm hoping a Riekan with an awful sense of humor might be up for helping me show the world who I am through his eyes."

Sylas gives him a playful smile. "Cocky? Short tempered? Sometimes a little stupid?"

"Maybe not those parts," Cal chuckles.

They both pause as someone bangs on the steel behind them. Unbuckling his seat belt, Sylas moves to open the small door. He locks eyes with Mercy who looked agitated and makes his way through the opening. Sylas goes back to his seat as Mercy sits on the console between the pair with the tablet in his hands.

"We're nearly there," he explains, his tone void.

"When was the last signal detected?" Cal asks, slowing the transport a bit.

"52 hours ago," Mercy shares, keeping his eyes on the small screen. "It's just up ahead, about 1000 feet."

Cal slows the vehicle down more as they begin to crawl toward the last known signal. Sylas and Cal exchange a look of concern, neither sure what they were about to find. As the beacon grew closer, their odds of finding Ruby seemed to dwindle. There was no sign of civilization or any others traveling along this road.

"Stop," Mercy orders.

Bringing the vehicle to a halt, they pause a moment. Mercy shoves past Sylas and opens the passenger door, stepping on his friend's foot in the process.

"You could of asked me to move!" Sylas snaps at him as Mercy exits.

"He has tunnel vision," Cal rationalizes, exiting on his side.

Moving to the back of the transport, Cal opens the doors so the rest of the party could exit with ease and grabs his blades from the luggage. As they jump out, the mixture of preparedness was clear. Zero was in a light tactical suit and weaponed up along with Shay while Pippa was simply dressed in a thick wool tunic and flowy brown pants, her crescent blade at her side. They follow Mercy into the trees, watching him as he keeps his eyes on the screen in his hands. Grabbing Zero's arm, Cal slows his pace to speak with him at the back of the group.

"If we find anything even remotely unsettling, I need you to use your peritia on Mercy," he instructs Zero. "Do not hesitate, just use it."

"If I can," Zero replies. "Guy's going haywire. I've been trying to get a read on him since the cabin."

"What do you mean by that?" Cal questions, glancing forward to the group, Sylas turning to see what was going on between the two.

"I can't explain it," Zero whispers, powering up and looking at Mercy. "Usually when I'm around him it's a wave of anxiety, but this is like a loud screaming with no emotion I can focus on. It's like he's feeling everything at

447

once. I could hardly stand sitting next to him in the transport. He's giving me a migraine."

"Well, you need to find an emotion and correct it," Cal instructs.

"Not that easy," Zero snaps, moving his eyes to Cal. He pauses and gives Caligo an odd look. "Your emotions are… You really do have the hots for the Nota."

"Stay out of my head, Zero," Cal growls. "Focus on Mercy. That's it."

"Maybe if your undying love for the fingerless archer wasn't screaming at me, I could," Zero smirks.

"I hate you," Cal mumbles as Zero's eyes go back to their silver color.

"You love me!" Zero shouts back as Cal speeds up.

Falling in line with Mercy and Sylas, Cal folds his arms with an annoyed look on his face. That was one thing he hated about Zero, but also why they had gotten so close. He could always gauge how he was feeling because of his peritia. Seeing the agitation on Cal's face, Sylas pulls on his arm and grabs his hand. The gesture seems to erase the annoyance on Cal's face almost instantly.

After a few minutes of walking, Mercy stops and looks around. It was clear there had been a camp here at one point, but it had since been packed up. A few remnants of fires once lit, and tent posts were scattered around.

Pulling away from Sylas and walking over toward one of the fire pits, Cal crouches down and hovers a hand over the ashes. There was still some residual heat, meaning they couldn't have been too far behind the group.

"It takes about ten to twelve hours for a campfire to lose its heat in this weather, so we cannot be far behind," Cal announces standing up and looking around.

Not saying a word, Mercy begins to wander forward, scanning the area. The rest take this as a signal to fan out and search for clues on where Malice may have gone. As Mercy begins to stray from his comrades, Pippa

448

rushes toward him and threads her arm through the crook in his elbow.

"In your vision you were alone," she mutters to him.

"Pippa!" Cal scolds, wary to let her go off alone with Mercy.

"I will be fine," she smiles at him.

With a worried look, Cal yields and moves the opposite direction with Sylas. Mercy gives her a small smile and lets her hold onto him as he walks. There had to be something here that could give them some indication on where they had taken Ruby. He feels Pippa let out a shiver beside him as sleet begins to fall. Now they were going to have the weather and time working against them.

He pulls away from her a moment and slides his yellow hooded jacket off that he had over his white Sentry suit and offers it to her. He didn't need it. If he felt cold, he could simply power up. Pippa on the other hand wasn't quite dressed for how cold the air was this far north.

"Thank you," she shivers, letting him help her put it on. "You have hardly spoken to me since we left Vermeer," Pippa notes as they move forward.

"Not much to say," he shrugs.

"Any updates from the capital?" she asks, glancing at the tablet on his hip.

"A few," he nods, clearing his throat. "The amendment to the Stopgap is in progress as well as the Refuge Act, which is one Cal had already been working on in Ozra. Basically, it's going to aid any mutts, humans, or Keepers who feel unsafe in their country to seek refuge from more accepting countries and cities like the Western Quarter," he explains, keeping himself alert. "Tris is also working on the Fair Schooling Proclamation which will-"

"Give every child a free hot breakfast and lunch," Pippa finishes with a smile. "As well as supply textbooks and offer advanced schooling for our educators."

"Exactly," he nods.

"Those all sound like fantastic things," Pippa shares, watching his expression.

Even though he was speaking about the good he was doing, his face was still showing agitation. Even the small smile he had was masking his true emotions. The worry begins to sink in for Pippa as she looks up at the forest around her. She couldn't help but wonder what her mother saw that had her so concerned for this assignment. With the warning to be wary with her friend, she wished she had been given clearer information on why.

"We got something!" they hear Sylas shout in the distance.

The two look in the direction his voice had come from and move toward it. As they approach Sylas and Cal, they see a small, white jacket in his hands. Pulling away from Pippa, Mercy bolts forward and tears the jacket from his friend.

"This is Ruby's," he mutters, moving it around in his hands until he could find the pouch he had sewn into the collar. He removes the tracker and lets it rest in his palm with a frown.

Zero and Shay join them, having rushed toward Sylas's voice as well. They watch as Mercy wraps his fingers around the tracking device in his hand and closes his eyes. This was his failsafe if something happened to his girls, and it didn't work. What was he going to do now?

Seeing Mercy's hands begin to shake, Cal asserts himself. "Keep looking," he orders. "All of you, spread out and keep searching."

"Pippa doesn't go alone," Mercy snaps, looking at his Alia with angry eyes.

Cal keeps his gaze on Mercy, seeing the rage filling his friend's face, a tinge of light showing he was on edge. With some hesitation, Cal nods his head. "Pippa go with Sy, please."

450

Sylas places his hand gently on Pippa's back and urges her forward with him, leaving Cal and Mercy alone. In one hand Mercy gripped the small jacket and in the other his fist was curled around the tracking device. Even with his connection to Mercy weak, Cal could feel the rage radiating off his Alia. He didn't need their Voca to see he was losing himself. Pippa was right with everything she had said. The Light Keeper in front of him was becoming a version of himself they needed to be cautious of. If Mercy's Source began reacting to the anger coursing through him, they were in trouble. With an unstable mind came unstable powers.

"What are you thinking?" Cal asks, prying to see where his friend's head was at.

"You don't even want to know," Mercy growls, his tone dark as he scans the area around them.

"Do you want me to get Zero?" Cal asks, as Mercy begins to walk.

"What for?" Mercy retorts.

"To calm you a bit?" Cal suggests as he keeps in pace with his friend.

"I don't even think his peritia could calm me down," Mercy laughs with a bit of craze. "You don't understand this, do you?"

"I understand your worry," Cal replies.

"You don't get it because you don't have kids, Cal," Mercy growls.

"We will find her," Cal comforts, his tone showing his concern.

Mercy glares at him as he moves forward. "Charity became my responsibility when I was 13, Caligo, and now she's gone because of me. I'm not about to let that happen to Ruby. I'm not letting another innocent child die because of my stupid Light Source."

451

"Bryer is just trying to get a rise out of you," Cal insists. "That is the only reason he took her. Do not give Bryer what he wants."

"You mean Emrys?" Mercy mocks.

"That man is not my father," Cal replies, looking to the ground that was now accumulating a thin layer of sleet. "His given name is Voltas. I'm unsure why he changed his identity, but I can assure you he is *not* Emrys."

The attitude coming from Mercy was testing Cal. Mercy had always been sassy and a little blunt, but this was different. The man his Alia had become since he had his vision in the conference room was not the man Cal knew. He was being reckless, rageful, and fueled by a need for revenge.

Cal pulls his Alia to a stop and locks his eyes on him. "We are both orphans because people could not stop fighting for what they thought was right," Cal states.

"You're not an orphan," Mercy differs with an eye roll.

"My mother died the day she murdered my father," Cal explains, his eyes showing the severity of his words. "We cannot be like our parents, Mercy. That cycle of blood will only end with our lives."

"What if blood is the only way to stop the cycle?" Mercy asks, his tone dark.

The remark prompts Cal to release his friend's arm and let him move forward. The look in Mercy's eyes wasn't something he had ever seen behind those silver irises. It wasn't just anger; it was a coldness he had only ever seen in the eyes of Mala. It sends a chill through him as he watches Mercy walk alone.

After about two hours of searching through the camp and surrounding forest in the sleet and chilly air, the group meets back where they had first entered the camp. The pellets of sleet falling from the sky felt like small bits of shrapnel pelting them. Sylas looks over to Cal who

452

shakes the sleet from his hair, leaning down to check the fire again. Cal could feel it was nearly completely cooled.

"Anything?" Cal asks, looking around the group.

"There were some tracks heading north, but they vanished after about thirty feet," Zero shares, folding his arms. "We could follow them."

"Perhaps I could find some information at the next village or city?" Shay suggests, keeping her tone low as Cal winces at her voice.

They all look to Mercy who was weighing the options. Sylas furrows his brow at his best friend. With the tracking being a dead end, he could see the Light Keeper was struggling to come up with his next move.

"Bryer is just trying to lure Mercy out," Sylas finally chimes in. "I say we turn back and wait for him to make the next move."

"We aren't going back," Mercy snaps in annoyance, his eyes filling with light.

Taking a shaky breath, Sylas stands his ground. Not only because it was the right choice, but because he could see Mercy was becoming agitated. Whatever was going on in his head was only going to make this more complicated. They needed to get his head level.

"Look around you, Merc," Sylas pleads, gesturing to the group. "You are asking the universe for directions to a place it doesn't want you to find. We should go back to Ozra and let Bryer make the next move."

"No," Mercy snarls, his Source coming to his eyes even more with rage.

This causes Sylas to pause a moment, wary to anger his friend anymore. Mercy felt like they couldn't stop. Stopping for even a few hours could put Ruby in more danger. He wasn't about to have her blood on his hands. He wasn't about to let anything happen to that little girl.

"We have humored this enough," Cal retorts. "Sy is right. We need to collect ourselves and find a better solution to finding her."

"You've humored me?" Mercy laughs. "It's your fault we're in this mess!"

"My fault?" he scoffs, anger coming through. "Have you lost your damn mind?"

"Cal, let me please," Sylas remarks.

With a low growl, Cal looks to the ground. Having short tempered Caligo try and reason with an unstable Mercy was a bad idea. Someone needed to try and talk some sense into Mercy, and Sylas was the best bet.

"Merc, I'm speaking to you as your Nota right now," Sylas explains, taking a step forward. "We are chasing the coat tails of someone who doesn't want to be found. If we go into this unprepared, you could be risking more than just Ruby. This isn't safe for anyone here."

"We're not turning back!" Mercy screams, a craze flooding him as he aims his hand at Sylas, his Source illuminating every vessel in his arm and his temples.

The group pauses in disbelief as Mercy begins to breathe heavily, keeping a stern look on his Nota. Cal's eyes watch Mercy as he takes a step to stand beside Sylas, putting his hands out to yield to his Alia. Cal grabs Pippa's arm and pulls her to stand behind him, fearful of what the Light Keeper was going to do next. Was Mercy really threatening his best friend right now?

They watch as the light continues to fill Mercy's eyes, and a white fog starts trickling from the hand at his side. Mercy was suddenly creating his own solis fog, the rage seeping from his fingertips.

Reaching over, Cal grabs Sylas's wrist. "Back down, Sy," he whispers as he urges Sylas to move behind him as well.

Moving slowly, Sylas heeds Cal's words and slowly steps back. If Mercy took a shot at Sylas, he had no way to counteract the strike. While Cal currently didn't offer much protection himself, he at least had his blades and his Sentry suit on. Plus, his Light Source would surely come into play if Mercy was a real threat to his survival.

"Does anyone else have anything they'd like to say?" Mercy snarls at Zero and Shay. "Anyone?"

Cal attempts to reason with him. "Mercy-"

To his shock, Mercy quickly shifts his hand and shoots his solis fog toward his Alia. Sylas registers the action and quickly pulls Cal to the ground. They both hit the frozen earth with a thud as Pippa's screams fill the air. Hearing her cries, Cal pushes Sylas off him and scrambles to her side as she falls to her knees screaming in pain.

"What the hell, Sy!" Cal snarls at his partner.

"I'm sorry," Sylas shoots back to Cal, but looking at Mercy.

In the same instance, Zero steps up sending a wave of his Light Source at Mercy. Mercy counteracts by putting up a shield around him, deflecting the surge. He shoots his fog forward again, wrapping it around Zero's wrist, twisting it, and shoving his arm back. The Light Keeper lets out a scream as the bones in his arm snap and he loses his footing. As Mercy pulls his fog back, Zero falls to a knee staring at his arm. He forces his Source to hold off healing as he collects himself to reset the crooked limb.

"Have you completely lost your damn mind!?" Cal snaps at Mercy. "What the hell is wrong with you!?"

"I'll go again!" Mercy retorts, his breathing heavy as he scans the group.

Sylas gets to his feet and keeps his gaze on his Keeper who was still holding his ground. He hears Zero let out a painful groan as he gets his arm back in place and promptly heals it before getting to his own feet. Taking a deep breath, Zero stands in front of Sylas and puts his palm out toward the Supra.

"Power down, Validus," Zero warns, his irises glowing with his own Source.

Shay comes up next him, her eyes dark, both prepared to fight Mercy. Sylas could hear Shay speaking softly to Zero over Pippa's screams trying to make sense of what was happening and figure out a plan. Quickly, Sylas begins to fear what Novi said was correct.

"Pip, let me look," Cal whispers to her.

"Zero," Sylas pleads, looking to his comrade, "bring him down."

The Light Keeper gives a shake of the head to signal he couldn't. Sylas's eyes go to his Keeper who was glaring at Zero and Shay. There was a clear anger radiating from him as he locked eyes with his comrades. Sylas felt overwhelmed himself. The emotions coming from Mercy were strong and hitting him in waves.

"We are moving forward," Mercy orders. "Do I make myself clear?"

"Do you even care what you just did?" Zero snaps at him.

"Do you want me to break your other arm?" Mercy scowls, his gaze cold.

"I only come on these assignments to get my ass kicked at this point, so sure," Zero shrugs, pulling more power to his hands, taking another step forward.

"Pip, you need to let me look," Cal begs.

She nods her head allowing him to pull her hands from her face. Cal's expression quickly shows unease at what he was seeing. Mercy had struck her right eye, the only eye she could see out of. The heat from the solis fog had burned her, creating a nearly perfect half circle over the right side of her face. The smell of singed hair filled his lungs as he took in the sight. He releases her hands in shock, they go back to the injury.

Taking his attention to Mercy, Cal slowly rises to his feet. He grabs his blades from his back and pulls them from their sheaths. The worry in his eyes quickly shifts to rage as the Light Source turns them a ghostly purple. Realizing what was about to happen, Sylas moves to Pippa to try and comfort her in Cal's stead. He wasn't even going to attempt to stop Cal. What Mercy had done deserved the beating Cal was about to give.

"Cal, don't be stupid!" Zero cautions, as he shoves past the two Keepers.

Even without his Shadow Source, Cal was a force to be reckoned with. The combat training he had was leaps and bounds above what Mercy was capable of, meaning he had some advantage in a fight.

Caligo wasn't sure he had ever been this angry in his life, but the longer Pippa cried the angrier he became. He was going to make Mercy pay for what he had just done. A small smirk comes to Mercy's face as he begins to pull an orb to his hand and thrusts it toward Cal. This wasn't going to be won with distance, this was going to need to be close combat. Dodging the orb, Cal charges at Mercy, a blade's hilt in each hand.

"You filthy little maddux!" Caligo snarls, slicing his blades at Mercy.

Realizing what was about to occur, Mercy pulls his father's sword from his waist and blocks Cal's advance. The sound of Cal's blades ricocheting off Mercy's rings through the air. Determined to continue forward, Mercy holds his ground. He had fought Caligo countless times, and without his Shadow Source it would be an easy match, or so he thought.

Watching the fight begin to unfurl, Sylas becomes apprehensive. The more he watched, the more antsy he became. He could feel his Nota instincts urging him to intervene, but he needed to let Cal do this. Someone needed to bring Mercy back down to Novus Aitus. He takes his attention back to Pippa hoping it would clear his head.

"I can't see," she whispers, reaching for him, panic in her voice. "Sylas, I can't see."

"We'll get you healed. It'll be fine," Sylas comforts, wincing at Mercy screaming. "Zero, can you lock in on him yet?"

"No," he responds, keeping his glowing eyes on the Light Keeper.

"I can't see," Pippa repeats.

Tearing his attention from the fight in front of them, Zero backs down and moves to Pippa. "Let me," he encourages, placing his hand on the girl's face.

He quickly draws his Source to his palm to heal Pippa's face. Letting Zero work, Sylas takes his eyes back to the fight and could see Cal had taken a swipe at Mercy, slicing a large gash in his arm and his leg. The blood stained Mercy's white suit, the contrast striking. With how Cal was going after him, Mercy had very little time to try and heal the wounds. He was giving Mercy hit after hit, the Light Keeper hardly able to keep up.

The pull in Sylas's gut was telling him to interfere, but he didn't want to. It was like a screaming in the back of his skull. His senses knew his Keeper was in danger, and he needed to act. Getting to his feet against his will, he moves toward the pair.

"Sylas!" Zero barks as Sylas pulls the mace from Zero's belt, his pace switching to a run.

As Cal goes to take another swing at Mercy, Sylas dives into the fight, using Zero's mace to deflect Cal's next blow. Seeing the Nota dive in, Cal attempts to pull back, but the force was already there. Luckily Sylas had enough strength to hold the weapon steady and block the hit. Seeing Sylas had intruded, Cal automatically falls back not wanting to hurt him.

"I couldn't stop myself," Sylas mutters to his partner.

Shoving Sylas away, Mercy gets to his feet, ready to take another hit from Cal. Instead, Cal sheaths his blades and turns away to tend to Pippa.

"Try that again and I'll kill you," Mercy growls.

As soon as Sylas drops the mace, Mercy goes to work on his injuries. The sight reminded them all of a feral cat tending to its wounds after a brawl. Moving his feet to check on Pippa, Cal glances to Sylas as he gives him apologetic eyes.

Recognizing the expression on Sylas's face, Cal lets out an exasperated sigh. He understood what Sylas had done, because Nex had done the same for him a dozen times. He hadn't realized the same drive that had been in Nex to protect her Keeper, also ran through Sylas. A Nota would do anything for their Keeper, including give their life. Even if Sylas wasn't willing to do that for Mercy, his Nota nature would force him. It was in that moment he truly realized just how connected Mercy and Sylas were.

"Caligo," Shay urges.

Darting the rest of the way, Cal crouches down beside Pippa. He could see the tears flowing as she held her hand to her eye. Pippa wasn't just hurt, she was scared. While he kept his attention on Pippa, pulling her into his chest, Cal listens to the argument unfolding between Mercy and Sylas.

"What the hell is wrong with you?" Sylas snarls, glaring at Mercy.

"Don't get it my way again," Mercy snaps back. "I could have handled that."

"Handled what?" Sylas gives his Keeper a firm gaze, his tone cold.

"Caligo," Mercy retorts, not even regarding what else he had done.

Rolling his eyes, Sylas lets out an annoyed scoff. "You seem to forget that even without his Source, Cal's a trained killer. Don't even try to act like-"

459

"At least I'm not sleeping with him," Mercy accuses, sheathing his sword.

"What did you just say?" Sylas barks back, anger clear in his tone.

Mercy laughs in disbelief. "After all the shit he's done to you… You still went back to him? You think I'm that stupid? You've been all over him since I brought him to Rieka. It's disgusting."

"What the hell is wrong with you?" Sylas repeats, completely bewildered by his best friend. "Do you even hear yourself right now?"

Mercy looks at him with rage filled eyes. "The last time you and Cal were together, you lied to me about every single thing," Mercy enlightens him. "For six months you told me lies."

"I never lied to you," Sylas denies, furrowing his brow.

"Yes, you did!" Mercy snaps. "The letters, Sylas. Did you forget about the letters? You wrote me letters about how great life was with Cal in Ozra, when in reality you were falling apart, and Caligo was watching it happen. He let you break down, and I had to come put you back together. I had to find you cold and alone, losing your damn mind in a barn and fix what he broke!"

This brings Cal into the quarrel. "That is enough!" he shouts at them.

"My breakdown was on me, Merc," Sylas explains, gesturing to himself.

"But he didn't fix you! I did!" Mercy shouts, with fire filled eyes. "He didn't stop for a second to help you figure yourself out and when things got hard, he ran."

"You have no idea what you're talking about," Sylas replies in frustration.

"Oh really?" Mercy scoffs. "Enlighten me then."

Cal pulls Pippa to her feet and interjects again. "Mercy, you need to back off before-"

"Before what?" Mercy questions, looking to Cal. "Before you take another shot at me or Sylas?"

The more Mercy spoke the more pissed off Sylas became. At this point he didn't even care if he was about to ruin their friendship. The things he was saying were lies and he needed him to know. This angry and childish behavior Mercy was showing and the reckless use of his Source, was enough to break him.

"I broke up with him because of you!" Sylas snarls at his Keeper.

"Let's not do this," Cal attempts to interrupt but is cut off by Sylas.

"The bottom line is always you!" Sylas barks, talking with his hands as usual. "My breakdown wasn't from Cal's lack of trying, Mercy, because he did. Sure, I was mad about the Arca Orb, but I was even more pissed about you." Mercy's face shifts to a frown as he takes in the new information. "He wanted to talk about my father and brother and Spheara and I… I didn't want to," Sylas admits. "I needed time to myself to come to terms with what happened. I couldn't do that locked up in Ozra playing the doting partner. I couldn't rule a planet with him when I had so much unresolved inside me and the common denominator in all of that is always *you*."

The two go quiet for a moment as Sylas continues to collect his thoughts. He could see the pain in his friend's eyes, but he couldn't stop. He wanted to stop, but he couldn't.

"Everything I was and am going through is because of you, Merc," he adds. "My father and brother died because of the choices you made." He lifts his shirt to show the scar on his stomach before dropping it. "This? I blamed it on Cal and Shay for a while, but this was you. I ran to protect *you*. I left Rieka to help *you*. We lost Charity because of *you*. My entire life got flipped upside down because of *you*, and the one thing I had for myself… The

461

one person I had, I couldn't be with because of *you*. But I have to just deal with it, right? I have to stay around because I'm your Nota. I have to help you keep your head on straight and help you learn your Source. I just defended you against a beating you deserved because I couldn't physically stop myself. I don't get to blame you for any of that though, because at the end of the day you're my Keeper and I know that."

"You two need to stop," Cal intervenes, letting go of Pippa gently, "before you say something you are going to regret."

Taking his attention to Cal, Mercy scowls. "You stay out of this."

"I'm not going to stay out of it when you are being a complete and utter idiot," Cal defends. "Unfortunately, that's been a majority of the time lately."

"Everything I've done the last two months has been for you!" Mercy barks at him.

"I didn't ask you to do anything for me," Cal growls back, approaching the pair.

The Light Keeper begins to move toward Cal, but Sylas tries to grab him. As soon as Sylas's hand touches Mercy's arm he heats it burning his Nota and ignoring the pain that rang through his own. He was too angry to even care about what Sylas had to say anymore.

"Bullshit," Mercy snaps, getting in Cal's face. "You put my name on that contingency plan!"

"And I am realizing now I should not have," Cal shoots back, backing away a couple of steps to protect Pippa. "I was foolish thinking I could trust you with my crown. Look at what you've done! Look at Pippa!"

"Zero," Shay mumbles.

His Source still in his eyes, Zero keeps his gaze on Mercy. Taking the shift in conversation Zero locks in on one of Mercy's emotions. Anger was the main emotion he was fronting in that moment and even Mercy couldn't hide it. Focusing on Mercy, Zero alters his mood and soothes him, shifting the anger within him to worry.

Mercy looks to Pippa as his eyes get wide and his Source dissipates. A sudden feeling of distress mixed with remorse was taking over. He hadn't even realized what he had done until that moment. Concern comes to the front as he moves toward her, Cal quickly moving to grab her and pulling her away.

"Pip?" Mercy asks, his voice small.

She pulls away from Cal's chest to reveal where he had struck. A burn scar covered the entire right side of her face, the girl keeping her eyes closed. His mouth goes slack at the sight. Not only had he injured her, but he may have blinded her. He suddenly becomes nauseous at his own actions and takes a step back. Cal looks at her face and the anger leaves his expression at what he was seeing. He hadn't even taken the time to register her face after Zero had healed it.

"I can't see," she whimpers, gripping at Cal's arms for guidance. "Cal, I can't see."

The realization of what Mercy had done begins to sink in. How could he have done this to her? How could he have hurt Pippa like this? Not only was he losing his damn mind, but he now may have rendered Pippa blind. Her left eye had been taken from her years ago and now her right. Cal pulls her into his chest, holding her tightly as her panic begins to reflect in him. His instincts to protect and sooth the girl he grew up with was all he could focus on.

Looking to Mercy, Cal speaks with resentment in his voice. "I don't know who or what you are becoming, Mercy, but I am ordering you to stay away from *my* family," he growls at his Alia. Cal looks to Sylas with soft eyes with a shift in his voice. "I have to take her home."

The comment makes Mercy's stomach drop. While he wanted to plead for forgiveness, he knew it wouldn't come. His eyes dart around the group of people who were now glaring at him. Even Shay seemed disgusted by his presence in that moment. There was no begging for forgiveness here. He wasn't going to get it.

"What's going on with you, Merc?" Sylas asks. "Elder Rom and Brokkr would be disappointed if they could see this right now."

Though he was completely shocked at his own actions, Mercy needed to stay on task. He would apologize later. Right now, they needed to find Ruby. Adopting his confident stance again, Mercy looks at Sylas sternly.

"If that's how you feel," he nods, trying to keep calm, "then maybe it's best for us to go our separate ways."

"What?" Sylas responds. While he was heated, he wasn't going to suggest splitting up. "We can't do that. You, me, and Cal... We're supposed to be a team."

"Maybe it's time the team broke up," Mercy retorts, pulling the tablet from his waist and dropping it to the ground. He turns and begins to walk away from the group to where the tracks had been mentioned.

"Mercy!" Sylas shouts at him.

He feels Cal place a hand on his shoulder to offer some support. Bryer was getting exactly what he wanted. Taking Ruby was enough to push Mercy over the edge. With each passing moment the Light Keeper was slipping more and more and none of them could explain why.

Sylas looks at Zero, "Why didn't you stop him sooner?"

"I definitely wasn't trying the entire damn time, Sylas," Zero snaps. "Of course I tried but his emotions are all over the place."

Picking up the tablet and looking toward the direction his Keeper went, Sylas shakes his head. "We can't let him go off alone."

"I'll go with him before he does anything else stupid," Zero sighs, getting his feet moving.

"I feel it would be wise for me to go as well," Shay nods, following Zero's lead.

Sylas turns to look at Cal, his eyes showing his confliction. "Go with him," Cal urges. "He is going to need his Nota."

"What about you?" Sylas asks, hearing Pippa try to suck in her tears.

"I need to take her home," Cal states his voice full of guilt. "I have to get her to Master Novi and Emidio."

"Cal," they both hear her whimper, gripping Caligo's shirt tightly.

"I am right here," he comforts, squeezing her tightly and kissing her gently on the top of the head. "I'm going to get you somewhere safe." He looks back to Sylas. "I will head back to the border and get her to Sintus. Do not let him near Malice until I come back. Who knows what he will do."

"You're supposed to be dead," Sylas reminds him.

"They still have Pippa's and my fake papers at the station," Cal states as he gives a nod of the head. "I will take the transport, which will keep them from questioning."

"Here," Sylas states, picking up the tablet and flashing the pendant around his neck. "You'll be able to find us. Be careful and stay alive," Sylas breathes, giving Caligo a quick peck on the cheek as he shoves the tablet into his hand.

"You too," Cal nods.

They share a worried glance as Sylas backs away and takes off in the direction the others had gone. Holding Pippa close, Cal leads her back to the transport. How was he going to explain this to Master Novi? Maybe this was why she didn't want her on this assignment.

He holds back his own emotions as she blindly follows his lead. He had failed to keep his promise to Master Novi. He couldn't protect Pippa.

Chapter Forty-Four

Cal watches Master Novi go to the door of Pippa's room to leave the two of them alone. Pippa asked to speak with him privately for a moment and they weren't going to deny her request. He was nervous about what she was going to say.

As the door closes, Cal adjusts himself on the edge of her bed. Pippa had a patch of fabric over her right eye to block out the light from the room in hopes it would bring her vision back in a few days.

"Caligo?" she questions.

"I'm here," he assures, fidgeting with his prosthetic as he spoke.

He hadn't really taken the time to make many adjustments since Mercy made them. Usually, Mercy sat with him while they adjusted the height and tension, to make sure they felt right. These were brand new though and in the last few weeks didn't feel quite right. Keeping up with the others, he ignored the irritating ache caused by the pain in his walk. Now he could take a moment to fix it, or at least attempt. The limp from the unfitted prosthetic also may have been aiding in his aching back, but he honestly wasn't sure. Either way, he needed it to be fixed before he tried to get into another brawl.

"You need to promise me something," Pippa whispers, keeping her voice low.

"Anything," he replies, taking his attention from his leg to her.

"You will bring Mercy back," she pleads.

"Pip…" he sighs.

"Promise me, Cal," she scolds.

He takes a moment to think. He knew how she felt about Mercy. The two discussed it multiple times since they had been introduced. Just like he had confided his feelings about Sylas in Pippa she had done the same about Mercy. While he appreciated her feeling comfortable enough to share that information with him, it had proven itself to be a problem. Every time he saw Mercy around Pippa, he thought about her words which always made him wonder if he would accidently reveal her feelings to Mercy through their Voca on several occasions. He wasn't exactly the greatest at turning it off, especially when under pressure or frustrated.

"Pip, do not let your emotions run this," Cal warns, rolling down his pant leg. "If he is-"

"Something is wrong," she cautions. "Something is not right with him. I can feel it and I know this is not his doing."

"Pippa, he hurt you," Cal replies.

"That was not him," she corrects. "His actions are not his own and you have to understand that."

"Zero or Sylas would know if there was Source magic at play here," he retorts.

"Then maybe it's not the Sources," she suggests.

"This is more than a mental breakdown," Cal argues, remembering the book she had given him. "Master Novi was right in her warnings. He is losing touch with reality, and I am not going to promise I will not-"

467

"You hurt him, and I will turn my back on you, brother," Pippa threatens.

He pauses. The two had been close since they met nearly ten years ago, but Pippa had never called him her brother before. Was she doing it to try and stress her point or did she mean it?

"You are letting your affection for him blind you," he shoots back. He winces at his choice of wording but keeps his stern tone. "You are smarter than this."

"You protect the things you love, Cal. I cannot protect him right now, so I need you to protect him for me," she pleads with him.

"Pippa-" he begins.

"Would you not let your love for Sylas blind you?" she retorts in a calm voice. "If this were Sy, would you not do everything in your power to help him?"

He opens his mouth to speak but pulls back. If this were Sylas, he wasn't sure what he would do. He loved Sylas, but would he let those feelings effect how he approached a situation if he were suddenly the enemy? He couldn't imagine hurting Sylas, even in the roughest part of their relationship. He cared for him too much. Even when he was under Shay's manipulation, his fondness for Sylas had been able to break him out of her control. In fact, he was certain he was the one protecting Sylas in his memories the entire time.

"Fine," he agrees.

"Promise me," she demands.

"I promise," he concedes. "I promise I will bring Mercy back."

"Thank you," she nods, laying down in her bed.

He waits a moment to see if she was going to say anything else, but the woman stays silent. Getting to his feet he gives her a loving kiss on the cheek before heading toward her door.

"I will bring him back, Pip," he states in a soft voice before exiting the room.

Once he closes the door behind him, he pauses and lets out a heavy sigh before looking up. As soon as his eyes go up, he locks them with Novi. When he had arrived at the house, Master Novi was more concerned about Pippa than anything, but that didn't mean she wouldn't switch to anger when alone with him. He felt lucky that Emidio wasn't home when they arrived, he certainly would have scolded Cal for his inability to protect the young woman.

Master Novi keeps her eyes on him as he averts his own back to the floor. He didn't even want to look at her. He had promised he would protect Pippa and had failed.

Master Novi had been in Pippa's room for nearly two hours before Pippa asked to speak with him, the first being spent with Doctor Sano. He wasn't sure what had been concluded, but he felt he knew the answer. While he was aware it had been done in the heat of the moment, he wasn't sure he'd be able to forgive Mercy for this. His Alia had lost control of his anger and Source and Pippa paid the price.

To his surprise, Novi moves forward and wraps her arms around him, holding him tightly. He returns the embrace with some hesitance; this only causes her to hug him even tighter. He lets himself return the tight embrace and squeezes his eyes shut. He couldn't even remember the last time Novi had hugged him. He wasn't even sure it had happened before. This felt strange and out of character. The woman was reserved and rarely showed any signs of affection, even to Pippa. They sit there a moment in silence until she pulls away and studies his face.

"I have failed you. I have failed both of you," she states to him, shaking her head.

"You have done nothing wrong," Cal corrects.

"But I have," she adds, looking to the floor in shame. "I did not heed my warnings about Mercy.

Whispers told me to be cautious with you children, and I did not pass along that message. I chose to keep the severity of my words to myself and look at what it has cost you both."

"This is my doing, and you know it," Cal retorts, keeping his voice low. "Mercy may have injured one eye, but I took the sight from the other."

He sees the pain on Master Novi's face at his words. This was something the Drors and Cal rarely spoke of. Pippa had come to a training session to observe and take notes for her studies when Caligo had just come into his Source. His foolishness and lack of training caused him to lose control of his spiritum fog for a moment and strike the girl, she was only twelve at the time of the incident. All these years later he was still ashamed of what he had done. While Pippa seemed to have moved past it, often trying to distract from her injured eye by using intricate makeup, he could never forget.

"Do not hold onto that guilt, Caligo," Novi instructs, shaking her head and heading toward the stairs. "Holding onto guilt will only cause you pain."

Following her, he maneuvers down the steps, keeping his hand on the railing to steady himself as he tries to keep up with her quick pace. "What did Doctor Sano say?"

He watches as Novi shakes her head again when they reach the bottom of the staircase. "She says there is nothing she can do to help her at this time. All we can do is wait and see if there is improvement."

"We will take her to Willa then," Cal offers, coming to a stop and folding his arms.

"I am afraid the damage has been done," Master Novi adds, looking to him with hurt eyes as they enter the living room. "I need you to listen to me carefully, Caligo. The path Mercy is on is not the path Orlo set for him. I fear the change in Orlo's Spheara prediction may have harmed your Light Keeper's future more than I originally thought."

"The change in Orlo's prediction?" Cal asks, furrowing his brow. "I did exactly as you instructed me. I mended the bond. You said-"

"The day of Spheara..." She pauses and takes a deep breath. "Sylas was meant to take your blade, not Trust," she explains, moving to him and placing a hand on his cheek. "I knew as soon as I heard whispers of the plan Sylas had crafted that the vision had changed. Sylas was not meant to live through that battle. Someone chose to veer from Orlo's instructions and create a new outcome that day."

"I was supposed to kill Sy?" Cal whispers, shock on his face.

"Yes," Novi confirms.

The idea of Sylas dying that day made his chest ache. Watching Sylas nearly lose his life at Cal's hand was shaking enough. His life being taken was something he wasn't sure he'd have been able to handle. The thought was frightening. He takes a deep breath trying to stay on subject and not let his emotions get the best of him. This wasn't about his relationship with Sylas; this was about Mercy.

"Trust knew this, as did I," Novi continues. "Your mother was meant to perish at Mercy's hand, another change in the future Orlo envisioned. With these shifts in the prophecy, Mercy's own path has changed. While before he was meant to be a protector of Novus Aitus, I fear he may now be what destroys it."

"No," Cal replies, shaking his head in disbelief. "This is Mercy we are talking about. He is quiet and keeps to himself and cares about his people. He would not hurt anyone, Master Novi."

"He did hurt someone," Novi stresses to him, her gaze stern. "He hurt my daughter."

He looks up to the steps to Pippa's door with a frown. What could have set off the spiral Mercy was currently on? Surely if the events of Spheara being altered was the culprit, it would have made itself known over a year ago.

"Master Novi, I-" Caligo starts, looking back to her.

"Whatever is happening to him will only end in tragedy, Caligo," Novi states. "With that exua rune scarred into Sylas's arm and your exposure fading your connection, the foundation Mercy Validus was built on is crumbling. I fear dark Source magic is at play here."

He looks up to Pippa's door again and takes in her words. As much as he wanted to blame this on the Sources or the exua runes, Pippa's words rang in his mind. Thinking through the last few days, something Zero had said stuck with him. He had been unable to get a read on Mercy's emotions. They were scattered and hard to get a handle on until Mercy shifted his attention to Cal, then his emotions were focused on his anger with his Nota and his Alia.

"He is frantic and scared," Cal mumbles, keeping his eyes on Pippa's door.

"Speak up, Caligo," Novi instructs.

"He is frantic and scared, Master Novi," he states, his tone louder and more confident, taking his eyes to her. "Before Spheara, Mercy lived his life by closing himself off from the world around him. Sy said until last year he had hardly spoken a word, and I could observe that as well when I met him. He was quiet and timid, not by choice, but by his need to survive. I don't think this has anything to do with straying from the vision or the exua rune or the Sources... Bryer and Iana are playing into his already existing internal crisis, not creating a new one. Mercy's mind cannot handle this kind of pressure."

"What are you saying, Caligo?" Novi asks.

Cal speaks quickly as he collects his thoughts, hoping they would make sense. "I don't think his actions are being fueled in a malevolent way, they are being fueled by his need to protect his people and his loved ones. He did not hurt Pippa out of spite, he struck her because he could not handle his own qualms with losing Ruby. He lost control of himself and his Source in that moment... He was trying to hit me, someone who could handle the strike, and he knew that. Hitting Pippa was a mistake."

She looks at her mentee as she nods her head letting him continue to think. He shakes his head and looks back up to the stairs again. When Pippa had brought that book into Sylas's room and asked them for help, she was onto something. She could see the mental toll this last year and a half had taken on Mercy, and she was pleading with them to try and offer him guidance.

"Pippa was right," he confesses to himself.

Novi attempts to speak. "Caligo, I-"

He darts his eyes back to her. "Master Novi, I know what it is like to be a slave of your own mind. I understand the amount of pressure he feels. It is dark, overwhelming, and cold," Cal explains, moving toward the door. "Tell Pip I will bring him back."

"Caligo, I wish you to stay out of this," Novi warns as he grabs the doorknob. "You do not understand wha-"

"It is Mercy," he assures her. "He cannot hurt me, Master Novi."

With that he exits the house. Putting his hood up, he moves to the transport parked outside. He pauses a moment to adjust his prosthetics again before climbing into the vehicle. He needed to get back to his comrades before Mercy got to Bryer.

Chapter Forty-Five

Moving through the streets of a village by the name of Lacero, the group followed closely behind Shay. Her eyes were dark as she searched through the townspeople's minds for any clue as to where Malice could be headed with Ruby in tow. They had been walking around for hours when the young woman finally comes to a stop.

"Find something?" Sylas asks, coming up beside her as her eyes go dull.

Shay watches a man as he walks toward them. He carried a basket full of vegetables and was avoiding looking at the group as they paused in the street. He was moving quickly, seeming to be in a hurry. Shay could tell he was avoiding their eyes simply because they were wearing Sentry Guard attire.

"He saw Ruby," she shares, glancing at Sylas.

Hearing the words come from Shay's mouth, Mercy's eyes automatically set on the man and power up. He pulls his sword from its sheath and shoves past Shay and Sylas. Sylas attempts to grab his arm but pulls back in shock at the sight of Mercy's hands lit up with his Source. The mention of Ruby's name and the idea this man had seen her was enough to set him off again.

"Mercy, wait," Sylas snaps at him.

With his free hand, Mercy shoots a wave of Source energy at his Nota, knocking him back into Zero. Zero catches him with a grunt and steadies his feet. The irrational and angry Keeper they saw in the forest was back. What was going on with him? Why was he acting like this?

The sound of the crack of magic coming from Mercy pulls the man's attention to the Light Keeper. His jaw drops as he abandons his basket and begins to bolt the opposite direction of the group. Putting his hand out, Mercy shoots a tendril of solis fog at the man and grabs him, yanking him to the ground with a thud. The amount of precision he was getting with his new ability was impressive but also terrifying to watch. They could hear the man scream in pain, the fog burning his skin. Mercy didn't care though; this man had seen Ruby.

Recalling the fog back to him, the man slides over the icy road screaming and coming to a halt at Mercy's feet. He pulls his fog back into his palm and puts his blade to the man's throat, his eyes cold and stern.

"Where's the girl?" he snarls at him.

The man looks at him with fear in his eyes, trembling at the sight of the Light Keeper. Unable to speak, he shakes his head, terror running through him. What he was seeing was horrifying. Mercy looked just as intimidating and powerful as Caligo.

"Where is she?" Mercy shouts at him, resting the tip of his blade on the man's neck.

The Light Keeper gives the man a moment to answer but he doesn't. His eyes begin to blaze brighter. Pulling his blade back, Sylas registers what his Keeper was about to do. Moving swiftly, Sylas uses his own sword to uppercut Mercy's, causing his Keeper to lose his grip on the hilt. Orlo's sword clatters to the ground as Mercy tears his eyes from the man and scowls at his friend. Why would

Sylas stop him? His eyes get wide as Sylas puts the tip of his own blade to Mercy's throat, returning the cold stare. He wasn't about to let Mercy hurt this man. Pleading with him to stand down, Sylas raises his brows.

"What're you doing?" Mercy snaps at him.

"What are *you* doing?" Sylas repeats back, glancing to the man on the ground.

"Getting answers," Mercy snarls, aiming his lit-up palm at the man.

"Zero, a little help!" Sylas shouts.

Sylas glances to Zero who was already powered up with his eyes on Mercy. Quickly a calmness washes over Sylas's Keeper, making his face relax and causing him to take several steps back. Keeping the tip of his sword toward Mercy, Sylas side steps and helps the man to his feet. The man scrambles, grabs his basket, and takes off running down the street and around the corner.

"What're you doing?" Mercy asks again, his tone innocent as he puts his hands up.

"You need to get your shit together," Sylas growls, sheathing his blade.

Moving a few steps, Sylas bends down and picks up Mercy's sword. The Light Keeper shifts his gaze to Zero who had a faint glowing in his eyes as he kept them locked on Mercy.

"You're manipulating me," Mercy accuses.

"Yup," Zero nods, his eyes fierce. "You're being a bigger dumbass than usual."

Mercy shakes his head, narrowing his eyes. "No, you were-"

"If you would have let me finish, I would have told you he saw Ruby, and his memories showed the woman she was with had moved north toward the mountains," Shay adds, folding her arms, irritation in her tone. "That man had nothing to do with her abduction."

"Sorry," Mercy mumbles as fear begins to bubble up inside him and he runs his fingers through his snowy hair. "I didn't... I'm sorry."

"What is going on with you?" Sylas asks, handing him his sword.

"I don't know," Mercy admits, shaking his head, taking the hilt as his thoughts begin to fog over. "I'm sorry. I can't... I just..."

"What's happening, Merc?" Sylas pleads. "Sure, you can be stupid sometimes, but this... and Pip... This isn't you at all. This isn't your usual stupidity and inexperience; this is something else."

Taking a deep breath, Mercy feels Zero pull his hold on him as the Keeper powers down. As soon as he felt the spell shift, Mercy could feel the fear, anger, and anxiety begin to come back. Putting his hand to his arm he lets out a hiss of pain. Why was his upper arm tender to the touch suddenly? He rubs it trying to relieve the pain, but it did little to stop the burning.

"We should keep moving," Mercy states, looking to the mountains north of the village.

"No. You need to stop and get your head cleared," Sylas corrects. "We're all exhausted, cold, and I don't know about them but I'm starving. Cal'll meet back up with us soon too. It'll give him some time to catch up..."

Locking eyes with Sylas, Mercy nods his head. Every inch of him wanted to keep moving toward the mountains, but they needed to take a break. They had been going nonstop since Cal and Pippa had left for Sintus nearly three days ago. He also needed to get his thoughts together. His mind felt like it was being run through a whirlpool right now and it wasn't pleasant.

Placing his hand on Mercy's back, Sylas guides his Keeper forward. They needed to try and get a handle on whatever was going on with him and pushing forward wasn't going to solve that. They all knew that Bryer had

477

taken Ruby to try and get a rise out of Mercy which meant he most likely wouldn't harm the girl until Mercy was in sight. That didn't make them feel much better, but it meant they weren't in a time crunch.

A few hours later the group had stopped at an inn. Mercy had gone up to a room to try and get some rest, Sylas insisting he needed to. Shay had gone up to make sure he didn't run off, which at this point they were worried he would. Zero and Sylas sat downstairs in the dining area finishing up a meal and a few drinks, trying to figure out what to do with their spiraling friend. Zero's eyes were lit up as he looked around the room.

"What're you reading on Merc anyway?" Sylas asks with a sigh, his own mind jumbled trying to come up with a reasoning for his behavior.

"It varies from second to second," Zero shares, leaning forward on the table. "He's angry then he's sad then he's guilty, then it switches to rage or anxious or shameful. Sometimes it's all at once. My head has been pounding for days... I don't even think he knows what he's feeling when he's not focused. The only reason I could get a handle on him when he hurt Pippa was because he was fronting anger, the same thing again with that man. He turned his attention to you and was angry."

"Could Iana have done something to him? Maybe another Shadow?" Sylas suggests.

"No," Zero sighs. "No one else is in his head but me. I'd be able to tell."

"Damn..." Sylas groans, leaning back in his chair.

"You can't just blame Source magic every time emotions get strong," Zero lectures. "All our minds work in different ways."

"I know," Sylas shrugs.

"Like you," Zero smirks. "Not all of us have a knack for staving off a mental breakdown with bad jokes."

This gets a small laugh out of Sylas. "I've gotten better about that."

"I can tell," Zero nods.

The pair go silent, both feeling a bit awkward. As someone approaches the table, they look up. Dressed in a black hood with a dark scarf over his mouth, there was no denying this was Cal. His dark eyes were peering at them as he takes a seat and pulls the shroud away from his mouth and nods to the pair.

"Welcome back," Sylas greets.

"Where is Mercy?" he asks, looking between the two.

"Upstairs," Sylas shares. "Shay is watching him, making sure he doesn't try to escape."

"Escape?" Cal questions with a raise brow.

"He nearly killed someone again. It was kind of cool but more terrifying than anything else," Zero informs, taking a drink.

"Sophos," Cal sighs.

"I don't know what's up with him, but it's gotten worse since you left," Sylas adds. "He's a time bomb."

"I think the bomb already exploded," Zero scoffs at the statement.

Cal takes a drink from Sylas's glass and gets to his feet swiftly. He needed to try and get Mercy to talk, well force him to. His friend didn't seem too interested in talking in the forest, but now he wasn't taking no for an answer. He'd endure the rude remarks if it meant he could figure out what was going on in Mercy's head.

"Where're you going?" Sylas asks, watching him take a few steps from the table.

"To talk to him," he states to the pair.

With a small exhale, Sylas gets up too. He gestures for Cal to follow him. They go up to the second level of the inn. Walking down the hall the two stay quiet. Cal drops his hood and lets out an annoyed huff. He was already tired of hiding himself. At least with the chilly air it wasn't hot wearing the hood and covering his face.

Spotting Shay sitting on the floor outside of a door, Cal waves to her. Caligo was still wary of her but seeing Zero and Sylas were confident enough to let her guard Mercy made him a little less distrustful. She seemed to be proving herself to be more than his mother's pawn.

"Good to see you again, Your Grace," Shay greets, getting to her feet.

He gives a small nod to Shay as Sylas moves to unlock the door. Pushing it open they are met with an empty room and a curtain blowing lightly in the breeze of the open window.

"Shit," Sylas mumbles, moving into the room. "Shay, what the hell?"

"I didn't think he could get out!" she defends herself, rushing in behind.

They walk around the room and could see he had left behind his tactical suit, while his boots, sword, and a few other belongings were gone. Glancing around, Sylas looks at the open window and moves over to it. Outside, the snow was blanketing the small village. Looking down he could see faint footprints below.

"He went out the damn window," Sylas mutters, moving away and grabbing his duffle bag, winter cloak, and sword before rushing out the door.

Cal and Shay trail him, moving down the steps and through the dining area. This catches Zero's attention who gets up and follows his panicked party. As they exit the building and rush around to the window below the room, they all come to a stop. Sylas looks at the footprints and frowns. The snow was already covering up the Light Keeper's tracks.

"We're gonna lose him if we don't move," Sylas states, starting to follow the prints.

"He's probably heading to the mountains," Shay instructs the group.

"Okay... Okay..." Sylas pauses and turns to the other three. "Cal and I will head north to try and trail him."

"What about us?" Zero asks.

"You two stay here," Sylas orders. "If he comes back, or is still in town, we need someone here."

"I should go with you," Zero encourages. "I'll be able to-"

"*You* will not be able to find Mercy," Cal states, backing up Sylas's orders. He pulls the tablet from his waist and hands it to Zero. "Put out an MPA on him. You can track me and Sy with this if you need to."

"Cal, I don't-" Zero begins to argue.

"You obey orders from your King and his partner," Cal snaps. "We will come back once we find him."

The comment causes Sylas to furrow his brow. Was Cal saying that to pull rank, or was he serious? Were they officially back together? Zero looks between the two for a moment and nods his head in defeat.

"Let's go," Sylas states to Cal.

Before they lose the tracks, Cal and Sylas take off following the faint footprints left behind. They needed to get to Mercy before he did anything else stupid. Based on what Sylas had been seeing, if Mercy found Bryer or Iana before they found him it was going to end in a blood bath. Either from Mercy or of Mercy.

"They're already gone," Sylas states, coming to a stop after a few minutes.

Taking a deep breath, Cal closes his eyes. If he was still marked with the Shadow Source, perhaps he still had a small connection to Mercy. Taking a few steady exhales, he attempts to find the taut rope in his mind that connected him to his Alia. It had always been so simple before. Was it really his connection to the Shadow Source that tied him to Mercy? There had to be more to being someone's Alia than just controlling their opposite Source. There had to be more of a connection, especially for him and Mercy. Their Voca proved they had something that no other Alias had.

"What're you doing?" Sylas asks, looking at Cal and pulling up his partner's hood.

He hadn't even realized they had run from the inn with Cal being so visible. While Caligo continues to search his mind Sylas pulls the scarf up around his nose and mouth to conceal his features from anyone who walked by. If anyone saw the King of Novus Aitus suddenly alive, it was going to make this more difficult.

After a few more moments, Cal opens his eyes and lets out a sorrowful sigh. There was nothing there. "Our Voca is truly gone."

Sylas could see the sadness on Cal's face at the realization as they begin to walk. His connection with Mercy got him through a lot growing up and losing it was not an easy thing to come to terms with. He had used his Alia's life in Rieka as an escape from his horrific time with Mala and now it was gone. Losing that closeness with his other half felt painful.

"If Mercy's a Supra, he can figure out why your Source isn't responding or bring it back," Sylas informs him. "At least he can with a traditionally drained Keeper. I'd assume if he's above the Elder Spirits rules, he'd also be above the Source runes."

"My Shadow Source is not on the top of my list of things to worry about," Cal admits as they reach the northern edge of the village.

They both pause and look up at the mountain in front of them. The large ominous peak was starting to build up with snow already. If Mercy had begun to climb it, they were in for a brutal hike.

"We're gonna die," Sylas laughs under his breath. "Have I told you how much I hate being his Nota?"

"You may have mentioned it," Cal laughs.

Unzipping his duffle bag, Sylas pulls out a tactical bow that had been tucked away inside and flings it open. He struggles with the holster for a moment before gesturing to Cal to help him. Getting used to his hand injury was going to take time. Cal watches him closely as he fastens the straps, and Sylas pulls his quiver out. The Nota preps his trigger release, his face stern as Cal locks the bow into place and moves away. Sylas was getting serious and was preparing for the worst.

Chapter Forty-Six

Hiking through the snow and freezing wind, Mercy keeps moving forward. He was keeping his Source powered up to stay warm as he climbed up the mountain, the burn in his veins and eyes feeling stronger than usual. He was following his own instincts on what would be a normal trail for someone to hike. Though honestly, with the weather getting this bad, it seemed like a bad idea to be out here in general. If it wasn't for his Source, he probably would have had to turn back at this point.

Pausing for a moment, he catches his breath and looks down the incline. He couldn't see much through the trees that littered the side of the mountain and the worsening storm. He wondered if the others had followed him. Surely, they would trail him once they realized he was gone. He was hoping that with his head start and his Source keeping him warm, he'd be able to move quicker than them.

The only thing driving him forward at this point was finding Ruby. He couldn't lose her, not like this. He couldn't imagine having to return to Ozra and tell Saphie he couldn't save her sister. Ruby was all Saphie had. Breaking that news to Saphie would surely break her heart.

Not only that, but he would feel like a failure himself. Ruby depended on him to keep her safe and he had failed. Leaving her in Rieka without him was a mistake. He should have never trusted the Sentry Guard to keep his family safe. Clearly it was foolish to trust Cal and Sylas with them as well.

Pressing on, Mercy moves through the small clouds of his condensed breath. Suddenly he feels the familiar ringing in his ears that presages a vision and stops. He quickly drops to the ground, knowing once he came back from the vision, he could easily fall down the slick incline.

Though he waited for the vision to come it didn't. As the ringing dissipates, he shakes his head and opens his eyes to see a pair of steel toe boots in front of him. Following them up, he quickly gets to his feet when he realizes Trust was there. He takes a moment to collect himself, having not seen his brother since his passing. After Trust died, his spirit seemed to have avoided him.

"What are you doing out here?" Trust questions, looking concerned.

"Where have you been?" Mercy replies, sounding almost angry.

"Busy," he states with a shrug.

Mercy studies his blurred image for a moment, losing his shock quickly. He didn't have time to deal with his dead brother. He needed to find his daughter.

"What do you want?" Mercy sighs, brushing the snow from his pants and continuing his trek.

"I don't know. You called me," Trust retorts, keeping pace with him. "Maybe I'm here to be your conscience. Seems like you could use one."

Continuing onward, Mercy doesn't reply. He closes his eyes trying to will his brother to leave. There was no use having him here. All he was going to do was put him even more on edge and fuel his already incessant guilt.

Adding another emotion to the confusing mix inside his skull was only making this worse.

"The Elder Spirits are worried about you," Trust shares. "Should I be worried too?"

"Probably," Mercy mumbles.

"That's encouraging," he sighs, his footsteps silent in the snow.

"I didn't ask you to come," Mercy snaps back, his Source lighting up his eyes brighter.

"Power down. Sophos," Trust replies, moving in front of him.

Whatever was going on with Mercy was causing a panic. The Elders had been trying to send him a guide for days but hadn't been able to reach him. The last thing the Spirits wanted was to lose touch with a powerful force like Mercy.

"Can you leave?" Mercy growls.

"I think you should stop for a bit," Trust suggests, staying beside him. "It's cold up here and the higher you go the thinner the air'll get."

"I'm not cold," he laughs, holding his hands up to show his glowing vessels.

"That doesn't mean you shouldn't stop for a few minutes. Give Sylas and Caligo some time to catch up with you," his brother cautions.

The Keeper rolls his eyes. Why was he trying to get him to stop? Maybe the others were closer than he thought they were. He looks over his shoulder and listens carefully but couldn't hear much over the wind howling. Closing his eyes as he continues up the mountain, he tries to get a lock on Sylas. The connection to his Nota felt faint, but he could tell he was near. He pauses and looks down through the trees wondering just how close he was.

"Just take a few minutes to catch your breath," his brother pressures.

He looks at Trust's blurred image and furrows his brow. Something about Trust felt off, but he couldn't place it. His eyes get wide at the sound of a small scream. He looks at his brother who shakes his head, not wanting him to go after the source. The scream cries out again, this time unmistakably coming from a little girl. Ignoring Trust's warning, he bolts in the direction of the cries.

"Mercy, wait!" his brother pleads.

Disregarding his cautions, Mercy moves through the trees. He could feel his Source creeping up his arms, to his shoulders. Without his fireproof tactical suit on he could smell his wool shirt begin to burn as he surged forward. With each step it seemed the screams were getting louder and louder until suddenly they stopped.

He freezes and scans the area around him frantically. His eyes lock on a red streak staining the white snow about 20 feet away. He looks around and could see that his brother had vanished, and he was on his own once again. Pulling a solis orb to his hand, he creeps forward slowly. Once he reaches the blood, he notices a set of footprints leading down the trail. Around the blood appeared to be a struggle before they continued forward.

Dissolving the orb, he pulls his father's sword from his waist and follows the crimson trail. Glancing between the trail and the forest he spots something moving ahead. As he gets closer, he sees a large bolder, blood dripping from the rock, staining the snow below. He narrows his eyes, not seeing a source of the blood just yet, but the closer he got the clearer the scene became. Once he gets within ten feet, he stops in his tracks and drops the blade in his hand. Within the pool of blood was a pair of soft brown leather shoes, ones he knew well. He feels his whole body begin to shake at the sight of the red stain and small shoes. This amount of blood meant someone was probably dead and that someone was Ruby.

"No," he mutters under his breath. His eyes dart around trying to locate her body.

"Mercy Validus," he hears Iana's voice chime.

His eyes shoot up to find the source of the voice, just above the rock, as the woman uncloaks herself. She was standing on the bolder, dressed in black from head to toe, and in her right hand she was holding Ruby by her hair. His breathing begins to go ragged as his eyes well up. He watches as Iana releases her and lets her small body drop the ten feet to the ground below, her head hitting the frozen ground with a thud. He stares at the girl with wide eyes, unable to move. His entire world felt like it was imploding all at once. His chest begins to lock up as his body begins to ache.

"Oh, don't have one of those attacks now," Iana frowns, crouching down on her rock. "It would be very inconvenient for everyone involved."

His chest locking up, combined with the cold air was making it hard for him to breathe. He wasn't sure if it was another panic attack or just the shock of what he was seeing or maybe both. He wanted his feet to move. If he could move, he could get to Ruby. Maybe he could heal her. Maybe he could fix what had been done.

"It took you long enough to get here," Iana complains, jumping down to the frozen ground. "I was told to wait until you got here, but you kept stalling and you were talking to yourself. I lost my patience."

He finally tears his eyes from Ruby and looks to the woman. He could feel his whole body shaking as his Source began to surge through him. He wasn't even calling it; the anger and shock was enough to get it to react to his current situation.

"Our leader says sometimes you have to lose everything to reach your full potential," she states, walking toward him. "What are your thoughts on that? Do you feel you've lost enough yet, Mercy?"

He looks back to Ruby's motionless body in the snow. No matter how much he willed himself to inhale, there was no air coming to him. He was stuck staring at her body, unable to help his little girl.

"It was easy," Iana states, coming into his line of sight. "They're so defenseless at that age."

He needed to move. He needed to do something. Anything. He couldn't just stand there like a useless doe.

As a shiver runs through him, he finally takes a breath. His eyes dart to Iana who was staring at him with an eerie grin. Pulling his Source to his hand, he slowly releases a tendril of solis fog. Just as Cal used his spiritum fog to grip a blade, he could use his solis fog to recall his weapon as well. Drawing his father's sword to his hand, he quickly moves to strike her, the woman easily avoiding his advances by creating a cloud of fog under her feet and using it to propel herself upward. His eyes follow her as she lands on another cloud about eight feet up.

He watches her closely with rage on his face. Yet another fighting style he had never witnessed before. While he had seen Cal use his spiritum fog to catch things or cushion a fall, he had never seen him use it as a platform. How was she even doing it? Was spiritum fog solid enough to hold a person?

"How does it feel to be the most powerful person on Novus Aitus, yet still not be able to save the child you swore to protect?" Iana taunts, aiming her hand out.

He drops his blade and covers his ears as a screech from an obscurum rings through the air. He lets out an angry scream as he begins to pull more of his Source to him. His irises turn completely white with light as he locks them on Iana. He could feel his shirt begin to burn more as the Source heating his skin moved from his arms into his chest. It seemed the more he powered up the more jumbled his mind became. At that moment, he was so angry and confused he was ready to kill Iana. A life for a life.

He turns quickly as the ground below him begins to shake and an obscurum comes plowing through the trees. He needed to be smart about this. With Iana here ready to fight and her beast keeping his attention, this could easily turn in her favor. Though at this point he wasn't even sure what she, Bryer, or Malice even wanted.

He needed to focus on the beast. Iana, he could take on with his Source. The obscurum on the other hand was something he wasn't too familiar with. There had to be a core to it though. Sander was in the center of the one by the Mors River which meant there had to be a Shadow at the center of this one as well.

Further down the mountain Cal and Sylas had picked up speed. They had heard the sound of an obscurum and knew that Mercy had to be nearby. Though the cry was giving them both flashbacks to the river, they needed to press forward and try to aid Mercy. They both skid to a stop as they hear Mercy let out an angry scream, the pain in his voice echoing through the trees.

"This way!" Sylas shouts, feeling his Nota drive push him forward as he bolts through the trees.

Mercy was in trouble and Sylas's gut was telling him where he needed to be. Protecting Mercy was in his blood and if he failed, he wasn't sure what would happen. Cal pulls the scarf from his face as he follows Sylas through the rugged landscape until they break through the trees and see Mercy flashing his Light Source at the obscurum.

They both pause a moment taking in what they were seeing. Hovering above Mercy on a cloud of spiritum fog was Iana and in front of the Light Keeper was one of her monsters. Mercy's eyes were lit up so bright they couldn't even make out his face. Taking his gaze to the obscurum, Cal notes what Mercy was trying to do and gives a small smile. His Alia was trying to figure out where the core was.

Pulling one of his blades from his back, Cal rushes forward. He knew exactly where he needed to hit it to get this beast to dissipate. Sylas grabs his other hand and pulls him back as they watch Mercy's Source wash over the beast. Feeling the tug, Cal keeps his eyes on Mercy as shock takes over. Mercy wasn't trying to find the core; he was converting the spiritum fog that built the obscurum into solis fog. It was exactly what he had done at Meera's cabin, but this time he was taking over the whole beast.

A sly smile comes to Mercy as the dark purple tinged fog begins to turn to the pearly white hue of his own weapon. After a few moments the beast had completely turned the same tone as the snow that covered the ground. The Light Keeper moves his hand back and forth to confirm the obscurum was following his command before turning his attention to Iana. If she wanted to fight with a monster, maybe it was time she met one.

"He's going to use it on Iana," Sylas mumbles to Cal.

"No, he's not," Cal argues, taking a step as Sylas grabs his arm again.

"We need to stay back," he warns. "If we get into this and Iana hurts either of us, it's going to push him more."

Looking between Sylas and Mercy, Cal falls back again. Sylas was right. Seeing Mercy like this only proved he was losing himself to the world Bryer was forcing him into.

Pointing the beast on Iana, the woman drops her spiritum platform and lets herself fall to the ground. She throws her own fog toward the beast hoping to regain control but as soon as her magic touches the white creature, it joins the glaring form. Keeping his eyes locked on her, the beast moves forward on Mercy's command. With his other hand, Mercy uses his solis fog to recall his father's sword, pulling it into his grasp once again. With Iana's attention on the obscurum, he could get in his shot.

Putting up a cloak around himself, Mercy moves toward the woman. Sylas and Cal scan the snow trying to locate the Light Keeper, both fearful of what was about to happen. They watch as Iana attempts to throw more fog at the beast, but it continues to move toward her.

"Do you think you can hit the Keeper in the center of that thing?" Cal asks, pulling Sylas's bow from his back.

"Maybe," Sylas admits, glancing at the bow release as he takes the bow from Cal.

"The Keeper is just below where it's heart would be," Cal explains as Sylas knocks an arrow into his bow. "You do not need to kill them, just hitting the Keeper powering this thing may be enough to stop it."

"Worth a shot," Sylas breathes, aiming his arrow.

He lets out a shuddering breath. He hadn't exactly practiced with his release since Mercy gave it to him. Nerves build in his stomach at the idea of the arrow straying and possibly killing the Keeper in this thing. He shakes the thought from his head and lets out a steady breath as he narrows his eyes. Keeping his focus where Cal had instructed, Sylas lets the arrow fly. As soon as it pierces the obscurum the beast shrieks. Its cries fill the air as it quickly dissipates, and a person falls to the ground with a thud.

"Perfect shot!" Cal praises.

"Don't get excited just yet," Sylas cautions, scanning the landscape.

He lets out a sharp exhale as his eyes go to the space behind Iana. With a scowl, he pulls another arrow from his quiver and readies his bow. He pulls the string taut, taking another deep breath.

"What are you doing?" Cal asks.

"Mercy's right behind her," he explains, keeping his focus. "He might be able to hide from her, but he can't hide from me," Sylas mutters to himself as the Light Keeper uncloaks.

Panicked, Sylas lets the arrow go as Mercy drives his blade through Iana's back. At the same time the blade goes through her body, the arrow strikes Mercy in the chest, causing him to fall to the ground with a cry of pain. Frustrated, Sylas relaxes his bow. He should have let his arrow go a moment sooner.

"Damn it," Sylas breathes, taking off toward his Keeper.

As he approaches Mercy, the Light Keeper yanks the arrow from his chest and lets his Source begin healing. He glares at Sylas who had his eyes locked on Iana as her hair faded to a light grey and the pewter left her skin. The stab to the back had killed the woman. Sylas turns his eyes to Mercy who gets to his feet, yanking his blade from the woman's corpse.

"Move," he snaps at his Nota, shoving him out of the way and running past him.

Sylas eyes his Keeper as he rushes away. His heart sinks as he sees where Mercy was going. Cal rushes forward to meet Mercy at the red stained snow where a motionless Ruby was lying. It becomes clear that Mercy had done what he just did in a fit of rage. This woman had killed his child and he wanted revenge.

"By the Elders…" Sylas mutters, following his best friend.

Cal and Sylas both stand over Mercy, the Light Keeper too in shock to even check the little girl over. All he could do was put a trembling hand to her face before having to pull back. His entire body begins shaking at the sight of Ruby's face and battered body, as the adrenaline begins to fade from his system.

"Damn it!" he screams, putting his bloody hand to his face to try and muffle his grief. "Damn it!" he screams louder as tears start to stream.

"Merc… I'm so sorry," Sylas whispers, crouching down to offer comfort.

Pushing Sylas away, Mercy leans back on the blood-soaked rock, completely losing it. He could feel the red snow seeping through his pants but didn't care. Ruby was gone. Brokkr's daughter was gone, and it was his fault. The little girl who had watched him work nearly every day after school and would come to him for comfort from her nightmares was gone. He had let his mentor down even in death. How was he supposed to protect all living things when he had let her and so many others die?

With Mercy's sleeves completely burned away, Cal could get a good look at the inflamed scar across Mercy's upper arm. Dark veins radiated from the roughly healed wound. He gives a small point of the chin toward it, bringing Sylas's attention to the odd mark. The Nota reaches for the arm and runs his thumb over the puffy scar, feeling the heat. Mercy lets out a hiss of pain as light surges through the vessels in his arm, disappearing into the darkened veins. It looked excruciating and unnatural.

"What the hell is this…?" Sylas mutters, keeping his eyes glued to the scar.

Mercy looks over to Iana's corpse and lets out a shaky breath trying to get his tears to stop. Not only did he lose Ruby, but he had killed someone. He had driven his father's blade through Iana and murdered her. He looks down at his hands and could see the faint glow still lingering in his fingertips. He really was a Supra. He was above a Keeper's judgement. He just consciously took a life, and the Elder Spirits gave him no punishment.

"What did I do?" Mercy asks, looking at Sylas as the panic sinks in. "Sylas, what did I do?"

Taking his gaze from the scar to Mercy's face, Sylas could see the fear in his friend's eyes. "You tried to protect your daughter," he eases in a soft voice. "You were protecting Ruby."

494

"I killed her," Mercy gets out, looking at Iana again. "I killed someone."

"Protecting your daughter," Sylas reassures. "Do you hear me? You were protecting your child."

"I broke the rules," Mercy states, clearly in shock. "I-I shouldn't- I broke the rules. I killed her," Mercy repeats again.

"Look at me," Sylas wills, grabbing Mercy's face with his hand to force his gaze, feeling the warmth in the Keeper's skin. "You were trying to protect Ruby. You were protecting your daughter."

"But I wasn't," Mercy confesses.

"There's nothing else to think on here, Merc," he assures him. "You are meant to protect all living things, and that was what you were doing."

The Light Keeper looks to Ruby again. While he had once offered her comfort and safety, now he was the nightmare. Looking back at Sylas he shakes his head and pulls away. "I killed her, Sylas. I wanted to kill her."

"No, you didn't," Sylas lectures, dropping his hand. "You are Mercy Validus, the peacekeeper. You wouldn't even kill Mala, the woman who took everything from you. There is no way you'd kill someone on purpose."

"I wanted her dead," Mercy stresses, his voice small.

"No," Sylas says again, shaking his head. "Don't say that. You don't kill people, Merc."

Taking his gaze back to Ruby, Mercy's grief shifts to anger. Sylas glances at the scar on his Keeper's arm as it begins to glow, the dark veins eating away at the Light Source coming toward it. The Light Keeper pulls away from Sylas and glances to Cal.

"Bryer's next," Mercy announces to them, getting to his feet.

This brings Cal's attention to the conversation. He couldn't let Mercy kill Bryer. Mercy wasn't a killer and Cal had questions for the man who had held him captive in that camp and tortured him for weeks. If he truly was his uncle, he needed answers.

"Merc, you can't let your anger control you," Sylas cautions, getting to his feet as well.

"I'm not letting him take any more lives," Mercy snarls, powering up. "I'm not letting *anyone* take any more lives. The killing is over."

"Merc, come on," Sylas pleads, grabbing him.

The Light Keeper turns swiftly, pulling his blade from his belt and putting it to Sylas's throat. "It'd be wise to stay out of this, Sylas."

Reacting to the threat on Sylas, Cal pulls his curved blade from his back and points it at Mercy. "And you would be wise to power down."

"You're not a threat to me, Cal," Mercy snaps at him, moving the blade closer to Sylas.

A small hiss of pain comes from the Nota as blood begins to pool on the blade. "We need to just take a breath here, please," Sylas begs, putting his hands up. "I really have no plans to die today, and I know you two weren't planning to maim each other."

"Power down, Mercy," Cal warns, pulling his other blade from his back. "You hurt him, and it'll be the last thing you ever do."

The words cause a falter in Mercy's serious face as he pulls his blade away from Sylas. He glares at both of them and raises his palm. He lets off a blast of his Light Source energy, sending them both flying backward into the snow with a wave of light. As they land on the frozen ground, both letting out groans of pain, the Light Keeper puts his cloak up. They both watch as the footprints in the snow flee the scene.

Getting to his feet, Sylas scans the area. "Shit. Merc!" he shouts. "Mercy!"

Getting up, Cal looks around at the damage in front of him. Iana was dead, there was a drained Shadow Keeper lying in the snow, still breathing at least, and then there was Ruby. He turns to look at the little girl whose eyes were starting to flutter open. Cal's eyes get wide as he realizes her chest was rising ever so slightly as she begins to look around groggily.

"She's alive," he mumbles, rushing over to the child.

"What?" Sylas replies, following Cal with his eyes.

Cal feels his lip tremble at the sight of the child. The guilt felt almost unbearable. He understood why Mercy was angry, that was the worst part. Wanting Bryer dead was fathomable as he looked at the small girl's injured body. This was Mercy's child. This was the girl he had dedicated over a year of his life to caring for and had a bond with. The rage the Light Keeper was feeling and the need for revenge was understandable.

"Don't move, Ruby," Cal instructs as her eyes flutter shut again.

"This is bad," Sylas mumbles, crouching down.

"We need to get her to Zero," Cal states, pulling his coat off and beginning to wrap it around her.

"A healer won't work," Sylas suggests. "If Iana did this, a Keepers Judgement is in play."

"Not if Iana didn't intend to kill," Cal enlightens. "We will stabilize her with what we have and take her with us. I'm sure Lacero has a decent doctor if Zero's Source doesn't work."

"Okay," Sylas settles, knowing in this situation Cal was going to be better at making the calls.

While Sylas had the training and field time, Cal had more experience with injuries like this. The years of fighting battles for Mala had given him ample time to figure out the best way to get the injured off the field and to a place they could heal. Since Spheara, there had been

497

hundreds of riots, but no battles like the one's Cal had seen. Sylas watches as Cal takes a knife out, cutting the scarf into strips, and wraps one around the wound on her forearm.

"Bryer is getting what he wanted," Cal states, shaking his head and continuing to wrap up the wounds with the fabric as Sylas crouches beside him. "He wanted Mercy to show Novus Aitus what he can do, and he is getting just that."

"This isn't him," Sylas breathes, shivering as he removes his winter cloak and hands it to Cal. "There's something else going on here. That thing on his arm…"

"I saw," Cal nods in agreement while refusing the cloak, knowing Sylas needed it to make the hike back. "We cannot let him get to Bryer. We need to get ahead of him and stop this before he loses it."

"I think he already has," Sylas states, putting his cloak back on and putting his hand to his neck, feeling the blood that was dripping down.

Seeing the red stain on Sylas's hand, Cal moves his attention to him. "It is just a scratch," he assures him, grabbing the edge of Sylas's winter cloak and using it to pat away the blood. "Zero can patch it up."

"We need to find Mercy," Sylas reiterates as Cal goes back to Ruby and finishes bundling her. "Maybe if we can tell him she's alive, he'll calm down and we can figure out what's going on."

"We need to focus on Ruby right now or we will not have that news to tell," Cal sighs, grabbing the pendant around Sylas's neck.

"What are you doing?" Sylas asks.

"We need to send someone to collect Iana," Cal states, taking the knife and cutting the leather open on the back of the pendant. "We can send them the coordinates of the tracking device."

Sylas nods his head, taking the pendant back as Cal gets up and moves to place the small device in Iana's pocket. He pauses a moment to study her face. If Bryer was truly his uncle, this meant Iana was his cousin. Perhaps like him, she had been manipulated into doing what her parent wanted. Maybe they truly could have been friends under different circumstances.

Leaving Iana's side, he goes over to the drained Shadow Keeper that had been in the obscurum and checks their pulse. They were still alive, weak, but alive. Beckoning over Sylas, he gestures to the Keeper. Maneuvering the unconscious person, Sylas gets them over his shoulder as Cal goes over and picks up Ruby carefully.

They needed to get to Shay and Zero to regroup. Suddenly Malice was no longer the enemy they needed to neutralize. The enemy was Mercy Validus.

Chapter Forty-Seven

Back at the inn, Cal was sitting at a desk in the room thinking through what he had witnessed on the mountain. He had his sketchbook out in front of him and a pencil in his hand. Instead of sketching though, he was writing down the sequence of events that had occurred trying to pinpoint Bryer's strategy with Mercy. Knowing that his central goal revolved around the Keeper made this all the more puzzling. He could understand the want to unlock Mercy's Supra abilities, but why? What was he intending to do with that power and how was he going to get Mercy to use it in the way he wanted?

The break-in was clearly done to get their hands on the genti plated tome. While it shook Mercy up, it couldn't have been a part of their main strategy. The next event was the attack on Sylas. Here, Iana was obviously trying to get a rise out of the Light Keeper and send a grisly message. She had been walking her obscurums around Orior hoping it would lure him out and when that failed, she took matters into her own hands.

He looks over to Sylas who was lying on the bed with his eyes closed and Ruby snuggled up next to him. Zero and the local doctor had patched up the girl nicely and she seemed to be doing okay. She had lost a lot of blood on the mountain, but at this point she was doing much better. The snow had made the injuries look much worse than they were, giving them both some relief.

After she woke up, she clung to Sylas for comfort and constantly asked where Mercy was. Sylas promised he would keep her safe until Mercy came for her, but they both knew he wasn't coming. Lucky for them, the girl seemed to have no memory of what happened after she left the house. Her memory being gone and the clear hit to the head was concerning, so they'd have to get her back to Ozra for a check over by Doctor Willa as soon as possible.

In contrast though, her survival confused Cal. Iana had a clear window to kill the little girl yet didn't. The injuries seemed deliberate, but she had no intention to kill the child since Zero was able to heal her. Certainly, they took her to get Mercy over the edge, so why not solidify their efforts by taking the child's life?

Cal could tell by the way Sylas was breathing that he wasn't asleep yet. How could either of them sleep after the day they just had? Their closest friend was running rampant with a strange pulsing scar on his arm and no one there to try and calm the storm in his head. Cal takes a deep breath and goes back to his sketchbook.

The next event was the attack on Meera. Iana had stated she had no plans to hurt Mercy's niece but had clear intentions to harm Meera. While the threat to Meera was enough to get Mercy to forge that document to release Shay, it wasn't a hard enough blow to set off his Supra Keeping. Crossing out the event, Cal continues forward.

Next was the incident at the Mors River. He shudders at the memory of going into the icy water. He had never felt that helpless in his life. Even now with his Source gone, he didn't feel anything close to the vulnerability he felt that day. Being batted around like a toy by that obscurum was horrific and seeing the way Sylas looked at him when he pushed him back to the bank was seared into his mind.

He furrows his brow as he continues to think. Though he couldn't remember much of what happened at the camp after he had gotten out of the tent, he did recall Pippa speaking to Zero in the infirmary. They were discussing how Mercy had attacked Iana and nearly Bryer before backing down. Was that a hint at the breakdown yet to come?

Lastly, Bryer and Iana went after the girls. Sprinkled throughout all this was a vision of Mercy's own death, which Sylas had suggested was a hoax as well as a prophesized attack on Pippa. Sylas had also told him that Mercy had said the visions seemed strange, like they were more metaphors of the future, which he could see when he saw the one in the conference room. He had witnessed many of his Alia's visions leak into his own mind in the past, but none were quite like that one.

"Hey, Sy," Cal whispers, turning to him.

"Hey, what?" he replies quietly, his eyes still closed.

"I have a query," he informs.

"Interesting way to present a question, but go on," Sylas notes.

"Do we know Bryer or Iana's peritias?" he asks.

Sylas opens his eyes and looks at him. "They're your relatives, shouldn't you know?"

"You are not helpful," Cal grumbles.

"I never claimed to be helpful," Sylas retorts, closing his eyes again. "Stop drawing and go to sleep."

"I'm not drawing, I am trying to figure this out," Cal explains, getting up and going to sit on the bed by Sylas. "Wake up and help me, then you can sleep."

"You Keepers ask too much of me," Sylas groans, adjusting Ruby carefully so he could sit up. "What?"

"What if Bryer or Iana were altering Mercy's visions?" Cal asks, looking at the page, keeping his voice low. "What if their strategy was to play into Mercy's already declining mental state to get his Supra Keeping unlocked? Perhaps that strange scar is amplifying it somehow?" Cal continues. "Perhaps Mercy was truly having visions from the Elders, but Bryer or Iana were somehow manipulating them into these altered visions to further push him."

Sylas ponders the theory but shakes his head as the conversation stays in whispers. "That's a lot of speculation."

"You love speculation," Cal points out. "Just look at this," he continues, showing his timeline to Sylas. "First the break in, minor. The vision of his own death... Shook him up, but not enough. Going after Meera? That was enough to get him to go rogue."

"I see what you're saying," Sylas admits.

"Taking me out of the picture..." Cal takes a deep breath. "That is when it started. That is when he started to slip. Finding me alive, seeing what Bryer had done... It made Mercy frantic. From the outside he looked like he was scrambling. Maybe this proved to Bryer he was starting to lose it. Once he had him close to the edge..."

"He made his final play," Sylas adds, resting his hand on the little girl.

"Ruby," Cal finishes, giving a shameful nod of the head toward the sleeping child. "This all happened in the course of just eight weeks. That is far too quickly for him to try and grasp onto anything to stabilize himself. Add what Master Novi said, crumbling his foundation by using the exua rune on you and me... Putting that divide between a Keeper and his Nota..."

"You think Bryer's using emotional manipulation to get him to do what he wants," Sylas realizes.

"Yes," Cal confirms.

"Shit." Sylas runs his fingers over his hair. "You might be right." He shakes his head in shame. "I never should've yelled at him or left after what happened at the river... This is my fault. I'm a horrible Nota and an even worse friend."

"You were upset," Cal defends, furrowing his brow at the statement.

"It wasn't just that time... I blamed him for..." he gestures to Cal. "I've been so caught up in myself and you, I've been taking things out on him... Sophos. I'm a bad friend, Cal. I'm a horrible friend."

Closing his eyes, Cal nods his head. He couldn't fault Sylas for being upset about what had happened. The man had thought he witnessed the person he loved dying. The fear and agony he was in would have been enough to push anyone over the edge.

"All this time I've been trying to get further away from Merc, but I shouldn't have," Sylas confesses. "Being his Nota is important and I shouldn't... Before I was told who I had to be for him, I did it willingly and without complaint. I enjoyed being around him and helping him with anything he needed. From combat training to threading the stupid needle when he needed to sew something. He always acted like he couldn't thread a needle... It didn't take me long to catch on he was only doing it so I'd feel helpful. I never should of pushed him away."

"You are in a difficult position. No one blames you for wanting to venture out on your own," Cal eases.

"I was supposed to be guiding and protecting him and instead I was leaving him to his own devices," Sylas continues, locking eyes with Cal. "Nex never left your side. She was always there. When I saw you, I knew that crow wasn't far behind. I should have been doing the same for Mercy and done it with pride. Being his Nota isn't a curse or an inconvenience... It's a high honor from the Elder

Spirits. They saw me and decided I could guide the most powerful Keeper this planet has ever seen, and how did I repay their gift? By letting him go off the deep end and kill a woman... I'm probably the worst Nota in history."

Cal stays quiet seeing if Sylas would continue. Realizing he was done; he closes his sketchbook and shakes his head. "If we are being honest, I have not been the best Alia either. Mercy and I were created to work as a team, and instead of doing that, I was sending him on assignments without me and giving him no say in any of the decisions being made for our people. I told you from the start I didn't feel I should be ruling alone... Perhaps I should have been doing it with Mercy. A Keeper of Light and a Keeper of Shadows are both needed to keep balance within the world. With just a Keeper of Shadows on the throne, where is the balance?"

"I mean... his reasoning for dissolving the National Council made sense," Sylas acknowledges. "Had you caught onto what they were doing?"

"I suspected they were doing it to try and keep power over me, not to corrupt the Tenebris name further or be working for the rebels," Cal discloses. "With Mercy aiding me, feasibly all the issues with the National Council could have been avoided."

"Pippa could see what was happening," Sylas shares, shaking his head.

"The number of times I disregarded her warnings..." Cal sighs.

"We both did," Sylas corrects.

Leaning forward, Sylas wraps his arms around Cal to offer some comfort as they sit in silence with their thoughts. They had a lot they needed to figure out. With Iana out of the way, they had no idea how they were going to track down Bryer. Their only option was going to be Shay, and even that was going to be rough. With Bryer

505

being a Light Keeper, he was practically invisible to the girl.

The two continue in their silence as Sylas's mind wanders. How had he been so clueless in what was going on with his Keeper? Now that he thought of it, being around Mercy had made him feel jumbled himself recently. Usually, he was keen to what Mercy needed and when, but lately it felt off. He had chalked it up to the exua rune on his arm, but perhaps it was more than that. Taking his eyes to Cal he lets out a heavy sigh. What else had he been ignoring?

"He's changing and I'm scared," Sylas admits in a small voice, releasing Cal.

"Another wise quote from Sylas Bellator that I have not forgotten," Cal smiles softly, beginning to remove his prosthetics. "People don't change, their circumstances do."

"Which is a scary thought when you think about Merc, isn't it?" Sylas breathes, laying back on the bed.

"Don't look at it that way," Cal stresses. "If pushed too far, we all have the aptitude to lose ourselves. Look at yourself."

"I'm still going through my quarter life crisis over here, King Charming," Sylas adds, kicking him lightly with his foot. "Don't bring it up, Tenebris, or I'll kick you where it hurts."

"I am just trying to help you understand," Cal sighs.

"You know what's the most terrifying part about this whole thing you just came up with?" Sylas states.

"What is that?" Cal replies, resting the prosthetics by the table and pulling his legs up on the bed.

"Bryer had to of been watching him," Sylas illuminates. "If this is manipulation like you're suggesting, then he had to of been watching Mercy's reactions. On top of that, the only people who knew the genti tome was in Rieka were you, me, Pippa, and the Validus home. Only

Mercy knew where Meera was. *I* didn't even know she was living near Opolis..."

"I did not think of that," Cal admits, grabbing his sketchbook and looking over the timeline again.

"Who else would have been able to figure out where Meera was?" Sylas asks, thinking to himself. "How on Novus Aitus would someone get that information?"

Tapping the pencil on his paper, Cal continues to think over the statement. The land Meera's cabin was built on was purchased by Mercy, but Cal had taken the records out of the public archives. It was a private purchase between Mercy and the capital. The cabin itself was built without him or Meera being directly involved so the workers wouldn't know who the occupants would be. Mercy had been very thorough with the entire ordeal. He wanted Meera to live there but for no one to know. His goal was to keep Velia out of the public eye, and it was the best course of action to do so.

The genti tome was given to Mercy to guard directly following Spheara. Pippa and Sylas would stop by somewhat frequently to work on translations, but it was required that the book was never to leave the Validus home, specifically Mercy's office. Neither Pippa nor Sylas spoke about the location of the book, so the fact Iana knew where it was, was concerning.

"Do you think they have a Shadow like Shay?" Sylas suggests.

Shaking his head, Cal takes a deep breath. "What if that information was being collected by someone a little closer to Mercy? Someone who knows him. Someone he trusted."

"Like who?" Sylas asks, sitting up again.

Continuing to shake his head, Cal writes down two names and lays the book down in front of Sylas.

"Charlyn and Sander?" Sylas laughs. "Are you nuts?"

507

"Sander was his personal Sentry," Cal clarifies. "He would have gone with Mercy to that cabin multiple times as well as known the genti tome was in his office."

"Why would Iana take him then?" Sylas differs. "Surely, they would want their weasel to stay in the inner circle and wouldn't punish him. Sander was used to power an obscurum."

"Yes," Cal nods, circling Charlyn's name. "Which is why I think we need to take our attention to Charlyn."

"She would never let anything happen to Ruby," Sylas argues, slightly offended by the accusation.

"Maybe she did not know," Cal suggest, looking at the little girl.

"So, what do you want to do then? Go back to Ozra?" Sylas questions, staring at the name.

"I think you, Shay, and Zero should stay here and continue looking for Mercy, and I will head back to the capital and confront Charlyn," Cal suggests.

"No," Sylas snaps back. "I am *not* letting us get separated. Not now. You and I are going to be the best bet at bringing Merc back down to solid ground. You know that as well as I do."

"Then what do you suggest?" Cal sighs in annoyance.

"Zero and Shay go back to Ozra, and you and I look for Merc," Sylas proposes.

"Sy, that is not-"

"Let me explain before you shit on my idea," Sylas snaps, cutting him off, continuing to keep his voice low. "Shay is going to be the quickest way to test your theory on Charlyn. It'll be quick and easy having her tap into her mind and give us an answer. We need to send someone with her because… well… we can't let a war criminal saunter around Novus Aitus alone. We both trust Zero, so sending him with her makes sense. Once they have the information, Zero can contact us. Meanwhile, I can tap into my connection with Mercy to try and track him down. With the obscurum queen gone, we have no need for a Light Keeper. We can send them on the transport they are sending for Ruby and that stripped Shadow tomorrow."

"You want to separate us from the two Source Keepers we trust?" Cal asks, skeptical at the idea. "We might need Zero to help with Mercy."

"Our biggest threat right now *is* Mercy, and he wouldn't hurt us. Not on purpose," Sylas states. "Even with that blade to my throat, I can promise you he had no intention to hurt me. When he hit Pippa, that shot was meant for you, and he knew you could take it. You were in a heat resistant suit, and you know how to take a hit. Plus, Mercy said it before; Bryer is going to expect us to go in with everything we have. If just you and I show up-"

"Bryer will kill us," Cal bluntly states in response.

"Will he though?" Sylas tests, giving a playful smile. "Bryer didn't kill you. Iana didn't kill me. If anything, they'd just use us to continue to play Mercy. As far as I'm concerned, Bryer and Malice aren't a threat to us."

"Okay," Cal yields, seeing the cleverness in the plan Sylas was creating. "You always have had the sense for a good plan."

"That's because I'm actually crazy and sometimes a good plan needs a little crazy," Sylas shrugs.

509

Chapter Forty-Eight

Fidgeting with the tablet in his hands, Cal looks up at Sylas from his chair. They had sent the rest of the group with Ruby back to the capital the day before and had been relaxing at the inn since. It was nice to get some time alone again, but at the same time their stress levels were far too high to even enjoy it. They were hoping to actually get out and do something to pass the time today.

Cal cocks his brow as he watches Sylas struggle with the laces on his boot, wearing the prosthetic Mercy and Doctor Willa fashioned for him. This was the first time he had seen Sylas put on the device and was curious how this was going to go. Sylas fumbles with the laces a few times before stopping and letting out an exasperated sigh. For the most part, Sylas had been ignoring what had happened, but this morning he seemed to have woken up with some determination to figure out his new hand, or maybe he was just going stir crazy.

After another few moments the frustration with the task was starting to get high. Sylas takes the prosthetic off and tosses it onto the bed and begins to try without it to no avail. It seemed the harder Sylas tried to lace the boot, the more mistakes he was making. Seeing him go through this upset Cal. Losing any part of your body wasn't easy to handle, and knowing Sylas, he had been putting off dealing with the reality of his injury longer than he'd admit.

"Let me help," Cal finally offers, putting the tablet on the desk beside him and gesturing to Sylas.

"I can get it," Sylas insists.

"I can do it for you," Cal asserts.

"I've done it before on my own just fine, thank you," Sylas snaps in irritation.

"It's okay to ask for help, Sy," Cal replies in a calm voice.

Taking a deep breath, Sylas looks to the floor in defeat. "That would be the logical thing to do, wouldn't it?" he admits. "You really want to lend me a *hand*?"

"Please don't tell me I just triggered the puns?" Cal groans with a small laugh.

"I feel it in my *sole* that you might have," Sylas snickers, but quickly goes to a frown. In that moment, joking didn't feel like the right thing to do.

"Please let me help you," Cal pushes. "Sometimes taking a step back and letting someone help you is the best solution."

Giving in, Sylas walks over to him as Cal pats his knee. He lets out a heavy exhale and gives Cal his foot. Usually when he struggled with a task like this he just gave up. Anything that took him too long to complete and wasn't vital, he simply removed from his routine.

"You spent six months hammering into my head that it is okay to ask for help when I need it, so please, for the sake of my sanity, do not make me hammer it into yours," Cal says, unlacing what Sylas had done to start fresh.

"Can you get the buttons on my shirt cuffs too?" Sylas asks in a defeated voice.

"Yes," Cal nods with a small laugh as he starts to lace. "Can I ask you something?"

"Sure," Sylas shrugs, watching him work.

"Have you accepted your fingers are not coming back?" he questions, focusing on the task.

"What?" he replies.

"Getting used to the missing part, accepting a new body image, the emotional toll," Cal lists. "I know you have not been talking to anyone about this. I noticed you have been tucking your laces into your boots or wearing shoes that don't require them and you have not been practicing with your bow release. I can't even recall the last time I saw you look at your guitar or write a single word, and you love writing. You are removing obstacles."

"You noticed, huh?" Sylas admits as Cal finishes up the knot and gestures to the other foot.

"I did," Cal discloses. "Can I give you some advice?" he enquires, beginning to lace the other boot.

"I guess," Sylas sighs.

"There is grief involved in losing any part of your body. Fear, sorrow, hopelessness... Let yourself feel those things and work through them. If you are frustrated, be frustrated. Cry a little if you must. You will need to find a new way to play your guitar and lace your boots and write your studies, just like you found an aid with your bow, and you need to practice those methods... If it's a difficult day, take a step back, yell at the sky, and know you can always talk to me. I have been there, and I know what you are going through."

He finishes up the laces and pats Sylas's boot. He looks up at him with a soft smile from his chair as Sylas takes in his words. Cal was right, he hadn't talked to anyone about it. He had isolated himself and when people asked how he was doing with his hand, he simply said he was fine. He declined any option for physical therapy and rarely showed up for his counseling sessions. He was getting stuck in his own head again like usual.

"If you simply focus on where you want to be, which is where you were before the incident, then you are going to struggle," Cal continues, buttoning the cuffs of his shirt. "It's the journey to that destination that matters the most. My first time walking in my prosthetics? Awful. It was not pretty to watch, and it was certainly unpleasant for me, but I was on my feet again and that was an accomplishment," he adds, getting up and looking Sylas in the eye. "That was something I was afraid I would never do again. That initial walk between those bars is one of the proudest moments of my life, because it was a step toward getting to where I wanted to be." He pauses a moment as Sylas looks to the floor. "I put in seven years of hard work, and I still struggle at times, you have seen that, but I am unstoppable when I want to be. Be in the moment and allow yourself to celebrate the small victories. You can be angry with the failures but keep trying. The things that test you the most are what make you the strongest."

"I think I actually needed to hear that," Sylas admits, looking at the cuffs on his shirt.

"You did," Cal smugly retorts, grabbing the tablet again to check it. "I knew you needed it when you called a life altering injury a 'minor inconvenience,' but we were not exactly on good terms then," he confesses.

"What terms are we on now?" Sylas prods.

"Regrettably, I think we are stuck with each other for the rest of our lives," Cal shrugs with a dramatic sigh and a sly smile, sitting down on the bed.

"Your sarcasm hurts me," Sylas bluntly retorts.

"You know I love you," Cal laughs.

"Good, because I haven't dealt with your cocky bullshit all this time for nothing," Sylas jokes, folding his arms and sitting on the bed beside him.

"I do so enjoy that your affection involves insults," Cal points out.

"Insults mean I love you," Sylas smiles. "Anything from Zero yet?"

"No," Cal announces, placing the tablet beside him. "What about you? Anything on Mercy?"

Sylas shakes his head. It had been two days since he had last been able to sense his Keeper. He was hoping he'd of felt some sort of tug toward his best friend but, for whatever reason, there was nothing. At least that meant Mercy wasn't in danger just yet. The more distance between him and Mercy, the less they could sense each other's whereabouts though. Then again, the exua rune could have finally severed what little was left.

"It feels stupid to just sit around waiting," Sylas admits. "Doesn't feel like we're doing much."

"Unfortunately, we are playing a waiting game, my love," Cal shares with him. "One I am sadly quite familiar with."

"What's that mean?" Sylas replies with a cocked brow.

"Do you have any idea how many times I was stationed somewhere waiting to kill on my mother's mark?" Cal asks, looking at him. "I was a weapon, remember?"

"I forgot about that," Sylas huffs.

Watching Cal pick up the tablet again, Sylas bites the inside of his lip. Since they had left Rieka, Cal had been acting fairly normal himself. Perhaps being back to work was bringing him out of his bout of depression.

"We talked about me... So now I wanna know how you've been?" Sylas pries.

Watching Cal's face, Sylas frowns again. As he goes to speak the tablet suddenly begins to chime. Cal shakes his head at the observation and scrolls through the device. He taps it with his finger a few times and begins to read. After a few moments he looks up to Sylas.

"I was right," he states in shock.

"About Charlyn?" Sylas asks, getting up and moving toward Cal.

"I wanted to be wrong," Cal adds in disbelief. "I really wanted to be wrong."

"I honestly thought you were," Sylas adds.

Cal hands the tablet to Sylas so he could read what Zero had sent. According to the information Shay was able to pull from Charlyn's mind, she had been working with Malice for the last year. While the reasoning wasn't given, they could only assume it involved Cal. His mother had taken everything from Charlyn, just as she did with many of their citizens. If what Bryer had planned could end the Tenebris name, then it was no wonder she fell into his trap.

As Sylas continues to read, he starts to feel sick to his stomach. After everything Cal and Mercy had done for this woman, how could she betray them? She had seen firsthand the kindness Caligo had and yet chose to aid in turning Mercy against him. His main source of disgust was in the fact his Keeper had done nothing but show compassion and offered refuge to this woman just to have her turn around and deceive him. Mercy had let Charlyn into his home, into his family, and she was thanking him by aiding in this epic meltdown and so much more.

"I wonder what her motives are?" Sylas asks, looking to Cal who takes the tablet back.

"We both know," Cal admits.

"She knew Mercy," Sylas states, his voice picking up speed. "She spent nearly every day with him. She knows he's a good man and a great father figure to those girls. He does everything for them and for her. How could she just turn on him like that? How could she do this to Ruby and Saph? I don't understand."

"Revenge can drive us to do unthinkable things," Cal replies, shaking his head as he sends Zero a response. The device goes off again with another message. This prompts Cal to get to his feet. "She gave them a location."

515

"Where?" Sylas asks.

Turning to look at Sylas, Cal lets out a heavy sigh. "The Source Temple."

"Mount Sacris?" Sylas asks for clarification.

"Yes," Cal nods.

Chapter Forty-Nine

Moving up Mount Sacris felt therapeutic. The last time Mercy had been there was the day his life had changed forever. The Source Temple was where he and Cal had connected for the first time and where he learned his abilities went beyond just self-defense. That day he had learned he could heal, and it had been eye opening. It proved that being a Keeper of Light wasn't a curse, but a true blessing.

Now he knew his hands weren't meant to just heal though, they were also meant to kill. That's what it meant to be a Supra Keeper after all. Being above the rules of the Elder Spirits meant he could take punishments into his own hands. He didn't need to let Cal handle his fights or have Sylas use his arrows. For once he could rely on his own Source to protect him and those he cared for.

Moving up the familiar trail he spots the watch post. He pauses and looks around, thinking back to the day Cal fought off the General of the UC Guard to protect him and Sylas. It was the first day he saw a true display of the Source of Shadows and realized how terrifying it was. Now he could be just as deadly as his Alia. If he had known then what he did now, maybe they wouldn't have needed Caligo to get to Mala. He could have handled the entire situation himself and kept both himself and Sylas out of the fight. Perhaps his brother would have even lived.

With a deep breath, he continues forward. There was no time to think on that. He needed to stay in the present and keep his mind on the goal. Right now, he needed to get to the temple and find Bryer.

Moving up the trail, he tries to shake the thought of his last visit here from his mind. For the most part, he had tried to forget the events that led up to Spheara. While he was glad to have met Cal and Pippa, he had wished it would have been under different circumstances. Then again, he wasn't sure what other circumstance would call for him to befriend the Prince of Ozra.

As he approaches the temple, he pauses. He could see that Cal had been working to restore the relic of a structure. The vegetation that had obstructed much of the temple had been cut away and the stone was in the process of being cleaned. The bits of moss, lichen, and dirt were now removed from the walls and roof of the temple. Overall, the temple had improved greatly compared to when he last set his eyes on it. It made it more breathtaking to look at. This temple was a work of art, and Cal was making sure others could see that.

Entering the structure, he takes another pause. The floors and walls had been cleaned recently, but the building was empty. He could hear the echo of his footsteps as he moved down the corridor, the intricate carvings surrounding him as he continued forward. He didn't remember such a prominent echo when he was last here, but then again, the place was new to him that day and he was on edge.

Pulling his Source to his hands he smiles as the torches in the hall begin to illuminate with him. He had missed this place. The power he felt when walking on these grounds was astonishing. The last time he was here he was at half power, now he had harnessed his full connection and he felt unstoppable. Maybe this was why Bryer was trying to lure him here. Putting him in a setting where his Source was at its peak would undoubtably unlock his Supra Keeping. With that in mind, maybe it would be smart for him to turn back.

"Finally," he hears a voice state from down the hall.

Moving his gaze forward, he locks eyes with Bryer. Looking at him with what he knew now, he could see Cal's features in the man's face. They had the same steely gaze and nose. Even the harsh jawline matched his Alia's perfectly. How he hadn't seen it before was shocking. This was definitely someone related to Caligo.

"I assumed Iana would beat you here," he states as Mercy continues forward.

"I took care of that problem," Mercy retorts, pulling an orb to his hand. He sees a small falter in Bryer's stern eyes. "She's dead," he coldly informs.

"I don't believe that for a moment," Bryer shoots back with a shocked scoff.

"You took something from me, so I took something from you," Mercy clarifies, dancing the orb around his hand. "Blood for blood."

"Keepers of Light don't take lives," Bryer frowns.

"A Supra Keeper does," Mercy shrugs, approaching the man.

As he gets closer, Bryer begins to take a couple of steps back. Hearing Mercy had killed someone wasn't something he expected, especially his daughter. While the goal was to push Mercy, they weren't trying to push him to slaughter their people.

"I don't see a reason I shouldn't kill you too," Mercy growls, coming to a stop. The look on his face was cold and full of anger. "King Emrys, right?"

"My brother is dead," the man corrects.

"Bryer Nitesems is an anagram," Mercy states with a raised brow.

"To honor my brother," Bryer informs. "The day Mala killed him was the day I vowed to avenge what the Tenebris rulers took from my family. I am just like you Mercy," he enlightens. "I lost everything to the Tenebris throne, just as you did."

"Bullshit," Mercy's snaps, the solis orb in his hand growing brighter.

"My first born, Mya," Bryer continues, putting his hands up. "She was one of the Shadow Keepers Queen Mala recruited and promptly disposed of. I assumed she would be safe in the hands of Mala seeing as she was Emrys's niece, but Mala gave little care."

Mercy eases as he listens to the tale. "You're lying," he accuses.

"Malice is only trying to repair what Mala destroyed and what Caligo is attempting to crumble even further," Bryer shares. "All we need to mend the damage of this planet is you, Mercy. Turn away from the throne and we will give you back everything you've lost. We will protect your family and end this torment."

"Why should I listen to you?" Mercy questions. "You're the one who tried to kill my family. You killed my daughter!"

The emotions in Mercy's mind begin to scramble again as he tries to make sense of what Bryer was saying. Seeing the upset in his face, Bryer frowns and changes his tactics. This is what they were riding on to sway Mercy to their side. The confusion and fear that was surging through him could be enough to help gain his trust.

"You want to put this blame on me, when the real villain is the Shadow Keeper you call your Alia," Bryer adds.

"Shut up," Mercy warns, squeezing his eyes shut.

"Caligo has always been the villain, Mercy," Bryer continues. "Look at what he's done to Novus Aitus. He has taken thousands of innocent lives. He killed Ezra and Berk Bellator. He took your brother from you and turned your Nota against you. Sylas blames you for all of his qualms due to the ideas Caligo Tenebris has put into his head. Think of the words your friend spoke to you, Mercy. Remember who the enemy is here."

"Sylas was angry," Mercy retorts, his hands shaking. "He had every right to be angry!"

"Anger is when your true emotions come to the surface," Bryer pushes. "Just as Caligo's come out. You are nothing but a filthy maddux to that man, and you always will be. He will turn your Nota into a killer soon enough, just as he is a killer himself."

"Cal isn't a killer," Mercy disagrees. "He's good."

"How could such a powerful Keeper be as unaware of his actions as he claims?" Bryer adds. "Why would he yield to his mother's wishes when he had the power to end her years ago? He didn't need you to end her tyranny, he had the ability to do it himself, but instead he painted an image of a broken man so you would do his bidding. He is a killer."

The Light Keeper narrows his eyes in skepticism at the statement and shakes his head trying to clear his thoughts. He knew Caligo. He knew Cal's fears and what drove him. He could tell when Cal was lying and when he was scared or frustrated. There was no way he would have taken any of those lives if he had a choice.

"There is no bigger threat to a Shadow Keeping King than a Light Keeper he can't control," Bryer stresses. "He is fearful of you and what you can become. Just like his mother and grandmother before him, fearing the Keepers of Light is in his blood, Mercy."

"Stop!" Mercy snaps, his head starting to pound.

"If Caligo truly was your ally then why would he keep the truth from you?" Bryer questions, his face sincere. "He killed your father. Myself and many others witnessed his death. Caligo murdered your father, Mercy. Why would he do that?"

"No, he didn't," Mercy's eyes get wide.

The anger Mercy felt begins to shift to panic. Was Bryer telling the truth? There was no way Caligo had killed his father. Master Novi said Orlo killed himself. That he took his own life that day. He had never bothered to look into the archives about his father, not wanting to reopen that painful wound, but this had to be a lie.

"Caligo Tenebris is nothing more than the heartless creature his mother fostered. He tried to keep you from pursuing me, didn't he? He refused to sign your documents to find me," Bryer adds, watching Mercy's face continue to break. "Then he tracked you to try and hold you back. He knows what you could be, and he fears you, Mercy. Malice on the other hand… We can help you. We can show the world your power and intellect isn't to be feared, but to be praised. We can help you, Mercy. We can teach you, train you in ways the capital never could… We can offer you refuge."

"Stop talking," Mercy warns, his voice louder.

The more Bryer spoke, the more confused Mercy felt. It was like his thoughts weren't his own. In line with the chaos in his mind, the more his Source powered up the more anxious he felt. There almost seemed to be a burning in his mind, like his thoughts were on fire. He lets out a gasp as he falls to his knees at the agony drilling through his body.

"You help us and this pain you feel can go away." Bryer pauses a moment for a response but could see the more he spoke, the more it was pushing Mercy's already clouded judgement. "There is more at stake here than you know. You have the ability to save lives and change this world, you just need to open your eyes to the person keeping you from fulfilling that destiny."

His body shaking, Mercy's eyes fill with light as his arm throbs. Whatever was happening he had no control over. His mind was racing as he tried to collect his thoughts. It was like a series of intense mood changes and flashes were running through him and he had no way to stop it. Every other second, he could feel his mind shift to something else that brought anger, guilt, fear, shame, or grief to the surface. Glancing at his arm he sees the dark veins pull the light from his upper arm. Each pump of his heart sent an excruciating pain through his body. He needed someone to ground him. He needed anyone.

"Mercy, get up!" he hears Trust shout.

The voice was interrupted by Bryer. "I want to help you, Mercy. I will help you. Just take care of Caligo Tenebris and you will be free."

Through the pain and confusion, Mercy quickly pulls a solis orb to his hands and thrusts it toward Bryer. He needed this man to get away from him. Bryer, not having time to react, takes the blow to the shoulder. Pulling another orb to his hand, Mercy collects his Source and pushes it toward Bryer again, hoping to knock him from his feet. Dodging the shot, the man bolts down the hall in fear of becoming the Keeper's next victim, giving Mercy a moment of peace to try and collect himself.

Feeling the pain in his arm begin to subside as he powers down, Mercy falls to his hands and knees. He needed to get out of here. Whatever was in his arm was reacting to his Source and the temple was only amplifying it.

Turning, Mercy locks eyes with Trust's spirit. He shakes his head slightly, unable to comprehend the fact his peritia was manifesting a spirit, especially on his command. Was this real?

"What is wrong with you?" Trust snarls, walking up to him. "What the hell do you think you're doing?"

"I don't know," Mercy admits weakly.

He had no idea what or how he was thinking. He lets out a groan of pain as his arm begins to burn again. He looks at the scarring and runs his hand over it. His touch causes the pain to increase.

"Why are you here?" Mercy demands, getting to his feet.

"You're the one who called for me," Trust retorts, shaking his head. "Where's Sylas? Why isn't he with you? Or Caligo? Where are they?"

Collecting himself, Mercy tries to refocus. He needed to find Bryer and end this before he even had time to talk. If he could get rid of Bryer, he could leave this place and figure this all out.

"Probably still in Summa," Mercy growls, beginning to walk down the hall.

"You're supposed to be working with your Alia and being guided by your Nota," Trust explains, walking beside him.

Mercy shakes his head, keeping his eyes firmly ahead. "They're better off far away from me. Everyone is." He pulls his Source to his hand as the pain rings through his body again. "I need to go take care of that sad excuse of a Light Keeper."

"What has gotten into you?" Trust questions, moving to stand in front of him.

Mercy stops and looks at his brother's spirit. His stomach ached seeing him again. The fact he was a spirit was his own doing. He was part of the system that took his brother's life. Trust should have lived that day, not him. His brother could have had a happy life after Spheara but was now nothing more than a lost and confused soul.

"That man killed my daughter," Mercy states, glaring at him.

"Your daughter?" Trust asks. "How long have I been dead?"

"I *had* one," Mercy snarls. "Brokkr's girls. My blacksmith Master. I took in his girls and- Why am I explaining this to you? It doesn't even matter."

"It does matter," Trust assures him. "Killing that man isn't going to bring anyone back."

"No, but it'll prevent him from hurting anyone else," Mercy retorts, trying to rationalize his thinking.

"You want to kill him, but you didn't want to kill Mala?" Trust questions.

"This is different," Mercy barks.

"How?" Trust asks.

"It just is," Mercy stresses.

"You're not thinking straight," his brother lectures.

"You want me to walk away from this just like everyone else, right?" Mercy asks, eyeing him. "I'm tired of running away from my problems. All I've ever done in life is run away, and I'm done. I'm stronger than that."

"Sometimes walking away has nothing to do with weakness, and everything to do with strength," his brother preaches.

"Says the man who kept fighting for something until it killed him," Mercy mocks.

"You need to stop," Trust barks at him.

Listening to him, Mercy comes to a halt and looks at his brother's image. Wherever Bryer was in this temple wasn't far, so he could spare a few moments to humor Trust. He folds his arms and gestures for him to continue.

"You are the last Validus," Trust informs him. "The rest of us are gone because we didn't get a choice. There comes a time where that cycle can end, Mercy. It can end with you. You can walk away from this, and you can live your life away from the pain and heartache and-"

"You don't think I tried that?" he snaps in response. "They won't let me!" he shouts, pointing down the hall.

"That man and Caligo and Sylas won't let me stop fighting! I don't get a choice!"

"If you don't want to fight anymore, then why are you?" Trust questions, furrowing his brow.

The harshness leaves Mercy's face at the statement. Why was he fighting? Why did he go on assignments with Sylas? He never took a step back to ask himself why he was putting himself into these battles. When he took his Source back, Sylas had even told him he didn't need to be on the battlefield to use his gifts. Why was he still fighting? He glances down the hall and then back to Trust.

"Let me get you somewhere you can think clearly," Trust assures, turning to walk down the hall.

"What?" Mercy asks, watching his brother.

"You need to clear your head," Trust stresses, gesturing for him to follow. "Move your feet. Come on."

Hesitantly, Mercy follows his brother. As they move down the hall, he feels the temple begin to shake. He looks around recognizing the sound from his last time here. The crystal room with the Keeper of Light altar made that same noise when the stone was pushed away from it. That seemed to be the direction Trust was leading him. Why would that room be opening though? The only way to open that was for a Light Keeper to heal a Shadow Keeper. That was how he and Cal had opened it over a year ago.

As they approach the open door, Mercy feels his stomach drop. He watches as his brother's spirit urges him toward the door and points into the room. While he wanted to trust his brother, this didn't feel right. This felt like a trick to him.

"Get in there," Trust orders. "It's important. You need this right now."

"Need what?" Mercy asks, coming to a halt in the doorway.

Studying the room, it seemed to be untouched. Unlike the rest of the temple, Caligo's restoration hadn't reached this room yet. Perhaps he had left it untouched for a reason or maybe he just couldn't open it.

"This door only opens when it's needed," Trust informs him, nodding his head toward the door. "Go."

Giving his brother a skeptical look, Mercy walks into the room a few feet and folds his arms. He turns to look at Trust again who gives him a small wave as the door slams shut behind him. His eyes get wide with shock as the space around him goes black, all the lights being extinguished. The only things giving off any glow were his hands, buzzing with the Light Source.

"Trust!?" he shouts at the door.

He gasps as the crystals lining the wall begin to illuminate around him. The dull glow from the stones casts an eerie hue throughout the room. He looks back to the door and scowls. What did the Elders want him to do in here?

He walks further into the dimly lit space, to the altar in the center. It was still coated in a thick layer of dust confirming Cal hadn't worked to restore this room in the least. He lets out a sigh and looks at the still open drawer from when he was last there. The Pura Blade had been nestled in that drawer for who knows how long before he had come in here and taken it.

"Now you can sit in here and cool down," he hears Trust's voice.

Looking up, he could barely make out his brother's form. "Cool down?"

"Before you kill anyone else," Trust shrugs. "You're off your path, Mercy."

"Not this stupid path shit again," Mercy groans with an eye roll.

"We all have a path the Elders have marked us to pursue," Trust shares.

"Free will means nothing and I'm just supposed to do what they want. I know," he growls. "Now get me out of here before I blast my way out."

"I'd pay to watch that," Trust laughs, looking at the large stone door.

"So what?" Mercy asks, looking around. "You're just going to lock me in here and let Bryer get away? I can't let him go."

"Just until Sylas and Caligo show up," Trust informs him. "You are desperately in need of some guidance."

"We don't work together anymore," Mercy laughs at the statement.

"That explains a lot," Trust sighs.

Mercy glares at his brother as he gives a little wave and vanishes again. Letting out an angry scream, Mercy's Source begins to power up. He jumps as the crystals around him react to the increase in power, their glow getting brighter with his own veins as the pain in his arm increases. He looks around the room slowly, taking in the illuminated spheres. Pulling the pendant from his shirt he could see his father's broken gem was reacting as well.

"What is this?" he whispers to himself.

Moving to one of the walls lined with the crystals he lifts a hand up. It seemed the crystals he was closest to were shining brighter than the rest. As he moves his hand along the shelves, they reacted in time with him. He lets out a small smile at the sight. This was an interesting discovery. It must have meant he was more powerful than he was the last time he was here. It made sense. Before he was only at half power, and now he was at full. Over the last year he had begun to master his Source, which brought an even greater power to him.

The pain shoots through his body again as another round of rage fills him. He looks to the door and narrows his eyes. He didn't care what the Elder Spirits had set for him. He was tired of letting the Elders run his life. While Cal had given him freedom to be a Keeper of Light, he was still chained to what the Sources demanded of him. As long as he allowed the Elder Spirits to continue to urge him to do their bidding, he was never going to be truly free. They were trying to let the man who killed Ruby get away with what he had done.

Pulling his Source to his hands, he could see the crystals begin to shine brighter around him. He creates a solis orb in his hand and pulls his energy toward the sphere, working through the pain in his arm. If he could create a large enough orb, he could break through the stone door with ease.

As he pulls more Source power to his hands, the orb grows larger and larger as the room begins to shine brighter and brighter. He needed to give this everything he had. This stone was built to last millions of years, and he needed to destroy it in a matter of seconds.

As he continues to pull the power to his hands, he could feel his veins begin to ache and his hair begin to move in the breeze he was creating. He spreads his feet apart to ready himself for the ripple that would come with the force he was about to release.

Taking a deep breath, he moves his aim toward the door. Now the crystals around him were shining nearly as bright as the large orb he had manifested in between his hands. The solis orb was almost bigger than his torso and buzzing with energy. Pulling his hands back slightly he lets out a scream as he releases the orb, and it bolts toward the door in a beam of solid light.

In the same instance he could hear the crystals around him shatter, the light from his orb and his skin reflecting off the pieces flying through the air. He feels a few bits of the gems cut him, but his Source goes to work healing the wounds. As the orb makes contact with the door, the blow back knocks him from his feet and into the altar. His head smacks into the smooth stone, the crack of his skull echoing through the room as it goes black around him.

Chapter Fifty

Sylas and Cal had found themselves climbing up Mount Sacris just as they did when they first met. This time though, neither of them were attempting to protect a weak Light Keeper, instead they were trying to calm one who was more powerful than they could have ever imagined. They had just passed the watch post which meant they were close to the temple.

While Cal was dressed in his tactical suit again, Sylas had opted for casual, warmer clothes with his bow on his back and his sword hidden below a thick cloak. The layers of cotton and wool garments were needed to keep him warm, unlike Cal whose Light Source seemed to activate as soon as a shiver ran through him when they left the transport. Even without snow on this mountain, the air was still putting a heavy chill in their bones.

"You haven't eaten today," Cal notes as they walk up the slope to the temple.

While to most this statement wouldn't mean much, it meant something when it came to Sylas. The fact he hadn't eaten was very out of character, especially considering the satchel he carried had more snacks than anything else in it. Seeing as it was getting close to noon, the realization that he hadn't touched a single bite of food was strange. It also probably meant Cal was going to be met with a very grumpy version of Sylas in the next hour or so.

"I have a bad feeling," Sylas states, shaking his head. "I haven't been able to shake it since we left Summa."

"You are away from your Keeper," Cal advises, keeping his eyes on the trail.

"It's more than that," Sylas admits, putting his hand to his head with a shiver. "Something doesn't feel right about this. Something with Merc doesn't feel right."

"It may be the fact he has lost his damn mind," Cal states, furrowing his brow as Sylas pauses his feet. "What is it? The injury on his arm? Zero said he was not influenced by another-"

"Keeper. I know," Sylas snaps with an annoyed eye roll, his teeth chattering from the chilly air. "There's something else going on here, Cal. I can feel it. It's more than just the thing in his arm."

Cal nods his head in understanding. "If there was another Keeper in his head, we would know, Sy. Zero would have sensed it. He has been around Mercy enough to know his energy and his Source connection."

"I know!" Sylas barks. "I think I'm a little more intuitive to my Keeper than Zero is. Something is wrong! The Elder Spirits have been screaming at me the last two days and I don't know what they're saying. I can't figure it out. I can always figure it out," Sylas adds, the frustration clear in his voice.

Cal's eyes get wide at the sudden snap and the agitation in Sylas's tone. There it was. There was the hunger fueled irritability he knew so well. He lets out a huff as he looks to his feet.

"Sorry," Sylas mumbles, shivering again. "I just don't have a logical explanation for once, other than I'm his Nota and I just know something is off."

Seeing the tremors from the cold, Cal lets out a sigh and puts his arms out. Knowing Cal was a personal furnace right now, Sylas gives in, opening his cloak and allowing Cal to wrap Sylas in his arms for a few moments while they spoke.

"That is a logical explanation, Sy," Cal assures. "You realize that Nex could tell when Shay was in my head, right? She knew before you or Mercy... Hell, she knew before me. A Nota's connection to their Keeper does not always appear to have sound logic behind it. I know you are one to seek answers, but the answer you are looking for is in who you are to your Keeper."

"I can't figure this out though," Sylas groans in frustration. "I'm trying to think through your timeline and-" Sylas pauses and pulls away from Cal to look up the slope.

"And what?" Cal asks.

Suddenly Sylas could feel that they needed to move faster. For some reason the Elder Spirits cries were coming through loud and clear. They were telling him he needed to get to Mercy before it was too late. Shaking his head, Sylas begins to run up the slope to the temple. Cal rolls his eyes in frustration and takes off after him. As they climb the remainder of the hill, they come to a stop outside of the temple.

The Elders' urgent calls for Sylas had stopped and he was flooded with a feeling of distress. He couldn't place why though. All he could do was stand and stare at the intricate structure. After another moment, he could feel the Elders sending him a warning. They needed to proceed with caution. The usual feeling of attentiveness and energy he felt during all his trips to the library with Pippa were gone. The temple felt void of a Source connection, but he couldn't explain why.

"And what?" Cal asks, panting slightly, trying to stretch out his back.

"Mercy's here," Sylas states in a low voice, getting his feet moving again.

"Why are you whispering?" Cal asks, lowering his voice to match as he follows.

"Something's wrong," Sylas informs him, shaking his head.

"Yeah, you may have mentioned that," Cal retorts. "That does not explain why we are whispering."

"This place feels different. The Spirits are worried for us," Sylas shares.

The shift in Sylas was making Cal uneasy. Why was he suddenly talking like he could sense the Sources like a Keeper? As they enter the structure, Sylas looks at Cal and studies his face for a reaction to the temple. He expected Cal's eyes to be lit up more than they already were or perhaps his hands, but there was nothing.

"You aren't reacting to the Source Temple," he mutters to Caligo.

"My Source connection is not exactly working right now, Sy," Cal shrugs.

"Your Light Source is though," Sylas differs, stopping and grabbing Cal's face. "There's no change in your eyes."

Pushing Sylas away in annoyance, Cal looks around the temple. They didn't have time for this. The pair keep silent, trying to stay unnoticed. Walking through the corridors, they glance into each open door hoping to see someone or something inside.

As they continue forward, Cal begins to grow uneasy. The restoration of the Source Temple was far from over, so why weren't they working on it today? Surely there would have been at least someone around. Even with it being winter, they still should have been monitoring the location for vandals or thieves.

534

"Do you know if Mercy canceled the restoration of this temple or took the staff off?" Cal asks in a low voice.

"I doubt he was worried about the Northwest Source Temple enough to make a ruling on that," Sylas replies, continuing to keep his voice down. "He was using his Source to *shrine* on better things." With a heavy sigh, Cal looks at him with disappointment. "Shrine... Kind of sounds like shine? Right?" Sylas explains.

Rolling his eyes, Cal lets off a small laugh. "That was bad, even for you."

"You haven't been giving me much to work with other than amputee jokes," Sylas shrugs at the comment. "Those get old after a while."

"You are supposed to be the comic relief," Cal states, as they turn the corner.

Spotting something down the hall, Cal puts his hand out in front of Sylas's chest, bringing him to a halt. Looking down the corridor, Cal could see a pile of rubble scattered on the floor. Sylas looks at him with confusion before following his gaze. His eyes get wide as the pair take off in a sprint toward the debris. They come to a stop and study the jagged rocks.

Taking his eyes to the wall, Cal's jaw drops. This was the crystal room he and Mercy had unlocked over a year ago. Now every gem that had once lined the walls was shattered and shards littered the floor.

"He was here," Sylas mutters, walking into the room absent mindedly.

Looking around, the pair were in shock. Whatever had happened in this room had rendered a large blast. As they walk around, they could hear the shards of crystals crunch below their boots. Scanning the room, Cal's eyes lock on a pool of blood by the altar. He moves toward it and kneels down. He puts his hand to the stain and could feel the residual heat. This was very fresh. Wiping it on his pant leg, he gets to his feet.

"He could not have gotten far," Cal states looking around.

"I wonder whose blood it is," Sylas notes.

"Hopefully not Mercy's," Cal states, looking at the entrance with a cocked brow. "Logically speaking, someone would destroy a door to get into a room... This was someone trying to get out."

Nodding his head in agreement, Sylas moves forward and runs his hand over what was left of the stone doorway. He could see the scorch marks made by the Light Source on the stone. He lets out a heavy sigh and looks to Cal. This room was sacred and now it was destroyed. It made his chest ache seeing someone had ruined such an important room for the Keepers of Light. This room was meant to help guide Keepers forward, gifting them with an ipdum, and now it was gone.

Going to the altar in the center, Sylas begins to shuffle through the drawers. With this place opened and little hope of restoring its sacred protection, he begins to remove the items. The value of these ipdums was unmeasurable and they needed to be kept safe.

"We need to get these to Ozra," Sylas states, feeling a wave of emotion hit him. "We can't let any of these relics fall into the wrong hands. Do you understand?"

Seeing the sudden importance, Cal moves to the altar and begins to shuffle through it with Sylas. Seeing this shift in Sylas and the panic that was clearly being hidden made him worry. He had seen this expression once before and it was the day Sylas came home to the Arca Orb. Sylas currently felt like his world was crashing in, and Cal needed to try and ease that, even if it meant wasting precious time going through the altar.

There were about thirty drawers, each housing a small item wrapped in cloth or within a box. Cal's hand pauses as he comes to an open drawer. "Were any opened before you started?" he asks, looking at Sylas.

"One," Sylas replies, his face serious. "The Pura Blade. Why?"

"There's another one open over here," Cal notes, pulling the drawer out entirely. "Someone else has been in here."

Handing the drawer to Sylas, the Nota furrows his brow and studies it. The cushion on the inside was set in the shape of a wide dagger. Cal grabs the last few ipdums and shoves them into Sylas's bag as he continues to stare at the drawer in his hand searching for an explanation. Could this have been another Pura Blade?

"You said Mercy was close?" Cal asks, taking the drawer from Sylas's hands, breaking his focus, and placing it back into the altar.

"Yeah," Sylas confirms, looking around.

The state of the room begins to weigh on him again. This was no doubt the meaning behind the sinking feeling he had when they entered the grounds. The destruction of this room took away valuable Source connectivity that gave this place it's strange buzz.

"Do you think Merc did this?" Sylas asks, locking eyes with Cal.

They both turn their attention to the hole in the wall as a large explosion goes off somewhere in the structure. The entire building shakes causing rubble to rain from the ceiling. Moving away from the altar, Cal takes off toward the entrance, losing his footing briefly on the crystal shards, but regaining it swiftly. He pauses looking down the hall, trying to locate the source of the explosion. He hears another rumble sound throughout the temple. Without hesitation, Cal takes off running.

"Caligo!" Sylas scolds, bolting to follow, the bag at his side heavy with the ipdums.

The two come to a stop inside a room trying to figure out who or what Cal had just heard. The room was large and had the Source runes marked on the floor at their feet and all over the walls. It was an intricate pattern that must have taken years to carve into the stone. Lining the room were a series of stone pillars, each carved intricately with vine like designs that snaked from the top to the bottom. They both jump at the sound of something sliding on the stone floor behind them, the sound echoing off each wall.

"This place is starting to give me the creeps," Cal whispers, scanning the room.

"Me too," Sylas laughs nervously as footsteps echo around them, their own feet still.

Scanning the room, Sylas could sense his Keeper. His best friend was close, and he was angry. Pulling a dagger from his belt, Sylas moves in closer to Cal and whispers, "Mercy's cloaked."

Pulling one of his blades from his back, Cal readies himself. "Show yourself, Mercy!" he calls into the room.

Both Sylas and Cal let out a gasp as a beam of light is thrusted toward them, the power stronger than anything they had seen their friend unleash before. It had the same presence as a solis orb, but it came across as a solid beam from the Keeper. They both jump out of the way, Cal tucking and rolling but feeling the heat singe the hair on the back of his neck. Sylas's dagger skids across the stone, coming to rest several feet away. Neither of them was ready to be back in a fight, but it was seeming they didn't have a choice.

Seeing another attack hurdling toward Sylas, Cal reacts and tackles him to the ground. This wasn't going to be a fair fight with Cal's Source gone and Sylas not used to his prosthetic yet. Especially when they couldn't even see who they were fighting. Regardless, Cal wasn't about to lose Sylas again. While he couldn't protect him at Spheara, he could now. The two get to their feet and look around the room again.

"This is not a fair fight!" Cal points out.

"Merc, if this is you, we don't wanna hurt you. We're just here to talk," Sylas adds.

Another blast comes at them, forcing both to drop to the floor again. Cal puts himself over Sylas to protect him in any way that he could, feeling the heat lick his back. They hear a pillar behind them begin to crack. Rolling off Sylas onto his back, Cal's eyes get wide at the sight of it shuddering in place.

As the pillar begins to topple toward them, they both scramble to try and get to their feet, but they couldn't get a grip in the rubble that now surrounded them. In desperation, Cal throws himself over Sylas again, pinning his partner on his back. Caligo braces himself for the impact, but it doesn't come. He breathes heavily, opening his eyes and locking them on Sylas who was staring past Cal with a shocked expression on his face.

"Move!" he hears Master Novi shout at them.

Looking over his shoulder, Cal sees his mentor straining to hold the beam up with her spiritum fog. He looks at her in disbelief as the room goes silent. When did she get there? How had she found them?

"Move, Caligo!" she snarls at him, forcing the pillar away, the impact of it hitting the ground shaking the entire temple.

Listening to her orders, Cal gets to his feet, grabbing his blade. He yanks Sylas up beside him, his partner just as confused by the sight of the Penumbra. The only explanation was Novi had heard of the outcome of this battle, and it wasn't going to be good for those involved.

"You need to get out of here," she warns the pair.

"No shit," Sylas retorts.

As Novi prepares to fight, Sylas sees Cal hesitate. This moment made Caligo feel just as helpless as he did at the Mors River, but he wasn't about to let Novi take on the threat alone. While he usually felt like he could get an upper hand in a fight, this one was different. He knew leaving Novi here alone was a death sentence for his mentor.

"Go!" she shouts at them.

Feeling the heat on their feet, Sylas looks down. He lets out a gasp as the other two watch the solis fog begin to seep out of the center of the room toward them. This causes their stomachs to drop as they begin to take several steps back. Solis fog confirmed this was Mercy. Why would he be trying to hurt them? Sure, he was angry Cal and Sylas got in the way in Summa, but what had they done to deserve being attacked like this?

"He is not his own," Novi informs the young men, herding them behind her. "Mercy is being influenced by dark intentions. This is a fight you will not win, Caligo. I need you to go."

Hearing her words, Cal looks at Sylas. Grabbing the hilts of both his blades and snapping them into a polearm, Cal locks eyes with his mentor and shakes his head as he speaks. "I've fought worse."

"You sure about that?" Sylas laughs nervously, trying to locate his Keeper, putting himself behind Cal.

Sylas should have thought this through. He was in no way prepared for a fight. While he did have his bow, he was wearing nothing but his travel attire under his winter wear. None of that was going to offer him much protection. He was lucky Cal was there to keep him from being lit on fire by their friend.

"Heed my words, Caligo," Novi pressures. "If you attempt to fight him, you will lose."

They watch as the fog becomes thicker. Glancing to Master Novi, Cal could see the severity in her expression. She was being vague with him as usual, but the pain in her eyes gave him all the answers he needed. If he tried to face Mercy in his current state, someone was going to die and that someone was probably him.

Scanning the room, Sylas searches for the shift in the scenery but his eyes couldn't detect one. Did a stronger Source connection mean an enhanced cloak? He gasps as another beam of light bolts toward them, this one seeming to move like a strike of lightning. Both Sylas and Cal grunt as Novi uses her spiritum fog to push them to the floor, Cal's polearm clattering to the ground beside him. They both wince as the bolt is followed by a crack of thunder, making their ears ring.

The pair get to their feet as Master Novi moves in front of them again, powering up even more. Her hair begins to jostle in the breeze she was creating as she searches the room for Mercy. She was going to protect Cal and Sylas from this version of Mercy, even if it meant dying in the process. The dark path she had been warned about was only getting darker, this encounter prophesizing a deadly outcome for the young men behind her.

Hearing another tinge of a blast, Novi quickly puts up a wall of fog to her left. The blast of Light Source hitting her spiritum fog is enough to lessen the blow, but the three still get flung back. Smacking his head on the stone floor, Cal's vision goes hazy as his ears begin to ring. He rolls onto his back as Novi gains her footing and goes to protect him again. While he could make out what was happening around him, everything felt blurred and muffled.

He sees Sylas come into his line of sight as another blast shakes the group, Novi doing what she can to lessen the blow. He watches as Sylas attempts to shield him from another stifled hit, the gust of wind littering the air with dust and debris. Closing his eyes tightly, Cal tries to get his senses back together. As another blast of rubble filled air comes his direction, his vision begins to clear. If they couldn't get Mercy to show himself, no one, not even Novi, was going to be able to get a hit in.

"Sy," Cal groans, as his partner pulls away to look at him, "please don't take this personally." Drawing his fist,

Cal punches Sylas in the face, hoping the pain in the Nota would echo through his Keeper.

"Sophos, Cal! What the hell!?" Sylas screams, as blood begins to pour from his nose.

The shout from Sylas gets Master Novi to turn and look at the pair, her hands still up and her eyes dark. She watches as Cal grabs his polearm and gets shakily to his feet.

"I'm trying to get him to stop," Cal explains. "I'm sorry in advance," he adds. Crashing the center of the pole down on Sylas's shoulder, they hear a scream from the other side of the room.

"I get it now," Sylas groans, nodding his head. "Good technique," he gets out as Cal brings another strike to his side. "Sophos…" Sylas groans falling to the floor.

"Understand I take no joy from this," Cal states as another scream cries out from his Alia. "Drop the cloak Mercy or I will hit him again!"

Scanning the room, Cal sees the cloak drop as Mercy appears, panting heavily and holding his side. His face was full of rage, his eyes still dancing with light. Cal shakes his head at what he was seeing. The man standing in front of them wasn't the Mercy he knew. He looked sickly and crazed, like a rabid dog. His shirt was nearly entirely burned away, and blood was trickling down from a large gash he had healed on his head, making him look even more wild. This wasn't Mercy, this was a mad man.

Getting to his feet beside Cal, Sylas wipes the blood from his nose and leans his head on Cal's shoulder, trying to collect himself. All he could focus on was the pain. He didn't even look at his best friend.

Glancing to Master Novi, Cal notes she was still powered up and on edge. Even with Mercy out of hiding, she wasn't ready to ease up her Source.

"They told me you'd come after me," Mercy states, keeping his attention on Cal.

"Of course we did!" Sylas snaps back, not realizing how off kilter his friend was yet.

"You want to stop me," Mercy accuses. "You want to keep me from reaching my full potential and saving our people."

"What are you talking about?" Sylas asks, confused.

"Don't play stupid! I know all about Cal's plans to strip my Keeping and put me into hiding again. They shared all the details," he snarls, his eyes shooting to Novi. "You knew too, didn't you?"

"What?" Cal questions as Novi shakes her head.

"He is not thinking for himself," Novi heeds in a whisper to the pair.

"Ya think?" Sylas snips back. "Merc, he's lying to you," Sylas groans, his stomach in pain.

"No surprise you'd take his side," Mercy barks, powering up again. "Sleeping with the enemy."

"Are we really back on who the hell I let in my pants again? For real?" Sylas questions, looking up at his friend finally. "Mercy, Cal's your friend. We don't even know what you're talking about!"

Sylas's eyes get wide at what he was seeing. The only way he could explain what Mercy looked like, was a wild animal. He had a craze in his eyes. The dark veins in his arm were now starting to trickle up his neck and down toward his hand. His best friend was in desperate need of help, and they needed to proceed with caution. With Mercy's power and skills increasing, he was a threat. A threat they were not prepared to take on. Novi was right. Whatever Bryer said was enough to pit Mercy against them and put him on a dark path.

"Mercy, you have to believe me," Sylas pleads, pulling away from Cal and taking a step toward him. "Cal would never do anything to hurt you or your family."

"Sy, wait," Cal pleads, grabbing his hand, Sylas batting him away.

"He killed my father," Mercy growls. "He convinced you to leave the house when they took Ruby. He let them take her," Mercy accuses.

"You cannot reason with him, Sylas," Novi warns, her tone harsh.

Ignoring her, Sylas takes another step. "You have it all wrong, Merc. I took Cal away from the house. That was me, not Cal. I took him to our spot... You remember our spot? The boulders? Whittington Point?" Sylas explains, putting his hands out to ease his friend. "Ruby's alive, Merc. Your daughter's alive and in Ozra waiting for you. Your girls are safe."

"Stop lying to me!" Mercy screams, pulling a solis orb to his hand and thrusting it forward.

Cal's eyes go wide as he bolts forward and wraps his arms around Sylas, turning him, and takes the orb to his back. Cal lets out a scream. Even with the tactical suit, he could feel the heat. Cal steadies himself as searing pain hits him. They needed to get out of here before this got worse. This version of Mercy was not going to listen to reason. Sylas untangles himself from Cal and keeps him stable as his mind races.

"We need to go," Cal mumbles, discomfort clear in his voice. "Master Novi is right. This is going to end badly."

"We can't just leave him," Sylas murmurs.

"I don't think we have much of a choice here, my love," Cal groans through the pain.

"I'm not leaving without him," Sylas snaps, locking his eyes on his Keeper, keeping Cal on his feet. "Merc, your arm. That pain you're feeling... That's Bryer. He put something in your arm that's causing you to feel confused right now. It's messing with your head."

"Shut up," Mercy snarls.

Pulling more power to him, Mercy's eyes turn to solid light as his veins surge with his Source. The more rage he felt the more powerful he became. Putting his palms out, he pulls his Source into his hands and readies another attack. As he thrusts the power toward Cal and Sylas, Novi rushes in front of them and attempts to use her fog to shield the pair, her fog seeming to absorb most of the impact being thrown at them. As the Light Source overtakes the trio, Cal pulls Sylas to the ground.

As Cal waits for the attack to end, it becomes clear Mercy was not going to let up with his beam of light. Keeping Sylas down, Cal attempts to make out where his mentor was. His eyes begin to water from the white light radiating around him as the faint silhouette of Novi becomes visible in front of them. While she was using her fog to shield him and Sylas, she was also trying to use it to overtake Mercy. The two of them seemed locked as Mercy pulled more and more Source to his attack. It doesn't take long for Cal to register Mercy beginning to convert the fog around him, each passing second taking valuable energy from the Penumbra. Novi had no chance against this.

"Stop!" Cal screams at his Alia in desperation. "Mercy, please stop!"

While Novi was strong, she was no match for Mercy. At this rate, Mercy was going to render her unconscious or dead within seconds. There had to be something Cal could do. He needed to try and help her.

"Mercy! Listen to me! You need to stop! Please stop!" Cal pleads, pulling away from Sylas.

As he goes to get up, Cal feels Sylas grab him, holding him down. The more he tried to squirm away, the tighter Sylas held on. The moment seems to go in slow motion as they hear Master Novi let out a shriek before the fog and light dissipates around them.

As their sight adjusts to the room, Cal's eyes fall to Novi just a few feet away. "No," he mumbles to himself, rushing to her.

On the stone floor, between him and Mercy, was Master Novi. Her hair was faded to a gray hue, and her skin mirrored Pippa's. In that moment it showed just how much the young woman resembled her mother. His gaze darts to Mercy who was staring at Cal, his hands at his side as he smirks. They all seem to freeze as they take in what Mercy had just done.

Turning Novi onto her back, Cal attempts to hold back the tears. Master Novi had given one last attempt to protect Cal as she always did, and in doing so gave her life. Trying to keep it together, Cal squeezes his eyes shut. Now wasn't the time to lose his composure.

"You took my father," Mercy finally speaks, lifting his hand and aiming it at Cal. "A life for a life."

Looking at Mercy again with pain in his eyes, Cal shakes his head. When he had taken Orlo's life, it was because he had no choice. It was kill or be killed. What Mercy had just done was out of spite. He had taken Master Novi from this world in a fit of rage. Mercy had a choice, and in that moment, Mercy chose violence.

"Blood for blood," Mercy states, his voice cold.

Shaking his head, Cal looks her over again. Her skin was mostly burned, some areas exposing bone. Her face was almost completely unrecognizable. If it wasn't for the fact he had seen her move between them and the blast, Cal wouldn't even believe this was her. How was he going to tell Master Emidio? How was he going to tell Pippa?

Registering Mercy was pulling his Source back to his hands again, Sylas moves to crouch beside Cal. He knew Cal was in shock, but they didn't have time to sit there and mourn this loss. If they hesitated too long, they were going to be next. He urges Cal away from Novi and attempts to pull him to his feet.

"We need to go," Sylas warns in a whisper, keeping his eyes on Mercy who was walking toward them. "We need to go now, Cal."

546

"I can't," Cal breathes.

"You can leave her, Cal," Sylas encourages, his eyes still on his Keeper.

"I can't," Cal repeats, his eyes glued to Novi.

"Leave her!" Sylas snaps, trying to break through to his partner. "Leave her or we die too."

Darting his eyes to Mercy, who was now just ten feet away, Cal's breath shudders. He gives in, getting to his feet and letting Sylas guide him. They begin to back away from Novi as Mercy continues to power up. Seeing he was about to let the attack go, Sylas jerks Cal to the exit of the room. As soon as they're through the doorway, they hear the blast as the temple quakes around them. The power that was coming from Mercy was like nothing either of them had ever witnessed before.

As they take off in a run and turn the corner, a wave of Light Source strikes the wall behind them. They feel the temple shake again as loud cracking becomes audible. Mercy was willing to completely obliterate this sacred location if it meant he could get to Caligo. They couldn't let him do that. They needed to get out of there, or Novi's life was given in vain. Feeling the tinge of the energy being pulled again, Cal jerks Sylas through a doorway trying to offer as much protection as he could. His main objective in that moment was to keep Sylas alive and in one piece.

They both wince as the attack crashes outside the door and their ears begin to ring at the impact. As they go to continue down the corridor, they could see Mercy wasn't far behind. Shoving the door closed, Sylas grabs Cal's hand and looks around. The room they were in was empty with nowhere to go. Not even a window.

"Shit, shit, shit," Sylas mutters, scrambling to get his tactical bow out of the holster on his back. He glances to Cal who was still visibly shaken. "Hold it together, Caligo," he begs. "I need you to keep it together. Okay?"

547

Nodding his head, Cal takes a deep breath. He needed to keep his focus on staying alive. If he let himself think too much on this, they weren't going to make it out of here.

Sylas looks to Cal with big eyes, breathing steadily with him to encourage him to calm down. He begins to speak frantically as he drops his winter cloak to the ground and flings his bow out. "Murdered by my best friend. Not exactly how I expected things to turn out. Well... Maybe it is with my reputation for near death experiences. They usually involve Mercy."

Sylas readies his release and an arrow and aims it at the door. Maybe he could get a shot in and buy them a moment to get past Mercy. Cal grabs his father's sword from Sylas's waist, realizing he had left his polearm in the other room. The pair separate to either side of the room in preparation for the door to fly forward.

"Ready yourself," Sylas breathes, narrowing his eyes on the entrance. He glances to Cal who still looked shaken up and lets out a slow exhale. "Cal, I need you to stay strong here or we're dead too."

Giving a nod of the head, Cal lets out a steady exhale as a blast rocks the room and the door shoots forward. Both Cal and Sylas try to stay calm as the door slams into the wall between them. Keeping his aim on the entrance, Sylas locks in on Mercy.

Seeing his best friend like this was horrific. There was so much pent-up anger and confusion in him he couldn't help but feel empathy for the man. All these years Mercy had been holding onto this much pain and he had no idea. It took someone compromising him for Sylas to realize just how confused and scared Mercy really was.

"What'd he do to you, Merc?" Sylas asks, keeping his bow aimed at his best friend.

"He told me everything he's done," Mercy snaps, looking at Cal, his eyes lit up. "You've made my life a living hell because you're a coward!"

Taking a deep breath, Sylas narrows his eyes on Mercy. Maybe he could hit the injury on his arm and dislodge whatever Bryer had put there. He pauses a moment, his mind going to the genti tome. He shakes the thought, but it comes back to him again. It was an annoying nagging feeling.

"Mercy, you need to just take a step back and look at all this," Sylas pleads. "Look at what you're doing."

At Sylas's words, Mercy rapidly lets off multiple orbs, his aim going toward each of his friends. Sylas releases his arrow, but the speed of the orb coming at him forces him to duck last minute, his arrow hitting the stone wall and dropping to the ground.

"Distract him," Sylas instructs Cal, dodging another orb.

With a small nod, Cal charges Mercy, the Light Keeper turning both hands toward his Alia. Recentering his aim on Mercy, Sylas lets out a steady breath. He needed to calm down. If he could just calm down, he could make the shot. He needed to.

"Cal!" Sylas warns, releasing the arrow as his partner ducks to the ground.

The shot imbeds in Mercy's upper arm, causing the Light Keeper to let out a scream. Sylas was just an inch or so off from hitting the inflamed scar. He scowls at his miss. Caligo scrambles to his feet and rushes back toward Sylas to stand between him and Mercy.

Yanking the arrow from his arm, Mercy heals the wound. While he was annoyed at Sylas's attempt at harming him, he knew he couldn't take a shot at his Nota. Hurting Sylas would only cause him pain, which would make it more difficult for him to take care of his actual problem.

He juts out a tendril of his white fog and yanks the bow from his friend's hand. The bow flies across the room and slams into the wall, bits of metal flying from it before it hits the ground.

"Shit," Sylas mumbles. Shifting his gaze to Caligo, Mercy begins to ready another beam in his hands again. "Cal, I think you're up," Sylas states.

"Great," Cal mutters as the blast shoots toward them.

Pushing Sylas out of the way and dodging the shot, Cal lets out an annoyed scream. There was no way he was going to best Mercy with distance between them. Mercy had the upper hand in that department, especially with his new attacks coming left and right. These were moves Cal wasn't familiar with and had no idea how to compete with. Mercy had learned a lot about his abilities and was figuring out more the longer he was powered up.

Charging toward his Alia, Cal takes a strike at him with his father's sword. The attack is met with Mercy putting his palms up to the blade and stopping it midair with about three inches between his hand and the weapon. Cal stares at the action in complete astonishment. He wasn't even using his fog in that moment; it was like he was a magnet repelling the metal in Cal's grasp.

The harder Cal tried to move it, the stronger the force was becoming. Seeing the annoyance on Mercy's face, he watches as his Alia's gaze shifts to the blade. The blade's tip takes on an orange glow as it heats. The glow moves rapidly down the blade causing Cal to release the hilt with a hiss of pain. Mercy finally grabs the blade in his fist, causing it to quickly pool into molten metal. With another wave of his hand, he forms the metal into a hot orange stake and flings it toward Cal, the sharp point imbedding in his shoulder. He lets out a scream of pain as Mercy moves his hand again to yank the stake from his

Alia and tosses it to the stone floor. The pain was coming in waves, but Cal needed to keep trying.

"Maybe even the odds here a bit, Mercy?" Cal grunts nervously, trying to hide his agony.

Pulling his short sword from his sheath, Mercy obliges to the request. With his Source giving him more strength than ever and his Alia's right arm now out of commission, Mercy was sure he could take on Cal without using his Light Source.

Mercy rushes at Cal only to see him duck beneath his swinging blade. As he ducks, Cal triggers the blades in his bracers, coming to his feet ready to defend himself. Mercy attacks with a flurry of strikes. Though Cal fends off the attack with his blades, he notes the increased strength in his friend. Or was he just weaker without his Shadow Source?

As the two dance, Mercy clearly using his Source to get the upper hand in the sword play, Sylas rushes to grab his broken bow. He collects the pieces with a frown at the fact it was going to be useless and places it back into its holster.

Taking his attention to the pair, Sylas could see Cal was tiring. The blows from Mercy were more powerful than ever and without Cal's Shadow Source, he was weaker than the last time he had sparred with Mercy. One thing Sylas knew for sure though, was Mercy wouldn't hurt him. Not only because of their history together, but because he was his Nota. Killing or harming him would only weaken the Supra or at least give him a moment of vulnerability.

As one of the blades snaps out of its position in Cal's bracer, Mercy pulls back his blade and begins a downward cut toward Cal. The dislodged blade clatters to the floor as Cal stares at Mercy's sword with panic in his eyes. Suddenly, Mercy spots his Nota bolt and move into his swing. Pulling back, the Light Keeper brings the blade to a halt on his best friend's neck, breathing heavily. The look on Sylas's face was one of understanding and concern, but also filled with frustration.

"Stop," Sylas breathes, feeling the cold metal on his skin. "You need to stop."

"Move," Mercy snarls, staring at his Nota.

"I'm not going to let you hurt him," Sylas states, putting his hands gently on the blade and shaking his head. "This isn't you, Merc. This is your fear and your anger and your grief. This isn't who you are."

"Move, Sylas," Mercy barks.

"Let's talk, Merc," his best friend pleads, his tone calm as he moves down the blade toward the hilt. "Just two minutes to rationalize this. Talk me through what's going on in your head, and I'll fix it. I *always* fix it."

"Move," Mercy warns again.

"Merc, listen to me," Sylas attempts again, slowly grabbing the hilt. "Whatever Bryer told you isn't true. Caligo cares about you. He cares about both of us He would never do anything to hurt you or those girls."

"Sylas, please," Mercy begs, a crack in his voice.

"No," his best friend replies. "I'm not moving until you drop your sword and power down."

Yanking his blade from Sylas, Mercy attempts to shove him out of the way. This prompts his best friend to hit the trigger on one of his own bracers to release a blade. Wrapping his arms around Mercy, he puts him in a headlock with the blade to his throat, pain in his expression.

"Please, don't make me hurt you," Mercy whispers through gritted teeth.

"If you want to hurt Cal, you'll have to hurt me too," Sylas warns him. "You're my brother, Merc, and I love you, but my future is with Cal and I'm not about to let you take that away from me again."

Again? Was Sylas still blaming Mercy for the events at the Mors River? A hurt expression comes to the

Light Keeper's face at the idea. If Sylas couldn't forgive him for that, what was the point?

"Sylas, please," Mercy begs one last time.

"Power down," Sylas warns.

Letting out an annoyed breath, Mercy lets off a surge of Light Source energy from his entire body, thrusting Sylas's arms forward and the rest of him back. Sylas flings away from Mercy and hits the opposite wall with a crack. He lets out a scream, feeling pain ripple through his shoulder as Mercy echoes the same reaction.

With a small growl, Sylas shakes it off and gets to his feet to go after Mercy again. He wasn't about to let his best friend kill someone else, especially Cal. Mercy had kept Cal from straying from his morals, so he was going to return the favor.

As Sylas bolts toward him, Mercy turns quickly and slices his blade through the air, Sylas ducking to avoid the hit. The Light Keeper takes another strike at him, this time using his Source to fuel the blow. Knowing he wouldn't be able to take the strike, Sylas attempts to deflect it with the blade on his arm. This prompts his Keeper to pause, not wanting to harm Sylas. He made those blades himself and knew if he hit Sylas too hard, he could break the smaller blade.

"I taught you a little too well," Sylas admits, taking a moment to regain himself as Mercy glares.

"Why are you even protecting him? He wants me dead, Sylas! You're probably next!" Mercy snarls at him.

"He won't hurt me, because he loves me, Merc," Sylas states, putting his hand out to urge Cal to stand behind him. "Cal would never do anything to hurt me. If he was there that day in Orior, he would have killed Iana himself. You know that. Deep down you know how he feels about me because he's told you... Bryer is lying to you. He's using you. He's been manipulating you from the start."

553

His words get Mercy to relax slightly. Nodding his head, Sylas eases as well. Perhaps he could take Mercy's usual approach and solve this with words instead of violence. Taking a small step forward, Sylas pushes his blade back into his bracer.

"Remember when Zero used his peritia on you? You were yourself again," Sylas continues, reaching toward his Keeper. "That thing in your arm... Whatever that is, is fueling this."

Glancing at the inflamed scar, Mercy flinches away from his friend. Easing forward and giving his Keeper a small nod, Sylas grips Mercy's arm gently. He feels the Keeper tense at his touch as the glowing below his skin increases. Being close to this thing made Sylas's skin crawl. How had Mercy let it get this bad?

"Caligo killed my father," Mercy whispers to Sylas.

Reaching for a knife in his pocket, Sylas nods his head in understanding. "I know, but he didn't have a choice. He was scared. Just like you're scared right now," Sylas comforts. "I know what he went through that day at the southern border, and he was terrified just like you are right now."

Mercy's expression shifts to a look of confusion as Sylas clicks the blade out. How did Sylas know where it happened? Had he known all this time and kept it away from him? Did he really know Caligo had murdered his father?

"You knew?" Mercy questions.

His eyes getting big, Sylas locks them with Mercy, realizing what he had just said. He just admitted to his best friend that he knew Cal had killed Orlo. Even though it was relatively new information for him, that wasn't going to matter. What he just foolishly said was going to be enough to set him off again.

"Merc," Sylas yields, touching the knife to Mercy's arm, "let me get this out and we can talk."

The Keeper shakes his head, pulling his arm from Sylas. His eyes dart around the room as he tries to collect his thoughts. If Sylas knew, why didn't he tell him? Was that just another thing his best friend was keeping from him? Sylas had already said so many hurtful things in the last couple of months, why was he even surprised? Why had Sylas said so many spiteful things to him? Why did Sylas hate him? Why did Sylas always choose Cal over him?

"You knew!" Mercy shouts.

"Mercy, please," Sylas begs, reaching for his arm again.

"You're against me too!" Mercy accuses, putting a shield up over himself. "You've been a part of this the whole time, haven't you?"

"No, Merc, I-" Sylas begins. "I'm- No- I didn't-"

Locking his eyes back on his best friend, Mercy uses his solis fog to pull the metal stake from the ground and hit Sylas in the back of the head with the rounded side. His vision going black, Sylas falls to the stone floor. Mercy echoes the blow as his hand goes to his head and he stumbles slightly, feeling the pain he had just caused. He quickly regains himself and raises his sword to Cal.

His eyes darting between Mercy and Sylas, Cal takes a deep breath. Having just seen Sylas making progress by attempting to talk this through, perhaps he could try. The real Mercy was still in there. Maybe he could reach him.

"I understand you're angry right now, Mercy, but killing me is not going to solve this," Cal explains, moving forward slowly, and coming to a stop at the tip of his sword. "I always said you deserve the right to choose, and I still stand by that." He pauses and looks at the coldness in his Alia's eyes a moment before speaking again. "Killing Master Novi was your choice. You can choose to take my life too and live with those consequences, or you can walk away from this, and I can get you aid. I can pardon what you have done and get you the medical attention you need, Mercy. You have a choice. This is *your* choice."

Mercy shakes his head and lets out a disdainful laugh. "I never got a choice in any of this, Cal." Furrowing his brow at the statement, Cal takes a step back as Mercy continues. "I didn't want this. I didn't want any of this. None of us ever get a choice in anything."

"Okay," Cal nods. "If you think your fate is to end me, I will respect that, but by the Elders, let Sy go," Cal pleads. "Let him go and you can kill me. I will not fight any more if you let him leave unharmed."

The Light Keeper looks down at Sylas. "He's *my* Nota but you somehow pulled him into your web of lies," Mercy accuses, calling his Source to his opposite hand and aiming his palm at his best friend on the floor. "He's no better than you are. Honestly, I'll be better off without the limitations of a spiritual guide."

"Mercy, listen to yourself," Cal begs in panic, taking another step back as Mercy takes one forward. If he lost Novi and Sylas today, he wasn't going to be able to handle this. "You are talking nonsense."

"I've never seen you clearer," Mercy snaps, forcing Cal to continue back. "I know who you are," he states, solis fog beginning to seep from both hands as the light in his eyes grew brighter.

"Mercy, please," Cal begs. "Do not hurt him. You can kill me, just let Sy walk away from this. Let someone I love walk away from this. Please."

"Can I let him walk away?" Mercy asks, raising a brow. "If I let him walk away, he'll still be against me. I can't have my Nota against me."

"I am your friend, Mercy," Cal stresses. "I am your Alia. We are bonded, you and I. We-"

"We are nothing!" Mercy snaps. "You and your family have done nothing but make my life hell for 24 years and I'm done. I'm done being a part of your game."

"Is that what you really think of me?" Cal asks, sorrow filling his eyes.

"I was stupid to think I could ever trust a Tenebris," Mercy adds, getting Cal's back to the wall and his blade to his throat. "You manipulate your people and cause nothing but pain and misery."

"I would never manipulate you, Mercy. I trust you with my life. I always have. Before we even met, I trusted you," Cal continues, staring at the blade. "You are giving Bryer what he wants. You need to realize you are playing into *his* game."

"And walking away from this would be playing into yours," Mercy growls.

Looking from the blade to Mercy, then to the dripping fog aimed at Sylas, Cal takes a shuddering breath. Hearing those words come from Mercy hurt him. From the moment they met he had done nothing but try to show his Alia he was an ally. They had created a friendship. They were family to one another. Though now it seemed no matter what he said he wasn't going to be able to alter the image of him Mercy had in his mind.

"Don't let them make you the villain, Mercy," Cal pleads.

"What if I already was?" Mercy breathes.

They both pause as Sylas comes to and attempts to get to his feet. Keeping his palm aimed at him, Mercy begins to power up another attack. Darting his gaze between Mercy and the blade, Cal takes a deep breath. He wasn't about to let Mercy take Sylas's life as well. Using the other blade still in his bracer, Cal pushes Mercy's sword to the side and bolts to protect Sylas.

Using his body to shield Sylas, Cal's thoughts were on protecting him. As the solis fog begins to burn, he feels a surge of power go through him as a blast of wind bursts around him. While Cal had hoped the lingering Light Source would attempt to protect him, this wasn't what he felt. The Light Source burning in his veins was accompanied by a sharp pain in his eyes. This was a familiar pain. This was something that he could control. This was his Shadow Source.

As Mercy pulls his attack back, Cal turns to look at him with a new wave of determination. He could feel his Source continue to reconnect as the energy flooded every muscle in his body. As he begins to stand up slowly, he could feel his injuries begin to ease as his Light Source went to work. In that moment, Cal felt more powerful than he ever did before.

"Holy shit," he hears Sylas mumble in bewilderment.

Whatever just happened was enough to call Cal's Shadow Source back to him. Not only call his Shadow Source, but also activate his Light Source's healing. Cal wasn't sure if it was the power of the attack or his fear of losing someone else that had recalled his power, but in that moment it didn't matter.

Dropping his hand, Mercy stares at Caligo, his eyes showing his own surprise. Glaring at Mercy, Cal puts his hand out and uses his fog to grasp the sword in Mercy's hands. With his Shadow Source back, he was ready to take Mercy head on.

"Still want to fight instead of talk?" Cal asks in a low voice, fog beginning to seep from his black eyes.

Putting his serious face back on, Mercy readies for a strike. With a small smirk, Cal pulls the bracers off. Mercy wanted to fight and since he had an equal match, it was going to be with their Sources. Cal had to be careful though. With Mercy being able to convert spiritum fog to his own weapon, his attacks needed to be thought out. Though maybe now wasn't the time to fight Mercy, maybe it was still the time to run. He just required an opening for himself and Sylas to get out of there so they could regroup.

As the two Keepers square up, Cal is met with a sudden droning in his head. The series of noises and voices were coming from Mercy's own confused mind. With his Source back that meant his connection to Mercy was also reinstated. There was so much going on in the Light Keeper's head that even Cal couldn't pull apart the messages he was getting. Clearly this wasn't intentional, but it was distracting. It was like having several people screaming in his ears while he was trying to focus. He puts a hand to his temple, trying to pull his attention to the task at hand and shut off the Voca. One message comes through clear though. Through all the noise he could hear a small "run," from his Alia.

"Your head really is a mess," Cal breathes, pulling his Source to his hands, coal filling his veins.

Watching Mercy and Cal prepare to fight, Sylas gets to his feet again. He was starting to feel the effects of his injuries, but at least he could move. He watches the pair of Alias with wide eyes, unsure what the next move was going to be.

As much as it pained Cal, he was going to have to hurt Mercy. He was going to have to use his Source to undermine him and get himself and Sylas out of there. Powering up more, he shoots as much of his spiritum fog at Mercy as possible, grabbing him and thrusting him into the wall. Looking at his fog, he could see small bolts of lightning laced throughout it. His Light Source was attempting to aid him. Watching Mercy, he notes the Light Keeper was unable to convert the light laced spiritum fog. This was perfect. This was the opening he needed.

"Sy, move!" Cal shouts, keeping Mercy pinned to the wall as he backs toward the door.

Grabbing Sylas by the arm he hears him give off a yelp of pain. The injuries to Sylas were piling up. Cal jerks him from the room as he drops Mercy to the ground. The two take off running through the halls. Hearing the feet rushing behind them, Cal lets out an annoyed scream as they turn down another corridor.

"Don't look back, just keep your feet moving!" Cal orders as they make their way out of the Source temple.

Sensing the tinge of another attack, Cal stops and puts up a wall of fog behind him and Sylas. They watch as the light laced fog surges with power when Mercy's Source meets the structure. Feeling the power hit his own magic, it almost felt painful in a way Cal couldn't quite explain. The Shadow pulls his fog back and locks eyes on Mercy for a moment before putting a cloak up over himself and Sylas. There was no reasoning with Mercy at this point. They're only choice was to run.

The pair take off in the cloak and as soon as they reach the grass outside, they are flung forward by a burst of energy from Mercy. The shock of the blow causes Cal to drop his cloak. Thinking on his feet, he uses his spiritum fog to cushion their fall, though both still hit the ground hard. The items in Sylas's bag scatter on the ground around them as they roll to a stop.

"This isn't fun anymore," Sylas groans with sarcasm and pain in his voice.

"Remind me to discuss the definition of fun with you later," Cal retorts, getting to his feet as Sylas begins to gather the ipdums.

Keeping his Sources at the ready, Cal watches Mercy exit onto the temple grounds. He observes his Alia pull his Source to his hands as he prepares his next attack. Waiting for him to release the bolt, Cal quickly puts up a wall of fog again. The spiritum fog takes the blow, a crack of thunder echoing through their bodies as Sylas gets to his feet. Cal could feel the charge from the Light Source trickle through his fog and into his hands as he drops the protection. As the fog clears, Cal locks his eyes on Mercy again as he begins to walk toward them.

Looking at Cal, Sylas could see his irises were ringed with the purple glow through the black in his sclera as his veins began to echo the same faint luminance. Cal didn't just have his Shadow Source at the ready, the Light Source in him was also reacting to the situation.

Sylas moves behind Cal as a solis orb, about the size of Mercy, comes barreling toward them. Cal uses his spiritum fog to divert the orb back, the blast sending a shock wave through the earth, rattling the mountain. Caligo takes a deep breath and puts up a cloak, moving slowly to the right, trying to buy them a moment to come up with a plan.

Scanning the area, they had limited options. They could rush down the slope and hope they could make it to the transport before Mercy. Cal could stand his ground and try to incapacitate him… or the less appealing of the three.

"Sy, I know you're afraid of heights but what are your thoughts on cliff diving?" Cal asks.

"My last experience with a cliff didn't go so well," Sylas shoots back, his eyes glued to his best friend.

"Do you have a better idea?" Cal asks, gesturing toward the drop off.

They both watch as Mercy pauses about thirty feet away and crouches down. He places his hands on the ground and closes his eyes. Concentration was evident on his face as the ground around them began to rumble. What was he doing?

Looking toward the cliff, Sylas could feel heat begin to radiate through his boots. "Sophos," he mutters, looking down. "Cal, he's heating the ground."

"He's what?" Cal questions, unable to feel the heat through his prosthetics.

"He's heating up the damn ground!" Sylas repeats in panic as Mercy looks up, hearing Sylas's voice.

Dropping the cloak, Cal begins to manifest fog at his feet. He knew what waited for them at the bottom of the cliff if he didn't use his Source right. The boulders that lined the valley would not be welcoming if his timing was off.

As Mercy gives them a sly smirk, Sylas grabs Cal's upper arm in fear. Knowing they wouldn't be able to survive the possible lava Mercy was making below the surface, Cal makes the decision for them. He lets out a frustrated sigh, grabbing Sylas and pulling him in a sprint toward the cliff on the edge of the grounds.

Suddenly they could feel and hear the rumbling increase as a wave of earth comes crashing toward them. As the wave of heated dirt and rocks hit his feet, Cal wraps his arms around Sylas and leaps from the cliff.

Sylas squeezes his eyes shut as the air rushes past him. This was nuts. Cal had seriously lost his damn mind. He knew he had said they were going to die together, but this was not what he had in mind. That was supposed to be many years down the road, not today. Especially not jumping off a cliff. Sylas grips the bag of ipdums to his stomach with one arm, fearful they would be lost in this insane idea, and Cal with the other.

With just seconds to pull this off, Cal keeps his attention on his Shadow Source. Keeping his Sources powered up he builds the fog up under them, pulling it up toward the sky. If he played this right, he could create a cushion and use his spiritum fog to slow the descent enough that hitting the bottom would be bearable. Without being able to see outside of his fog, this was a dangerous gamble. It didn't matter though; Mercy was going to kill them regardless.

Feeling them slow, Cal could tell what he was doing was working. He turns midair so Sylas would land on top of him as they hit the ground with force. He lets out a scream feeling his ribs crack and his chest lock up from the impact. Keeping himself alert, Cal uses his spiritum fog to avert the falling debris away from them. Knowing they had just a few seconds to get it together and move out of sight, Cal collects himself and gets to his feet. Pulling Sylas beside him, he scrambles through the boulders and rushes toward the tree line, Cal letting survival mode take over. Once they got out of sight, they could breathe.

Dragging Sylas by the hand, they find cover in the forest several yards away. They both drop to the ground, gasping for air, Cal keeping a hand to his ribs as his eyes lit up, the Light Source healing its Keeper. Leaning back on a tree, Cal steadies his breathing, each inhale feeling less painful.

"Are you insane!?" Sylas finally gets out.

"A little," Cal laughs breathlessly, leaning his head back on the trunk of the tree. "At least you're alive."

"*We're* alive," Sylas stresses.

"Yeah, that," Cal chuckles again, trying to regulate his breathing as the adrenaline eases.

Opening his satchel and checking the items in the bag, Sylas breathes a sigh of relief. Nothing seemed to be broken or damaged, so that was good. These items were precious and needed to find a new home in the relic room at the estate.

Looking to Cal, Sylas could see the tears dancing in his eyes. He watches as Cal squeezes them shut, trying to reel in his emotions. "Filthy little maddux," Cal mumbles to himself, hatred in his voice.

"Cal," Sylas whispers, "I'm sorry about Novi, but you know that wasn't him."

Cal looks at Sylas as he shakes his head in defeat. While Sylas was trying to keep it together, Cal could see the tears in his eyes as well. They were both a mess after what they just witnessed.

"Fuck," Sylas breathes in frustration. "Fuck!" he shouts, his voice echoing.

Both of their eyes shoot to the valley as a crash of lightning strikes just outside the trees.

"We need to go," Cal states, getting to his feet. "We can grieve our losses later."

"Stating the obvious there, King Charming," Sylas retorts, letting Cal pull him to his feet with a groan.

Chapter Fifty-One

Rushing into Cal's office, Zero locks eyes on both Sylas and Cal sitting on the sofa. Sylas's arm was in a sling, his shoulder looking discolored with various scrapes, cuts, and burns all over his body. The pair had hardly been able to make it to Pogu with Sylas's injuries. It was frustrating, while Cal's body had been able to heal itself, he was unable to heal Sylas during their journey back. Zero looks to Cal who was working on drawing something in his sketchbook while Sylas gave him notes.

"That line's not straight," Sylas notes.

"Well, neither am I," Cal remarks in an annoyed tone, pulling his eraser out and starting again.

"Sophos! Did you get hit by a transport?" Zero asks as Cal gets to his feet to hug his friend. Zero moves to Sylas who halfway gets up and accepts the awkward embrace and gives off a hiss of pain. "Suck it up, Bellator. Are you two okay?"

"If that's what you wanna call it," Sylas remarks with sarcasm.

"I already contacted the National Council about your rise from the dead," Zero shares, pulling a folder out of the bag at his side. "Pippa's summoned to the capital per

Sylas's request. She's in the Dror suite. Can I ask why I wasn't told to summon Master Novi too?"

Giving Zero a pained expression, Cal looks to the floor and shakes his head. "I will fill you in later," Cal states with a heavy sigh.

Nodding his head, Zero clears his throat. "You should be able to make your broadcast within the hour."

"Perfect," Cal nods, sitting back down, his voice sounding defeated. "I knew I could count on you."

"I know you're suicidal half the time, but you aren't supposed to act on it," Zero remarks, his eyes falling to Sylas. "By the Elders... Let me heal you. This is painful to look at."

"I'm fine," Sylas states. "I want Mercy to keep feeling every ounce of pain he put me through."

"Sy," Cal scolds.

While Doctor Willa had patched up Sylas, he still looked awful. The stiches that held the gash on his forehead closed were uncomfortable to look at. His broken nose had been reset and the blood cleaned away, but the black bruising remained.

"I'm petty," Sylas states with a scowl. "Let me torture him for a few more hours, okay? Zero can take care of me later."

"Alright," Cal chuckles at the remark.

"Mercy did this?" the Light Keeper asks.

"Yeah," Sylas confirms. "He's completely lost it and we were target practice."

"Clearly," Zero retorts. "I always knew he was a little shit, but this is a bit excessive."

Cal shakes his head. "Bryer planted something in his arm," he explains, nudging Zero the drawing he had made of the injury. "We think it's some sort of ipdum, but we're honestly not sure. Whatever it is, it's feeding on the Light Source. Ever seen anything like it?"

"By the Elders..." Zero breathes, studying the image carefully for a moment. "No..."

"And it gets better," Sylas smiles, his voice sarcastic. "We're pretty sure he's unlocked his Supra Keeping. He killed at least two people with no repercussions. He also somehow knocked Cal's Source back. By accident I think, but he was throwing some pretty horrifying attacks."

"Wait, who'd he kill?" Zero asks in concern.

With a heavy exhale, Cal speaks. "Iana Nitesems and," Cal pauses, closing his eyes for a moment, not wanting to speak the words himself, "Master Novi Dror."

Hearing Cal speak her name causes the room to go silent. Zero glances between the pair in shock at what he was just told. It was no surprise Mercy had the fuel to kill Iana, but Novi?

"Are we going after him?" Zero asks, locking his eyes on Cal.

"I don't know," Cal sighs, taking the sketch back. "We have not really discussed that yet... I need to make the broadcast about my return first." He looks at Sylas as he gets to his feet, trying to keep his professionalism. "Sy, can you go meet with Pippa, please?"

"Yeah," he nods, getting up as well.

With a pained look, Cal pauses a moment. He closes his eyes and takes a deep breath. "Could you ask Dolus to please call Master Emidio as well? I don't think I can handle making that call myself."

"Of course," Sylas agrees.

Cal gives Sylas a quick peck on the cheek before locking eyes with him. His partner gives him another nod, knowing that look was to just see if he was okay to be left alone. With the okay from Sylas, Caligo gestures for Zero to follow him. The two Keepers exit the office as Sylas grabs the sketchbook and picks up the bag of relics from the temple before leaving himself.

After finding Dolus, Sylas makes his way to the Dror suite. He knocks on the door, his hand shaking. He waits a moment for the door to open as someone appears. He smiles at the familiar face.

"Meera," he greets.

"Nice ta see yew, Sylas," she smiles at him. "Yew... don' look well."

"I know," he admits.

His eyes automatically go to Pippa who was sitting on the sofa in the sitting room. There was a book open on the table in front of her that she seemed to be ignoring. He frowns as Meera moves to the table and picks up the book, closing it. Scanning the room, he notes Shay wasn't around, the young woman should have been in the Drors' care once she was returned from the assignment.

"Where's Shay?" Sylas asks, looking to Meera.

"I don' know. I haven' seen her in a few days," Meera discloses. "I'll leave yew two ta et."

"Thank you," Pippa nods.

With a heavy sigh, Sylas walks over to her and gives Meera a forced smile. The woman moves to the bedroom to presumably check on her sleeping daughter. Sitting beside Pippa, Sylas places the bag on the table as her hand grabs his arm.

"Where is Mercy?" she asks.

"We don't need to-"

"Caligo promised he would bring him back," she speaks quickly. "Did he not?"

"It's complicated," Sylas discloses. "I need to tell you something, Pip."

"Okay," she nods turning to look at him.

Looking at her face he smiles feeling relief wash over him. While the right side of her face had scarring from the burns, her eye appeared to be completely unharmed.

"Can you see?" he asks in a quiet voice.

"Yes," she nods. "Reading is difficult, but I'll adapt. Are you okay?" she asks, noting the injuries.

"Thank the Elders," Sylas exhales in relief. "I'm better now seeing you're okay."

"Doctor Willa said the Light Source had caused temporary blindness," she explains with a small smile. "It should return more over time, but for now I'm content with what I have."

He puts a hand on her face and studies her eye closer. While it was slightly bloodshot, her yellow iris seemed unscathed by the blast. He gives her a soft smile and clears his throat, knowing full well he needed to break the news to her before he could even feel relief.

"Pip, Mercy... He..." he looks down, setting the sketchbook on the table as well. "Your mother..."

"She is gone, isn't she?" she questions with a pained smile.

"You know?" he asks, his eyes darting to her face at the words.

"I assumed when you returned without her," she confesses. "She was speaking with Meera a few nights ago and I overheard her words. She spoke of the loss of Caligo. At first, I thought maybe she was looking for answers on the events at the river, but..."

"Pip, I'm so sorry," Sylas breathes, letting her take his hand.

"She was doing what she was sworn to," Pippa assures with a small smile. "Protecting her child and ensuring the survival of our ruler."

"He was going to kill Cal, wasn't he?" Sylas asks, a tinge of fear in his voice.

Not wanting to answer him, Pippa pulls her hand away and shifts her gaze to the floor. While she appreciated the confirmation of what she feared, she was not going to allow them to dwell on it. Sylas watches her a moment, seeing her deflect the topic.

"Do you want me to call your father?" Sylas offers. "I'm sure he's already on his way but-"

"He will be here soon enough," she states, glancing at the satchel he brought. "I am sure this is not the only reason you came here, darling?"

With a heavy sigh, he nods his head. "I need your help, Pip," he announces. "We need two book nerds for this one."

"I will try," she nods, her voice sounding empty.

"I know we don't know much about ipdums, but do you know of any that could be stuck under the skin and used to mess with people's emotions or maybe their Source?" he begins.

"That is oddly specific," Pippa notes. "I told you we cannot just blame this on the Sources, Sylas. We need-"

He nudges her the sketchbook, hoping she'd be able to make sense of the image Cal had scrawled on the page. It was a fairly accurate depiction of what the relic in Mercy's arm looked like when they saw him last, the dark veins leading from the raised scar were frightening.

"This scar was reacting to his magic somehow," Sylas explains.

Narrowing her eyes, she shakes her head. "Is this on his upper arm?"

"Yeah," Sylas confirms.

"I asked him about this weeks ago," she states in shock. "I thought the scar looked strange... Usually his healings are precise and clean, but this appeared jagged and raised. He blamed it on not being able to focus but..."

"You could see the Light Source travel to whatever this is through his veins and the dark bit would just destroy it," Sylas explains. "Almost like a parasite."

"Curious," she admits, shaking her head again. "Ipdums can be used in many ways. I would not be surprised if there was one that could do such a thing. If Bryer has a peritia that already can be used to alter

570

emotions, perhaps like Zero, a specific ipdum may exist to aid in a projection of that power, or in this case, to focus it when the Keeper is not near their victim."

"Bryer's gone. We think Merc killed him, and he did kill Iana and your mother. He all but destroyed the Northwest Source Temple and was going to kill me and Cal," he shares, his voice heavy.

"Did you bring him back?" she questions, her eyes darting to his face.

"Did you hear what I just said? He's lost his mind, Pippa. We had to leave him to have a chance at living," he explains.

"So, you left him at the temple?" she frowns. "And my mother?"

"I'm sorry, Pip, but we didn't have a choice. We either ran or let him kill us," he defends, his tone sympathetic of her worry.

"I understand," she sighs.

"He's gone, Pip. Mercy is...," Sylas sighs, closing the book with a shudder.

"We will figure this out," Pippa assures, taking his hand and giving him a soft smile. "We simply need to remove that item from his arm, and we may be able to get his mind back."

"We have to get close enough to do that," he notes. "The attacks he was using... It's unlike anything I've ever seen. Anything Novi or Cal tried to throw at him with the Shadow Source just bought us time."

"Cal's Shadow Source?" she asks, her eyes wide.

"Yeah," Sylas confirms. "Mercy tried to attack me, and Cal jumped in the way. When Merc pulled back, Cal's Source connection was working again. I don't know if Mercy-"

"Cal was able to recall his Source connection," Pippa gasps, getting to her feet quickly. "Do you know what this means?"

"No?" Sylas discloses with a shrug.

"If Cal could overcome his exposure to the exua rune, that means he's also above the laws of the Sources," she explains, moving to the bookcase and pulling out the book she had shown him in the library. "That would explain why he has the Light Source. It wasn't a lingering of Mercy's connection or a hoax; it is, in fact, his own. Caligo's a Supra, Sylas. You were right."

"Not to brag, but I'm usually right," he retorts as she sits back down beside him and hands him the book. "Maybe losing your mother and the idea of losing me made him desperate enough or maybe fearful enough to…" he trails off, rationalizing the experience.

"Open this to page 448," she instructs, shoving the book into his hands.

Opening the book, Sylas does as he is told. He flips through the pages until he finds the correct one. Reading it he furrows his brow. Written in the margin was a note from Pippa herself.

"His ability to overcome the exua rune proves he's a Supra," she shares. "He may not be as powerful as Mercy, but he may be able to take him in a fight if we can train him in his Supra Keeping."

Unequaled power = Proven

Light connection = Proven

Exua rune = Inconclusive

"From what I've gathered, unlocking it seems pretty dangerous," Sylas adds, shaking his head. "Seeing Mercy with all that power…"

"Caligo already has a better handle on his connection than Mercy," Pippa assures. "Unlocking his Supra Keeping, he will be much more in control. I do fear this means Bryer has something bigger planned for Mercy though."

"Yeah," Sylas agrees, closing the book and rubbing his temples. "Even when Cal was against us, I knew I could bring him back. Mercy though? I don't know."

Reaching toward the bag, Pippa begins to shuffle through it, placing the items on the table. It was almost like she knew Sylas needed the distraction, she probably needed it herself. He suddenly understood the fear that had been plaguing Mercy since his fight against Cal in the courtyard, because he had felt the same thing in the temple. Seeing someone he trusted, someone he cared for, want him dead was a truly terrifying experience.

"I... uh... They're the ipdums from the Source Temple," Sylas shares, helping her remove the rest of the items, each one still wrapped carefully. "There were two items missing, the Pura Blade, which Mercy still has, and another dagger I think."

She unwraps one of the items to reveal a simple blue crystal. The gem was thin and smooth, fitting in her palm comfortably. She studies it and shakes her head again.

"Unfortunately, many of these will be difficult to find the meaning behind. Not many are depicted in the tomes we have here at the capital," she explains. "A Keeper tends to be drawn to an ipdum or perhaps it is gifted with its abilities shared. That is how Mercy came into possession of the Pura Blade. It was bestowed on him by his father with Trust's aid... It's also how my mother gained the Arca Orb Mercy's power was stored in during your journey," she shares, her voice heavy. "The item was gifted to her, and its properties shared. These ipdums were in that temple to be retrieved by the Keepers of Light destined to use them. With the temple destroyed... They will never find their Keepers now."

"There was a special room, one that only opens under specific circumstances," Sylas shares, unwrapping another to reveal a black knapped dagger. "I think Mercy may have used his Source to destroy it. The crystals that lined the walls were shattered. Every single one. It made me sick to my stomach."

"The grounds have been fouled," she states, shaking her head. "Mercy, what have you done?" she whispers placing the gem in her hand back into its wrapping.

"I don't know what to do, Pip," he sighs, placing the black blade back into its fabric.

"We will figure this out, Sylas," she comforts him. "I will speak with the other acolytes, and I am sure we can make sense of this."

"I think this might be beyond us," he admits, shaking his head. "His mind is... I looked at him and I didn't see Mercy, Pip, I saw a stranger."

"You fear he is too far gone?" she adds, studying his face.

"Did Master Novi tell you anything before she left?" Sylas pries. "Did she give you any idea on what she heard from herself about Mercy?"

"Unfortunately, no," Pippa explains. "She was there to protect her son. Whatever she heard, she was protecting Caligo."

She could tell Sylas's mind was racing while he tried to sort through this. Surely if Mercy's mind was as scattered as he stated, then Sylas's was just as chaotic. The Nota mirrored his Keeper, unable to escape the other's strong emotions. It was both a blessing and a curse.

Shaking his head, he gets to his feet. "I'll take these to the relic room," he announces.

"That sounds like a good idea," she affirms.

Helping him put the items back in the bag, Pippa's hand pauses on the sketchbook. "Do you mind if I hold onto this?"

"Sure," Sylas replies. "Just get it back to Cal."

"Of course," she smiles softly to him.

Sylas gives a broken smile in response before exiting the suite. Nothing felt right in that moment. Looking at the image on the paper again, Pippa furrows her brow. Something about the injury seemed familiar to her, but she couldn't quite place it.

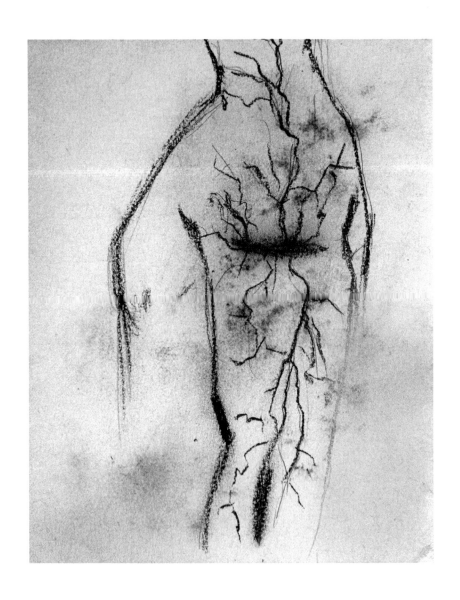

576

Chapter Fifty-Two

Cal had just updated the Missing Persons Alert throughout the Sentry Guard, hoping that private updates within the military would be the right move. Putting an Active Danger Alert on Mercy felt like the wrong choice with how sensitive things were. He needed to handle this delicately and with grace. One wrong move and he was going to have a true uprising on his hands.

Entering his suite, Cal lets out a heavy breath. He closes the door and leans his forehead on the wooden frame a moment to try and collect himself. He had hoped he would have been able to speak to Pippa before turning in for the night, but when he stopped by her room there was no answer. No part of him wanted to let Pippa mourn Master Novi alone. He wanted to be there for her while she waited for her father. The man would surely be on his way to the capital after being given the news, but that meant Pippa was left alone to go through this devastating situation for the night.

Turning, he scans the room. He could see Sylas's winter cape and hat were hanging beside the door and his boots flung across the floor, looking to have been removed in a frustrated manner. He grabs the boots and places them neatly by the door as Dolus appears from the bathroom, used towels in hand.

"Hello," Cal greets with a forced smile.

"Sorry to still be here, Your Grace. Master Sylas requested I stay until you arrived," he bows to him, placing the towels in the hamper. "I have prepared the washroom for your nightly routine. Master Sylas is resting in your room. I hope that is acceptable."

"Thank you," he states with a soft voice, his exhaustion showing through. "You are dismissed, Dolus. I apologize for keeping you."

"Not a problem at all, Your Grace," he bows again and heads toward the door to leave. He pauses a moment and looks to Cal beside him. "If I may be so bold as to offer some advice for you, My Lord?"

"Of course, Dolus," Cal nods with a light smile, not sure he wanted to hear what he had to say.

"It is not uncommon for one to experience guilt or a need for control in times like this," he consoles. "I'm unsure exactly what happened with Master Novi, but I can see the guilt in your eyes, and I can see your struggling for control in your actions. The only way you can move forward from this is to remember you have always done what you were capable of for those around you in the moment."

"Right," Cal sighs, looking at the floor.

"My King, I have watched you grow into a strong and brave young man. I have no doubt you will figure this out," Dolus adds.

Keeping his small smile, Cal nods his head again. That was one thing he appreciated about his senior staff member. Dolus had been around long enough to know Cal, having been on staff since he was an infant. After the removal of Mala, Dolus had become much more open with him when given the chance and always seemed to know just when Cal needed some encouraging words.

"Thank you, Dolus," he replies.

"Get some rest, My Lord," Dolus encourages. "I feel a good night of sleep will aid you and Master Bellator."

"Have a good night," Cal waves lightly.

"You as well," Dolus chimes. He pauses once more. "And know that Master Novi would be proud of the man you have become. She is the proudest of us all, Caligo."

Feeling his words hit him, Cal's smile falls to a frown. He watches as Dolus leaves the suite and lets out a heavy exhale. Maybe Dolus was right, perhaps he was struggling for control of the situation but what choice did he have? He locks the door behind Dolus and begins to remove his formal wear. Going to the bathroom he gets ready to turn in for the night.

After washing up and slipping on the pajamas Dolus laid out for him, he heads to the bedroom. He frowns seeing both Saphie and Ruby nestled under the blankets, but Sylas nowhere to be found. There was no doubt the girls were there to seek comfort from Sylas with Mercy and Charlyn both unable to care for them. The housekeeper was sitting in the prison, waiting to be tried.

He moves over to the bed and tucks the blanket over the girls. He pauses seeing a small brass tube held in Ruby's hand and gently nudges it from her grasp. He looks at it and furrows his brow before placing it on the side table. He turns the light off beside them and goes to look out into the sitting room. He spots Sylas's boots and winter wear still where they had been placed.

As a small shiver shoots through him, he looks to the balcony. The glass door was slightly ajar, letting the cool night air into the room. He huffs and walks over to close it, wondering where Sylas was when he spots his foot through a separation in the dark curtains. Pausing, he opens the door to see Sylas sitting on the cold balcony floor in loose shorts and a brown shirt, staring out at the city.

579

Quietly, Cal ducks back inside and grabs a blanket from the foot of his bed and goes to join him outside.

Seeing the sling was gone and the bruises had faded, it was clear that a Light Keeper had offered their healing abilities to Sylas. It was a relief to see he let someone take care of the injuries finally. Cal lets out a heavy sigh looking at Sylas as he stared blankly out into the city, not even acknowledging Cal's presence.

"What are you doing out here?" Cal asks, draping the blanket over Sylas's shoulders.

Ignoring the gesture, Sylas shakes his head and speaks softly. "Trying to find Merc."

"How is that going?" Cal questions.

"I could feel him this morning, but now there's nothing," Sylas admits with a frown, his voice void. "Just... nothing."

Awkwardly getting to the ground beside him, Cal looks out at the city. They sit in silence for a couple of minutes as Cal adjusts the blanket to drape over his shoulders as well. Feeling Cal beside him, Sylas moves closer, becoming aware of how cold he was. He shivers a bit as Cal pulls the blanket around him more snugly, trying to offer some sort of comfort.

"You should come inside and get some rest," Cal whispers. "We both need it."

"I can't sleep," Sylas discloses.

Taking a deep breath, Cal nods as Sylas leans his head on his shoulder. Reacting to the action, Cal wraps an arm around him. Ever since they had gotten back from the temple, Sylas hadn't been himself. Neither of them had been. Was it the separation from Mercy or the distress of what happened that day weighing on them?

"I'm sorry about Novi," Sylas mutters. "I'm sorry that Mercy-"

"You do not apologize for his actions," Cal states in a calm voice.

With a heavy sigh, Sylas goes quiet again. He felt like he had to apologize. If he didn't apologize to everyone for his Keeper's actions, who would? What Mercy had done was unforgivable, so maybe there wasn't even a point. His best friend had taken the life of a woman who meant the world to Cal and Pippa. What Mercy had done was wrong and proved how lost he was.

While Cal wanted to claim he understood what Sylas was going through, he couldn't. The bond a Nota had with their Keeper was unlike anything else. The fact the Elders forced such an emotional bond on a person seemed cruel in a way. The complex thoughts and emotions of a person could only make these feelings worse for Sylas. Not to mention he probably wasn't even sure why or how he was feeling the way he did. All Cal could do was sit there and watch him suffer until they could figure this out or the exua rune completely severed his connection to Mercy, if that was even possible.

"If you need to talk, I *will* listen," Cal reassures him, rubbing his shoulder. "Just as you listen to me."

Sylas shakes his head numbly. "I don't think I want to talk right now."

"Okay," Cal responds, taking a deep breath.

Sylas had been trying his hardest to be open with Cal, but this situation with Mercy was different. This was something he felt talking about would only make it worse. Mercy had killed someone they both cared for, someone who had raised Caligo. There was no easing this empty and confusing feeling and if he opened up to Cal about it, it would only hurt his partner. He was stuck with it until he was able to find Mercy, or their connection was gone.

The pair stay silent as Cal stares at the floor. His mind goes to Novi as his gaze moves back out to the city. His mentor had given him everything she could. The Drors were his real family. Novi had shown him what a true mother could be. She had given him his first taste of a real family by accepting him into her home. While he still had Tristia, the bond with his blood relative was never as strong as the sisterly bond he had forged with Pippa.

After another moment, Cal's mind wanders to Nex. Part of him hoped that the crow shown to him in the tent wasn't Nex. If that were the case, surely the part of him that felt hollow inside wouldn't be there. While he didn't feel the loss of his Nota at the time, he could feel it now. Even with his Source back, something still felt lost. Perhaps that was how Sylas was feeling as well.

"Sy…" Cal breathes, kissing his head. "I know I don't fully comprehend your relationship with Mercy, but I can try to understand," he comforts.

Pulling away, Sylas shakes his head again. It was more complicated than Cal could understand. While Mercy was his Keeper, and there was no negating that, he was also his best friend. Mercy was his brother, his favorite person, the one individual on the planet who knew him better than he knew himself. He was sure one day Cal would be the same thing, but a romantic partner wasn't the same. The Light Keeper saw him through his most difficult times and his highest points. He couldn't imagine life without Mercy because he never had to. From the day he was born, Mercy was there.

"Sy, please," Cal begs.

He shakes his head once more and gets to his feet slowly. Talking to Cal wasn't what he wanted to do right now. He was still trying to process what Mercy had become. How was he supposed to just accept that his best friend was a murderer? How was he supposed to accept any of this? What was the plan anyway? Surely Cal was working on a way to locate Mercy and bring him back. Having Cal tell him the plan felt just as ominous though. No part of Sylas wanted to know what was in store for his Keeper when he was finally found. With that thought, Sylas lets out a heavy exhale and goes back inside.

Following Sylas, Cal keeps pushing. "Sy, talk to me," he pleads, closing the balcony doors and keeping his distance. "That is why I'm here, is it not? I'm here to listen and be there for you."

"Quiet," Sylas whispers, gesturing to the girls.

Moving out of the bedroom and into the sitting space, Sylas tries to keep it together. The last thing he wanted right now was Cal to push his limits. While he knew Cal was only doing it out of love, that didn't matter. At that moment he preferred to just sit in silence rather than talk through the storm in his head.

Pursuing Sylas, Cal keeps trying, pulling the pocket doors to his bedroom closed. "Sylas, please," he pleads. "Just try to-"

"No," Sylas states, keeping his eyes away from Cal.

"Sy," Cal scolds, "I refuse to stand by while you-"

"I said no," Sylas repeats, turning to look at him. "Can't you respect that?"

"I do respect you," Cal retorts with raised brows. "I just don't want you to think you are in this alone. Neither of us are alone, Sy."

"Cal, don't," Sylas breathes.

"Telling me how you feel is not supposed to end in an argument," Cal notes.

"And Mercy isn't supposed to be a homicidal maniac, but here we are," Sylas shoots back, folding his arms with a scowl. "He killed Novi, Cal. He killed her, his mentor. Your mentor. The woman who cared for you, Cal. She was like a mother to you, to all of us, and he killed her. He didn't even react. There was no remorse there... There was nothing."

Taking a deep breath, Cal nods his head and looks to the floor. It was one thing for Mercy to kill their enemy, it was another for him to kill their friend. Master Novi was only there to protect Cal, and now she was gone. How was he supposed to explain to Pippa that her mother was gone

583

because he chose to pursue Mercy? Shaking the thought, Cal takes his attention back to Sylas.

"I just want to understand how you feel," Cal explains with a heavy exhale.

"What if I don't understand?" Sylas asks. "What if I don't even know how I feel, Cal?"

"Then we figure it out together," Cal assures him, walking over and putting his hands on his shoulders. "We figure all of this out together."

"He killed Novi!" Sylas repeats, anger in his voice. "How are you so calm about this?"

"I'm not," Cal admits. "I am simply trying to keep my composure for the sake of those around me. You and Pippa and my people need my strength right now and-"

Their conversation is quickly interrupted by someone banging on the door. They both pause as the pounding persists. With a furrowed brow, and an annoyed sigh, Cal walks to the entrance to answer it. He gives a look of surprise as Pippa frantically enters the room. Looking at her, Cal gives an expression of confusion as he closes the door, Sylas mirroring the reaction.

"I apologize for the intrusion," Pippa states with a small bow, fire in her eyes, "but I fear this couldn't wait," she shares.

Without thinking, Cal goes to hug her, Pippa accepting the embrace. She feels him squeeze her tightly, trying to offer her comfort. Feeling the emotions come to her stomach, she takes a moment to bury her face in his chest. At least she still had Caligo. If she was thankful for anything in that moment, it was that her mother succeeded in keeping him alive. She could make it through the loss of her mother if she still had her best friend and brother.

"It's fine," Cals says as she pulls away, exhaustion clear on his face. "You are always welcome to interrupt us. Are you okay?"

She shakes her head, keeping her eyes locked with his. She could see the pain in Cal's expression. She could see the guilt he felt reflecting in his dark eyes. No part of her wanted him to feel responsibility over her mother's actions.

"I am okay, because you are standing here," she assures him with a broken smile.

Looking Pippa over, he locks his eyes on his sketchbook held in her hands. "Why do you have this?" he questions, as she returns the book.

"The injury you depicted," Pippa answers. "I fear this may be more serious than an ipdum."

"How?" Cal asks with a raised brow and a laugh. "He nearly killed me and Sy. He has killed your mother and probably Bryer. I don't think it can get much more serious than that..."

"It can, and it will," Pippa warns them.

Seeing the severity on her face, Cal slowly sits down on the sofa waiting for her words. Whatever Pippa was about to tell them wasn't going to be good. Glancing to Sylas he could see his partner's eyes shift from confusion to concern rather quickly.

"I have seen this before," she shares with the young men, pulling a tablet out.

She hands the device to Cal. Moving his eyes from her to the device his brow wrinkles in confusion. On the tablet was a case study from nearly fifteen years ago. A study with something familiar to him.

"What is this?" he asks, running his finger over the screen to read.

"A trial Mala did when we were just children," Pippa explains as Sylas moves behind the sofa to read over Cal's shoulder. "Remember when you came into your Source, and my mother spoke with us about the effects of genti? How do you think she came into this knowledge?"

Keeping his eyes on the screen, Cal frowns. This depicted the effects of genti as more than what he knew. What he was reading was making him physically ill. Mala was experimenting on these people. She was doing trials on Keepers and genti exposure.

"I have touched genti before," Cal argues as Sylas snatches the tablet from his hands. "This was not-"

"You have experienced the short-term effects," Pippa corrects him with sadness in her eyes. "Mala knew the effects of genti on a Keeper's skin could cause anywhere from irritation to severe burns. She wanted to know what long term exposure could do."

"This is disgusting," Sylas adds, his face showing the nausea he was feeling as he continued to read.

"She tested on Keepers like animals," Cal breathes, putting his hands to his temples. "By the Elders…"

As Sylas continues to poke through the tablet he grimaces. Scrolling through the files, he comes across a name he recognized. "Skerrick," he states, looking to Cal. "Zeer Skerrick. Any relation to Zero?"

Cal's eyes shoot to Sylas as his partner hands the tablet back to him. "Zeer is Zero," Cal informs, studying the file himself.

"Zero's name is Zeer?" Sylas asks in confusion.

"You really thought his given name was Zero?" Cal shoots back in annoyance.

"I guess I never thought about it," Sylas admits.

Pippa puts her hand out for the device. Looking to her palm, Cal gives her the screen as she begins to click through it. He was sickened by what he was seeing. Mala was forcing them to swallow the dangerous metal, holding it to their skin, injecting it, and more. It was just another form of torture. A torture she was putting at least a dozen Keepers through based on the names listed in the file.

"This is how they learned it could be toxic," Pippa continues. "Long term exposure to the metal can create fits of mania, paranoia, severe changes in mood, irritability, dissociative episodes, and in some cases, death."

"That sounds like Merc," Sylas notes.

After another moment, Pippa hands the tablet back to the King. "Look familiar?" she asks.

Cal's eyes go wide at the image she had brought up. It depicted an injury similar to the one Mercy had on his arm. The dark veins running from the raised scar in the center of someone's back were just as frightening and grotesque as what was seen on his friend during their last encounter.

"You think this is genti poisoning," Cal whispers, opening his sketchbook and comparing the two images beside each other.

"Yes," Pippa confirms.

"How much do you know about this study?" Cal asks, locking his eyes on Pippa.

"Not much," she admits. "Mother would have known more," she frowns. "Genti reacts to the Sources though. This means whenever Mercy powers up, willingly or not, the genti will attempt to destroy the Source flowing toward it. The more Source power he pulls the quicker the effects will take over."

"But when he touched genti in the past it just burned him," Cal argues. "It would blister. How could that be in his arm and not-"

"The Sources are constantly trying to protect their Keeper," Pippa snaps, cutting him off. "This is why your connection to the Light Source unlocked when it did. In a way, the Source in a Keeper's body is an entity in and of itself. This means wherever the genti touches Mercy, his Source is working to repair the damage. I am willing to bet he felt pain around the injury every time he powered up since the metal was planted."

Cal glances to Sylas who was standing behind him looking to the floor with his arms folded taking in the information. He wasn't sure if Sylas was simply listening or perhaps was beginning to go numb to the news. His partner was shaken up enough the way it was, this information was bound to cause more of an upset.

"The more he uses his Source the more severe the effects will become," Pippa warns with fierce eyes.

"When did the injury occur?" Cal asks, looking between the two.

Sylas shrugs. He hadn't noticed the scar until that day on the mountain. Mercy had hardly mentioned anything to him about the pain. His Keeper probably wasn't even aware he was infected.

"The night of the break in," Pippa answers.

"Sophos," Cal whispers at her words. "We need to locate him and bring him back to Ozra for treatment as soon as possible."

"Easier said than done," Sylas notes, shaking his head in disbelief.

"Difficult or not, he must be found," Pippa warns, looking between Sylas and Cal.

"Or he'll die," Sylas mutters, looking at Caligo.

Scanning the room, Cal takes a deep breath and nods his head in understanding. "How much time do we have?"

"I am unsure," Pippa admits. "If he was exposed the night of the break in, that is over two months of exposure. It could be several more months or just days."

"Okay," Cal mumbles. "We need to page Zero. If anyone can give us details on this, it's him."

"He left on the recovery mission at the temple after he healed me," Sylas shares, his tone void.

"Under whose authority?" Cal asks, giving Sylas a raised brow.

"I don't know," Sylas replies blankly.

"I told him I needed him here," Cal groans, taking his attention to Pippa. "Does anyone else know about this study?"

"I do not know," Pippa shares. "The trials ended eight years ago, so perhaps someone in the senior staff would know."

Cal sighs, putting his hands to his temples. "Why on Novus Aitus can't something be simple for once?"

Sylas begins to move away from the group, their voices fading out. Hearing them talk about Mercy like this was making this all the more terrifying. Mercy tried to kill him. He tried to kill Cal. If Cal hadn't been able to call his Source back when he had, his best friend would have succeeded in killing them all, not just Novi. Now on top of that, his best friend's life was on the line. He was going to have to face a confused and scared version of his Keeper if he wanted any chance of him living.

Trying to hold back his emotions, Sylas feels his hands begin to shake as his breathing gets ragged. This couldn't be happening. How were the Elders allowing this to happen? Mercy was the last person he had left. He couldn't lose him.

"Cal," he gets out, his voice cracking.

Hearing the distress in the sound of his name, Cal stops talking to Pippa and looks to Sylas with worry. Pippa's eyes shoot to him as well. As soon as Cal's eyes meet Sylas's, he could tell something was wrong. While moments ago, Sylas had been numb, now he was on the verge of completely losing it.

"Cal, come here, please," Sylas whispers, biting his cheek to try and hold back the impending tears.

"What is it?" Cal asks, getting up slowly.

Sylas gestures for him to come more urgently, feeling the tears hitting his eyes. This prompts Cal to pick up the pace. Once he approaches him, Sylas throws his arms around him and buries his face in Cal. Perplexed, Cal returns the embrace feeling sobs begin to wrack Sylas.

Looking to Pippa for help, Cal's eyes showed his unease. What was he supposed to do? The woman gives him a look in return like he should know, but he didn't. He had never had to experience an emotional Sylas before. Sylas always held it together. Suddenly he feels Sylas's legs buckle, the weight causing Cal to go down as well. They both clumsily make their way to the ground, Sylas not letting go of Cal.

Looking at Pippa with pleading eyes, Caligo begs for help. He had spent so much of the relationship wanting this type of emotion from his partner but now he was at a loss for how to react to it. Pippa mouths for him to "talk" as Sylas curls up beside him, tears still coming in full force.

Giving a nod of the head, Cal clears his throat. "What do you need?" he asks, keeping his voice quiet.

"I can't lose him," Sylas admits through his gasps. "I let him fall apart and now I'm gonna lose my best friend. I fucked up, Cal!"

Mercy and Sylas had grown up together, spent holidays and birthdays together, and spent nearly every day with each other until Spheara. The two had spent their entire lives around the other. Cal had never had that kind of companionship with anyone before and while he saw Mercy as family, he hadn't spent much time with him outside of assignments and meetings.

Sylas on the other hand knew Mercy in and out. The Light Keeper had been there for him through it all. From the awkward childhood moments to his mother leaving, and even through his breakup with Cal. Mercy was all Sylas had left of his childhood, of his family, and the last moments he had with him, Mercy had wanted him dead.

"You are not going to lose him," Cal comforts.

"He's been dying in front of us for months, Cal!" Sylas rebukes in anger, suddenly trying to push Cal away, but Cal not allowing it, holding him tighter. "Months! And we were too stupid to see it!"

Wincing at his words, Cal takes a deep breath and looks to Pippa again. He wasn't good at this. Maybe this was why Sylas rarely opened up. Sylas was the empathetic and comforting one in the relationship.

"I messed up!" Sylas continues, trying to squirm away, but Cal holds him tight. "I was supposed to be there for him, and I wasn't! I was supposed to help him and keep him on the path the Elders chose, and I didn't do that! I screwed us all over! I let him murder someone! I let him kill Master Novi! This is on me."

Seeing Cal struggle and Sylas in tears, Pippa approaches the pair and places a hand on the Nota's shoulder. Seeing that Sylas had hit his breaking point was beyond shaking. He was a pillar of strength, and that pillar was crumbling. She grabs Cal's hand to offer him some comfort as well and gives him a soft, broken smile.

"I have you," Cal comforts, remembering the words Sylas had said to him before. "You are safe. What can I do?" He feels Sylas shake his head, giving up trying to get away. Taking a deep breath, Cal starts again. "Listen to me, Sy," he begins in a soft voice. "You can question your actions, but don't for a moment question your loyalty or dedication to Mercy Validus."

With Mercy turned against them, nothing felt right. Sylas's entire world felt like it was about to implode. Being away from Mercy had never felt this empty before. It was like every single cell in his body was screaming for him to go find his best friend, but he couldn't. If he valued his life, he had to stay right where he was.

"What can I do?" Cal repeats.

"Don't leave," Sylas mutters.

"Okay," Cal nods, locking eyes with Pippa. "I'm not going anywhere."

Through all the mess in Mercy's head, one message did stand out to Cal. His Alia had told him to run. That meant somewhere within his chaotic and scared mind, his friend was there, and he knew he was dangerous.

Chapter Fifty-Three

Sitting in the snow, Mercy closes his eyes. His whole body was on fire. It felt like lava in his blood as he rocked back and forth trying to figure out what was happening to him. The static in his brain was blaring and he couldn't even focus long enough to make sense of where he was.

He lets out a shuddering breath as he puts his hand to his arm again. The heat resonating from the scar was intense and hurt to the touch. He needed to get this thing out of his arm. Sylas had to have known something he didn't when he tried himself.

With another shaking breath, he pulls the Pura Blade from his belt. He studies the knapped blade carefully, feeling tears come to his eyes. What was he doing? What had he done? Why was he doing this?

Looking at the tattered, burned remains of his shirt, his eyes fall to the dark veins radiating from the scar on his arm. Taking a deep breath, he grips the blade in his hand and puts the crystal dagger to his skin. He lets out a hiss of pain as he cuts the skin on his arm, his Source automatically trying to heal the wound. He lets off an annoyed groan as the cut heals over, still throbbing.

"Come on, Validus," he mumbles to himself.

He takes another deep breath and digs the blade into his arm again, this time using the blade to dig out whatever was in his arm. He lets out a pain filled scream as a piece of shiny metal falls into the snow beside him. He takes a few steadying breaths, trying to calm himself. He closes his eyes hoping to feel the pain subside in his body as his Source heals his arm. While the throbbing pain was leaving, he still felt nauseous, and his joints ached. Opening his eyes, he studies his hand, the dark veins still radiating under his skin making him look like a corpse.

"Sophos," he breathes, letting his arm go limp.

He looks to the metal beside him and goes to run his finger over it. He lets out another hiss of pain at the stinging sensation it gave on his skin. He releases a sharp breath as he studies his fingers.

"Genti?" he questions to himself.

As the words leave his lips, his head begins to throb. He closes his eyes tightly, knowing another wave of agony was about to overtake his skull. How had he let this happen? Why didn't he realize what was happening until now? What were the effects of having genti in his arm this long? How did it not burn him?

He scoops the metal up out of the freshly fallen snow and throws it as hard as he can. That stupid little piece of metal was making him lose his damn mind. He feels the tears come to his eyes as anger takes over. He couldn't even control what he was feeling anymore. Why was he even angry?

"Mercy," he hears Trust whisper.

He opens his eyes and looks at his brother. Looking at Trust he understood why he felt grief. At least this emotion made sense. Nothing else did.

"You need help," Trust whispers to him.

Mercy nods his head in agreement. He did need help, but how was he going to get it? The two people who

594

could have helped him, he tried to kill. He had killed Master Novi in that temple. He was probably on Ozra's Most Wanted list again, this time for a good reason. He had killed Master Novi, then attempted to slaughter the King and his own best friend. Did he kill Bryer? He couldn't even remember. Not to mention he destroyed a sacred temple. He was a horrible person. He was a monster.

"Where's Sylas?" Trust questions.

The Light Keeper shakes his head. He didn't know. Did Sylas and Cal even survive the fall from that cliff? He wasn't sure. His memory felt blurred and by the time he realized what had happened he had thrown so many blows at the boulders below, he wasn't even sure he'd be able to make out if Sylas and Cal had survived. Did he kill them? He might have killed them.

Even if they were alive could he go back to them? Maybe they would help him, but would they forgive him for all the suffering he put them through. Would Cal and Pippa forgive him for taking Novi's life? Maybe they were better off without him. They probably were better off without him. Look at what he did.

Closing his eyes, tears begin to run down his cheeks. What had he done? His daughter was dead. His friends were probably dead. Master Novi was dead. Pippa probably hated him.

He looks at his hands that were glowing faintly, trying to keep him warm and lets out a scream. Nothing made sense. Caligo should have never given him his Source back. Look what giving him his connection back had unleashed on this world. He couldn't control this. Whatever he was he couldn't control.

"Mercy, look at me," Trust begs.

Looking at his brother again the tears grow. As he studies his brother the grief is suddenly replaced with anger again. Why had Trust come up behind him like that during Spheara. If he hadn't done that, then he'd still be alive. He left a daughter behind and Meera. How was Meera supposed to move on with a child? A child she probably didn't even want. Why would Trust do that to her?

"You need help," Trust repeats. "You need to get up and you need to find someone to help you."

Hearing his voice, Mercy closes his eyes. Why was he sad now? What was going on? He jumps at the sound of footsteps in the snow behind him, his brother looking up to see who was approaching.

"You," Trust growls.

As Mercy turns to look at who was approaching him, a blow comes to his head and the world goes black again. He couldn't even make out the face, all he saw were the black boots in the snow.